After a career in national newspapers, Rory Clements now lives in a seventeenth-century farmhouse in Norfolk and writes full time. ~~When not immersing himself in the Elizabethan world~~, he enjoys village life and a game of tennis with friends. He is married to the artist Naomi Clements-Wright.

Praise for *Revenger*:

'A historical thriller to send a shiver down your spine. Atmospheric . . . it demonstrates energy, élan, a fine ear for dialogue and a grasp for the intrigues of Elizabeth I's court. Clements also demonstrates the compelling eye for detail and character that Bernard Cornwell so memorably brought to Rifleman Sharpe . . . I could not tear myself away, it is that good' *Daily Mail*

'The sights, sounds and smells of Elizabethan London are resurrected in Rory Clements's marvellous *Revenger*, in which intelligencer John Shakespeare (brother of you know who . . .) administers what can only be described as ruff justice' *Daily Telegraph*

'Step into the world of Elizabethan intelligencer John Shakespeare and you put your very life in peril, whether it be by the blade, the rope or the rack . . . High adventure has never been more exciting, and a life-and-death shoot-out . . . makes for a storming climax' *Northern Echo*

Revenger

RORY CLEMENTS

JOHN MURRAY

First published in Great Britain in 2010 by John Murray (Publishers)
An Hachette UK Company

First published in paperback in 2011

1

A CIP catalogue record for this title is available from the British Library

ISBN 978-1-84854-085-9

Typeset in Adobe Garamond by Servis Filmsetting Ltd, Stockport, Cheshire

Printed and bound by Clays Ltd, St Ives plc

John Murray policy is to use papers that are natural, renewable and recyclable
products and made from wood grown in sustainable forests. The logging and
manufacturing processes are expected to conform to the environmental regulations of
the country of origin.

John Murray (Publishers)
338 Euston Road
London NW1 3BH

www.johnmurray.co.uk

To Emma, Sarah, George and Madeleine
with love

Elizabethan England

London (inset):
Whitehall · Westminster · Shrewsbury Ho. · Chelsea · River Thames · Isle of Dogs · Greenwich

Scotland

Wales

Zervaulx Abbey · Masham · York · Hardwick Hall · Chartley · Blithfield · Shrewsbury · Burghley House · Norwich · Sudeley Castle · Gloucester · Oxford · St Albans · Theobalds · Wanstead · Bristol · Windsor · London · Canterbury · Southampton · Exeter · Plymouth

Elizabeth

Shoreditch

City of Londo

Southampton House
Spitalfields

Aldersgate   Cripplegate   Bishopsgate

Holborn
Moorgate

Essex House
Newgate   Fylpot
Ludgate   Lane   Aldgate

CITY WAL

Bridewell
Dowgate
St Magnus
Cross

Gun
foundry

Whitehall
Palace

London
Bridge

Gatehouse
Prison

Bankside

Tower

Bull~baiting

Topcliffe's
House

St Mary Overy
Water~stairs

Gully
Hole

St Thomas
Hospital

Westminster

Lambeth

Southwark

0   ¼   ½   ¾   1

Mile

Bull~b

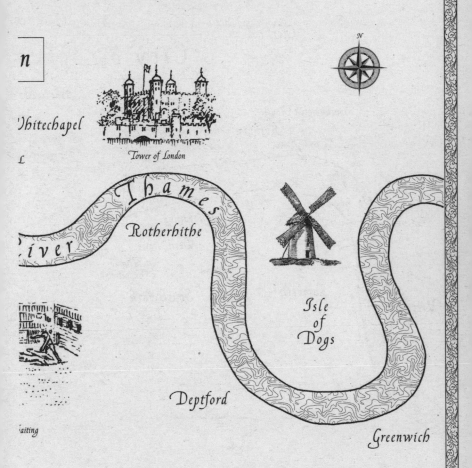

n

Whitechapel

L

Tower of London

Thames

Rotherhithe

River

Isle
of
Dogs

Deptford

aiting

Greenwich

Chapter 1

Iᴺ ᴛʜᴇ ʜᴇᴀᴛ of the evening, just as daylight began to drift into dusk, Joe Jaggard took Amy Le Neve's hand in his and pulled her willingly away from her wedding feast.

Amy was slight, little more than five foot and less than a hundredweight. Her fair hair shone in the last of the light and her skin was as clear and soft as a milkmaid's. She was sixteen, yet her hand in Joe's great right hand was like a child's. He was eighteen years, six foot or more, lean and muscular and golden. In his left hand he clasped a wine flagon.

They ran on, breathless, until her bare foot struck a sharp flint and she faltered, crying out in shock and pain. Joe stopped and laid her down in the long grass. He kissed her foot and sucked the blood that trickled from the sole.

Tears flowed down her cheeks. Joe cupped her head in his hands, his fingers tangling in her tear-drenched hair, and kissed her face all over. He held her to him, engulfing her.

She pulled open his chemise of fine cambric, he pushed her wedding smock away from her calves, up over her flawless thighs, crumpling the thin summer worsted. It was lovemaking, but it was warfare too; the last delirious stabbings in a battle they knew to be lost.

Joe took a draught from the flagon. 'You know what, doll,' he said, and his voice became high-pitched, 'I do believe you are an abomination. Get you behind me, daughter of Satan, for you are profane and impure and as frail as the rib of Adam. Verily, I say you are fallen into corruption.'

She jabbed him sharply in the ribs with her elbow. 'I'll abominate you,' she said, laughing with him. She sobered. 'The funny thing is, though, he *really* talks like that.'

'Winterberry? Winter-turd is what I call him. He's a dirty, breech-shitting lecher of a man, I do reckon. Puritans they call them. He's as pure as swine-slurry, steeped in venery and lewdness. He's got a face like a dog that's never been out the kennel and a suit of clothes so black and stark they'd scare the Antichrist back into hell. He's buying you, paying for you as he might bargain for a whore at a Southwark stew.'

They were silent a few moments. In the distance, they could just hear the occasional whisper of music caught on the warm breeze.

'We'll go,' said Joe. 'We'll go to London. I've got gold.'

'I can't leave my family. They'll get the law on us. You'll be locked away and whipped. Strung up at Tyburn. I don't know what.'

He turned to her, angry now. 'Would you rather go to *his* bed? Would you have *him* play with you?'

'You know I don't want that! They forced me to marry him.'

He turned his gaze from her. 'I'll kill them all, Amy. I'll do for them – your kin, the lot. I'll scrape the figs from Winter-turd's arse and push them down his throat.'

She kissed him. 'It's hopeless. I'll have to go back there tonight. I'm a married woman now.'

His eyes were closed. Then he opened them and smiled at her. 'No, doll,' he said. 'There's stuff we can do. *I* can do. I promise you I can make it so we can be together forever. Trust me. Now kiss me again.'

✠ 2 ✠

They kissed, long and lingering. It was the last thing they ever did. They had not heard the creeping footfalls in the grass.

The first blow killed Joe. He knew nothing of it. Amy had no more than two seconds to register the horror, before the second blow came.

Chapter 2

JOHN SHAKESPEARE FOUND his wife, Catherine, in the oak-panelled school hall, teaching their four-year-old daughter Mary her alphabet from a hornbook. Catherine met his eye but she did not smile. She tossed back her long dark hair as if ridding herself of a fly. Shakespeare sensed her anger and did his best to ignore it. He knew what she wanted to discuss, so he deliberately avoided the subject and said, 'Rumsey Blade is set on flogging Pimlock yet again.'

'Yes,' she said curtly. 'I know. Six stripes. Blade has it in for the boy.'

'Pimlock takes it with fortitude.'

'Well, I don't, John. How can boys study when they face such punishments?'

There was nothing more to be said on the subject. It was merely another worry for Shakespeare to deal with as High Master of the Margaret Woode School for the Poor Boys of London. Like it or not, they were stuck with Rumsey Blade and his beloved birchrods; he had been inflicted on them by the fiercely Protestant Bishop Aylmer to ensure no Roman Catholic teachings burrowed their way into the curriculum. Catherine's Papist leanings were well known and disliked.

'But there *was* the other matter . . .' Catherine continued.

Shakespeare's neck muscles tensed. 'Must we talk about such things in front of the child?'

Catherine patted her daughter. 'Kiss your father and go to Jane,' she said briskly. Mary, delicate and comely like her mother, ran to Shakespeare and stood to receive and give a kiss, then ran off to find the maid, Jane Cooper, in the nursery.

'Now you have no excuse to avoid the subject.'

'We have nothing to discuss,' Shakespeare said, painfully aware of how brittle he must sound. 'My position is plain. You must not go to the mass.'

Catherine stood up and faced her husband. Her blue eyes were cold and unloving. 'I have surrendered to you on every aspect of our lives together,' she said quietly. 'Our daughter is brought up conforming to the Anglican church, we run a conformist school and I entertain no priests under our roof. I even attend the parish church so that I incur no fines for recusancy. Do you not think I have played my part, John?'

'I know it, Catherine, but . . .'

'Then why forbid me this one boon?'

John Shakespeare did not like to cross his wife. Usually it was pointless to do so, anyway, for she had a stubborn way. Yet this request was one he would fight to the bitter conclusion. He could not have her putting herself and the family in jeopardy.

'You know why, Catherine,' he said, his face set.

'No, John, I do *not* know why. I need you to explain it to me again, for I am but a mere woman and of simple wit.'

It would be a secret Roman Catholic mass. Such events were fraught with danger; simply to know the whereabouts of a priest, let alone harbour one, could lead to torture and the scaffold. And this mass was yet more perilous, for it was to be said by the fugitive Jesuit Father Robert Southwell, a man Catherine Shakespeare knew as a friend. He had evaded capture for six years and was regarded by Elizabeth and her Privy Council as an irritant thorn to be plucked from their flesh at all costs.

'Catherine,' he said, trying to soften his voice – the last thing he wanted was this rift between them to escalate into an unbridgeable gulf – 'I know you have made many compromises. But have I not done likewise? Did I not forsake my career with Walsingham to marry you?'

'So I must obey you?' Catherine said, almost spitting the words.

'I would rather you made your own – considered – decision. But, yes, I say you *must* obey me in this.' He had never spoken to her like this before.

She glared at him. When she spoke, her words were harsh. 'So, as Thomas Becon says in his *Christian State of Matrimony*, women and horses must be well-governed. Is that how you are guided?' She laughed with derision. 'Am I a *mare* to be so treated by you, Mr Shakespeare?'

'I have no more to say on the matter, Mistress Shakespeare. You will not go to a mass, especially not one said by the priest Southwell. He is denounced as a traitor. To consort with him would taint you and the rest of us with treason. Would you give Topcliffe the evidence he needs to destroy us and send our child in chains to the treadmill at Bridewell? Let that be an end to it.'

Shakespeare turned and strode away. He did not look back because he had no wish to meet her withering glare. He went to the courtyard and sat on a low wall, in the shade. He was shaking. This was bad, very bad. She was being utterly wrong headed.

Behind him in the courtyard, he heard unequal footsteps and turned to see his old friend and assistant Boltfoot Cooper shuffling towards him, dragging his club foot awkwardly on the cobbled stones. It occurred to Shakespeare that Boltfoot was becoming slower in his movements as he neared the age of forty. Perhaps this quiet life as a school gatekeeper did not suit an old mariner and veteran of Drake's circumnavigation.

'Boltfoot?'

'You have a visitor, Mr Shakespeare. A Mr Charles McGunn would speak with you. He has a serving-man with him.'

'Do we know Mr McGunn? Is he the father of a prospective pupil?'

Boltfoot shook his head. 'He says he is sent by the Earl of Essex to treat with you.'

Shakespeare's furrowed brow betrayed his surprise. He laughed lightly. 'Well, I suppose I had better see him.'

'I shall show him through.'

'Not here, Boltfoot. I will go to the library. Show this McGunn and his servant to the anteroom and offer them refreshment, then bring them to me in five minutes.'

As Shakespeare climbed the oaken staircase to the high-windowed library, with its shelves of books collected by the founder of this school, Thomas Woode, and, latterly, by himself, he considered Essex. He was famed throughout the land as Queen Elizabeth's most favoured courtier, a gallant blessed with high birth, dashing looks, courage in battle, sporting prowess and the charm to enchant a princess. It was said he had even supplanted Sir Walter Ralegh in the Queen's affections. What interest could the Earl of Essex have in an obscure schoolmaster like Shakespeare, a man so far from the centre of public life that he doubted anyone at court even knew his name?

McGunn was a surprise. Shakespeare had half expected a livery-clad bluecoat to appear; but McGunn looked like no flunkey Shakespeare had ever seen. He was of middle height, thick-set, with the fearless, belligerent aspect of a bull terrier. He had big, knotted hands. His face and head were bare and bald, save for two greying eyebrows beneath a gnarled and pulpy forehead. A heavy gold hoop was pierced into the lobe of his left ear. He smiled with good humour and held out a firm, meaty hand to John Shakespeare.

'Mr Shakespeare, it is a pleasure to meet you,' he said.

'Mr McGunn?'

'Indeed.'

Shakespeare guessed his accent to be Irish, but from which part or class of that dark, forbidding island he had no way of knowing. His attire struck him as incongruous; a wide, starched ruff circled his thick neck, a doublet finely braided with thread of gold girded his trunk and he wore hose of good-quality blue serge and netherstocks the colour of corn. It seemed to Shakespeare that he had a working man's face and body in a gentleman's clothing.

His serving-man at his side was introduced merely as Slyguff. He looked no more the bluecoat of a great house than did McGunn, though he was less richly dressed, in the buff jerkin of a smithy or a carter. Slyguff was smaller and thinner than his master. He was wiry like the taut cable of a ship's anchor, with a narrow face and a sharp, gristly nose. Though smaller, he looked every bit as formidable as McGunn. One of Slyguff's eyes, the left one, was dead and the other betrayed no emotion at all.

'I hope that Mr Cooper has offered you some ale. It is another hot day.'

'Indeed, it is and indeed, he has, Mr Shakespeare,' McGunn said, smiling warmly. 'For which we are both grateful. To tell you true I could have drunk the Irish Sea dry this day.'

'How may I help you, Mr McGunn?'

'Well, you could start by giving us yet more ale. No, no, I jest. We are here because we are sent by my lord of Essex to escort you to him at Essex House. He wishes to speak with you.'

'The Earl of Essex wishes to speak with *me*?'

'That is correct, Mr Shakespeare.'

'Why should he wish to speak to an unknown schoolmaster, Mr McGunn?'

'Perchance, he wants lessons in Latin, or a little learning in counting. Could you help him with that, now? Or maybe you could show him how to command his temper, for certain he is as moody as the weather.'

'Mr McGunn, I fear you jest again.'

'I do, I do. The truth is he wishes your advice on a particular matter of interest. But for certain you don't do yourself credit when you call yourself an *unknown schoolmaster*. Who has not heard of the brilliant exploits of John Shakespeare on behalf of Queen and country?'

'Mr McGunn, that is ancient history.'

'Not in the Earl's eyes, it's not. He is mighty impressed by the tale of your fierce courage in the face of an implacable foe. As am I, may I add. You have done admirable work, sir.'

Shakespeare accepted the compliment with good grace and bowed with a slight smile on his lips. 'And what sort of advice is the Earl of Essex seeking, Mr McGunn? He must know I am retired from my work as an intelligencer.'

'That is for him to say, Mr Shakespeare. I am merely his humble servant.'

McGunn did not look at all humble, thought Shakespeare. Were it not for the fine clothes, he and Slyguff were the kind of duo an honest subject of Her Majesty might well cross the road to avoid. Yet for all his brutish appearance, McGunn seemed a good-humoured fellow and Shakespeare had to admit that he was intrigued. Who would not wish to meet the renowned Essex? 'Well, then, let us make an appointment, and I will be there.'

'No, Mr Shakespeare, we are to accompany you to him *now*. My lord of Essex does not wait on appointments.'

'Well, I am afraid he will *have* to wait. I have a lesson to conduct within the hour.'

McGunn smiled and clapped Shakespeare on the shoulder with a hand the size of a kitchen wife's sieve. 'Come now, Mr Shakespeare, are you not High Master of this school? Delegate one of your lesser masters to take over your tutoring for the morning. The earl is a busy man and I know he will make it worth your while to take the time to meet him. Here.' McGunn took a gold coin from his purse and spun it in the air. He caught it and held it between thumb and forefinger in front of Shakespeare's eyes. 'That's for starters. Take it. There's plenty more where that came from.'

Shakespeare did not take the gold coin. He stared McGunn in the eye and saw only gently mocking humour. 'Very well,' he said. 'I will come with you. But give me a few minutes to arrange my lesson and let my wife know where I am going.'

As he spoke the words, he experienced a sense of dread; the battle with Catherine was far from done.

Chapter 3

Rumsey Blade, a small man with a pinched, unlovable face and thinning hair, was not happy about taking on Shakespeare's lesson. He was in the yard, swishing his birch cane in preparation for flogging Pimlock, who was awaiting his punishment, hose about his knees and bent forward over the low wall where Shakespeare had recently been sitting.

'I am called away on urgent business, Mr Blade. You will take my lesson.'

Blade frowned. 'Indeed, Mr Shakespeare?'

'Indeed, Mr Blade.'

'Well, I cannot allow you to make a habit of such things. It is a bad example to the boys when masters fail to keep to the roster.'

Shakespeare did not have time to argue. 'Mr Blade, you are forgetting who is the High Master here, to speak to me thus.' He looked at the boy. 'And I would suggest you go easy with Pimlock.'

'Would you so, Mr Shakespeare? And what use do you think a flogging would be if it did not draw blood?'

'It is of little or no use, whether blood be drawn or not.'

'At Winchester, Friday was always flogging day and a failure to stripe them with blood was considered not at all acceptable. Do you consider yourself superior to Winchester, sir?'

'Good day, Mr Blade.'

As Shakespeare turned away, Blade went rigid. His birch rod ceased swishing. 'And have you discussed this matter with the Bishop? He will not be happy with such a lax attitude to discipline and the good governance of boys.'

Shakespeare walked away.

McGunn and Slyguff were waiting for him in Dowgate, mounted on their horses. Boltfoot held the grey mare, saddled and ready. Out here, in the full blaze of the late morning sun, the heat of the day hit Shakespeare like the blaze of a Smithfield pyre. He swung up into the saddle, then pulled his cap down on his head to shield his brow and neck. McGunn had already removed his ruff and opened the front of his fine doublet in an attempt to cool off.

'Let's ride,' McGunn said.

Fragrant summer flowers and herbs – lavender, rosemary, bay and a hundred other species – grew in profusion in the city's many gardens, yet they did little to counter the overpowering stench of the dung-and-slop-strewn roads as Shakespeare and his companions trotted their horses slowly along Thames Street then up to the City Wall. Rats scurried brazenly, picking at the discarded bones from kitchens. Kites circled overhead or perched on walls, feeding at will from the bodies of slaughtered cats. 'Makes you long for the fresh air of the countryside, does it not, Mr Shakespeare,' McGunn said. 'They say the plague will come hard this year.'

Shakespeare nodded. He had already wondered whether they should close the school while summer lasted and head for Warwickshire to escape the pestilence. It would be good to visit his family. It might also be good for the health of his marriage.

At Ludgate a team of dog-catchers was rounding up strays to slit their throats, a sure sign that the City Aldermen were worried about the possibility of the sickness blowing up into a general plague. It was a terrifying thought.

All along the way beggars and rag-clad doxies stretched out thin, bony hands and stumps, hoping in vain for coins from those driving the heavy midday traffic of farm wagons and timber carts. It was a dismal sight, a sign of what England was coming to as crops failed and the demands of the war chest ate into treasury funds. As they approached Essex House, Shakespeare saw a group of a dozen or so vagabonds surrounding the open gateway. McGunn stopped by them and handed out alms liberally, for which many of them thanked him by name and doffed their caps. 'They may be only beggars, but they are *our* beggars,' McGunn said by way of explanation to Shakespeare, and then roared with laughter and kicked on through the gates.

Essex House stood on a large plot of land between the Thames and The Strand. Its gardens swept down to the river-bank, where there was a high wall with a gated opening to some water-steps, a landing stage for boats and barges.

Shakespeare and his companions dismounted in the fore-court under the watchful eye of a troop of halberdiers, their axe-pike lances held stock still at their sides. The house was a hive of bees, so energetic were the comings and goings. An ostler quickly came forth and took their horses. 'This is the Essex hovel, Mr Shakespeare, how do you think it?' McGunn asked, standing back to admire the enormous stone-built house.

Shakespeare looked up at its towering frontage.

'Forty-two chambers, one hundred and sixty servants and retainers, but day-by-day you will find twice that number and more entering and leaving. Kitchens large enough to cook a feast fit for a monarch and a banqueting house great enough to entertain one. All built by his mother's late husband, the Earl of Leicester.' McGunn strode towards the steps to the main doorway, his bull neck seeming to lead the way with the rest of him following. A halberdier stood either side of the doorway, shoulders back and unmoving. They clearly knew McGunn well for he was not required to ask leave to pass. 'Let us go in. You will be meeting my lord of Essex in the Picture Gallery.'

Essex stood in the middle of the high-ceilinged, intricately plastered gallery. To his right, casting him in a half-shade that accentuated his fine features, were four south-facing windows that stretched almost the full depth of the walls. The room was bathed in brilliant light by the high midday sun and the windows were opened at every available casement to allow in what breeze was to be had.

The earl looked magnificent. He stood tall in a rich costume of white silk and mother-of-pearl, his curled hair combed back from his wide forehead, his full-length red beard tumbling over his ruff. He had a slight upward tilt to his chin, his gaze fixed on a small volume that he held at arm's length in his left hand as if he were a man of letters, not war. Lest anyone forget his cannon reputation, however, his right hand nonchalantly cupped the hilt of his ceremonial sword.

All around him the room was hung with portraits: Essex in military armour with wheel-lock, sword and poniard; his beautiful mother, Lettice Knollys, in a baudekin gown of bejewelled glory; Essex's sisters, Dorothy and Penelope, reckoned by many to be the match of their mother in beauty . . . and in wildness of spirit; his father, the late Walter Devereux, first Earl of Essex, who died a mysterious death in Ireland, some said of poisoning; Lettice's new husband, Sir Christopher Blount, a handsome man with what John Shakespeare took to be an untrustworthy eye; and dominating them all, Essex's late stepfather, Leicester, the man who first won Queen Elizabeth's heart but betrayed her by marrying Lettice (and, some said, was guilty of poisoning her husband Walter in order to do so).

It occurred to Shakespeare that this was the most formidable family of the age, a clan to match the Tudors themselves in power and majesty. Leicester, in particular, seemed to survey the scene from his portrait with supreme contempt.

A few yards in front of Essex stood a painter at his easel, paint-loaded brush in hand. Essex's eyes rose languidly from his book and drifted to Shakespeare and McGunn. He nodded to the painter, who wiped his brush on a rag and put it down on a coffer beside him, where he had his pigments and oils and other tools of his craft, then stood to one side.

Essex closed his book and stepped forward, his posture slumping slightly as he did so, making him now appear to have the ungainly stoop so often associated with extremely tall men.

McGunn, whose man Slyguff had remained outside the door, ambled forward, grinning. 'My lord . . .'

Essex smiled back and clasped him like an old friend. 'You are well met, Mr McGunn.'

McGunn turned towards Shakespeare, then swept his arm to introduce the guest. 'And this is Mr Shakespeare, whom you asked me to find.'

Shakespeare bowed to him in deference. 'It is an honour to meet you, my lord.'

'Mr Shakespeare,' Essex said, his eyes lighting up. 'What a pleasure to meet you. And the honour, may I say, is mine. Let me shake you by the hand.'

The grip almost crushed Shakespeare's knuckles.

'So, Mr Shakespeare, this is the hand that brought down Philip of Spain's hired assassin and saved Drake. You are welcome in my home.'

Shakespeare bowed. 'You do me too much honour, my lord.'

'Come, sit with me. Take some wine. It has been cooled in ice.

Your face betrays your surprise, Mr Shakespeare. Have you not heard? We have an ice cave here; it is a conceit of antiquity that I heard of from a correspondent in Italy. In the cold of winter, you collect ice and store it in the depths of the cellar, protected with straw and horsehair. Then in summer, even in a *furnace* summer such as this, it remains in its solid state to cool your wines and salads. It is an excellent device for keeping the freshness of fish, I am told.' Essex snapped his fingers and a servant stepped forward to take his order. 'Now, Mr Shakespeare,' he said. 'You must wish to know why I have asked you to come here.'

Shakespeare inclined his head, but said nothing.

'And in due course I shall reveal all to you. But first let me ask about your circumstances. I believe you have a grammar school for poor boys?'

Shakespeare explained about the Margaret Woode school. Essex was clearly bored. At last he shook his head slowly. 'This is all very well, Mr Shakespeare,' he said. 'But do you not miss the excitement of your former life?'

Shakespeare sometimes wondered this himself, but he would not admit as much here. 'It was of its time, my lord, and I am glad to have served; but now my life has taken a different turn.'

'But your career as an intelligencer ended in an unfortunate manner. I believe you fell foul of the late, much lamented Mr Secretary over the question of your wife's Catholicism. That is certainly the tale bruited about.'

Shakespeare stiffened. 'It is all a long time ago, my lord.'

'Yes, Mr Shakespeare, I do understand that quite well. But, I say again: is schoolmastering enough?'

'It is, my lord.'

McGunn and the painter listened in silence. Essex turned to them now. 'What say you, Mr McGunn? And you, Mr Segar? Can a tiger so lose his stripes that he become a household cat?'

Both men laughed. 'Quite impossible,' McGunn said. 'What man could turn from the art of war, even a war of secrets, to the world of dusty books? Impossible, I say.' The painter signalled his agreement with a slight bow of the head.

The bluecoat arrived with four glasses of sweet and light canary wine. As Shakespeare sipped he noted that the drink was indeed cold, a refreshing and remarkable indulgence on such a hot day.

'Now then,' Essex said. 'To the matter in hand. The reason I have asked you here. Does the word *Roanoke* mean anything to you, Mr Shakespeare?'

Roanoke. Who had *not* heard of Roanoke? The mere word conjured up an image in Shakespeare's mind of a far-distant, exotic shore, of strange plants, venomous creatures and yet more dangerous men. Roanoke: the lost colony. One of the most mysterious tales of the age.

Shakespeare let a second draught of the cool drink slip down his throat. 'Roanoke. Why, yes, my lord. I have heard the tale, and a curious one it is.'

Essex gestured Shakespeare to come and sit with him on a wooden settle beside the window. 'Before we proceed, let me tell you the story as I know it. I am sure that much has been said about Roanoke in the taverns and ordinaries of London, and most of it probably embellished for the sort of gulls who buy the penny broadsheets. Few people know the plain facts, so I shall rehearse them for you. Roanoke is a small island off the Virginia coast of the New World, reckoned to be some five hundred sea miles north and east of the Spanish colony of St Augustine. Sheltered by sandbanks, it had been thought so well favoured that it would do well as the site for England's first colony in the New World. It seemed to offer natural protection from the Spanish, who would dearly love to see it done away with, and to offer a base for English privateers.'

'That is much as I had heard it, my lord.'

'Five years ago, the first permanent English colony was founded there: about one hundred and ten men, women and children – and two babies, I believe – left to fend for themselves, hopefully to prosper and grow. But even before the ships had set sail, leaving them there, it was clear things were not running smoothly. There were disagreements with the savages. And there were shortages of supplies. Because of this, the governor of the colony, John White, came back to England with the ships. His mission was to assemble supply vessels to return the following year, 1588. But, as the world knows, he was unable to do so.'

'Because of the Armada.'

'Quite so. It wasn't until three years after the colonists were left that an expedition was mounted to help those one hundred and ten souls. But when the ships arrived they found no trace of them or their belongings.'

Shakespeare ran his finger around the cool rim of the elegant wine glass and looked closely at Essex. How could this story possibly involve him? 'Was there not some clue as to their disappearance, my lord? Some mark on a tree indicating that they might have gone to live with the savages? Or is that a tavern tale?'

'No, you are correct about that, Mr Shakespeare. There were three letters carved on a tree – *CRO*. And on a fence there was carved the word *Croatoan*. That is the name of a tribe of savages living at that time on an island to the south of Roanoke. It is said they had been helpful to the colonists in the past, but that they were losing patience with the white man's demand for food. Would the colonists have gone there under such circumstances? Perhaps they were starving and did so, and perhaps they are all alive and well and living happy, productive lives in harmony with their hosts. That is certainly the most comforting explanation. For my own part, I do not believe it. Had they made an orderly departure, they would have had time to leave a more comprehensive message for those who came to find them. So there we have it, Mr Shakespeare. There is, of course, much more to it than I have told you, but before we move on I wish to be sure you have a clear understanding.'

'I believe I do, my lord. But I confess that I am less certain how it affects me.'

'Which is what we are now coming to.' Essex rose from the elm-wood settle, took Shakespeare by the elbow and stood with him gazing out of the high window. Shakespeare was a tall man, six foot by anyone's reckoning, yet Essex overtopped him by a good three inches. For a few moments they looked out at the Thames together. It teemed with the traffic of barges and tilt-boats, blanched sails dazzling in the midday sun, oars clipping splashes from the surface that burst in iridescent plumes. On the opposite shore, among verdant pasture land, stood the palace of Lambeth, residence of the Archbishop of Canterbury. Not far off, they could hear the cries and sounds of the City. 'What would you think, Mr Shakespeare,' Essex said, 'if I told you that somewhere out there, walking the streets of London, is one of the lost colonists.'

Shakespeare was not sure he had heard the question aright. 'What are you asking me, my lord? Forgive me, but I fear I do not understand what you wish of me.'

Essex let out a loud snort of laughter and then turned back to McGunn and Segar. 'You see, it is madness. No one will believe this.' And then he said slowly, directly to Shakespeare, 'What I am saying is that we have evidence that one of the so-called lost colonists is alive and well and is now here in London, thousands of miles from Roanoke. Now, how do you explain that?'

Shakespeare had no idea what he was supposed to say. The question seemed moon-mad. 'Well, I really don't know. But if he is here, then I imagine others are, too, and that they have been brought here. Somehow they must have sailed here.'

'It is not a *he*, Mr Shakespeare. It is a *she*. And we have her name. She is Eleanor Dare – and she is a woman of great interest on two counts. Firstly, she was born Eleanor White and is the daughter of John White, the colony's leader who came back to England to secure supply vessels. And secondly, she is the mother of the first-ever English baby born in the New World, a girl aptly christened Virginia. As to the suggestion that all the colonists have come back, I hardly think that is feasible. I cannot believe a hundred or more people have somehow slipped into England unnoticed. One, yes, perchance two, but a hundred, no.'

'Perhaps Eleanor Dare returned with her father five years ago when he came for the supply vessels.'

'Impossible. The other colonists would not have let her or her child leave. She was their hostage, if you like. She it was that made certain their governor – her father – would move heaven and earth to secure supply ships and return. No, if it is indeed Eleanor Dare who has been sighted here in London, then she has somehow found her way across the ocean alone. Mr Segar, please, *your* tale if you will . . .'

The artist rose from his bench. He was a man of middling height and breadth with a tight mouth and lips like a woman's, half hidden behind a wide moustache that closely resembled a cat's whiskers. He wore a long painter's smock from neck to heel to protect his valuable court attire from paint splashes. He took a deep breath. 'I have little to add to the story as told by my lord of Essex, save to say that the tale emanates from a maid in my own household, Agnes Hardy, who swears to me, hand on Bible, that she saw Eleanor Dare in London no more than a week since . . .'

'People can make mistakes,' Shakespeare suggested.

'Of course. And that is what we must find out,' Essex said. 'Now, Mr Segar, tell Mr Shakespeare where your housemaid saw this woman.'

'She was outside the theatre in Southwark, dressed as a strumpet touting for business. It was certainly in the area where the whores gather. Agnes told me she was so taken aback to see Eleanor, knowing her of old and knowing her to be lost in the New World, that for a moment she merely stood there open-mouthed in astonishment. By the time she had gathered her wits to approach her, the woman had joined arms with a man and they had gone, vanished into the theatre crowd. That was the last she saw of her.'

'What time of day was this?' Shakespeare asked.

'Mid-afternoon, I believe. You would do best to ask her such details yourself.'

It was the sort of question Shakespeare would have asked in his days as an intelligencer, to determine how much daylight there was and how clearly this Agnes Hardy might have seen this woman she took to be Eleanor Dare. But what had any of this to do with him now? McGunn read his thoughts.

'So, Mr Shakespeare, why have we brought you here? That's what you want to know.'

'Well, of course any man would be curious about this strange tale – but it really has nothing to do with me.'

Essex clapped his hands. 'But you are *just* the man for the job, Mr Shakespeare. The perfect intelligencer, a man used to digging in the most putrid of middens to find bright red rubies of betrayal. Everything I know of you suggests to me that you are the man to find this woman.'

Shakespeare set his face very determinedly. 'Oh, no . . .'

'Oh, yes, Mr Shakespeare. A thousand times yes. And you will be paid well for your troubles. I am sure that a handsome sum of gold would help your school, would it not?'

·Indeed, who did not need gold in these straitened times? 'But *why*, my lord of Essex, are you so concerned about the supposed sighting of this woman, especially when she is most unlikely to be the person identified?'

Essex looked at Shakespeare as if he had lost his wit. He sighed with great exaggeration and turned to McGunn. 'You talk to him, Mr McGunn. Answer all Mr Shakespeare's questions. Knock sense into him. I have other matters to attend to. Come, Mr Segar.'

Without another word he strode with proud yet ungainly gait towards the entrance door, Segar following in his wake. And then they were gone.

Chapter 4

IT SEEMED TO Shakespeare that he had been assailed by a whirlwind. He looked at McGunn and saw something unpleasant in his eyes.

'Well, there we have it, Shakespeare,' McGunn said with weary resignation. 'God has spoken and so we mere mortals must obey.'

Shakespeare held up the palm of his hand. 'I really don't think you and my lord of Essex quite understand—'

'Oh, we understand all right. We understand, too, that you are in sore need of funds – funds which we can provide in exchange for a small service that may take you no more than a few days. An old colleague of yours informs me that you are the perfect man for the task.'

'An old colleague?'

'You will meet him soon enough.'

Again Shakespeare demurred. 'Mr McGunn, I still feel as if there is something I am missing here.'

'Well, let me say just two words to you: Walter Ralegh. Now do you understand my lord of Essex's interest in the matter?'

Shakespeare knew, of course, that the Roanoke colony had been Ralegh's child. That it was he who had won patents from the Queen granting him permission to sponsor the colony and had raised the necessary gold for ships, crews, supplies and settlers to make it work. It had been a critical investment for the great courtier, for he had persuaded the Queen that the colony – and his plan to found a great town in Virginia grandly called The City of Ralegh – would bring untold riches to *her* coffers. But what had all this to do with Essex?

'The point is, Shakespeare,' McGunn said slowly, as if spelling out the obvious to a small boy. 'The point is that my lord of Essex and Sir Walter Ralegh are not easy companions. In truth – and I do not care if you repeat this – they would happily plunge red-hot pokers up each other's arses if in so doing they could cause the other pain and further their own influence at court. For you must know that they see each other as chief rival for the Queen's favour.'

'But that does not explain why it is so important to find this Eleanor Dare.'

McGunn ran a leathery hand over his sweat-dripping bare forehead. He pulled at his gold hoop earring, all the while staring at Shakespeare with an expression on his fleshy, canine face that hovered somewhere between condescension and intimidation. 'Because Ralegh is already in bad odour,' he said quietly. 'He has impregnated and married the Queen's lady-in-waiting Bess Throckmorton, and Elizabeth is in a towering rage. She has had them arrested and held under close arrest. Ralegh is on the ground; he will not raise himself up with poetry *this* time. Only treasure will buy his way back into the Queen's heart. Treasure from Roanoke. That is why we must find Eleanor Dare – for she alone knows what happened. Is the colony still alive? Does it thrive? Can Ralegh expect a fleet of gold? Or have all perished – and with them his hope of redemption? Do you understand *now*, Shakespeare? My lord of Essex does not want Ralegh ever to get off the ground again.'

Shakespeare acknowledged the logic. Ralegh's fate depended on Roanoke. With the colony not proven dead, he had hope still. With the colony gone, he had none. This was court politics. No one cared about the missing men, women and children. This was about power and position. Shakespeare understood it all now, and saw too that there was danger here, extreme danger.

To get caught up in an affair such as this between two of the most powerful men in the land was like finding yourself trapped in a burning attic; do you die by burning or by jumping? This was a deadly game between Essex and Ralegh. Leave them to it. 'I am sorry, Mr McGunn,' he said. 'This task you ask of me is out of the question. Please apologise to my lord of Essex on my behalf, but I cannot possibly accept his kind offer.'

There was no longer any ambiguity in McGunn's face. His lips curled back and his yellow teeth moved against each other so that Shakespeare could hear an unholy grinding noise, as if they would crack like glass against each other. 'Did I mention the twenty sovereigns?' McGunn said as if it were the last offer before a knife under the ribcage.

'Twenty sovereigns, two hundred sovereigns. I cannot be swayed, Mr McGunn. The task is not for me.'

McGunn's hand flashed out like a serpent's jaws and clasped Shakespeare by the throat. With just the one hand he lifted him clear off the floor. Shakespeare's hands went to his throat to try to dislodge the enormous hand that was choking him, but without effect. McGunn's hand was rigid and of immense, unmovable strength. He looked up into his eye and mouthed words that Shakespeare could not hear as blood rushed to his brain. Of a sudden, McGunn dropped him and he fell in a heap to the wooden floorboards. Shakespeare gasped for breath; his hands rubbed his throat. He knew now what a hanged man felt in the moments before death took him.

'You don't understand, do you, Shakespeare,' McGunn said, his soft Irish brogue dripping malevolence. 'No one – and I mean no one – turns down my lord of Essex. And more than that – no one turns me down, either. In death's name, this isn't an offer, we're making you. It's an order.'

McGunn relaxed and smiled his easy smile once again. He patted Shakespeare on the back. 'There we go. No hard feelings, Mr Shakespeare. We're all men of the world. And I am certain we shall work very well together and share a drink or two in the tavern when our toil is done.'

Chapter 5

THERE IS NO cold like that which a man feels when he is in the midst of an unresolved lovers' quarrel and yet must try to sleep. Catherine did not join her husband in their bed. When she did not appear, Shakespeare went to the nursery, where he guessed she would be. In the flickering light of his candle, he saw her lying on blankets beside their child's cot, her face turned away from him. He stood there a minute, watching her, not sure what to say. He said her name, but she did not respond.

He knew she was awake, perhaps feeling as desolate as he. He sighed inwardly, watched her a few moments more, then quietly left the room, shutting the door after him. In the morning, he decided, he would apologise to her for his intransigence. Whatever the risks, he should have let her accept the invitation of her friend Anne Bellamy to attend the mass, see this Jesuit priest Southwell one last time, hear him say his superstitious words. What harm could a few words of Latin do? All over the country, seminary priests and Jesuits hid in secret places and said hundreds of masses every day in defiance of the laws that branded them traitors. Surely it would be safe enough for Catherine to have gone, just this one time. Did he not owe her that much?

The sun was still low when the four boys ran out into the meadows near the village of Wanstead in the county of Essex. They had a pig's bladder from the shambles, blown up tight and tied secure so that it made a football. The first boy, a strong lad of twelve, kicked the ball far into the grass and they all chased after it.

As one, the three fastest boys fell on the ball, pushing and punching each other to get to it. The fourth of them was close behind and snatched up the bladder from under the pile of laughing, grunting bodies. They lunged for him, but he was too nimble for them and punted it away into the oaks and ash at the edge of the wood. Once more the chase was on and they ran into the wood, hitting and tripping each other as they went.

The wood was thick with bracken and brambles that scratched their legs. At first they could not find their ball. Then the big twelve-year-old, his nose dripping blood from the sharp elbow of one of his friends, put a finger to his lips for the others to be silent. Crouching low, he crept forward, down a slight incline. He could hear the light babbling of a stream and he could see naked flesh.

'Over there,' he whispered. 'They're swiving, I'm sure of it. I can see them. Let's get a look.'

The boys stifled giggles and followed him silently through the ferns. All were tense with excitement at the thought of catching a man and woman at their business, here in the open air, like rutting farm animals.

'Look at the tits on that,' the nimble lad said.

Suddenly the big boy at the front stopped. He sniffed the air. 'I don't like this,' he whispered. 'I don't think they *are* swiving.' Ahead of him, a startled fox scurried sideways, its ears pricked. It loped off into the darkness of the wood, something in its jaws. The boy took no note of the fox; his eyes were fixed on the naked flesh. He stood up and gasped at what he could see. A few yards ahead of him, half in and half out of the stream, was a pair of entwined human bodies. Their unclothed flesh was bloated and blood-flecked. Flies buzzed around them and other insects crawled over them and into them. The boy felt bile rising in his throat at the overpowering stink and put a hand to his mouth.

'God's bloody teeth,' the nimble one said. 'God's bloody teeth, they're dead. Both of them.'

Chapter 6

SHAKESPEARE HAD BEEN stricken with gloom all morning. On waking, he had wanted to apologise to Catherine, but she was already up and gone.

'I believe she went to the market,' Jane, their maid, said.

'Did she tell you that?'

'No, but it is the day she likes to go, and she left Mary with me.'

As Shakespeare picked at his repast of cold beef and onion pie, with a beaker of ale, Boltfoot Cooper brought a message from McGunn. 'I suspect it is by way of a warning or threat, Mr Shakespeare.'

'What exactly did he say?'

'He said, "Roanoke calls. Fetch your mangy English arse to Essex House by dusk tomorrow and there shall be gold. Fail me and there shall be penury and pain."'

Shakespeare laughed without humour. 'Yes, it is fair to assume that is a threat, albeit couched in playhouse terms, Boltfoot. Did he not wish to talk with me himself?'

'I asked him. He said there was no point. He said he was sure you would see things his way.'

'And what did *you* say, Boltfoot?'

'I told him to go piss his Irish breeches, sir.'

'Thank you, Boltfoot. I could not have put it better myself.

However, I fear we have not heard the last of Mr Charlie McGunn.'

Boltfoot turned to go, then thought better of it. 'Excuse me, master. I wonder whether you have heard the news today.'

'What news is that, Boltfoot?'

'The Jesuit priest Southwell is taken. It is bruited all about town. Topcliffe discovered him at a manor house in Middlesex, then brought him in a cart to his Westminster torture chamber this very morning with a guard of fifty pursuivants on horse.'

Though he sat at the table, Shakespeare felt his legs turn weak as though he would not be able to stand. 'Southwell taken in Middlesex?'

'In the Bellamy house.'

Where was Catherine? He had seen her curled up beside Mary's cot late last night – surely she could not have somehow slipped out and gone to that house? Shakespeare was seized by fear, a terror so intense he felt his chest encircled by icy tentacles. There was a hammering at the door and Boltfoot shuffled away, dragging his clubfoot, to answer it.

Richard Topcliffe stood there, alone, incongruous in his court satin and ruff. Richard Topcliffe – white-haired priest-hunter, torturer, prosecutor and executioner – a man who had his sovereign's ear and gloried in no title other than Queen's Servant.

'Boltfoot Cooper. What, not dead yet? We shall have to attend to that.' He pushed past Boltfoot into the antechamber and stood a moment, hands on hips, legs astride, looking about him. 'So, this is Mr Shakespeare's spawning ground for Papist traitors.'

In the next room, Shakespeare got up from the long oaken table. He knew instantly who it was; that cur-like voice, which he had not heard in five years, would always fill him with fore-boding. He went straight through to the anteroom to confront him. 'Topcliffe,' he said. 'You are not welcome in my house.'

'Hah, Shakespeare. You did not think I had forgot you, I hope? A pretty pile you have here, pleasingly placed beside the river. I believe this building will be mine one day, when I secure your conviction for treason. And that cannot be long in coming.'

'Why are you here?'

'Why, sir, I bring you information. There have been complaints lodged against your school. The Bishop does fear that you are in breach of your licence, teaching of saints and relics and superstitious treason. I am to report to him whether this house of easement should not be closed down.'

'You lie, Topcliffe. These are nought but lies.'

Topcliffe put his hand inside his green doublet and brought forth a paper. 'You will see. But I have good news, too. News to delight you, I am sure. This very day I have disturbed a hill of Romish ants and plucked forth the chiefest among them, one Robert Southwell, also known as Cotton. And all in a house I believe your Papist wife knows well. Are you not pleased, Shakespeare, that traitors have been apprehended and will be questioned by me?'

Shakespeare stepped forward, closer to Topcliffe. 'What has this to do with my wife? What do you know of her?'

Topcliffe laughed and tapped his silver-topped blackthorn stick against the dark panelling and the boards. 'Why, is she somewhere here, perchance, hid away?' He unfurled the paper he had withdrawn from his doublet. 'Do you know what this is, Shakespeare? It is a tree of your dog-mother wife's family in Yorkshire, sent me by friends. Did you not know that there are Topcliffes in Yorkshire? Your wife, it seems, does come from a veritable litter of dog-mother Papists.'

Every muscle and sinew in Shakespeare's body was taut. Topcliffe was here to gloat, but gloat about what exactly? There was nothing new in Catherine's Catholicism; Topcliffe had known of it for years. Was it the taking of Southwell that he came for or something else? Shakespeare felt a pang for the Jesuit, but his problems were of his own making; he knew the penalty of entering the country illegally, he must understand that in law he was guilty of high treason and would be dealt with by the full weight of Her Majesty's unforgiving authority.

There was a movement and the door to the antechamber opened. Suddenly, Catherine was there, in front of him, dressed in a light summer kirtle and smock, clutching a basket filled with fruits and salad vegetables. She glared at him, then noticed Topcliffe and her angry expression deepened to red fury. Shakespeare let out a long breath of relief; so she *had* been to market, not caught at the Bellamy house.

'Catherine?'

'What is *he* doing here?'

'Thank God you are safe.'

She ignored her husband and focused her attention on Topcliffe. 'I hear you have taken Father Southwell. You must be proud of yourself. Did my husband tell you I wanted to be there, Mr Topcliffe, and hear the mass said? I wish I had been there when you called with your band of cowards.'

'I wish it, too. For certain I had expected you there. But fear not, your time will come, as it will to all the Antichrist's whores. Southwell, the boy-priest, is already talking, squealing like a pig that is being relieved of its sweetbreads. Why, he can scarce get breath enough to tell me about the treasons of Mr and Mrs Shakespeare, and I do not even have him against the wall yet.'

'And what of Anne Bellamy and her family?'

'Anne Bellamy?' Topcliffe thrust a pipe of smouldering tobacco between his brown teeth and furled back his aged lips in a corpse-like grin. He drew deep of the smoke, then belched it out in a cloud. 'Why, she was the dirty slattern that told us where the sodomite Jesuit traitor was hid, under the eaves. I smelt the greased priest by his farting and plucked him out from his stinking hole. Her Majesty will double up in mirth as I tell her how I tickle his parts in my own strongroom. I will put him down like a plague dog so that he can no longer spread his evil pestilence. As for Anne Bellamy, we shall make a Protestant of her yet.'

'Get out,' Shakespeare said, pushing Topcliffe in the chest. 'Take your stench from my house.'

'I shall have you all against the wall, too. And then I shall prosecute you in court and when you go to the scaffold, I will be beside you with the filleting knife in my hand, drawing out your entrails and feeling your blood run through my fingers into the dust where it belongs.'

Boltfoot Cooper was behind Topcliffe now, wrenching at his elegant, green satin doublet, dragging him backwards towards the door as Shakespeare pushed from the man's front. Topcliffe was laughing all the while, prodding at Shakespeare with his blackthorn. 'This house, this maggoty den of Papistry, is no longer protected, Shakespeare. Walsingham is cold in his grave and no one will look out for you. When you are dead, your child and Woode's orphan spawn will be taken to Bridewell and handed to the taskmaster to have the Antichrist's demons flogged out of them forever.'

Topcliffe was strong, but Boltfoot was powerful, too, and with Shakespeare's assistance he soon had the intruder out on the front step. Not that he put up much resistance, for he had said what he came to say and he had other business to attend to. Even as he strode away for the barge to Greenwich, his dark good humour was evident in his cruel face; he had the prize he had waited six years to secure and he would bask in his sovereign's favour.

Shakespeare watched him walk away along Dowgate, then

went inside and slammed the door shut. He was shaking. Catherine eyed him coldly.

'You see what you have brought us to, Mistress Shakespeare?' he said. 'You see what peril you bring to this household.'

For a few moments they stood facing each other like two fighting fowls about to be let loose with spurred talons. 'Mr Shakespeare,' she said sharply. 'A man whom I am proud to call friend has been taken by that brute and *you* shout at *me*. He will destroy his body and use all his power to break his soul, and he will have the full panoply of this heretic government behind him. It is said in the marketplace, where none talk of aught else, that the Queen danced for joy this morning when word reached her of Father Southwell's arrest.'

'Then you must see the danger, madam. He had a chart of your family in Yorkshire with their Papist leanings ringed in ink. He meant to snare you. That is what we are dealing with.'

She pushed a hand back sharply across her long, dark hair. 'I have had enough of this dissembling, attending your preposterous church on fear of a fine. I will have no more of it. You can keep your pseudo-religion, sir, with its pseudo-bishops and sham ministers and a sovereign who arrogantly places herself above God's vicar on earth. Why, I expect she will pass an act of supremacy over God himself next. Good day to you, sir.' Without waiting for a reply, she swept into the house and out of her husband's sight.

Shakespeare wanted to follow her, but it was pointless. This storm, if it were to pass, would not be calmed by harsh words. He still felt angry. He had been right all along. A trap had been set for Southwell and Catherine had almost walked into it. But who was behind it? A suspicion was clawing at the back of his mind, scratching like a terrier's paws at the earth. The name McGunn would not go away.

He looked at the squat figure of his man, Boltfoot Cooper, as if he might find some solution to his problems there. But Boltfoot had his own concerns: Jane, his wife, was heavy with child, and they had already lost their first-born at birth.

Boltfoot did not smile. His rugged face was weather-beaten into permanent lines and creases, set hard like the furrows on oak bark, the reward of many years at sea.

'I am going for some air, Boltfoot. Remember, spend time with Jane. One disconsolate wife in a household is more than enough.'

Outside, he walked by the river. A light breeze brought some relief from the sun, now high in a cloudless sky. He looked east towards the bridge and watched the cormorants fishing.

A man appeared at his elbow. 'At least the waterbirds keep cool, do they not, sir?'

Shakespeare turned towards the voice. It came from a man of advanced years, perhaps fifty, with a generous face beneath a thinning pate of white hair. Shakespeare knew him, but could not place him. He wore a poor shirt and breeches beneath a farm worker's felt hat. Shakespeare smiled at him. 'Forgive me, I do not recall your name.'

'Clarkson, Mr Shakespeare. I was Lord Burghley's man for many years.'

'Yes, of course. I am sorry, Clarkson. Are you pensioned now?'

'Not exactly, sir. Let me speak plain, though quietly, if I may. This meeting is not an accident. I am here to talk with you, privately.'

Shakespeare frowned. 'You wish to talk with me? Why not come to my house?'

'The same reason that I am not in my livery, sir. I must not be seen with you. This is a matter of some delicacy and it is not possible to know who might be watching.'

'You had better tell me more.'

'Indeed, sir. Perhaps if I were to walk off eastwards and you were to turn back alone up Dowgate, taking care to see if anyone dogs your footsteps, then we could meet again out of the public glare. Might we say the church of St John in Walbrook in five or ten minutes' time, sir? It will be cool in there and we can talk without being observed or overheard.'

'Clarkson, you have me intrigued. I will see you there.'

Shakespeare liked Clarkson and believed him trustworthy. As he walked slowly along Dowgate north towards Walbrook, he looked about him to see if he was followed. The streets were thronged with noisy crowds and clogged with wagons and carts that could scarce move for the poor parking of other wagons and the scaffolding on houses in the narrow lane. It would be difficult to discern the prying eyes of a stranger among this sweating mass of humanity.

St John's in Walbrook was empty when he entered. But as Clarkson had predicted, it was pleasantly cool, a sanctuary on this baking-hot day. The church was sparsely furnished with only a few three-legged stools to sit on and a table where once a great Catholic altar had stood. All the finery of Rome had been torn out and burnt; the rood-screen and the confession boxes, the bones of saints and painted panelling, all long gone in a great bonfire. The stained glass had been smashed years ago by Protestants and not replaced.

Shakespeare sat on one of the stools and waited. When he had been there a minute or two and no one else had come in, he heard a noise, like a whispered call, from a small chapel to the side and went to investigate. There was a door to the vestry. He went in and found Clarkson there.

'I am sorry for the secrecy, sir,' he said. 'But as you will discover, it is entirely necessary. I hope that neither of us has been pursued here.'

'I am afraid I have no way of knowing, Clarkson. Now, pray, tell me what this is about.'

Clarkson looked grave. 'I am now in the employ of Lord Burghley's son, Mr Shakespeare. I am sure you know of him: Sir Robert Cecil, a privy councillor and already taking on much of the workload of the late Sir Francis Walsingham. Some say he is already Principal Secretary in all but name.'

Cecil? Of course Shakespeare knew of him. He was probably the most influential of the younger men in Elizabeth's government, even if he lacked the raw physical power and dash of courtiers such as Essex and Ralegh. 'And what has that to do with me, Clarkson?'

'He wishes to see you, sir. On a matter of great import to the realm, I believe, though I am not in a position to tell you what it is.'

'And when and where am I to see him?'

'He is at Theobalds, sir, his country home in the county of Hertford. He asks that you come straightway to him and he apologises for the inconvenience to you.'

Shakespeare shook his head. First Essex, now Cecil. But he had no choice. When such men summoned you, you obeyed the call. 'May I return to the school first, to reorganise my lessons?'

Clarkson shook his head. 'I fear not, that would be too hazardous. Just follow me now. I have horses waiting.'

In a remote house on that bleak and lawless tongue of swampland known as the Isle of Dogs – though it was no island, being surrounded on just three of its sides by the Thames – a frightened man sat, stripped to the waist, on a high-backed wooden chair. His wrists were strapped to the chair arms and he clenched his hands in fists. His upper arms and shoulders were bound tight to the back struts. He was a strong, muscular man but he could not move. He shivered uncontrollably, though the day was sweltering. Sweat poured from his thinning black-grey hair and forehead into his eyes and piss trickled down from his breeches to a puddle on the floor.

Slyguff stood in front of him, holding a pair of tanner's shears – powerful iron clippers that cut through leather with ease. The man on the chair shrank into himself, terror in his wide brown eyes. He was about thirty, with the honed body of a mariner. Slyguff prised apart the clenched fingers of the man's left hand. With practised art, he pushed the blades of the shears over the soft, sinewy web of flesh between the thumb and forefinger. With his one working eye, he looked into the man's eyes for some sign of cooperation, then snipped.

The blades sliced through the flesh, splitting the two digits yet further apart. The man screamed. He would not be heard, for no honest beings came near this desolate place on the marshes, save wading birds and the feral dogs that roamed here free. Blood shot out from the man's cut hand on to Slyguff's apron and face. He wiped it with the sleeve of his shirt, then moved the shears to the next arc of webbing between the forefinger and the middle finger.

'Mr Slyguff, please, I beg you in God's name. I do not know where Bramer is. I have not seen him these five years.'

Snip. A deep groan of pain and terror. It was an unnatural noise, a roar of despair. Slyguff pulled back the clippers and looked into the man's eyes again. Still he did not see what he wanted. He moved the shears back to the bloody morass of gore that was the man's left hand, on to the next arc of webbing, the flesh between the third and fourth finger. The cry of seabirds and the distant barking of dogs and the man's fevered breathing was all he could hear as he carried on with his morning's work.

In the corner of the room, a man looked on impassively, his hand on the hilt of his glittering sword of finely honed Spanish steel.

Chapter 7

SHAKESPEARE AND CLARKSON managed the fifteen-mile ride in under three hours. The going was hot through the clogged north London streets, but then a little cooler once out in the open countryside, where they could break into a light canter and enjoy the breeze in their faces. The heat had been oppressive over the past few days and weeks, and the fields and woods they passed were dry and crops were already failing.

A short distance north of Waltham Cross, they turned their mounts left along a well-worn road, then slowed to a trot along the last two hundred yards through a formal avenue of elm and ash, ranged alternately along a raised path, up to the main archway of Theobalds.

The house was magnificent, thought by many to be the finest palace in all England. Lord Burghley, Elizabeth's most trusted minister throughout her long reign, had started building it twenty-eight years earlier, within the first year of his son Robert's life. Since then he had spent many years and much silver improving and expanding it into a pile fit to entertain his beloved sovereign.

After grooms took their horses away to be watered and fed, Clarkson led the way into the first of the two great courtyards, around which the house was constructed. The whole palace was set within pleasure gardens so extensive and exquisite that one could walk for miles without tiring of the scene.

Sir Robert Cecil was in the Privy Garden to the north of the house, where the heat was less intense and the plants had been watered. Shakespeare was struck at once by how small and neat and still Cecil was; an extraordinary contrast to Essex, the bustling giant of a man he had met a day earlier. He stood, almost statue-like, on the beautifully sheltered lawn, its borders bursting with flowers. The garden was enclosed on three sides by hedges of yew that towered over a man's head, and on the fourth side by the redbrick and expansively windowed façade of Theobalds itself, a wall richly decorated with trees of fig and apricot and other exotic fruits.

Clarkson bowed low. 'Sir Robert, may I introduce Mr John Shakespeare.'

Cecil smiled quickly, his small mouth immediately reverting to its serious stillness. His face was thin and doleful, his head small like the rest of his body. He had a short beard and moustache, dark and severely trimmed. He was, thought Shakespeare, a man made in miniature, like one of Mr Hilliard's delicate little paintings.

'Good day, Mr Shakespeare. Thank you for coming so far,' Cecil said. His clothes were dark, even on a day like this, and his left hand was gauntleted and held square and a foot or so away from his body. On it was perched a peregrine falcon with a hood of soft leather to cover its eyes.

Shakespeare bowed. 'It is an honour, Sir Robert.'

'That will be all, Clarkson. Send a footman with wine. Now, Mr Shakespeare, will you walk with me?'

As Clarkson bowed again and made his way back to the house, Cecil turned and it was only then that Shakespeare noticed the hunch of his shoulder. People often spoke of him as Robin Crookback, and rarely in flattering terms. Shakespeare knew from gossip that he was reckoned by his enemies to be as quiet and venomous as a serpent. His allies, however, saw him as a straight-dealing, hard-working administrator who would not harm you as long as you were never foolish enough to cross him. Certainly, he had the trust of the Queen, just as his father, now ailing with gout, had enjoyed her confidence throughout her years of power.

'Let us take the Mulberry Walk. To my mind, they are the finest of God's trees. I love the sunshine but even I need some shade in this heat. And the fruit is ripe and sweet.'

From the Privy Garden they proceeded along a lovely avenue of mulberries, hemmed in on each side by a high wall of mellow red brick. Occasionally Cecil plucked a rich, dark berry, alternately handing one to Shakespeare, then popping another into his own mouth. 'This day I sentenced a man to die, Mr Shakespeare. Sir John Perrot, of whom I am sure you have heard. I would have saved him, but alas, I was unable.'

Perrot. Of course. Reputed to be the bastard son of Henry VIII, making him Elizabeth's half-brother. He was cursed with a tongue so loose that in any other man, he would have met the headsman's axe many years since. He had the roughness and enormous frame of his royal father, but none of his great political power or cunning. It seemed his luck had run out.

'I am afraid he insulted his royal sister one time too many. He called her "a base, bastard, pissing kitchen woman".' Cecil smiled grimly. 'No one can say words like that about their sovereign lady and hope to survive long.'

'Is that why you have called me here, Sir Robert?'

'No, no, Mr Shakespeare, by no means. I merely mention it in passing to explain my humour, in case I seem at all melancholic to you. It was not a duty that gave me pleasure.'

'Of course.'

With a gossamer touch of his pale, slender fingers, Cecil

stroked the wing feathers of his falcon. 'I believe you do not hawk, Mr Shakespeare. It is a shame, for it is the finest of sports. To watch a peregrine in flight, then see it fall in its stoop on some unsuspecting rabbit or mouse, is a wonder of the world.'

Shakespeare found himself involuntarily raising an inquiring eyebrow. Was he the rabbit and Cecil the falcon? He was certainly surprised that Cecil should have any knowledge about his liking for hawking or otherwise. If he knew such a detail, then what else might he know?

'But you must be impatient to know why I have asked you here. Let me say that I know much about you. I know you have a wife, child and a fine school to look to. And nothing, in my estimation, should stand in the way of family and education. My father always brought me up to believe more in the encouragement of children than punishment, and it seems as though you are of a mind with us. I should like to help you. But in the meantime bear with me and hear me out. Come, sit with me beneath this tree.'

They sat together on a wooden bench at the end of the Mulberry Walk, close to the Great Pond, where waterfowl of all kinds cooled themselves and foraged. Being seated brought the two men eye-to-eye for the first time, for Shakespeare was nine or ten inches taller than his host when they stood.

'Another thing I know about you, Mr Shakespeare, is that you went to Essex House yesterday and did meet there my lord the Earl of Essex.'

'Indeed, Sir Robert.'

'He had a task for you, a most curious mission to seek out one Eleanor Dare, one of the lost colonists of Roanoke. And you declined his offer because you have a school to run and also, I suspect, for other reasons more political than educational.'

'You have an eye to men's souls, Sir Robert.'

'No, no, Mr Shakespeare. There is no sorcery here. Merely

careful thinking. I would feel exactly as you do, that there is little to be gained from such a mission and much to be lost. In helping one powerful man, you may cross another. But that brings me to the point of why you are here. I wish you to accept my lord of Essex's commission.'

So that was what all this was about. Where the strong-armed threats of Charlie McGunn had failed to persuade Shakespeare, Essex used his powerful ally on the Privy Council to intercede and order Shakespeare to do as he was bidden.

'Please, Mr Shakespeare, wait until I have spoken further before you pass judgement. Let me say at once that I have little interest in Roanoke or the fate of the so-called lost colonists, other than, I suppose, a mild curiosity. Nor is it my intention to twist your arm on behalf of my lord of Essex; he can do that quite well enough on his own. No, Mr Shakespeare, I have a different task for you altogether, but in order to do it, you must say yes to the Earl, accept his gold and do his bidding. Only then will you be able to help me and, much more importantly, our sovereign lady the Queen.'

A footman arrived with a flagon of wine and poured two glasses. Shakespeare was glad of the refreshment; his head was befuddled by the heat and the extraordinary request from Cecil. Was he asking him to *spy* on Essex?

'Mr Shakespeare, it is my nature to think the best of people where I may and speak no ill of any man or woman. But in these difficult circumstances, I will speak plainly to you because I think I know you to be trustworthy. The things I am about to tell you are state secrets. You will repeat them to no one. Not even to your wife.'

Shakespeare was not at all sure that he wished to hear any state secrets, but he merely nodded. Cecil was not going to be stopped now.

'Mr Shakespeare, I fear there is a plot against the Queen . . .'

Cecil spoke the words slowly and clearly so that they should not be misunderstood. He paused to gaze a few moments at Shakespeare, as if awaiting some sort of reaction. When none was forthcoming, he continued, '. . . with the aim of proclaiming Essex as king of England in her place.'

The clatter of hooves through the dusty streets was a common sound – but the progress of the great lady through the thoroughfares of London drew all eyes and stopped all commerce. She sat alone, majestic, in a new coach of gold, resplendent with a beplumed canopy. Few had ever seen its like and stood in wonder and awe, convinced it must be carrying the Queen herself. It was drawn by four white stallions, all proudly harnessed with feathers and shields, their forelegs trotting high and in time.

Ahead of the carriage, on black horses, rode two outriders in white silk livery. With swords drawn and held vertical in front of them, they cleared the streets of laggardly carters and draymen.

Eastwards along Lombard Street they made their stately journey, past the church of St Dionis and into Fen Church Street. Finally, the outriders turned right into Fylpot Lane. The chief coachman, realising the carriage would never fit into such a narrow street, crowded as it was with untended wagons between corbelled houses, tugged at the long reins and pulled the four white steeds to a stamping, noisy halt.

The man beside the coachman got down from his perch and opened the carriage door, bowing low with a sweep of his cape. He was a strong-muscled man of African features, with black skin that matched his employer's eyes. 'I fear we can go no further to Dr Forman's house, my lady,' he said.

She raised the tip of her beautiful nose and smiled distantly, as she had been taught always to smile at those of lower rank. 'Well, I shall have to walk then, Henry. If it is not too far.'

With the assistance of her servant, who held his head high and proud, she stepped down from her carriage and looked about her. They were in the beating heart of London, the merchants' quarter whence all wealth emanated, yet to her it all seemed small and dirty and constrained, so used was she to the palaces of the aristocracy, especially her own great homes of Wanstead, Essex House, Leighs and Chartley in Staffordshire.

In her jewel-encrusted shoes of white kid, she picked her way carefully through the dung and the dust along the narrow confines of Fylpot Lane. Bays of shops pushed out into the road and, above her, the jettied chambers of fine houses blanked out much of the light. To her nose, she held a pomander of lavender and rose.

'Which house is it, Henry?'

'I believe it is the next door there, my lady, Stone House.'

She smiled her condescending smile once again. She had met the celebrated Dr Forman on occasion but never, until now, had cause to use his services and certainly not visit his house. His magic tricks and bedtime services were, however, famed among her friends, the ladies of the royal court. She nodded and the coachman beat with the pommel of his whip at the oaken door.

Inside the house, Simon Forman had recently finished a late lunch and was enjoying his third swiving of the day with his new mistress, Annis Noke. He liked to call this pleasant occupation a *halek*, for he kept a record of his daily doings, his alchemy and his experimentations and wrote in cipher so that none should steal his secrets or ideas. The word *halek*, which he had invented, seemed as good a code for intercourse as any and appeared many times in his diaries.

Above him, her eyes closed in bliss, Mistress Noke suddenly screamed in ecstasy and he chose that moment to reach his own heady pitch of excitement. She collapsed, shuddering, on to his hair-matted chest and kissed his yellow-red beard and freckled face all over. Panting heavily, she clenched her sweat-glistening thighs about his waist and shuddered once more, grinding her plump body down on to him. She smiled at him, satisfied in a way she had only ever found in *this* bed, with this strange, squat and hairy man. For his part, he knew that this giving of pleasure was a gift to him from God, and one he was happy to dispense liberally to any woman who cared to know what heaven was like without dying.

There was a hammering at the door. With a last kiss, he disengaged himself from Mistress Noke, swung his legs off the bed, scratched his member and his balls and stood up. The infernal sores were still there; the herbal tincture he had devised for the clap was not working. Still scratching, he ambled to the window, then pressed his naked body against the glass panes to get a better view of the street below. A maid in the house on the other side of Fylpot Lane chose just that moment to look up and got a clear view of his diminishing – but still extraordinarily well-sized – tumescence. Forman waved to her cheerily and she met his eye with an immodest gaze. She would make a pleasant repast one day soon. He looked away from her and his eyes turned down to the street below, where he saw a neatly coiffed head of fair, wavy hair that he recognised instantly. 'God's teeth, it's the She-wolf's daughter!' he said. 'And she has a blackamoor with her. What's she doing here? Get yourself dressed, Mistress Noke.'

Hurriedly grabbing a shirt and breeches, he stumbled downstairs to the door, fastening hooks and ties as he went. As he opened the door with a dishevelled flourish, she swept past him into his antechamber. She stood for a moment looking about her. Lady Penelope Rich. The most beautiful young woman in England; wife to the fabulously wealthy Robert, third Lord Rich; sister to the great Earl of Essex; daughter to Lettice Knollys; stepdaughter to the great Robert Dudley, Earl of Leicester; believed by many to be great-granddaughter to Henry VIII by Anne Boleyn's sister Mary.

'Well, Dr Forman,' she said at last. 'I seem to have found you quite *déshabillé*, if not to say *in flagrante delicto*.'

He bowed low to her, then looked nervously at her servant. 'A thousand pardons, my lady. I was merely couching a hogshead away from the afternoon sun. I had not expected you.'

'Couching a hogshead, Dr Forman?'

'A little afternoon sleep, my lady.'

'Ah. Well, no, of course you were not expecting me, for that would have spoiled the surprise. I wished to see how you lived, Dr Forman. And I now know. I have certain friends, ladies of breeding, who speak very highly of your . . . prowess.'

'My lady?'

'But that is not why I am here, Dr Forman. I am here because I wish you to prepare a chart for me.'

'Ah, charts, my lady,' Forman said warily in his deep Wiltshire drawl. 'Charts are dangerous things. Perhaps some refreshment would be in order while we discuss the matter.' He clapped his hands. 'Mistress Noke, would you come, please. We have an honoured guest.'

Annis Noke appeared at the bottom of the stairs, took one look at Penelope Rich and curtsied as low as a penitent at a shrine.

'A flagon of our finest claret, please, Mistress Noke – and some ale for the manservant.'

Forman led Penelope upstairs to his chambers and through to the hall where he did his work. It was a chaos of books and papers, charts and instruments, glass vials and powders – all the strange clutter of an alchemist and astrologer. 'My humble hall, my lady. Please accommodate yourself on the settle.

You are most welcome. Most welcome, indeed. Shall I fetch cushions?'

Penelope Rich did not sit down. 'So this is where you do your work, Dr Forman. This is where you cast your spells.' Her gaze lighted on a pentacle drawn on parchment and pinned to the wall above a coffer.

'My lady, there is no witchcraft here. I deal only in the ancient and honourable sciences of astrology and alchemy.'

'And what, pray, are you working on at the present time?'

'A cure for the plague. Soon there will be much call for it and it will make my fortune. As well as saving many good Christian lives, of course.'

'And charts?'

'I am wary of charts, my lady. No good tends to come of charts.'

'But I know that you make astrological charts, Dr Forman. And I am certain that you are just the man to make one for me.'

He bowed. No one denied the She-wolf's daughter. 'As you wish, my lady. I will, of course, require a few details. Let me make a few notes, if I may.' Among the rubble of books and papers he found a quill, which he proceeded to sharpen. Then he scrabbled around until he found an inkhorn. At last he dipped the quill tip into the ink and smiled ingratiatingly at his aristocratic visitor.

'Is it a new-born babe, my lady? Might I have the birth date?'

'The birth date was September the seventh, Dr Forman.'

'And the year?'

'Fifteen thirty-three.'

Forman looked up at her from his parchment again. This time, his lined brow was inquisitive yet fearful. 'Do you know what date this is, my lady?'

'Indeed, Dr Forman, I do. It is the date for which I require a chart. I can also tell you the time of birth, which was a little after three of the clock in the afternoon. And I am sure you needs must have the place too, which was Greenwich.'

'My lady, I cannot do this thing for you.'

'Cannot, Dr Forman? Do you say "cannot" to me?'

'I mean I would rather not do it.'

'And if I insist?'

'Then I would have to ask you a great deal of money. A man might lose his liberty, perchance even his head, for divining such a chart.'

'Shall we say three gold sovereigns, Dr Forman?'

Forman rubbed his throat beneath his red, bushy beard, and grimaced. 'I have great reservations. My neck, my head . . . I feel the sharp edge of the axe and the rough edge of the rope. This is not the thing for those among us who would sleep well in our beds at night.'

'My information, Dr Forman, is that you do very little sleeping when you are a-bed. I hear tell of exceeding energetic nights with much cavorting.'

'My lady, you flatter me. There is much gossip and rumour about in these troubled days. The broadsheets, madam, they print calumnies.'

Penelope threw back her head of blonde curls and let out a great laugh. 'It is not the broadsheets, sir, it is my friends that tell me this. Now, let us say five sovereigns and be done with it. You will take this offer, or you are like to have a visit from the sheriff who may wish to lay a charge against you of necromancy.'

'Of course, my lady, of course. I will produce the chart you require.'

'And would you like me to give you the name of the person whose chart I am asking you to divine?'

'My lady, I would like it very much if you would *not* give me the name. It would not be at all good for my health to know it.'

Penelope laughed again. 'You are a droll little man, Dr Forman. I like you very much, very much, indeed. Perhaps another time you will show me more of your famed trickery.'

Chapter 8

'TELL ME, MR Shakespeare,' Cecil said. 'Why do you think I have called you here to Theobalds and entrusted you with this information regarding my lord of Essex?'

Shakespeare sipped his wine. He felt distinctly ill at ease. 'Well, Sir Robert,' he said at last. 'I confess I really do not know what to say.'

Cecil looked at him coolly. 'You know, of course, Mr Shakespeare, that Sir Francis Walsingham felt obliged to dispense with your services because of your marriage, but he admitted to me in his latter days that it had been a mistake. He said his secret operation was never so strong again. That is how highly he valued you. England needed you then – and I believe it needs you again.'

'You flatter me, Sir Robert.'

'I am not here to flatter you. There is a vacuum, Mr Shakespeare. If nature, as we are told, abhors a vacuum, how much more so does the world of secrets. If I do not fill it, others will, others less scrupulous.'

Shakespeare knew the truth of this. Though he was no longer part of that world, it was the one he understood better than any other.

'I need you for this. There are few enough men of your calibre. Yes, there are many spies, men who can be set to a task with the lure of gold, but are they trustworthy? Can any of them inquire, organise and pursue as, I believe, you can? With relentless energy and attention to detail. With such talents, you are needed. These are dangerous days.'

Shakespeare nodded. These were the most perilous times since the dark days of the Armada – one hundred and thirty warships wallowing slow and purposeful down the Channel under the weight of heavy cannons, culverins and thirty thousand battle-hardened Spanish troops, all hungry to descend on England with fire and steel. 'Yes, I am sure King Philip burns with desire for vengeance,' he acknowledged.

Cecil smiled thinly. 'Good. It is good that you understand. I have firm information that forty great galleons are being built in the ports of Spain – forty fighting ships and each one finer than the best vessels of war that Philip threw at us before. He is strengthening his ports; he is preparing to attack again. The prospect of a second armada sent against us is very real, Mr Shakespeare. Like a pack-dog, Philip watches England closely for signs of weakness. When he sees us tired, sick or divided, he will go for our throat.'

'But we are strong at sea.'

'Not as strong as we were. The war chest is bare. Many of the great ships are laid up in port, neglected and in need of refitting, others are sent fishing or trading. At home the country grows weaker. Our crops fail, the plague comes upon us, armies of vagabonds roam the land bringing terror to villages and towns.'

Shakespeare knew all this. By the same token, he knew that Spain, too, had her troubles. The endless war in the Spanish Netherlands had drained Philip's treasury. Nor could Spanish morale have recovered from the beating inflicted on the Armada by Drake. But this was no time to argue such points.

'The worst of it, Mr Shakespeare, is this constant speculation about the succession. This is what makes us seem feeble. Courtiers and ambassadors talk of little else when they huddle in corners or dine together. Maids of honour twitter and gossip and examine the Queen's face for every wrinkle, every lost hair, the state of her teeth, any perceived diminishing of powers that might signify the end is near. What, they wonder, will become of them when the Lord takes her? It is a contagion of fear. King Philip sees it and plots how he may exploit it.'

'How then, Sir Robert, does this bring you to your conclusion regarding my lord of Essex?'

'Let me tell you a little about Robert Devereux, the Earl of Essex. He is a strong man, valiant in war, formidable at the tilt, charming and amusing. That is why the Queen loves him. That is why so many cluster around him. When a strong man rises up in times like these, he becomes a lodestone that draws weaker men in. Especially when, as in France last year, he personally knights twenty-four of his men, much to the dismay and fury of his sovereign. Why does he do such a thing unless he would build up a power base of men who owe him everything?'

'But he is not of the blood royal,' Shakespeare pointed out. 'The Scotch king, James VI, must surely have a prior claim. The young Lady Arbella Stuart, too. Even the Countess of Derby or her son Lord Strange . . .'

Cecil interrupted. 'Many do not want a Scotchman as their king. The Countess of Derby is long in the tooth – or what few she has left – and has no support. Her son is tainted with suspicion of Catholic sympathies. There are those who believe it must, then, be Arbella. She is English-born and has youth and, some say, beauty to commend her.'

'Then Arbella must look most likely to succeed.'

'What would you say if I were to tell you that she is being wooed, secretly, by Essex?'

'I would say that my lord of Essex has a wife. He is married to Frances, daughter of Sir Francis Walsingham and widow of Sir Philip Sidney.'

Cecil stood and signalled to a flunkey to take their empty glasses. He began to walk again through the gardens, basking in the dappled sunshine and warm air. Shakespeare followed him, studying him intently. Never since his days working for Walsingham had he met a man so utterly in command of himself and his surroundings. It seemed almost that he did not blink without first weighing up the consequences. He would be a hard man to warm to, but an easy man to respect.

'You are not so innocent, Mr Shakespeare. You did not work for Mr Secretary for nine years without learning something about the dark heart of man. Do you think this Devereux family is one that cares for such legal niceties as a mere marriage contract? When Essex's mother, the regal Lettice, married Leicester, was he not already wed to Lady Douglass Sheffield? He tried to claim it was some false marriage, but no one believed that. And what of poor Amy Robsart, Leicester's first wife, who had a most unfortunate – yet convenient – fall down the stairs to her death while her husband was trying to win himself a Queen for his wife? What is one little life against a matter so great? What is a little fall down the stairs? It cured all poor Amy Robsart's ills and might have won Leicester the crown. Do you think the Countess of Essex will fare better?'

Shakespeare was thinking fast. He was astonished that Cecil should reveal his suspicions in this way.

'A small thing like a wife is but a minor inconvenience to such men, Mr Shakespeare.' Cecil's face was hard-set now. This was no jest. 'Let me tell you more about my lord of Essex.'

They approached a wooden bench that stood against a wall of the house beneath a peach tree. Cecil gestured for Shakespeare to sit. Sunlight glanced off his shoulder. Cecil perched himself on the arm of the bench, one foot touching the ground.

'I have known my lord of Essex since we were boys,' Cecil said. 'He was my father's ward after his own father died. We were schooled and brought up together. We never liked each other. Though I was three years the elder, he was always bigger than me and greater at the manly sports. On the tennis court he was exquisite in his grace and skill, while I could only watch and wonder. And, of course, he taunted me for my physical weakness, as boys will.

'But I also knew that I had advantages over him. He could never hope to match me at the classics, at the languages of our continental neighbours, at law and the study of governance. He lacked rigour. When I was fourteen and he was eleven he challenged me to a duel. He had made some foul remark about my crooked back being a result of my mother conceiving me at the time of her flowers and I responded that at least my mother had not poisoned my father. I should not have spoken to him thus, but it was said in the heat of the moment. I tried to laugh off his challenge of a duel, but he insisted and said that it was my right to choose the weapons and the battleground. And so I said, "If that is the way it is to be, then I choose chess pieces as my weapons and the squared board as the battleground." He became angry, very angry, and said I was a coward. I told him that, clearly, it was he who was afraid to take up *my* challenge and I went off to fetch the chess pieces and board. We played and I was beating him with considerable ease. He went away and said he would be back anon. He returned with a morgenstern. Are you familiar with a morgenstern, Mr Shakespeare?'

'Of course, I know of them. I have never seen one.'

'They are maces, much favoured by the Habsburg troops. The word *morgenstern* means morning star, for they have a heavy iron head, spiked like a star. My lord of Essex took his morgenstern and swung it with all his great might down on to the chess board, which was a fine piece, cut from marble and brought from Verona. The board was smashed into fragments, as were many of the playing pieces. He then kicked the rubble away with his soft-shod foot and said to me, "Checkmate. That is what I shall do to you one day, Robin Crookback."'

Cecil paused for effect. Shakespeare knew that there was no love between the two men, but he had no idea it stemmed from such an episode.

'I spotted something in my lord of Essex that day, some dark ambition that even he could not understand, let alone control.'

Again, Shakespeare said nothing.

'My father has seen it, too, Mr Shakespeare. The Queen will *not* see it, however. She takes pleasure in the attentions my lord of Essex pays her and is beguiled by him. He swoons and affects a swain's devotion to his maiden love, his Queen. So we must protect her without her knowledge.'

'Protect her from *what* exactly?'

'His dark desire. My lord of Essex would be king. And those around him – his family, his friends – would crown him. Arbella, though she does not know it, is the route, the conduit, to that crown.'

'You have information?'

Cecil paused. 'Mr Shakespeare, please,' he said evenly, 'do not ask me to reveal the source of my intelligence. If I were to tell you such a thing, how would *you* ever trust me?'

It was a good point. But Cecil clearly had an informant operating within the Essex circle. Shakespeare tried to recall all he knew of Arbella Stuart, the princess with England's future weighing heavily on her tender young shoulders. Great-granddaughter of Henry VIII's elder sister, Margaret, she was the child of the scandalous marriage of the young Charles Stuart and Elizabeth Cavendish (he was nineteen, she twenty); the match was illicit because the Queen had not licensed it, and she erupted in one of her customary furies on hearing of it. For Charles was in line of succession to both the Scots and English thrones, and such a man might never marry without his sovereign's consent.

So Arbella was born into trouble, and it had followed her like a hungry dog ever since. Her father died of consumption within a year of her birth and her mother died of a sudden illness five years later, leaving the little girl an orphan. Her maternal grandmother, the Countess of Shrewsbury – better known as Bess of Hardwick – took on the care of the six-year-old. She brought her up a princess, insisting she be served by kneeling retainers and addressed as 'Highness'.

At the age of eleven came the moment to bring her to court, to meet the Queen and her dazzling array of courtiers here, in this house, Theobalds, during the summer progress of 1587. It was a triumph. Elizabeth took the girl under her wing and made much of her, almost – but not quite – seeming to proclaim her heiress to her own throne. Perhaps it all went to the sweet little girl's head, however, for soon she was breeding resentment among senior courtiers with her haughty ways.

What Arbella had not realised was that the Queen was not affectionate towards her without purpose. Elizabeth wielded smiles and favours to win obedience the way her father used an axe. This was politics on a grand scale, aimed at spiking the planned invasion by a great armada from Spain. Arbella had no way of knowing that behind the scenes of the great theatre of European politics, negotiations were under way for her to marry Rainutio Farnese, son of the Duke of Parma, Spain's all-powerful general in the Low Countries. The hope was that the marriage would cause a rift between Parma and his King, Philip II, and wreck the invasion plans.

The marriage never happened and the invasion armada was swept to destruction by Drake. But now, so Cecil said, a new armada was being assembled. Where did that put Arbella? It was an open secret that in the past few months the Spanish wedding plans had been resuscitated. Hilliard the portraitist had painted miniatures of the girl to be carried to Parma and his son. Anyone who knew Elizabeth well realised it was all vanity, signifying nothing; she would rather have cut off her right hand and hurled it into the fire than allow a Spanish claimant to wed a possible successor to *her* throne.

'Sir Robert, these are complex international affairs . . .' Shakespeare began. 'What are you asking of me?'

'Prevent this marriage between the Earl of Essex and Lady Arbella Stuart. Take on this Roanoke investigation and you will have cause to stay close to Essex and his household. Watch what he does, observe every move he makes, worm your way into his circle. Find evidence against him. You must work for him, but in truth you will be employed by me, on behalf of your Queen and country. There is something else, too, Mr Shakespeare. You will recall Sir Francis Walsingham's library and his collection of correspondence and charts?'

Shakespeare could never forget it. For nine long years, Mr Secretary and his library full of secrets had been the centre of his world. He recalled the austere, silent room at Barn Elms in Surrey, the Principal Secretary's country home where he kept so much of his correspondence; hundreds, if not thousands, of papers and documents from Madrid, Paris, Rome, Delft and Antwerp. Even from the Orient, the Indies and the New World. But most of all from here at home – intimate information about the thoughts and deeds of men and women in every corner of society; what was said in the taverns and theatres, the prisons and the bawdy-houses; who was swiving whom in the palaces and great houses. Who was plotting, who was loyal and who was not. It was a unique collection of information and only one man knew it in its entirety – Walsingham himself.

'I remember it well, Sir Robert.'

'The question is: where is it? When he died, Mr Shakespeare, it all disappeared. Every last scrap of paper, every nautical chart, every intercepted secret from the Escorial and the Vatican. All gone, spirited away from his house.'

'Surely you do not suspect my lord of Essex?'

Cecil affected an expression of scandalised shock. 'Tut-tut, Mr Shakespeare, *suspect* is a strong word. It seems to suggest a crime has taken place, when nothing could be further from the truth. I am sure the Earl has these documents – but you may very well think he is entitled to them, for he is married to Mr Secretary's daughter. And why should she not inherit her father's papers?'

'Are you saying that you want me to find these papers and bring them to you? I would need several wagons to carry it all.'

'God's wounds, no, Mr Shakespeare. I merely want you to find them and gain access to them, examine them if you can – and find out what information he held about Arbella Stuart and those around her. I would be astonished if there were not extensive and important information to be had. This is a game of chess, Mr Shakespeare. It is a game we must win. Like chess, it has clear rules, the main one being that the sovereign must be protected at all costs. To that end, we must use every ounce of our wit to best our foe.'

'And what if my lord of Essex should wield his morgenstern and break your pieces, Sir Robert?'

Cecil stroked his unlined brow with the slender fingers of his ungloved right hand. 'The morgenstern, Mr Shakespeare, is an unsubtle weapon. It was effective when I was not expecting it. Now I know he has it and we shall be prepared. And, anyway, you will be with him to make sure no such thing occurs.'

'It will be like working for two masters – and betraying one of them.'

'I understand your misgivings, but that is the intelligencer's art, is it not? That is what Mr Secretary saw in you.' Cecil rose. He lifted his head, almost imperceptibly, and his falconer appeared and took the bird and gauntlet from his arm. 'Come let us walk just a little further, Mr Shakespeare. I am keeping you from your school, but look how the sun shines. Every man must play truant once in a while. I want the sun to shine always on England. Though the times are dangerous, there is much cause for hope, too. We have a new Pope in Rome, one that may yet prove more amenable to peace between the old religion and the new; Henri of Navarre may soon grasp the whole of France and bring peace to his blood-stained country. These are today's men. They are, hopefully, men like you and me; men who would rather send ambassadors than armadas. But the peace that you and I both crave will not happen by accident, for there are other men, men of a martial bent who would rather kill and destroy than talk. Will you let them hold sway, or will you join me? Do you wish eternal war with Spain, or would you like your daughter to grow up in a world of peace?'

Yes, thought Shakespeare, I am like Cecil. In some ways. 'But I have put this life of secrets behind me, Sir Robert.' Even as he said the words, he knew he spoke without conviction.

'I can be of great assistance to you. I can protect you.'

Even in the heat, a cold shiver ran through Shakespeare's neck. 'Do I *need* protection, Sir Robert?'

'Do *you* think you do?'

He knew he did. He needed protection from Topcliffe, a man whose lust for Catholic blood ran unchecked. And Cecil clearly knew it, too. 'Yes, sir, my family does need some protection,' he admitted. 'There are those that would harm them. My own safety is of little concern to me, but as for those I love . . .'

'Then join me, Mr Shakespeare.'

Spy on Essex? That would bring yet more danger. Why then

did he nod his head to signify his agreement to the mission? For a moment, he thought that Cecil might clap him on the back, but then he realised that Sir Robert had never clapped any man on the back and had never had a jovial feeling in his life.

'I shall do all in my considerable power to protect you and yours from enemies,' Cecil continued. 'We both know who they are. Being in the service of the government again, you will have all the authority that goes with your post. But I do not need to tell you that you – *we* – must be circumspect in that regard. No one must know for the present for whom you work. My lord of Essex must believe that you are *his* man. He must never know of this meeting and you must only come to me covertly and in exceptional circumstances.'

Shakespeare felt somehow as if he were accepting five guineas for a horse he knew to be worth ten. Why would he work for one powerful man against another? The reason was clear. He still cared about this realm and his instinct told him that only one man, truly, had its interests at heart. Sir Robert Cecil. Pray God he was right in this. 'Very well,' he said. 'I am your man. Whatever that entails.'

'That is good.'

'But what of the Countess of Shrewsbury and Arbella? Will you assign protection to them?'

Cecil hesitated, as if weighing up how much to reveal. 'Bess is aware there is a problem,' he said at last. 'But she believes the danger is from Spain, that Catholics would kidnap Arbella and carry her abroad, to mould her as a figurehead for their own cause and insurrection. There may be truth in this. But you must remember, she has ambitions for Arbella. She would wish her to be queen and has always raised her with that in mind. She nearly ended her days in the Tower when she ill-advisedly agreed for the girl to be betrothed to Leicester's late son, Denbigh. The question is: has she learned her lesson well – would she countenance another illicit marriage proposal? The answer is that I do not know – which is why I cannot enlist her assistance in this, but I would have *you* go to her and get her away from London to one of her northern estates. She will be safer there. I warn you, though, Bess is a hard woman, as any of her displaced tenants or debtors will tell you. It is not for nothing that her late husband called her a sharp, bitter shrew.' Cecil paused and chuckled lightly. 'Fear not, though, Mr Shakespeare. You have wit and charm. Use it.'

Shakespeare bowed his head. Cecil had stirred something in him, something long buried beneath the daily round of Latin verbs and domestic comings and goings that now made up his life. It was the thought of returning to the fold, working in the world of secrets once again: the old days of Walsingham and his covert dealings and the thrill that went with them. Yes, he could admit it now: he *did* miss those days.

'Now ride home, for the world and your wife will be wondering where you are. Clarkson will accompany you, to bring back our horse.'

'Thank you, Sir Robert.'

'As you go, think on this. I have no way of knowing how advanced is this plot. I know, however, that it centres on the belief that the Queen cannot live much longer. Essex wishes to position himself as the next in line. At the moment, I do not believe he plans an assassination. He hopes to marry Arbella, intending to take the crown when Elizabeth dies a natural death. But we all know that it is but a short step from wishing her dead to making it happen . . .'

Chapter 9

BOLTFOOT AND JANE looked an ill-assorted couple as they entered the school refectory. He dragged his foot while she waddled, her distended belly pushed forward proudly in this her thirty-fifth week of pregnancy. Shakespeare, sitting alone at an early evening supper after the ride back from Theobalds, smiled at the sight and called them to him.

'Jane,' he said. 'I imagine you have had enough of this ugly old ruffler getting under your feet.'

Jane laughed. 'He is worse than useless, Mr Shakespeare. He thinks I am made of glass and as breakable, and will scarce let me do my work. Please find him some task away from here. It will bring us all peace of mind, I am certain.'

'A fine thought, Jane. I will do that.'

Jane and Boltfoot had been married five years. She was young still – perhaps twenty-two – while Boltfoot was in his late thirties and looked older, his short, grizzled body carved and battered by harsh years at sea. Yet this disparate pair suited each other; their mutual devotion was there for all to see. Sometimes, Shakespeare caught them looking at each other with unabashed affection. If only his own marriage was in such good repair.

Boltfoot appeared disconsolate. He treasured Jane above pearls and was worried about the baby that swelled her belly. He could not bear the thought of losing this one. Yet he felt helpless to do anything except be with her. Fighting Spaniards and savages was easy compared to this. He blamed himself for the loss of the first child, as if somehow the boy had inherited his bad blood, just as he had taken on the sins of his own father and forefathers in his club foot.

'What say you, Boltfoot? Will you undertake a task for me? Can you bear to be parted from Jane's side for five minutes?'

Boltfoot hunched into his shoulders, his face a picture of gloom. 'You are the master, Mr Shakespeare,' he said in a low voice that betrayed his reluctance to be anywhere but with his wife.

'So I am, Boltfoot. And I have a simple but intriguing mission for you. I wish you to go to all your old shipyard haunts – the taprooms, taverns, chandleries and wharves of Southwark, Deptford, Blackwall and beyond – and there talk to whomsoever you may about Roanoke and the New World.'

Boltfoot grunted, which Shakespeare took to be a 'yes'.

'Find me a mariner who has been there, one from the very first voyage when the colonists were carried to their new home, if you can. Or listen for tales. Discover what is being said, what the seafarers believe happened to the souls now lost. Are they dead or alive? If dead, how did they die? If alive, where might they be? I want to know the conditions out there, how they might have survived. Most of all, I wish to know whether any of the colonists might somehow have returned to England.'

Boltfoot looked at Jane, as if hoping she might tell his master that he could not possibly go on such a mission because he was needed here, to look out for her in these last few weeks.

'Thank you, Mr Shakespeare,' Jane said. 'I am sure it is useful work and it will do us both a world of good. He needs something else to think on.'

'Good. Well, that's settled. I will talk with you alone regarding the details, Boltfoot.' Shakespeare turned back to Jane. His voice softened and he hesitated, unsure. 'Pray tell me, Jane, do you know where Mistress Shakespeare is this afternoon?'

Jane could not meet her master's eyes. Her mistress had clearly said she had no wish to speak with her husband. 'I do not think she is herself today, master. She says she wishes to be alone. She is with Mary.'

Shakespeare accepted the situation with a smile. 'Thank you, Jane. When you see Mistress Shakespeare, please tell her that my thoughts are with her and that I understand. I must go to Essex House but I would see her later, should she wish it.'

'Yes, master,' Jane said, her gaze still averted, then hurried away as fast as her swollen belly would allow.

The sun was dipping and the sky had a hue of golds and reds. Tomorrow would be another hot day. 'Let me finish my meats and then we will share a quart of ale, Boltfoot,' Shakespeare said. 'I will tell you more of this Roanoke inquiry. It seems we are to go intelligencing again, my friend. You will have to dust down your caliver and hone your cutlass for the fray.' As he spoke, Shakespeare thought he saw a sparkle in the eye of his old copesmate. Perhaps Boltfoot would be happier away from the cares of impending fatherhood after all.

Shakespeare had never seen a woman more lovely. His first sight of her was at a distance, in profile, along the evening-shadowed long gallery of Essex House and he was transfixed. The room had fine elmwood panelling and frescoed walls with pictures of nymphs and satyrs in woodland scenes. She was laughing and her fair hair fell back across the soft skin of her nape and shoulder blades. Her neck was adorned by three strings of precious stones that looked to him like diamonds and rubies.

He was a married man and Catherine was to him the loveliest of God's creations. And yet he could not take his eyes off this fair woman.

Slyguff walked a step ahead of him, his hand gripped on the hilt of a dagger that was thrust in the belt buckled tight about his narrow, wiry waist.

Only at the last moment, as they came near, did Shakespeare avert his gaze from the woman and see that she was with Charlie McGunn, deep in conversation.

The woman looked up with nonchalant curiosity at Shakespeare's approach. Her eyes were black, like still, dark water. She raised an eyebrow questioningly. McGunn turned to him, too, and a grin broke across his fleshy, bald face. 'Ah, Mr Shakespeare, I believe you have seen sense. Welcome to the fold.'

'Thank you.'

'I hope you will introduce us, Mr McGunn,' the woman said.

'My apologies, Lady Rich. This is Mr Shakespeare. Mr John Shakespeare.'

Shakespeare bowed. 'My lady.' Of course, he had seen her portrait. Penelope Rich, sister of the Earl of Essex, was said to be the most beautiful woman at court, if not in the whole of England. It was an assessment that Shakespeare could not dispute.

'Mr Shakespeare,' she said, 'you must be brother to the other Mr Shakespeare, the Earl of Southampton's poet, for I can see that there is a little family likeness in your eyes and brow, though you are taller.'

'Indeed, my lady. And I am a little older, too.'

McGunn clasped his arm around Shakespeare's shoulders. Too tight for friendship. Shakespeare winced at the memory of his vicelike hand taking him by the throat. 'Mr Shakespeare has agreed to join our great enterprise of all the talents, Lady Penelope. He is to seek out and find the mysterious lost colonist, if one such really exists.'

'Oh, I am sure she exists, Mr McGunn. It is an intriguing tale. Do find her, Mr Shakespeare. I should so like to hear what she has to say for herself, about the perils she has endured in the New World and how she came to make her crossing of the ocean home to England. It will be the talk of the court. And, of course, it is certain to discomfit Ralegh, which will be most amusing.'

'I will do my utmost.'

She smiled the sweetest smile he had seen. 'And I want you here tomorrow evening for the summer revels. Do say you will come.'

'Well, my lady . . .' He thought of Catherine, back home, turning from him, not even admitting him to her presence. How long was it since he had seen her smile at him like that?

McGunn's grip about his shoulders tightened. 'He'll be there, Lady Rich. I'll vouch for him.'

'That will be wonderful. I believe you were an intelligencer for Mr Secretary Walsingham and saved Drake from some Spanish hellhound. I want to hear all about it from your own lips, Mr Shakespeare. But for the moment, I am afraid I have to leave you.' She reached out and touched his face with the fingertips of her gloved right hand. 'The She-wolf summons me and I must obey . . .'

He watched her move away from him along the hall. She wore a dress of gold and deep burgundy, almost brown in its intensity, with full embroidered sleeves and a sharply pointed bodice. From behind she seemed to glide, like a slender royal craft upon the Thames.

McGunn loosened his grip, then slapped him playfully on both sides of his face. It stung. 'Watch yourself, Shakespeare. You're a married man and she's a married woman, and no good can come of it.'

'You do Lady Rich a disservice.'

McGunn laughed aloud. 'But then you don't know the Devereux women, do you? It's not for nothing that she calls her mother the She-wolf.'

'I heard it was Her Majesty the Queen that gave her the name.'

'Yes, but it was the She-wolf herself who earned it. Except that she hunts and eats men, not lambs in the field. And her daughters are no different.'

'I am astonished at your temerity, Mr McGunn, to speak of the Earl of Essex's mother and sisters so.'

'Would you have me kiss their feet?'

Who exactly was McGunn that he could display such disrespect and familiarity to Essex himself and to the ladies of his house, Shakespeare wondered? And how would the Lady Lettice take it if she heard this man and her own daughter refer to her as the 'She-wolf'?

McGunn opened a purse of soft leather and took out coins, which he handed to Shakespeare. 'Here, fifteen marks in gold. Now, come with me. I run things for Essex and I have something to show you.'

Shakespeare took the coins, though he felt unclean in doing so. 'Are you his steward? His factor?'

'What do you think, Slyguff? Is *steward* the word for what I do for Essex?'

Slyguff said nothing.

'Ah, call me what you like, Shakespeare, I care nothing for titles. But a little warning before we proceed: never cross me. Never. For I always repay a slight. But if you are a good fellow, you will find me the truest friend a man ever had.' He grinned broadly, as though he had never made the threat. 'Come. I will arrange letters-patent in my lord of Essex's name. That will grant you access wherever you require it in your inquiries.'

They left Slyguff in the long hall and went up a narrow,

twisting stairway of stone steps to a high room in a square turret at the back of the house. The room was tall-ceilinged with deep oriel windows, and lit by many candles. The three men seated there, poring over papers, looked up as they entered. Shakespeare recognised them all.

'Old friends, Mr Shakespeare,' McGunn said. 'They insisted you were the man to help us with this little task.'

The three were Francis Mills, Arthur Gregory and Thomas Phelippes, all senior intelligencers with Walsingham in the old days. The last time they had all been together was five years since. They had been an effective if incongruous crew, each working directly to Walsingham rather than as a team.

The room was a mass of documents and books, a sort of library. What, exactly, was Essex trying to do here? Recreate Walsingham's intelligence network?

Shakespeare looked at them each in turn. He shook Gregory by the hand but hesitated over Mills's proffered hand, recalling the problems he had caused by being too close to Topcliffe. Phelippes did not rise to shake hands, but merely pushed his glasses up his pox-scarred nose and returned to his papers. Shakespeare thought it unlikely that either Mills or Phelippes had suggested his name to Essex or McGunn. Perhaps Arthur Gregory was the man.

'Mister Sh-Sh-Shakespeare,' Gregory stammered. 'It is a delight to s-s-see you once more.'

'And you, Mr Gregory.' Shakespeare liked him. His face was as pink as a young pig's and he was clearly suffering in these hot days. His expertise lay in his careful hands and his uncanny ability to open a sealed letter, read it and replace it so that the intended recipient was none the wiser. He also devised invisible inks and could easily reveal the supposedly invisible writings of others.

Mills was another matter. He and Shakespeare had been

equals under Walsingham. Like Shakespeare, he was tall, but he was stick-like and more stooped than Shakespeare remembered him. He had been an interrogator, sometimes working together with Topcliffe in the Tower rack room. Mills would speak with soft, coaxing words while Topcliffe raged and foamed and turned the screws tighter on the rack and uttered unspeakable threats and obscenities. Yet this was not the sum of Mills's abilities: he also had a cold, inquiring mind that could sift through the mass of intercepted correspondence from Spain and Rome and spot what was of importance. He was as valuable at a table of documents as he was in the tormenting chamber.

Phelippes, though, was the undisputed master of the intelligencer's craft. His face was so pockmarked and unpleasant to look on beneath his lank yellow hair that children would shy away in fright, but his brain was as taut and beautiful as an athlete's sinews. His talent was with ciphers and the breaking of them, be they French, Spanish, Latin, Greek, Italian or English; it was Phelippes who had enabled Walsingham to bring Mary of Scots to the headsman's block.

'Surprised, Mr Shakespeare?' McGunn said. 'You had not expected to find these old friends here, I would happily wager.'

'Yes, *surprised* is the word.'

'Well, feel free to use their expertise, for I want this woman found. My lord of Essex will allow for no failure in this. You will find much of the information you need among these papers. Come and go at will, Mr Shakespeare, and report to me what you find. Sooner rather than later, if you will. Good evening to you.'

Shakespeare watched McGunn leave the room, then looked about him. This was Walsingham's old library, he was certain. All his papers were stacked here, high on shelves and over tables – a great mass of secrets that any spymaster would kill for.

'Here, Mr Sh-Shakespeare,' Arthur Gregory said. 'Come, perch yourself with me, for I have gathered some information for you.'

Shakespeare sat on a bench beside him 'How have you been keeping, Mr Gregory?'

'Scratching a living, sir. Times have not been easy since Mr S-S-Secretary passed away, but I have found gainful employment with my lord of Essex.'

'And Mr McGunn . . .'

Gregory stiffened at the name. 'He comes and g-goes.' He took a deep breath as if trying to relax and control his stammer; also, Shakespeare thought, to change the subject. 'Anyway, take a look at these papers if you wish. They may help your inquiries into the st-st-strange case of the lost colony.'

Shakespeare was not to be fobbed off so easily. 'But I would wish to know a little more about McGunn, Mr Gregory. Who is he – and what has he to do with all this?'

Gregory glanced around him, as if fearful of prying eyes. His voice lowered. 'I can tell you this much, Mr Shakespeare. He is a dangerous man and not one to gainsay.' He moved yet closer to Shakespeare's ear. 'He had young Jaggard working for him, looking for this Eleanor Dare. Mr McGunn says nothing, his demeanour rarely changes, yet the boy went missing and McGunn was most aggrieved. That is where you came in. Mr McGunn wanted the best inquirer in the land. He takes a great personal interest in the matter.' He caught Mills gazing at him and stopped. 'I can say no more except that we hear the boy is dead, murdered in the woods.'

Chapter 10

IN THE MORNING, Shakespeare reached out for Catherine. She wasn't there. He jumped up from the bed, suddenly wide awake. He must have this out with her, settle things once and for all. He could not go on in this way.

She wasn't in the nursery, nor in the refectory. He began to panic and found Jane, who looked uncomfortable.

'She has gone out, Mr Shakespeare.'

'Gone where?'

'To find Mistress Bellamy, sir.'

Shakespeare mouthed a silent curse. This was madness. It had been Anne Bellamy who invited Catherine to the mass where Southwell was apprehended by Topcliffe. If he, Shakespeare, had not stood firm she would now be in Newgate or some other putrid hole awaiting trial for treason. What did she think she was doing going to see the Bellamy woman now? Was it not obvious to her that Southwell had been set up by Topcliffe and that Anne Bellamy was his instrument?

'She said she needed to find out the truth of what happened, Mr Shakespeare.'

This was becoming too much. On arriving home from Essex House the night before, he had apologised to her. He had not admitted any wrongdoing, but he conceded that he had, perhaps, been insensitive towards her feelings; yes, it was important she be allowed to worship in whatever way she wished. But . . . it was the 'but' that hung in the air between them. She thanked him for his apology, but said she would prefer to sleep alone for the present. There was no smile on her face, no warmth.

He had stayed awake for hours thinking of the day, thinking of what he had found in the turret room at Essex House: Gregory, Phelippes, Mills and, perhaps most importantly, the collected papers of Sir Francis Walsingham, not lost at all but openly displayed. Clearly the three intelligencers were going through them in fine detail and cataloguing their contents. Did Sir Robert Cecil know of this? Had he known all along? Shakespeare began to fear he was being played like a mummer's doll – but who was the motion-man, the puppet-master?

Arthur Gregory had shown him some Walsingham papers he had uncovered relating to Roanoke and the lost colonists. They charted the development of the little colony from its tentative beginnings. First there was the foray of 1584 when two of Ralegh's captains found a land of fertile soil and friendly natives and returned to England with two captured chieftains, Manteo and Wanchese, who caused a sensation at court. The two captains spoke so highly of the land that Elizabeth agreed it should be named after her: Virginia.

The story did not run as smoothly as Ralegh had hoped. A second expedition under the command of Ralegh's friend Sir Richard Grenville explored the region before leaving a garrison of one hundred and eight troops.

Their mission was to find gold and set up a base from which Spanish shipping could be harried. But the promised land had begun to turn ugly; there were violent clashes with the Indians.

Within months, the soldiers and their hosts were openly hostile, all except the tribe known as the Croatoans – the tribe of Manteo's mother – who lived on an island twenty miles to the south of Roanoke.

It was with great relief that, a year on, the soldiers saw the ships of Sir Francis Drake arriving with relief supplies. That was the summer of 1586. But instead of accepting the offer of supplies, they opted to go home, and Drake took them.

Back in England, Ralegh remained undaunted. He would try again the following year, only this time the colony would be made up of a very different sort of settler. Instead of men-at-arms, there would be ordinary families – men, women and children, and men with useful skills: carpenters, farmers, crafts-men, cordwainers, wrights, skinners, fishermen and ironsmiths. Their leader and governor of the new 'City of Ralegh' would be John White, an artist and surveyor who had been on the earlier expedition. It was a fateful choice, for he was no leader of men.

In the summer of 1587, while the ships and mariners that had carried this new colony were still at Roanoke, preparing to depart once more for England, trouble was already bubbling up like a brewer's mash. One of John White's assistants was killed by Indians while fishing for crabs, his body pierced by sixteen arrows and his skull smashed by clubs. But there was happiness, too, for on August 18, White's daughter, Eleanor Dare, gave birth to little Virginia and, a week later, Margery Harvey gave birth, too.

The cloud billowing over the island was a lack of supplies, particularly farm animals and salt for preserving food. It was decided that White should return to England with the ships and organise a relief expedition. He agreed, reluctantly.

That was where the Walsingham papers left the story, for he had died in early 1590, before White's futile relief expedition had finally got under way. As the world now knew, they had found the island of Roanoke deserted, the settlers and their houses vanished without trace.

The question was: what happened to the colonists between

being deposited in 1587 and the arrival of the supply ships three years later? And why, now, was someone reporting seeing one of their number – and not just anyone, but that same Eleanor Dare – here in Southwark, thousands of miles across the Western Sea? Shakespeare's first call would have to be on the woman who had made the sighting – Agnes Hardy, maid to Essex's portrait painter William Segar.

Over a light breakfast of herrings, manchet bread and ale, Shakespeare spread out the paper with the list of settlers and looked again at their names. Seeing them there, scraped in black ink, somehow turned them from a strange tale that titillated the public curiosity into real human beings: John White, governor; his assistants Roger Bailey, Ananias Dare, Christopher Cooper, Thomas Stevens, John Sampson, Dennis Harvey, Roger Pratt, George Howe. And more than a hundred other names, many in family groups.

In the margin was a note in a hand that Shakespeare recognised as Walsingham's own: 'SWR's great wager.'

SWR: Sir Walter Ralegh. Yes, clearly it had been a great wager. If the venture was a success, his credit at court would soar. If it were to fail – and Elizabeth herself had invested money and expected a good return – his star would fall faster than a shot game bird.

Shakespeare finished his breakfast and stepped out into Dowgate. The artist Segar lived two streets away in a half-timbered home in the cramped and narrow thoroughfare known as Windgoose Lane. The housekeeper showed Shakespeare into the antechamber and went to fetch Agnes Hardy from the kitchens. A minute or two later she trundled in, a big, coarse woman with hands that were bony and muscular like a plough-man's. Her face was indeterminate of sex, being more male than female, and it was only her drudge's garb of linsey-woolsey smock and apron that gave her away as a woman. Shakespeare could scarcely guess her age, but thought she must be in her early twenties if she was a childhood friend of Eleanor Dare.

'Mistress Hardy?' Shakespeare said.

'Yes, master.'

'Tell me about Eleanor, if you will.'

Agnes sighed as though she had told this story a hundred times and was mightily fatigued of it. 'Do you mind if I sit down, master? I ache all over and my head's a-throbbing like a faulty harrow.'

'Of course.' Shakespeare smiled. He remained standing, away from her, for she had an unpleasant smell. 'I believe you knew Eleanor as a child, Mistress Hardy?'

'I didn't like her though. She thought so highly of herself. My mother worked for her parents as a kitchen malkin, but Eleanor and me played together when we were small. When we were older, though, I wasn't good enough for her.'

'Describe Eleanor to me.'

'Above herself, sir. Like she was somebody and I was nobody.'

Shakespeare closed his eyes momentarily in frustration. 'And her appearance? The colour of her hair. Was she fat, well-formed?'

'Too thin for my liking. I last saw her when she was sixteen and she barely had tits to speak of. Some might have thought her pretty, but I reckon a man would have to be a poor sort of fellow to go after a hop-pole like that one. Her hair was like straw. And I couldn't abide those clothes she wore. Worsteds and velvets and such like, with lacy lawn coifs all above her curls. Little Mistress Nose-in-the-Air is what I called her. Blue eyes she had, very blue with a strange grey ring around the middle if you looked close.'

'And what happened when you saw her recently? Where were you?'

'I was by the bull-baiting, waiting to go in, with my friend, when I saw Eleanor White – Dare – in the crowd. I couldn't believe what I was seeing, because I knew her to be lost in the New World, sir, with all those others, killed by savages. I thought it was a ghost. But then she moved a little closer and I saw that it *was* her, in the flesh. I stepped towards her, but then a man approached her and I held back and watched. They spoke half a minute, then she took his arm. That's when the gates to the baiting opened and the crowd surged together and she disappeared with the man.'

'The bull-baiting you say, not the theatre?'

'No, sir, the bull-baiting. I like to see the bulls tossing the dogs on their horns, sticking them in the belly and their bowels spilling out, sir.'

'What time of the day was this?'

'Why, mid-afternoon. A bright day like today, sir.'

'So you had a good view of Eleanor Dare?'

'Clear as I can see you, Mr Shakespeare.'

'And how was she apparelled?'

'Now there's the funny thing. She was dressed like a strumpet. She had no cap or coif. Her head was uncovered. And her breast was uncovered, also, as though she were an unmarried woman, sir, when she is not. Perhaps Mistress Nose-in-the-Air has become Mistress Eyes-on-the-Ceiling.' Agnes Hardy slipped off her shoes and rubbed her aching feet.

Shakespeare was becoming increasingly irritated. 'And the man she met. What was he like?'

'I paid him little heed, but I would say he was not as tall as you. He had a long beard and long hair, and quite red. I couldn't tell you more. Except he was in workman's clothing.'

'Very well, Mistress Hardy, that will be all. If you see her again, send word to me.' He had had enough of the woman. She was a poor witness for detail, but he was left believing that she did, at least, honestly believe she had seen Eleanor Dare.

As he walked towards home, he realised he was being followed. Each time he turned around, a darkly clad figure on the other side of the road also stopped and melded into the busy crowds. He was not unduly concerned, except that it would make it a little more difficult to travel to the Chelsea household of Bess of Hardwick and the Lady Arbella Stuart undetected.

Chapter 11

CATHERINE SHAKESPEARE KNOCKED at the door of the house in Holborn where last she had seen Anne Bellamy. An old man opened it slowly and shuffled forward into the daylight, carrying a stick. Somewhere behind him, from the depths of the house, a dog barked. The man was bent forward but looked up at Catherine from dull, watery eyes.

'Yes?'

'Mr Basforde, it is I, Catherine Shakespeare. We have met before. I am seeking Mistress Bellamy.'

He paused, as if trying to recall where he had heard her name before, then said curtly, 'She's not here.'

'When will she be back, pray?'

'She won't be back. You'll find her at Westminster. Gone to Mr Topcliffe's fine house.'

Catherine felt uneasy. Anne had been arrested in January and held for questioning by Topcliffe in the Gatehouse Prison, but she had been freed on bail within the bounds of Holborn. Catherine had visited her twice at these lodgings, been welcomed here by this old man, Basforde Jones. Then, last week, Anne had told her that Father Southwell was living nearby at the home of a great family, where he was safe, but was preparing to go further afield in England, to bring the sacraments to the faithful in the Midlands and West Country. Anne said she had begged him to say a mass at her family's home in Uxendon before he set out on his journey. She would break her bail and slip away for one night and meet him there. Would Catherine come, too? Catherine immediately said yes, the idea both thrilling and terrifying her, for she was well aware of the possible consequences. Only the overbearing – intolerable – intervention of her husband had prevented her going.

Catherine frowned in disbelief. 'Topcliffe? Has he taken her again?'

The man's grumble turned to laughter. 'No, she went of her own accord. Have you not heard? Her belly swells by the day, so Nicholas tells me.'

'Nicholas?'

'My boy Nicholas, Nick Jones.'

Catherine felt sick. Nicholas Jones, Topcliffe's contemptible assistant. And was he saying that Anne Bellamy was with child? How could such a thing have happened? She looked closely at the leering old man.

'May I enter your home?' she said. 'I would wish to speak more on this.'

The old man stepped aside. 'By all means, mistress. All are welcome here at my humble abode.'

She stepped into the dark hallway. She saw the eyes of the man's mastiff in an inner doorway and sensed malevolence. The dog barked louder. The old man hobbled over to it and beat it about the head with his stick. It whimpered, then lay down and was quiet.

'Did I tell you that my Nicholas is to come into money? A scryer with a glass ball told me my boy would be rich one day, and so he is to be. A very grand gentleman he will be, I am sure.'

An awful thought took shape in Catherine's mind. If Anne really was with child, could Nicholas Jones be the father? He was thick-set, sly and shared Topcliffe's taste for cruelty and the shedding of blood. Could sweet, innocent Anne have allowed herself to be debauched by such a monster?

'I am sure she will have a pretty baby and we shall save it from the clutches of the Rotten Chair. The dirty little drab . . .'

Catherine exploded in a rage. She pushed the man full in the chest with both her hands. 'How dare you talk of her like that? It is you that has brought her to this! You, and your foul son and Topcliffe.'

The old man slunk back into the shadows, his stick raised defensively. 'She is a grubby little whore, mistress. A grubby little whore. We have all had her, so that none will know who is the father of her bastard.'

'No. It is not true.'

'She's a bitch on heat, that one, dripping for it. All the time . . .'

For a moment, Catherine believed she could summon up the strength to kill this man. Take his stick from him and beat him to death with it, just as he beat his dog.

The urge terrified her. She froze where she stood. She had nothing more to say; she must kill him, or go. She looked at him there, cowering in the shadows with his surly mastiff cur at his side, four eyes in the dark like the eyes of Satan's little demons. Then she turned on her heel and walked away, back out into the street. She closed her eyes a moment and stood there, shaking. Her heart pounded and she felt faint. She had seen into the first circle of hell, here on Holborn Hill, just outside the city walls of London.

The great hall at Essex House blazed with light. Extravagant candelabra, each with dozens of candles, glowed and flickered like a sea of sparkling gemstones. Liveried servants hovered everywhere with goblets of the finest wine and trays of delicate sweetmeats. Music from two dozen viols wafted in the air above the drowning chatter of three hundred revellers.

John Shakespeare stood at the doorway, at the edge of the throng. Even at the royal court, he had not seen such splendour, and his attire – he had taken out his old court doublet of embroidered blue, black and gold – seemed poor stuff in comparison to the magnificent clothes on display here.

'Well, well, Mr Shakespeare, you have made it to the court of Queen Lettice, I see.'

He turned to find himself gazing into the mound of flesh that was Charlie McGunn's ill-formed face. '*Queen* Lettice, Mr McGunn?'

'Be under no illusion, she is the sovereign here. The She-wolf reigns. We are all her subjects.'

A tumbler bounced past, springing from hands to feet, then over again on to his hands. But Shakespeare hardly noticed. He was more astonished – dismayed even – by McGunn's irreverent language. If Sir John Perrot was sentenced to death for calling Elizabeth 'a pissing kitchen woman', how much worse would it be to pay homage, even in jest, to the Queen's cousin and sworn enemy Lettice Knollys? 'I should be careful of your tongue, Mr McGunn, lest it be cut out. I fear even my lord of Essex may not be able to save you.'

McGunn clapped him hard on the back. 'You are an innocent doddypoll, Shakespeare. I cannot believe Walsingham ever had such a simpleton as intelligencer.'

Shakespeare had heard enough. He walked away into the crowd, taking a cup of wine from a bluecoat on his way. The viols stopped and a man took to the richly draped stage, which encompassed the width of one end of the hall, not ten feet from him. At the two sides of the stage heralds blew trumpets and the crowd immediately hushed and turned to see the man.

He was dressed as a jester, in multicoloured costume. Bells

jangled on his cap and brightly patterned sleeves. 'My lords, ladies and gentleman, pray silence for the She-wolf.'

A slow drumbeat sounded and a bier was born on stage by four men dressed as Indians from the New World. They wore breech-clouts – loincloths – of soft hide and their hair was shaven on the sides and raised into a bristly central strip from front to back, all topped by a single pheasant's tail-feather. On the bier, a woman reclined in state. She was adorned in fine court clothes and a wolf mask. The crowd of guests roared with laughter.

The bearers lowered the bier to the stage floor and the She-wolf alighted. With a delicate step, she threw back her head and let out a great howl, like a wolf baying at the moon. She removed her mask and spread wide her arms, her long, elegant fingers upturned: Essex's mother, Lettice Knollys, granddaughter of Anne Boleyn's sister Mary, and red-haired like her cousin Elizabeth. Yet far more beautiful. Her features were soft and fair, her eyes aslant, her mouth set in the warm smile that had enticed men all her adult life.

Shakespeare took a long sip of his wine and watched as Lettice, almost fifty years old but as lovely as a woman half that age, welcomed her guests and invited them to enjoy 'a little masque for your delight, penned by one of our most estimable poets and players . . .'

Lettice left the stage to a thunder of applause and was immediately followed by a cast of tumblers and players hurling themselves on to the stage in a riot of knockabout entertainments. Then, suddenly there was silence again and all the players stood as still as trees in the forest. 'But hush,' said the jester, cupping his ear with a hand. 'Who do we hear coming into the wood? Why, methinks it is the queen of the faeries.'

As the viols started up again, quietly at first, all eyes turned to the stage entrance at the right, where three figures emerged, two of them dwarves dressed as monkeys, both with chains about their necks. The chains were attached to leashes held by the third figure, black-clad like a witch with pointed hat and boils about her haggard white face.

'Bow down, bow down, kneel one and all,' the jester said. 'It *is* the queen of the faeries! And she has her familiars, little William and Robert Puckrel.'

Shakespeare was aghast. One of the monkey figures had a long white beard; the other a hunch-back. It was plain for all to see that they were meant to be William Cecil – Lord Burghley – and his son, Robert. As for the queen of the faeries, ancient and haglike with red hair and a whitened, pox-ridden face, it was intended to be taken as none other than Her Majesty, Gloriana, Queen Elizabeth of England. This was high treason. This could cost a man or woman their bowels and their life. You could be put in the Tower just for watching and have your eyes scraped out with a spoon for laughing. Shakespeare looked around him, expecting to see mouths agape in outrage. Instead he saw a sea of faces creased in laughter and hands coming together in deafening applause.

He watched what followed in a kind of trance. Half of him wanted to flee as far and as fast as he could and never return for fear of being separated from his head, yet the other half was fascinated. Could Elizabeth's credit in England have fallen so low that her courtiers dared stage such a masque behind her back? And doubly astonishing was the thought of who was behind it: Elizabeth's most favoured pet, the Earl of Essex himself, in league with his mother, the She-wolf Lettice.

As he looked around the hall, Shakespeare saw faces of great fame: Essex was at the centre of things, surrounded by a pack that included the Earls of Southampton and Rutland; the brothers Francis and Anthony Bacon; the dashing and dangerous Sir Henry Danvers and Gelli Meyrick – all known to be his close associates at home and on the field of battle. Somewhere in the distance, too, he saw Charlie McGunn, conversing like a conspirator with Essex's straight-backed military aide Sir Toby Le Neve. Nearby, Essex's sister Penelope Rich – four years senior to her brother – talked animatedly with the handsome Charles Blount. And then, with a mixture of relief and alarm, Shakespeare saw his own brother, William, in a group that included Essex's wife, Frances.

On stage, the hag rattled the chains of her monkeys. 'I know I have the body of a weak and feeble woman,' she said, her voice ringing out falsetto like some eunuch from the seraglio. The crowd laughed with brazen humour, then the hag's voice turned deeper, like a market stall holder calling out his wares and she – or he – threw up her skirts to reveal a pair of bare, hairy legs and a pizzle that would not have shamed a bull. 'But I have the balls and prick of a king, and of a king of England too.'

Shakespeare, horrified, made his way through the crowd of revellers to his brother's side. He nodded towards the stage and spoke quietly in his ear. 'William, I hope this is nothing to do with you.'

His brother raised an eyebrow. 'It's that fool Greene. Look at him over there, preening with his villainous friends as he puts his neck further into the hangman's halter.'

Shakespeare followed his brother's eyes. The playmaker Robert Greene was holding court with his mistress Em Ball and various other unsavoury characters. This summer revel of Essex's had certainly brought out a curious array of pleasure-seekers. Will touched him on the shoulder. 'Take care, brother.' Shakespeare raised his eyebrows. 'And you,' he said softly. He watched as Will wove his way towards Southampton, where he was immediately welcomed by that group. He, in turn, switched his gaze to a settle at the side of the room. Frances, Essex's pretty mouse of a wife, was there now, sitting alone, fanning herself.

'Mr Shakespeare, how lovely to see you,' she said as he approached to pay his respects.

He remembered her from her childhood days when, as the well-loved and cosseted daughter of Sir Francis Walsingham, she seemed like a perfect doll, assisting her mother Lady Ursula with her embroidery and the running of the family's households in Seething Lane and Barn Elms. Shakespeare had always liked her quiet ways and vaguely thought that, in a previous age or another place, she could have made a rather splendid Mother Superior in a convent.

'It must be five or six years, my lady.'

'Oh please, Mr Shakespeare, you always called me Frances as a girl. It seems very strange to me now to be called aught else by you.'

Shakespeare smiled. 'As you wish, my lady.' He thought she did not look at all well, very pale and drawn.

'There,' she said. 'You see, you cannot even manage a little thing like that.'

'Well, you would have to call me John by way of return, and that might not be at all proper. People might talk.'

She laughed lightly. 'Indeed, I had not thought of that. What would the gossips make of such a thing? Do come and sit with me. You are so much taller than me and I feel a little too weak to stand. I have not been well. My mouth burns and my bile is bitter. I see little things in the air, flying things, but my physician tells me they are not there. Do *you* see them, Mr Shakespeare?'

Shakespeare sat down, two feet or so from her. 'Do you mean bees, my lady, or birds? Or butterflies? Moths, perhaps?'

'No, no. These are lovely little things. They have tiny candles in their wings, which are made of gossamer silk.' She patted the settle next to her. 'Though I am not at all well, I do not have the pestilence, Mr Shakespeare. You may safely sit a little nearer to me.'

He shuffled a bit closer. 'My lady, I had not thought such a thing,' he said, though her face did, indeed, look worryingly pale and moist.

'No? Well, many other people nowadays do think so when one has a little summer sweat. If it had been the plague, I fear I would be in my grave by now for I have been feeling weak and sick for some two weeks and I believe the pest is more like to take a mere three days to kill one off.' She swatted at something in front of her eyes with her fan. 'You see they are everywhere.'

'What are, my lady?'

'The little flying things with the tiny lights. You must see them. Do you not think them pretty?'

'I do not see them, my lady,' Shakespeare said slowly.

'Oh well, you are fortunate then, for though they are lovely to look on, I consider them over-familiar. Dr Forman says they are sprites and has given me tinctures to ward them off.' She broke off. 'Mr Shakespeare, you are looking at me as if you think me quite mad.'

'I am sorry, my lady. I am a little bewildered. I do not see these little flying things.'

'Well, let us say no more about them. As for the plague, you must burn herbs in all the rooms. You must go from room to room with rue and herb of grace and throw water outside the doors and along the street.' She smiled but it seemed a strain for her. 'But I cannot bother with it. I might as well have the plague for all the attention my lord and master pays me. You know, Mr Shakespeare, it is a curious thing, we were all with child together in this year past. My lord's sister, Penelope, good Bess Throckmorton – now Lady Ralegh, of course, to the Queen's disquiet – and my lord and master's concubine, whom I cannot bear to name, though she stands here in this room. Why, tell me, is it that my own little Walter lived but a few days and died in my arms, while theirs lived? Do you think his spirit lives in the flying things?'

Shakespeare did not know what to say. He knew, of course, of Ralegh's child and illegal marriage; he knew, too, that the ever fecund Penelope had brought forth a new babe into the world, and he had heard gossip of a bastard born to Essex's amour Elizabeth Sewell. But the fact of Frances's new child, and its death, had eluded him. In the end, he merely said, 'I am sorry, my lady. The ways of God are mysterious indeed.'

'Yes, they are. And now I might follow my little Wat and lie beside him at All Hallows, for I grow more feeble by the day.' They were silent together. Shakespeare would like to have comforted her, but had no way of doing so. She gave another of her heavy, sickly sighs, then spoke a little quieter, as if imparting a confidence. 'Tell me, Mr Shakespeare, what do you make of the revels?'

He tensed. 'They are interesting, my lady.'

'The crowd makes my heart beat so fast I can scarce breathe at times. The revels . . . I do hope you are not uncomfortable with my question.'

'I confess I have not seen their like.'

'My father, if he were alive, would be in a very dark humour indeed to see such drolleries. I pray that no word of this reach Her Majesty's ears, for she would take it very ill, I fear. I did not like those monkeys. They were malign.'

'I cannot disagree with you, my lady.'

She patted his hand again. 'Still, it is harmless, I am sure. No one could be more devoted to the Queen than my lord of Essex. He would not allow anything untoward.'

Shakespeare knew otherwise, but confined himself to remarking neutrally, 'Indeed, your good husband is noted for his close attachment and loyalty to Her Majesty.' He watched as Essex hove into view like an ungainly galleon. The Earl's white silk and gold thread doublet, heavy with diamonds, pearls and other stones, glittered in the candlelight so that he quite outshone his wife.

'Mr Shakespeare, I hope the countess is keeping you well entertained. I am delighted to hear you have joined my merry band of intelligencers.'

Shakespeare rose to his feet and bowed. As far as he was concerned, he had accepted just one commission from Essex, but this was no time to argue the finer points of his employment. 'My lord, it is my honour and pleasure.'

'Good man, good man. And how go your inquiries? Have you found Eleanor Dare yet? Where has she landed following her long flight from the Americas?'

'Not yet, my lord. But soon, I hope. If she is here to be found.'

'Well, keep me informed. I shall have yet more important tasks for you soon enough. But tonight, make merry. I fear it is all a little strong for my constitution, but my beloved mother and sisters would have it thus. And I dare not argue with the She-wolf. What man would? If she wants monkeys and hags, then monkeys and hags she shall have . . .' With that he laughed, and strode away with his curious gait towards his adoring guests.

Shakespeare watched him go and wondered, with distaste, just how long he had been poisoning his wife.

Chapter 12

B Y MIDNIGHT, THE outrageous masque was long finished (the queen of the faeries having been mounted most obscenely by her gibbering monkeys) and the celebrations were spreading from the great hall out into the gardens and even on to the river, where revellers fought mock sea battles from barges and tilt-boats, all lit by pitch torches and blazing cressets planted along the bank. Wherever Shakespeare moved there was a different group of fiddlers and balladeers playing and singing. In the great hall, the dancing was a riot of galliards and voltas, in which young gentlemen threw their ladies high into the air and hoped to catch them.

Shakespeare watched the gaming in a side room. He had taken very little wine; he needed to preserve his wits.

Southampton and Rutland were betting large sums of gold coin against each other. Southampton plucked a diamond from a chain about his neck and planted it in the middle of the table. 'This for your carriage, Roger. One turn of a card and the highest wins.'

'Very well, Henry. But I must have the idle wench turn my card.'

Penelope stepped forward and flipped up a ten. She was, thought Shakespeare, even more beautiful than when he first saw her. Her eyes darker, her hair more fair.

'Then I shall have Dorothy,' Southampton said. 'Where *is* Dorothy?'

'My sister has retired to bed,' Penelope said.

'Retired to bed? Then she is an idler wench than you.'

'I did not say with *whom* she had retired to bed; nor did I say anything about *sleep*.'

'God's blood, then I shall turn it myself and be damned.' Southampton flipped another card and brought up a king. 'Aha, I have your coach, Roger. The idle wench is no charm to you.'

Shakespeare wandered from the room. He had heard once that Southampton had lost five thousand pounds at tennis in Paris. It was said he had not cared about the fortune, but did care very much that he had succumbed to a Frenchman.

Casually looking about him, Shakespeare stumbled like a sot through the doorway at the far end of the hall, taking a fresh glass of wine from a bluecoat as he went. The servant showed no interest in another high-born drunk. Once outside the great hall, Shakespeare glanced around. At the bottom of the steps there was an ornate oaken coffer, with a flickering candlestick atop its lid. Putting down his wine glass, he took the candle and cupped his hand around the flame to keep it alight, then quickly padded up the narrow winding stone stairway. He was in the square turret that housed the high room where McGunn had taken him to meet Phelippes, Mills and Gregory. Though he was certain he had not been seen, he held back a few moments to make sure no footfalls followed him, then slipped into the room of secrets.

It was a vain hope that he would soon find what he wanted among this mass of documents. What he sought were pointers to the layout of the place, the possible location for the information he needed. He knew that Walsingham would have collected extensive files on both Arbella Stuart and the Earl of

Essex. It was a matter of narrowing down the search area. If he knew where to look, he could return here on other days.

When Cecil had given him the commission, he had had doubts. Those had been swept away by this evening's revels. There was something rotten here, a brazen contempt for the established order. Neither Essex, his haughty mother Lettice nor those around them cared who knew it. They were imperious, so sure of their high status that they felt themselves immune to the normal laws of the land. This Court of Queen Lettice was, indeed, like a court-in-waiting.

Shakespeare put the candle on a table. Working at speed, he moved with method along the shelves and piles of papers, taking down a document at a time, scanning it for any possible relevance and then replacing it. It soon became apparent that there was some sort of order here. Documents and correspondence from Rome were stacked together, so were the intercepts from Madrid and, likewise, Paris and the Netherlands.

What he needed was a home section. That must be where – if anywhere – he would find what he wanted. To the left of the tall oriel window, at the east of the room, was a table laden with charts. To the left again was a stack of large, leather-bound books, all upright and leaning against each other. Above them was a series of shelves. He reached up to these shelves and took down a small packet of papers at random. He quickly looked through it. There was correspondence from Walsingham's old intelligencers from years ago; Shakespeare recognised the names: Poley, Berden, poor Harry Slide, knifed through the throat in a Southwark whorehouse. Shakespeare flinched at the memory and put the packet of papers back where he had found it. He took another pack from the shelf above. This was more promising; a letter from the Earl of Shrewsbury concerning the daily routine of Mary Queen of Scots. The letter was dated December 1586, just two months before her execution. Shrewsbury, who had died a few months after Walsingham in 1590, had been Bess of Hardwick's estranged husband.

Shakespeare read quickly. The letter warned Walsingham of his wife's ambitions for her granddaughter Arbella. 'I fear, Frank, that the girl will heap much trouble upon our family. She makes the girl a shrew, in her own image.'

He heard a faint noise. Soft footsteps on the stairs coming up to the room. He thrust the packet of papers back on to the shelf and snuffed the candle. The darkness was intense, but he knew where he was going. Carrying the candlestick with him, he edged further left, where there was a doorway into an adjoining chamber. The door to the room was ajar and he slipped into the room. In the darkness, instinct took over. His heart pumped fast and yet he was utterly calm.

Crouching like a hunting cat, he slid backwards into a small space between the cold stone wall and a settle. Shakespeare was a tall man, but he was small now, consciously shrinking into himself, and ready to pounce.

The footfalls were closer, in the main turret room. Through the slightly open door he saw a flicker of light. He heard a light sniffing noise; whoever was there could smell the snuffed candle. Yet he or she had a candle of their own and could not be sure whether it was the guttering flame of that one which they scented.

For a moment all was still. The hunter stood motionless, listening for breathing or a slight sound. Shakespeare, too, was completely still, every muscle tensed. The flickering light moved close towards the doorway, then stopped again. There was something dark and strange about this presence. Why did the man – he was now sure it was a man – not cry out 'Who is there?' like any normal watchman? Why maintain this ghostly silence?

The light came through the door now. From his hiding

place, Shakespeare could see a vague shape and shadows as a figure advanced further into the room. It was McGunn's man Slyguff, thin and dark-clothed. In one hand, he carried a candle that threw its strange light here and there, in the other a short sword. Around his shoulder was a thin, loosely coiled rope. He stood stock still, his eyes moving slowly around the room. He sniffed the air again.

From below, out in the garden, sounds of laughter and music and loud chatter rose in the air, but here it was as if time and life was suspended. There was no sound of breathing or move-ment from hunter or hunted. How long did he stand there like that? A minute? Five? Of a sudden, Slyguff turned on his soft leather-clad feet and walked towards the doorway and out again into the main room. Shakespeare listened for his light footsteps, counting them as he went out into the stairwell. He heard the faint sound of clothing being adjusted, then the tinkling and grunt of a man peeing.

Shakespeare began to count the seconds in his head; slowly. He counted to three hundred then stopped and listened to the silence again. Then he counted three hundred more before easing himself forward from his hiding place and standing up. He had a cramp in his leg, but paid it no heed, moving crablike, sideways, to the door, his hand on the hilt of the ornamental dagger in his belt.

His eyes were adjusting to the dark. A filling-out moon gave a little light to the room through the oriel windows and he could see his way out on to the stairwell. The door was large and made of oak and was open enough that he could slip out without pushing it. But what – who – would he find on the other side? He pulled the dagger from his belt and held it in front of him, then moved on out. No one there, only a puddle of piss. He allowed himself the release of a deep breath.

From the bottom of the stairs, he shunned the entrance

to the great hall and went, instead, a round-about route towards the garden. Whenever he came across a servant or reveller, he resumed his drunken act. In one dark corner he stumbled upon a guest whom he instantly recognised as Francis Bacon, his breeches dropped low, with another guest, whom he vaguely thought to be the celebrated scholar Henry Cuffe, standing boldly in front of him. Bacon turned and saw Shakespeare, his perpetually worried and ambitious eyes staring into Shakespeare's yet not really registering who he was. His eyes closed as he embraced Cuffe and concentrated on his pleasures.

Stepping outside into the balmy evening air of the garden, Shakespeare's heart still roared like the London conduit. It was time to hail a waterman at the river stairs to row him home. But first he needed wine. He took a glass from a serving-man and drank it down in one gulp. Around him there was much laughter. In the darker, more shaded areas of the large but intricate gardens he heard the rustle and giggle of frolics and trysts.

McGunn appeared in front of him, standing square and puffed out, his mouth turned up in a snarling smile. 'Still at it, Shakespeare?' His eyes were sober, his voice was businesslike. 'Where have you been? I have been seeking you.'

'I cannot say, Mr McGunn,' Shakespeare said, taking care to slur the words. 'I am a gentleman and a married man.'

'Swiving, is it?'

'I cannot say.'

McGunn drew back his fist as if he would punch him. Shakespeare recoiled instinctively. The fist hovered then lowered.

'Be very, very careful. Tonight they make merry, but they will want results fast, as will I. Remember, you are here for one purpose and one purpose alone – to find Eleanor Dare.'

Did McGunn suspect him of something? Had he sent Slyguff

to follow him? The answer had to be no, for Slyguff would not have given up so easily in the turret room if he had known for certain he was there.

'Do you understand?'

Shakespeare contained his anger. 'Yes, I understand.'

'Good, then sober yourself and get hunting on the morrow.' He looked hard at Shakespeare one more time, then strode away into the house.

As he watched McGunn stride away, Shakespeare felt two arms slide about his waist and caught a waft of sweet briar perfume. A pair of soft female lips touched the nape of his neck. He knew immediately who it was, without turning to see her face or hear her voice.

'Mr Shakespeare, you seem all alone.'

Penelope's arms lingered for a few moments, then she slid them away from him.

'I was about to summon a tilt-boat, Lady Rich.'

'So soon. Where are you going so early at night, and to whose bed?'

'To my own.'

'Ah. What a tragical waste.'

Shakespeare said nothing.

'You know, Mr Shakespeare,' Penelope continued. 'My brother needs a man with skills such as yours.'

'He has me, my lady.'

'No, not just over this Roanoke affair. There are greater matters.'

'My lady?'

'We will talk in due course, Mr Shakespeare.' She smiled and touched his face with the tips of her fingers. 'Tonight, we make merry.'

'I can think of no better way to idle away the hours . . .'

She threw her head back in laughter. 'Mr Shakespeare, you

must know that I am a married woman, as I know that you are a married man.'

'Why do they call you "idle wench", my lady? If I may ask.'

'It is my mother's idea of mirth, Mr Shakespeare. She calls me that in her letters to my brother, and he bruits such things about among his friends. And I suppose it is true; I am idle. I have never milked a cow nor scrubbed a pot in my life, and I fancy I never shall.'

'A great disappointment for pots and kine, my lady.'

'My husband has often said I am no more use than a farm maid, which I always took to be a great insult to farm maids.'

'Your husband?'

'Fear not, Lord Rich is not here. He would rather die than dance and make merry. He keeps the company of his God-fearing friends at our home in Leighs, while I flit about like a barnybee, supping honey from the flowers. Do you know about my marriage, Mr Shakespeare? It is a most instructive tale.'

He had heard the gossip. It was impossible to live within the city walls and not hear everything. Her marriage to Lord Rich had been forced on her, when she was a girl of eighteen. Not only had her parents insisted, but the Queen had ordered it. She had not fought nor screamed nor stamped her foot, for it was not her way, but she had made her feelings very plain, even protesting her objections in the nave of the church, before relenting and saying the words which wedded her to an austere man, for whom she had felt no warmth.

'But not tonight. However, there is something I would mention.' Her voice lowered. 'Henry – the Earl of Southampton – has asked me to speak with you, for he knows you have a particular interest in a friend of his.'

'My brother?'

'No, Father Robert Southwell, recently taken by Her Majesty's pursuivants and presently held in Mr Topcliffe's delightful chamber of all the pleasures. I know I can talk to you plainly about this, Mr Shakespeare, because I know of your wife's inclinations. The truth is that until very recently, Father Southwell resided in Southampton House, close to the countryside at Holborn.'

'I know the house, my lady.'

'I think Topcliffe knew he was there, but was powerless to do anything about it. Father Southwell was not only safe there, but he was cherished for his good works among the poor and for his poetry, and by many among us who are not of his faith, myself included. He is a fine man, whatever you think of his religion, Mr Shakespeare – a poet of wondrous wit. Even your brother has met him there and admired his writings. Topcliffe waited until he left, then pounced. It is dark news for all of us that he has been taken in this way.'

Shakespeare put up his hand defensively. 'My lady, there is no way I can help. My influence ended when Mr Secretary terminated my employment. It is your brother and my lord of Southampton who have the Queen's ear. Surely they can do something?'

Penelope shook her head. 'Sadly, Mr Shakespeare, they are just the men who *cannot* help him, for they would be compromised. Any intervention by them would merely play into their enemies' hands. Such is the royal court. I am approaching you because I know you too have history with Mr Topcliffe and it is generally thought you had some hold over him, that is all.'

Shakespeare tried to smile, but it looked like a scowl. He tried to laugh, but it came out as a bark. 'I fear any power of persuasion I might once have had with Topcliffe died when Mr Secretary was taken from us, my lady. I am as much in peril from him as Father Southwell.'

Chapter 13

SHAKESPEARE WAS PREOCCUPIED as he banged at the door of the whore Starling Day. He was thinking about the events of the previous evening at Essex House. There had been a fevered air of treachery, billowing like the dark clouds of an approaching storm. In particular, the open defiance and mockery of the masque seemed to confirm everything Sir Robert Cecil had said about Essex and his ambitions.

Mostly, though, Shakespeare thought of the Countess of Essex and the strange disturbance of the mind that afflicted her. She was being poisoned, he was certain of it. *What is one little life against a matter so great?* Her sickness had less to do with the loss of her child and more to do with something she had been fed.

As the door was opened, he tried to put the thoughts aside. He smiled at Starling Day, surprised by the change in her. She had gained a well-rounded figure since last they met. She had also gained a great deal of money and a well-favoured house in the middle of the great bridge between London and Southwark. She welcomed him effusively.

'Come gaze with me out of the windows eastwards, Mr Shakespeare. I love the morning sun. See the birds diving for fish and the proud argosies setting sail for the spice islands. I could stand here the day long just watching and listening. At times I fancy I can hear the timbers creak and the shrouds sing.'

'Your life has certainly changed, Starling Day.' He was particularly struck by the change in her voice. Where once her Nottinghamshire tone had been difficult to decipher, even to a Midlander such as himself, now she could almost pass for a London lady. Almost, but not quite.

'Mr Watts has taught me much. He has told me proper ways of speaking and is even teaching me to read a little. He promises that one day soon he will present me at court, though I should *die* to meet the Queen. Indeed, it is a fine thing to be the plaything of a wealthy merchant, Mr Shakespeare. Mr Watts looks after me very well and I am always here for him, as is meet and proper in a *courtesan*. That is my new word for *whore*, Mr Shakespeare. Do you like it?'

'It suits you very well, Mistress Day.'

'Mr Watts learned it in Italy, where it implies a certain respect.' She clapped her hands and a maid came quickly to her side, a sweet-faced girl perhaps five years younger than her mistress. Starling herself was dressed in a fifty-mark dress of gold and silver with a voluminous bum-roll and a low neckline that let loose her expanding, milk-white breasts. The garment, which she said was confected by Tredger the tailor, of Cheapside, was clearly intended to mark her out as gentry, but sadly only marked her out for what she really was, a gaudy strumpet whose cards had turned up kings.

'Winnie, fetch us malmsey wine and saffron cakes.'

The maid bowed and went out of the room. It was a room rich with tapestries from Arras and cushions of colourful silks from the Indies, a room befitting the well-fed whore of a wealthy, piratical merchant like John Watts.

'How may I help you, Mr Shakespeare?'

'I am here with a most curious request, for I know you have friends in the bawdy-houses of Southwark.'

'Oh dear, I am not so familiar with bawdy-houses as once I

was. My trugging days are over since Mr Watts took a liking to me, although I would happily take *you* to my chamber for the joy alone, Mr Shakespeare.'

Shakespeare smiled at the offer but shook his head. 'I am looking for a woman named Eleanor Dare, born White, though there is a good chance that she no longer goes by either of those names. She was seen by the Bull Ring last week, where the Winchester Geese parade for customers. It was said she wore the attire of a street woman touting her wares.'

'What does she look like?'

'Pretty, from what I am told. Slender with fair hair and strange, piercing blue eyes with a grey ring.'

'And can you tell me why you want her?'

'It is a strange tale.' As the maid returned with wine and saffron cakes, Shakespeare told Starling the story of Roanoke and of the sighting of Eleanor in Southwark. 'It is so curious that I do not really wish it bruited about. If this woman Eleanor *is* in England – and if she were to hear of my inquiries – I fear she might well disappear.'

'Then I shall ask about quietly, Mr Shakespeare. And I shall send word to you as soon as I have heard aught of interest.'

Shakespeare took his leave of Starling Day and walked the short distance home to Dowgate to fetch his horse, sure all the while that he was watched. Another man might have felt intimidated, but you could not work in a world of secrets and be too concerned by such things. Shakespeare knew how to spot the observer who wished to remain unseen; the shadow on the wall that stopped when you stopped, the figure in the crowd that did not quite flow with the surging of the mass, the face that was cowled despite the warmth of the day. More importantly, Shakespeare knew, too, how to lose the watcher when it became necessary.

At the mews he ordered the groom, Perkin Sidesman, to ready his grey mare, then went through to the house for a brief refreshment and to fold a change of garments into a pack-saddle. He also met his deputy, George Jerico, and told him that for a short while he was to assume the duties of high master. Jerico looked shocked and a little worried, but Shakespeare merely shook him by the hand and thanked him for his forbearance. 'I will see that you are properly recompensed, Mr Jerico,' he said, then left him to contemplate his new responsibilities without a chance to make objections.

On his way through the courtyard, Shakespeare encountered Rumsey Blade. His narrow face sneered.

'Ah, Mr Shakespeare, might I have a few words with you?'

'Later,' Shakespeare said sharply, not breaking stride as he made for the mews.

Blade scurried to keep up with him. 'It is only proper to inform you that I have this morning sent a report to Bishop Aylmer. You can expect to be disciplined in the most severe terms.'

'Good day, Mr Blade.'

'The Bishop does not take these matters lightly, so I have recommended him to revoke the school's licence. I am sure of a fair hearing in this, for the Bishop is my kin.'

Shakespeare stopped. He looked Blade in the eye. 'And I have information for you, sir. You are dismissed from your post as a master of this school. You will leave the premises this day and will not return.'

Blade's pinched face creased even more, shocked to be spoken to thus. 'You cannot do this, Shakespeare.'

Shakespeare gestured to his servant, who was carrying a water butt towards the house. Jack Butler was a giant of a man, well over six feet tall. He set down the butt and came to his master. 'Mr Butler, will you please ensure that Mr Blade is off these premises before sunset.'

Butler bowed. 'As you wish, master.'

Rumsey Blade looked aghast. 'This is intolerable. The Bishop will not allow it. Not when he hears about your failure to beat the boys, your absences, your wife's Papism.'

Shakespeare clapped the man on the shoulder and smiled broadly. 'The Bishop knows all that, Blade, and more. And I trust that in time he will come to support me wholly in this, my decision. So goodbye. And if you wish for advice, look for some new employment that does not involve the flogging of little boys.'

The grey mare was saddled. The groom held the reins while Shakespeare stepped on the mounting block and slid nimbly aboard. Below him, Rumsey Blade stood stone-faced in shock. Shakespeare took the reins from the ostler, then leant over and whispered towards Blade, 'And you may take your birches with you, sir, for they will no longer be used at the Margaret Woode school.'

Boltfoot Cooper sat in a corner of The Hope, on the south bank of the Thames, directly facing the western edge of the Tower. He was dismayed.

In his younger days, this was one of the taverns he and his crewmates frequented. It gave a fair welcome, offered beds at reasonable prices, and soft flesh with a welcoming smile. Now the only girl in the taproom was scrawny and had a sullen aspect. The landlord scowled as he slopped the beer. Even the daub of the walls was breaking away from the wattles and you could see sky through the thatch. It had been a similar story in a dozen or more other taverns he had visited. He was getting sick of such places. With Jane growing larger, he did not enjoy staying away from home.

But here in The Hope he had at least found Will Legge, an old companion from the three long years aboard the *Golden Hind*, when they sailed the world.

Legge, who had been a steward to Drake, could barely raise a cheery word of greeting. 'Well, look at us. Reduced to misery. Left for dead after the great bloody Armada victory. Victory for who? Not the common mariner, Boltfoot.'

'You always did complain a great deal, Will Legge.'

'And did I not have cause? Did Drake not treat us like dogs the way he took and kept *our* gold, which he had promised to us? You too, not just me. Twenty-nine ounces. I could be living in a fine manor-house with that.'

Boltfoot could not argue the point, for he knew he spoke the truth, even if he exaggerated the value of the gold a little.

'Come, meet the fellows,' Legge said. 'Hear what they have to say, if you don't believe me.' He led Boltfoot across the taproom to join half a dozen long-bearded, weather-hardened men, all with wound scars. One was tall, well over six foot and had a peg leg and a vivid red scar along his forearm; another had just one arm and no legs and was propped inside a crate, a third was blind in both eyes.

'These are the men as did for the Armada, Boltfoot. Look at them now in their rags. Many more are dead, starved on the shores where they were off-loaded when the fighting was done. And did the Queen whose skin we saved send food and gold to us in thanks? Did she buggery! They'd string me up if I said what I thought of that poxy old bag of rancid mutton.'

'You've said enough, Will Legge.'

'Report me, will you, to your fine friends on the Privy Council?'

'No, but you've said enough. Now, stow you while I stand these fellows ale and talk with them awhile.'

Boltfoot bought the group ale and beer, then questioned them what they knew about the voyage that had taken the colonists to Roanoke.

'They was Puritans, so I heard,' the blind man said. 'Drove

the poor mariners Bedlamwards with their sermonising and praying and damning the world to hellfire. It's the poor savages of the New World I feels sorry for, having to listen to their zealous ranting and roaring the whole day long.'

'And what do you think might have happened to the colonists?'

'Disappeared up their own zealous arses, I reckon,' the blind man said.

Their theories went on and on, none of them surprising or original. 'What I most want to know,' Boltfoot said. 'Is whether any of you ever heard tell of any mariners that were on the voyage that took them there. And if so, would you know where they are now? There would be gold in it for the man that could find me such a one.' It was an offer Boltfoot had made several times already that day without success.

'Gold?' the tall one said. 'We don't want gold, we want tobacco.'

'If you've got a name, tell me and I'll give you a mark – and another when I've found him. You can buy your own sotweed.'

The seafarer turned down the corners of his mouth dismissively. 'Can't get it. All goes to the royal court. Mariners used to have as much as we liked, now it's nowhere to be found.'

'I'll get you tobacco,' Boltfoot said reluctantly. 'I have some.'

'In that case I might just be able to help you, Mr Cooper. But it would have to be a good half a pound.'

'Six ounces. Who is he – and where?'

The man shifted uneasily in his seat. He looked from one to another of his comrades. Then he thrust out his enormous grimy hand. Boltfoot felt most disgruntled as he fished into his jerkin pocket and brought out his prized pouch of tobacco. The landlord fetched scales and Boltfoot weighed out six ounces as if he were being forced to give up his vital organs. He looked disconsolately at the few strands of leaf that were left him. 'Here.' He handed over the tobacco. 'That's best verinshe, that is, so this had better be good.'

The big mariner sniffed at it and his eyes brightened. He was about to pat some of it into his walnut-shell pipe, but Boltfoot stayed his hand. 'You can smoke it when you've spoken – if I like what you say.'

'As you will. But none of this comes back to me if he's unhappy. It's dangerous business telling stuff like this. Don't want anyone thinking I've got a loose tongue, not in days like these.'

'You've got the sotweed. Get on with it.'

The seafarer's eyes flickered this way and that. Boltfoot could understand his fears; he had himself worried that there was something more to this, something sinister, and had done his utmost to avoid being followed or observed as he journeyed between these seamen's haunts.

The man with the information sniffed again at the tobacco. 'Very well,' he said. 'His name was Davy. I recall him from the end of the year the Scots queen was headed when all the yards and docks were getting in a frenzy about the Spanish fleet they said was coming. There was a taproom out at Blackwall, and he was in there telling the whole world of that voyage when they put them poor souls down in the New World. We was all giving him ale to keep him talking with his tales of warlike savages and mad-prattling Puritans. He was a caskwright, like you Mr Cooper.'

'What use is any of this to me? That was five years ago.'

'That's the point. I saw him a few weeks since in Gully Hole and I did hail him. But it was as if he was deaf, for he just hurried on and paid me no heed.'

'How will that help me find him?'

'Because I saw where he came from, Mr Cooper. And I reckon he'll go back there again, being as how he's a cooper like you and he was wearing his workman's belly-cheat.' He patted a pinch of tobacco down hard into the walnut shell, put the straw sticking from it into the side of his mouth, begged a lighted taper from the landlord and inhaled deeply of the fragrant smoke. He closed his eyes and sighed with the luxury of it. 'Ah, that'll keep King Pest at bay,' he said, basking in the pleasure.

'Well?' Boltfoot demanded irritably.

The man held out his pipe and his fellows all looked at it appreciatively, hoping to savour some of it themselves. At last the smoker grinned. 'He came from Hogsden Trent's. That's where I saw him come from, Hogsden Trent's.'

Chapter 14

SHAKESPEARE'S PURSUER, WHO was on foot, wore a dun-coloured cowhide jerkin, black woollen breeches and grey hose. There was nothing to distinguish him from any other working man, but Shakespeare had not lost his skill in spotting the one who wished not to be noticed.

He kicked his grey mare into a trot and soon saw the pursuer floundering behind him, walking fast, occasionally breaking into a run, but losing ground the whole time. At last, he felt sure he was in the clear and turned westwards through New Gate, then along the Strand, past Westminster and out into open country towards the little village of Chelsea. He stopped and looked about him. The road was busy with drays and carts and postriders.

He rode on a little further, then reined in some distance short of Shrewsbury House, tethering his horse to a sycamore on a piece of common land. He walked the last quarter mile to the north side of the building.

Shrewsbury House was an opulent, brick-built manor, facing the Thames on its southern side. Most visitors arrived by river at the landing stage, but Shakespeare went to the postern gate, where he was met by a guard.

'I would speak with the Countess of Shrewsbury.'

'Are you expected, sir?'

'No. But say I am sent by Sir Robert Cecil with a message which I must convey to her in person.'

'And your name, sir?'

'Marvell,' he said, giving his wife's birth name. 'John Marvell.'

'Please wait here.'

The guard returned in a few minutes and led Shakespeare into a magnificent hall, adorned with shields and splendid tapestries, many threaded with gold and silver. It well befitted the second most wealthy woman in the land. A liveried footman appeared and took over Shakespeare's care from the guard, leading him through to another chamber.

Cecil had described Bess of Hardwick as a hard woman. From all he had heard, Shakespeare certainly knew her to be formidable: married four times, mother of eight children of whom five survived, grandmother to a host of well-bred grandchildren, sometime companion of the captive Mary Queen of Scots when her late husband, the Earl of Shrewsbury, was her keeper, and good friend of Elizabeth herself.

In the flesh, Bess of Hardwick did not disappoint. She was examining bolts of cloth laid out on the floor in front of her by a richly clad mercer and his three assistants. There were great lengths of taffeta and black damask, satins and silks. A tailor and haberdasher stood close by, with their own assistants, beside a table laden with quantities of intricate white and black lace, gauze, black velvet and cambric.

She looked up at Shakespeare's entrance and smiled warmly.

'Mr Marvell? I don't think I know you.'

Shakespeare bowed. 'I am sent on an errand from Sir Robert Cecil, my lady. It is a matter of some urgency.' He glanced at the tradesmen. 'May we speak alone?'

Bess nodded to the mercer and haberdasher and their

assistants. 'Gentlemen, if you would. And think on those prices I have offered, for they are fair.'

'My lady,' one of the merchants pleaded. 'You will ruin us.'

'I will go no higher. Take it or leave it.'

They all bowed low and hurried from the room.

The Countess was not tall, neither was she a beauty, though she was very slender and healthy for an old woman of nearly sixty-five – six years senior to the Queen. She was strikingly dressed in black velvet and a broad ruff and wore a black coif atop her still golden hair. Long strings of perfect pearls adorned her neck, cascading down to her narrow waist.

'This is all very secretive, Mr Marvell. Please proceed.'

'It is a delicate matter, my lady. It concerns your granddaughter, the Lady Arbella.'

'Is Sir Robert still worried about Arbella?' Bess's attentive eyes revealed her intelligence as she spoke. 'I do think he imagines I neglect my duties as guardian.'

'Indeed, I am sure he does not, my lady. He speaks most highly of your loving care for her upbringing and education.'

'But he fears Spanish plots. He thinks King Philip will send his mercenaries to spirit her away and make an infanta of her and use her as a tool to steal the crown of England.'

'My lady, that *is* his concern. He wonders if you would agree to remove Lady Arbella to your holdings in the Midlands and North, that you might better protect her there.'

'Well, if that is what Sir Robert desires, then I shall do so. I hold Sir Robert in the highest esteem. We shall leave for Hardwick at the earliest opportunity.'

'Might I tell him how soon that will be?'

Bess smiled her warm smile once more, but Shakespeare thought he detected a hint of irritation. She was not one to be commanded.

'Well, let me think,' she said. 'I have much to pack up and

take with me – perhaps twenty wagonloads. I have two hundred and thirty household staff who must be provisioned for the long journey. There are clothes, linen, livestock, hangings and wondrous new paintings and tapestries to transport. It cannot be done in a midnight flit, if that is what you mean, Mr Marvell.'

'Forgive me. I did not mean to discomfit you. I asked only that I might report back to Sir Robert.'

'Let us say two weeks then. Two or three weeks at the most. Would that suit the next Principal Secretary?'

Shakespeare was certain that Cecil would not be at all happy, but there was nothing to be gained from argument. 'I am sure he will be pleased at your cooperation, my lady. And most relieved that the Lady Arbella will be out of harm's way.'

Bess frowned, and though the smile was ever present she was obviously put out. 'Mr Marvell, I would have you know that I ensure my granddaughter is safe at all times, wherever we are. When we are at court, I never let her out of my sight. She is constantly chaperoned. And here at home, she is either with me or with my maids or her tutors. She is no more in harm's way in Chelsea than she will be in Derbyshire.'

He bowed and said nothing.

She raised a hand. 'But I have said I will do Sir Robert's bidding. Let that be an end to it.'

Shakespeare began to understand how, from relatively humble beginnings, this woman had accumulated such wealth and power. He had one more question.

'May I ask about your household staff, my lady? I think it would be well if you were to re-examine all credentials and letters of recommendation of those close to her. I know that such a course of action would set Sir Robert's mind at ease.'

'Then yet again I shall do as he wishes. And if I see one word in Spanish, or even the semblance of a Spanish name, I will dismiss them on the instant.'

Shakespeare found himself laughing. She was mocking him, but he supposed it was earned. He guessed, too, that she would do as he asked. If she had ambitions for her granddaughter, it was as much in her interest to keep her safe as it was for Cecil.

Shakespeare bowed low, thanked her once again for her forbearance and the bluecoat appeared and escorted him out.

At the postern gate he turned briefly and looked back at the house, with its intricate patterns of brickwork, its soaring chimneys and its tall windows. He saw a girl at one of the windows. A girl in a cream and yellow dress. Her face was serious before its time. Her large, unblinking eyes seemed to be gazing into the distance, across the fields and woods, as if looking for someone or something. It was a face of the most unutterable sadness. As he looked, her eyes turned down and met his. Briefly, for two heartbeats, their eyes locked. Her expression did not change, but she looked away and moved from the window, back into her cavernous prison.

Shakespeare waited in a private antechamber at the palace of Whitehall. He wore artisan's clothes and a cowl, having changed from his formal attire in a spinney on the common land at Chelsea; he could not afford to be recognised in this vast palace of gossips.

At last he was shown through to the office where Sir Robert Cecil was busy planning the Queen's annual progress west. Concerned by the plague, she had insisted plans be hurried along so that she might be away from the city as soon as possible.

Cecil was issuing instructions to an assistant on the route to be taken and the provisions required. Elizabeth's luggage would be carried on four hundred wagons. She would need stabling and feed for her two thousand five hundred horses on each stage of the journey. She would be accompanied by hundreds of guards, knights, courtiers and other dignitaries, many with entourages of their own. It would be like a town on the move.

It occurred to Shakespeare that Cecil's office was the sort of room Walsingham would have favoured: austere and business-like. Yet this was more ordered than Walsingham's office had ever been. Tables were bare save for the document Cecil was working on at that moment; files of correspondence were neatly stacked on shelves. The neatness told much about the precise workings of Cecil's mind. Also telling were his quiet, though costly, clothes. On his feet he wore elegant *pantoufles*, slippers faced in dark blue velvet with a gold braid.

He did not seem pleased to see Shakespeare. 'I trust you were not followed here,' he said abruptly.

'I was not, Sir Robert.'

'Be wary, Mr Shakespeare. If you are seen to be evading their watchers, they will become suspicious very quickly.'

'I needed to speak with you, Sir Robert.'

'The masque?' Cecil picked up a paper and read aloud. 'Two monkeys, one with a long white beard, the other with a crook-back.' He looked up and smiled bleakly. 'It must have all been exceedingly mirthful. For myself, it is of no significance; I have been pricked with such barbs all my life. Yet making sport of Her Majesty is another matter. I wish I were surprised by it, that is all.'

So Cecil did have someone else reporting to him from Essex House. Shakespeare said nothing.

The young privy councillor shuffled the paper away into a file, then brought down another, which he kept folded. 'Let me emphasise, Mr Shakespeare, this is not about me or my feelings. I say to you just this: Essex has worn a crown in his heart all his life.'

'But he lacks organisation.'

'He has powerful friends. He is brave in battle. Soldiers flock to him for he is one of them. Look who surrounds him – Sir Roger Williams, Gelli Meyrick, Le Neve, Danvers – martial men, quick to take sword and fiercely loyal to their chief man.

'His family shares his ambition and urges him forward. You saw his mother last night, Mr Shakespeare. It is with good reason that the Queen calls her cousin *She-wolf*, for the lady Lettice has sharp teeth as well as great beauty and sees herself as every bit as regal as Her Majesty. It is not just for marrying the Queen's beloved Leicester that Lettice was banished from court. It was her arrogance, her presumption. What did she think she was doing riding to court in a coach drawn by four white stallions, attended by four footmen in black velvet, and all followed by her knights, friends and retainers in great coaches? Did she think her cousin would be pleased to be so eclipsed? Or was she then – as now – so proud and assured of her own royal blood that she thought nothing of trying to out-glory her sovereign?

'Nor has it stopped with her banishment. She merely creates her own court and thinks to mock and surpass Her Majesty. She rides in her gold carriage around London and waves to the crowds who think she must be the Queen herself. Her daughters are the same. They are a coven, Mr Shakespeare, and they will not cease casting their spells until they have wed Essex to Arbella and have the throne within their grasp.'

Shakespeare knew he spoke the truth. He had seen what they were doing to Frances, Countess of Essex.

'Come, Mr Shakespeare, you seem quite drained. Let us take a little walk in the central court and you can tell me more. We will be undisturbed there. Are you hungry?'

They went outside into the intense heat of day. Cecil summoned Clarkson and ordered ale and boar pie. There was a small table and chairs in the shade close to the southern wall and Cecil led Shakespeare there. 'I like to work here. The open air and a warm day are good for the soul.'

'I have just been to Shrewsbury House, Sir Robert.'

'And?'

'The Countess of Shrewsbury listened attentively but revealed nothing.'

'But she has agreed to go north?'

'Not as soon as you might wish. Two weeks, three . . .'

'That is something, at least. The girl will be away from court. She is a curious young lady. She does not help herself with her haughty ways. Many among the Queen's courtiers despise and shun her for demanding precedence over them, which serves Essex's purpose well, for he is the only one to pay her much heed. I have watched him this summer courting her with little smiles and touches, which he thinks no one sees. In any other man, it might seem a Christian kindness for a girl in need of friends, but I know Essex too well. I have seen, too, the way she looks at him – with the adoring eyes of a lovesick calf.'

Clarkson arrived with the pie and ale. Shakespeare ate hungrily and brought the subject around to the turret room at Essex House. 'He has some of Walsingham's old staff there – Phelippes, Gregory, Mills. And you were correct about Mr Secretary's papers. It seems they are all there. One section commands my especial interest, but I have not been able to study it unobserved.'

Cecil nodded gravely. 'That is good to know. Very good. I knew that Mills and Gregory were there. I had not realised Mr Phelippes was also employed by Essex. He came to me asking employment after Mr Secretary's death, but I had no use for him then. Perhaps I should have taken him on.'

'The brothers Francis and Anthony Bacon are involved with the Earl.'

'Oh yes, I know all about that.' Cecil laughed. 'They do not know which way to turn. Francis Bacon would have the Principal Secretaryship and he ties his fortune to the mast of the Essex ship, but he flaps in the wind. Watch him and marvel how he turns and bends. Pay the Bacons no heed. The others interest me, though. I would know more about Mills, Gregory and Phelippes. Do you think they might work for me?'

'Mr Gregory, I would think. As to the others, I cannot say.'

'And what do you make of Mr Charles McGunn?'

'You know of him?'

'How could I not, Mr Shakespeare?'

Shakespeare weighed up his words carefully. 'He seems to hold powerful sway in the Essex household,' he said. 'I have never met his like before.'

'Do not underestimate him.' An expression of distaste flickered momentarily across Cecil's face. 'I believe he funds Essex's ambitions. Essex requires a great deal of gold. Even with his income as Master of the Horse and the considerable customs duties he receives from sweet wines, he is deep in debt. He lives like a king and I am certain McGunn is paying for it. That is one reason he cannot wait for the crown.'

'But what does McGunn get in return?'

'That is for you to discover.'

'I am certain McGunn would demand much. He is a dark, villainous creature.'

Cecil finished his small slice of pie and unfolded the paper he had been carrying with him. 'This is a letter, in cypher, from an intelligencer in Spain, one that used to correspond with Walsingham. He says that McGunn has been there in Madrid "with the displaced Irish nobles and is much respected and feared by them, so much so that they will not betray him for twenty ducats. They shy away at the very suggestion of talking about him, as if he has some secret which would be death for them to speak on. What little I have heard comes to me in hushed voices. He affects to be a merchant and flits here and there at will – England, France, Ireland, Spain – but it is whispered that he trades in flesh and gold. I know not where his sympathies lie, but he is not the common villain you might suppose. He has supped with King Philip at the Escorial Palace and has the benefit of whatever he requires from that quarter. I believe him to be presently in London."' Cecil looked up from the paper. 'That must give us all pause for thought, Mr Shakespeare.'

Shakespeare shook his head uncertainly. 'When was this letter sent?'

'Eighteen months ago. I would bring in McGunn for questioning – but he would tell us nothing and we would merely stir up a hornet's nest in Essex House. It is said he has the manner of a Hackney cutpurse, but the contacts and riches of a courtier.'

'Yes, I would say that is the measure of the man.'

For the first time, the strain showed in Cecil's face. His brow was tense and the corners of his neat mouth twitched. 'Is he working for Philip or for Essex, or both? Or neither?'

'Perhaps he offers them each different things. If he funds Essex's ambitions, he will certainly help Philip, for his actions will destabilise the English realm.'

'That is possible. Perhaps he sees it as a stepping-stone to removing the English from Ireland. Anyway, we must take him seriously. Find out what you can. And I say again, fetch me the proof I need that Essex is wooing Arbella, for only that will give us the power to stop him in his tracks. Is that clear?'

'Yes, Sir Robert. There is one other thing I must mention in that regard. The Countess of Essex has some strange sickness – of body and mind.'

'Poison?'

'Yes. I am certain of it.'

Cecil nodded. 'I am not surprised, Mr Shakespeare. I will ensure she is protected. Find out what you can. Take what you know of her condition to one well-versed in such things and report to me. Here, this is for you.' Cecil handed him a book, *The Profitable Art of Gardening*. 'This is a fine volume. I am sure you will find it excellent reading one day when you have more leisure. But for the moment I am giving it to you because I do not want you coming to me again; it is too dangerous. Use this as a cypher book. Just mark the page, the line and the number of each letter on your paper and I will be able to find the corresponding letter in my own, identical, copy of the book. Every fourth letter should be a null. It is a simple cypher, but only breakable if the code-breaker has the book. Keep it safe. Do you have a trustworthy servant to bring me messages, one that can move about unseen and make himself disappear when followed?'

'I have a servant called Jack Butler. I trust him.'

'Good. I shall be at Greenwich until the Queen's progress begins. Be strong, Mr Shakespeare. I am depending on you.'

Shakespeare put up his hand, before he could be dismissed. 'Might I talk of one more matter, Sir Robert?'

'Be quick. I have a Council meeting to attend.'

'It is the question of Father Robert Southwell.'

Cecil's mouth turned down in displeasure. 'You can do nothing to help him. He knew when he arrived in England as a priest that he was committing treason. He has brought this on himself and will perish for his stubborn foolishness.'

'But in the meantime, Sir Robert, must he be held in the private strongroom of Richard Topcliffe, where he is subject to wanton and un-Christian cruelty? If he were to be removed to the Tower, his examination would at least be scrutinised.'

Cecil's face displayed no kindness, no compassion. 'This was your undoing before, Mr Shakespeare. Learn from that and keep away from it now. I know *you* are not a Papist, but you are too lenient with those like Southwell who would subvert the state.' He eyes lightened a little. 'I am doing what I can. The

Queen curses Topcliffe as a fool for his unsubtle examinings, so I have already had Father Southwell removed to the Gatehouse Prison. For what it is worth, I have met him and think him an impressive man. He is my cousin, you know. There is a torture which it·is not possible for a man to bear, hanging against the wall. And yet I have seen him hanging by his hands in the iron gyves and no one is able to drag one word from his mouth. No wonder the Papists trust these Jesuits with their lives.'

'Thank you, Sir Robert.'

'But Mr Shakespeare, I beg you, take no more interest in Southwell's fate. It is out of all our hands now – and crossing Topcliffe can do you and yours no good. No good at all. Even *with* my protection.'

Chapter 15

JOSHUA PEACE STOOD back from the two bodies laid out before him on the slab of stone in the crypt beneath St Paul's. Their flesh was bloated and ruptured and gnawed by animals, yet he could see that they had been a handsome, well-formed couple. Even for a man as used to death as he was, it was sad to see two young human beings come to this. On the floor nearby stood an earthenware flagon, which had been found beside their bodies on the edge of a stream in the woods.

The stench of mouldering flesh would have overpowered a lesser man. Yet as Searcher of the Dead, Peace was accustomed to the smell and went about his business, examining the bodies, looking for curious-shaped cuts that could have been made by a blade, examining their mouths for the telltale signs of burned lips or bitten tongues, sniffing them to determine the date of death. From years of experience he was able to tell whether they were dead a day, a week or a fortnight, depending on the season of the year.

Even in the heat of this blistering day, it was cool down here beneath the great cathedral. Peace worked alone and in silence, his soft shoes padding silently across the stone floor. He heard the creak of the oaken door being pushed open and turned to see who was there. He smiled in welcome.

'John Shakespeare. Well, well.'

Shakespeare gagged at the smell and covered his mouth and nose with his hand.

'Why, John, I have not seen you in a year or more. Do you not say good day? How goes the world of learning?'

Shakespeare could scarcely breathe. He backed out of the room.

'Come on,' Peace said, laughing. 'Let us leave these two unfortunate souls and go outside. I don't want you bringing up your luncheon over my floor.'

Peace covered the bodies with their winding sheets, then took off his surgeon's apron, hung it on a hook, and together they wandered over to the Three Tuns for a tankard of ale.

'So what brings you here, good friend John?' Peace was a little older than Shakespeare. His head was almost devoid of hair, save for a rim of fine brown locks along the sides and back. His face was questioning and full of wit. Amusement played around his eyes.

Shakespeare gulped in the fresh, warm air, trying to rid his lungs and nostrils of the foul stink from the crypt. 'Why, the thought of a pint of ale with an old copesmate, Joshua,' he said. 'What else?'

'What else, indeed. I know you better than that, John Shakespeare.'

'Let us drink first to clear our throats and cleanse our souls.'

They settled down in a booth, away from the noisy chatter of lawyers and clerks and booksellers doing deals. As a taproom wench brought them ale, Shakespeare came to the point. 'It may not be within your reckoning, but I thought to try you anyway. And if you cannot help, perhaps you might point me towards one who can.'

'I will do my best.'

'Would you be able to tell, Joshua, whether someone was being poisoned?'

'If you were to tell me that a man was doubled up in pain and convulsions beyond enduring, and that he was puking blood the colour of dark rusty filings of iron, and shitting a flood, then yes, I could tell you that he might well be suffering poisoning, especially arsenic. But it could just as well be caused by some miasma in the air, or by bad food or water – particularly if others were similarly afflicted. A foulness or blockage in the bowel could cause similar effects to poisoning – the pain, the vomiting, the wish for death.'

'And what if the symptoms were more general and lasted for weeks?'

'Yet more difficult to say, for the poison may be delivered in small doses to give the impression of natural causes. As the patient wastes away, a physician might think it to be some strange disease or an evil in the blood. As Paracelsus said: "the dose makes the poison". He meant, of course, that everything will kill you if you take too much of it. What sets a poison apart is that it will kill in relatively small amounts – perhaps small enough to slip into food or drink without the intended victim noticing.'

'And what if the person seemed to be going mad, seeing strange flying creatures with lights in their wings?'

'Interesting. Wolfsbane poisoning can bring on strange imaginings and disturbances of the mind. Is it accompanied by a tickling or burning sensation in the tongue, perhaps. And sickness and pain.'

Shakespeare nodded slowly. He felt a chill, his suspicions seemingly confirmed.

'I see from your face that I am the harbinger of bad news, John.'

Shakespeare grimaced. 'Indeed. But, Joshua, how might one counteract this?'

'Remove the intended victim from those that would kill him.

Ensure that all food and drink is prepared by one you trust, and pray to God that no damage has already been done.'

Well, that was now in the hands of Sir Robert Cecil. He should have the means to save her. In the meantime, Shakespeare would send urgent word of this conversation.

Peace stayed him with his hand. 'Before you go, John, it is interesting that you talk of poison, for the two bodies on the slab in the crypt were thought to have killed themselves with poison. It was believed by the constable and sheriff and those that knew the young girl that they took their lives by arsenic because they could not be together.'

'A sad story, Joshua.'

'But untrue. Someone has gone to a lot of trouble to make it *seem* that they killed themselves.'

'Well, then, you have a mystery to solve.'

'And an extremely interesting one, for the girl is Amy Le Neve, daughter of Sir Toby Le Neve.'

The name brought Shakespeare up with a start. Sir Toby Le Neve was known as a fine general, had been an aide-de-camp to Essex on his recent expedition to bolster Henri of Navarre in northern France. More than that, he had been present at the summer revel at Essex House.

Shakespeare sat down again. 'Joshua, tell me more. What are the circumstances of these deaths?'

'They were found by a stream in the forest of Waltham out by Wanstead in Essex. Not my jurisdiction, but the Essex coroner is an old friend from Cambridge days. He was unhappy about the deaths and came to ask me to take a further look at the bodies. I had them brought here along with the flagon that was found with them. It has a large quantity of arsenic in it – enough to kill a dray horse – mixed with wine. There was also some arsenic in their mouths. It is nasty stuff. No scent, no taste.'

'Then how do you know it is arsenic?'

Joshua Peace gave the guilty smile of a schoolboy. 'I fed a little to my neighbour's cat. It was a wretched, brindled animal, infected with mange, and would have been done for by the plague men soon enough anyway. It is undoubtedly arsenic.'

'So why do you not think it was the poison that killed them?'

Peace downed the last of his ale. 'If you can bear to come to the crypt with me, I will show you.'

As they walked back towards the cathedral crypt, Shakespeare saw a woman selling pomanders. 'Herbs and blooms to ward off the pest,' the woman cried. 'Pest pomanders a penny.'

Shakespeare bought one and held it close beneath his nose as they entered the crypt. It was of limited use, but gave him just enough strength to stave off the nausea that threatened to overwhelm him. Peace pulled back the shrouds and Shakespeare gazed on the two bodies. They were covered with injuries and bite marks. In their faces were bloody pulps where once sat bright, hopeful eyes. Yet even in death, bruised and snapped at by vermin, the girl's face retained its youthful innocence. The boy's naked body did not even have the pallor of death. His muscles had tone and the skin that was not torn glowed with a healthy tan that almost made him seem alive.

'Do you know who the boy is?' Shakespeare said, and immediately regretted speaking because the bile rose in his throat and he brought up an acid wash of ale over the stone floor.

Peace laughed. 'Do not concern yourself, John. I have worse eruptions to contend with here. And yes, the boy's name is Jaggard. Joe Jaggard. More than that, I have no idea who he is. I examine bodies, nothing more.'

Being sick eased Shakespeare's discomfort. He still held the sweet-smelling pomander close to his face and stepped nearer the bodies. 'So how did they die?'

With his left hand, Peace gently raised the girl's head from the slab and held it forward so that they could both see the back, which was thickly matted with blood. Peace pushed the three middle fingers of his right hand into the hair and Shakespeare saw that beneath the blood was a deep indentation in the skull.

'Could that not have happened when she fell? Could an animal not have done that to her after death?'

'There would have been no bleeding after death. Now, look at this.' He lay the head back on the slab, then walked around to the left side of the boy's head. His temple was caved in. Peace put the same three fingers into the bowl-shaped hole. 'Almost identical to the girl's injury. This is what killed them or, at least, rendered them unconscious so that arsenic could be forced into their mouths. I still don't believe the poison killed them, however, for there would have been signs that their bowels had been purged – and there was none. They were both bludgeoned once with a club with a very heavy, rounded head. These wounds could not have been self-inflicted. If they did not die immediately, then they must have been left unconscious and died within two or three hours. No one could survive such blows. I would venture to say that whoever did this must have come upon them and surprised them. They probably did not even see their killer. The poison is an inept afterthought, a desperate attempt to make it seem they took their own lives.'

'Why did the constable and sheriff not note these head injuries?'

'There are many injuries on the bodies. The corpses had become carrion. Their flesh was clawed and bitten. And the girl's thick hair disguised the true nature of her head wound. With the presence of the arsenic flagon, they simply didn't look any further. More than that, I believe her parents wanted no ado. They wanted her buried and forgotten. Perhaps they were ashamed – either at her being found naked with this boy or because they felt dishonoured by her self-destruction.'

'What of their clothes?'

'No sign of them. Either the killer took them, or they might have been stolen away by a vagabond. The girl's gown would have been of fine quality. Such items are worth much gold.'

Shakespeare was thinking fast. This was nothing to do with him; he was already neglecting the Roanoke inquiry and needed to get word to Cecil about the wolfsbane. Yet these killings worried him. There was the link to Essex and there was something else, jangling in his mind. The name Joe Jaggard. Arthur Gregory had spoken of a murdered boy named Jaggard. Not just any boy, but a lad with connection to Charlie McGunn. A boy who had been seeking Eleanor Dare on his behalf.

He knew what Walsingham would have said: leave no dung-hill unforked. He looked once more on the tableau of death in the wintry crypt. 'Whoever did this must have been a man of immense power, to kill them with one blow each.'

'I don't think so,' Peace said. 'Given the right weapon, any man or woman of reasonable strength could have inflicted these injuries. These two young people had been swiving. It is not beyond the bounds of likelihood that on a warm summer's day it made them nod off to sleep, which would be why they were left so open to attack. Certainly if they had not been caught unawares, that lad would have been strong enough to defend himself against most men. He had the build of a pugilist.'

'Thank you, Joshua. I must go.'

'One more thing. If your friend is being poisoned with wolfsbane and if he or she is already having vivid imaginings, it might already be too late . . .'

Chapter 16

THE ENTRANCE TO Hogsden Trent's brewery and cooper-
age in Gully Hole, Southwark, was littered with hoops and
staves. The thick walls of the old stone building were perme-
ated with the smell of fermenting barley and the bitter tang of
hops. It was a scene which would never cease to give Boltfoot
an uneasy feeling. He had spent many years as a cooper, both
by land and sea, and had no desire to return to that life.

Boltfoot looked about him. There was some good craftsman-
ship here; he would have been proud of this work himself in the
old days when he sailed the world. A couple of men wandered
past in open-necked shirts and rolled-up sleeves, with leather
tool-aprons about their waists. One of them stopped.

'Can I help you?' He was sixty or so, with short-cropped
white hair and welcoming eyes. 'I'm Ralph Hogsden.'

'I'm looking for a man called Davy.'

'Davy Kerk? Dutch Davy? Yes, he's here somewhere. Come
in and I'll find him.'

They found Davy in the yard, sawing long staves for
puncheon casks. Boltfoot watched a moment, admiring the
work. Davy finished his cut, ran his palm along the edge to
feel the smoothness, then looked around at Hogsden and the
newcomer.

'Davy, this fellow was after talking with you.'

The cooper dusted down his hands. 'And why would that be?'

Davy was a man in his mid-forties, but well kept. He stood an inch or two taller than Boltfoot, his face partially obscured by a long carpet of greying hair that hung about his head like a helmet. He had the same salt-weathered lines to his face as Boltfoot – the look of a man who has been to sea for many years. His nose – or what you could see of it beneath all that hair – was long and hooked down sharply at the tip. His ears, which protruded through his mane, were large and festooned with bristly hair like a man twice his age. It seemed to Boltfoot that if the man ever bothered visiting a barber, he might be fair-looking. His accent was broad and foreign, but betrayed no animosity. He met Boltfoot's eye and held it.

'My name is Boltfoot Cooper. I'd like to talk with you a while, about a voyage.'

Boltfoot thought Davy stiffened, but the man said evenly, 'A voyage? I've been on a few voyages in my time, what voyage would that be?'

'Aboard the *Lion* to the island of Roanoke in the New World.'

'And why would you be interested in that?'

'Do you want to speak here?'

'I've got no secrets.'

'As you wish. I am here on the orders of Mr John Shakespeare, an intelligencer working for the Earl of Essex.'

Davy put down the saw. 'You'll have to tell me more than that.'

Ralph Hogsden was watching the proceedings with a keen interest. 'Well, Mr Cooper? What exactly is the great Earl's interest in Davy's seafarings?'

Questioning wasn't what Boltfoot did. He was good with his cutlass and deadly with his caliver, but he had always been a man of few words; interrogation was for men like Shakespeare, not him. But he had never shirked a task in his life. 'All right, I'll tell you true,' he said brusquely. 'There's one as says that a so-called lost colonist has been spotted, here in Southwark. I'm looking for her on Essex's orders. Don't ask me why. I do what I'm told. And I do believe you were on the voyage that took them all there.'

Davy Kerk frowned, then he looked towards Hogsden, and both men broke out laughing as one.

'Is it true or isn't it, Mr Kerk? Were you on the *Lion*?' Boltfoot persisted.

'Well, Dutch Davy,' Hogsden said. 'Were you?'

'Yes, course I was. So were a hundred others. What's any of this faffling nonsense got to do with me?' Kerk had stopped laughing and was starting to look angry.

'Tell me about it then. Tell me about the voyage and the people on it. Or come with me to John Shakespeare at Dowgate and tell him.'

'I'm not going anywhere, Mr Cooper. I have work to do to put food on my table.'

'Then tell me what you know. Answer a few questions and that's it.'

'And what if I don't?'

'Then I shall return with a warrant.'

Kerk did not look concerned. 'And what charge would that be? Refusing to talk to a stump of a man with a club foot asking me questions that mean bugger all to anyone, with some cat's piss notion of lost colonists turning up? Is that a new crime in England?'

Boltfoot felt the weight of the caliver slung about his back and the cutlass at his belt. Something in the movement of his body gave away his thoughts.

'Shoot me, will you? Or cut me down?' Davy Kerk bared his

teeth aggressively, but then softened as quickly as the heat had risen in him. 'Come on then, Mr Cooper, let us have done with it. Of course I remember the *Lion*.'

'Thank you, Mr Kerk. I am most glad to hear it. Now, as I have been told, the settlers were mostly Puritans, and given to sermonising.'

'God's blood, but that was a voyage of the doomed. They preached and ranted and got in the way of good, honest privateering. Made us travel away from the Carib Sea up the coast of Florida to that forsaken lump of land Roanoke. It is a place I would not have stayed for all the gold in the Spanish Main, a place of murder and evil. Bleaker than the Waddenzee in winter.'

'Murder?'

'Aye. Poor George Howe, cut down by Indians with arrows and axes while fishing. He was one of the better fellows. When you were there, on the island, you found yourself thinking those savages were behind every tree. Standing there or crouching, watching you, waiting until you crept out to the pit for a shit in the night. Never have I seen darker nights.'

The three men stood silent as if imagining a black night on the farthest of shores, knowing that you were observed by a hundred eyes. It was a feeling Boltfoot remembered all too well. There had been times ashore on coral strands and the coast of Peru and in the Spice Islands, when he too had felt open to sudden death.

'There was one name,' Boltfoot said, breaking the spell. 'Eleanor, daughter of John White, wife of Ananias Dare. Do you recall her?'

'Of course. She did give birth to the first child there, named for your virgin Queen. If the child is alive she must be nigh on five now.'

'*My* virgin Queen, Mr Kerk?'

'I am not English, Mr Cooper. She is no Queen of mine.'

'So why is a Dutchman here in England, Mr Kerk?'

'Escaping, Mr Cooper, like every other stranger in this city of strangers.'

'So you're a Protestant, are you?'

'Would I be here if I were not?'

Boltfoot noted that Davy spoke good English, probably better English than most Englishmen spoke, albeit with a Dutch accent. There were plenty such men here in London, fugitives from the horrors of war in the Low Countries, a conflict that seemed to have been raging forever.

'Tell me more. What do you recall of Eleanor?'

'She was fair, blue-eyed I'd say. A pretty young lass. Wasted on that sanctimonious Ananias Dare.'

'It is said she is alive and here in England.'

'Then that is good news. Did someone find her and bring her home?'

'Not that is known. But she was seen, not far from here in Southwark.'

'If she is here, then someone must have brought her. Or perchance, the settlers built a boat and sailed home. Either that or she sprouted faerie wings and flew the Western Sea.'

'You sound doubtful, Mr Kerk.'

He rubbed a hand across the back of his tousled mane of sand-grey hair. 'You are making merry at my expense, Mr Cooper. Yes, I have heard the tales and the gossip the same as you about what happened to those settlers. The truth? She's dead. They are all dead, done for by the savages. What chance do you think they stood – a hundred or so men, women and children surrounded by thousands of natives who had fallen out of patience with them? We didn't like leaving them there, for we all feared that they were to have a miserable fate in that Godless land. On the last day, when we said our goodbyes, there was many a tear shed, and not just by the womenfolk. The settlers' faces on the shore as we pulled away were drained and terrified, Mr Cooper. They looked at us as a man on the scaffold looks at the block, for we were leaving them to a dreadful fate and everyone knew it.'

'So you do not believe she is here in London?'

'No, Mr Cooper, I do not. Is that enough for you? May I now return to the sawing of my staves before Mr Hogsden deducts a groat from my pay for idling the day away in chatter?'

'One last question, sir, and I will myself give you a groat for your time.'

'Go on, Mr Cooper.'

'Do you know of anyone else now in these parts who was on the *Lion* voyage with you, someone else with memories that I might inquire of?'

'And why would I tell you if there was such a one? I do not think any man would thank me for it.'

Boltfoot said nothing; Davy was right. As he turned to leave, however, the Dutchman stayed him.

'There is one, though – a Portuguese gentleman, by name of Fernandez, commander of the expedition. And for that groat you promised me, I shall tell you where you might find him.'

Using *The Profitable Art of Gardening*, Shakespeare scraped a short coded message with quill, ink and paper and handed it, sealed, to his servant Jack Butler. He instructed him to take it to Greenwich Palace and place it in the hand of Sir Robert personally, and to no one else. No one must see him going there, no one must ever know that he had been.

Jack Butler had been with Shakespeare five years. He was a big man, six inches taller than his master, with strong arms beneath his frieze jerkin. Now, high on his large bay steed, he towered over Shakespeare.

'You have the letter safe, Jack?'

Butler patted his pack-saddle.

'Wait to see if there is a reply. And God speed.'

Butler grinned. 'Have no fears on my account, master.'

Shakespeare slapped the horse's flank and watched Butler disappear. He thought of the message he had written and wondered how it would be received by Cecil. It contained two points: one was the confirmation that the Countess of Essex was being poisoned, almost certainly with wolfsbane, and was probably now at a critical stage; the other was the mysterious death of Amy Le Neve, the daughter of Essex's aide-de-camp and associate, and the worrying possibility of a connection to McGunn.

With Butler gone on his mission, Shakespeare headed for Essex House.

In the intelligencers' turret, he eyed the shelf of papers he wished to examine. Nearby, Thomas Phelippes peered through his thick-glassed spectacles at a coded document and seemed to take no notice of anything else. Arthur Gregory was not here today, but Francis Mills was, and it seemed to Shakespeare that his narrowed eyes followed him like little torches.

He had already encountered McGunn this day, and it had not been pleasant. 'You are too slow,' he had growled. 'We'll all have left London before long. Get on with it, Shakespeare. Find this woman.'

'And what if she does not exist?'

'Find her.'

Now he reached up his hand, close to the papers he had seen during the summer revel. Instantly Mills was at his side, his fetid breath smelling like pig manure. 'You'll find nothing of interest there, Shakespeare, nothing about the colony.'

Shakespeare's hand hovered. 'I am trying to discover where to look, Mr Mills.'

'Not there. You will find nothing there.'

'I think I will decide for myself where to look, Mr Mills.' Shakespeare gave Mills a hard look. Their mutual dislike went back a long way. How could he search this place with such a man always in attendance, a man he knew would betray him without a flicker of concern? He reached for a package of papers.

Mills touched his arm to stay him. 'There is no need, Mr Shakespeare. Mr Gregory has collected some more documents for you.' Mills indicated a pile of papers on the floor. 'There. Take them away and look at them at your leisure.'

The package was already in Shakespeare's hand.

'You certainly won't need that,' Mills said, taking it from him. 'That is ancient correspondence from Stafford in Paris. There,' he nodded once more towards the papers Gregory had collected, 'that is what you want.'

Shakespeare clenched his jaw, trying to contain his fury.

Mills gave him a curious look. 'There is a great deal of interest in you in this house, you know, Mr Shakespeare. The Bacons keep telling Essex that information is power. And someone has said that you are the man to help them acquire it.' He laughed mirthlessly. 'I cannot imagine where they got such an idea.'

Shakespeare collected up the papers and charts Mills had indicated. There was no more to be done here today. Cecil had set him an impossible task.

Back at Dowgate, George Jerico asked for a word. He complained that the workload was become too great with Rumsey Blade departed and Shakespeare engaged on other matters. Shakespeare said he sympathised, but that it would not be for more than a few days, for he had decided to close the school for the summer, before the plague took hold.

Catherine and Jane were in the nursery, sewing. Jane

immediately rose from her stool to scurry away. Shakespeare let her go. He wanted Catherine for himself. At other times he would have embraced her. This day, he stood his distance and spoke briskly, like a stranger. 'So, you went to find the Bellamy girl?'

'Yes.' Catherine was mending her best kirtle. Her needle stopped in mid-stitch.

'And?'

'And she was not there. Gone to Topcliffe's at Westminster.'

'Which means she was part of a plot to snare Southwell. And to trap you.'

'No. It is not as you make it seem. I believe her to be as much a victim in this as Father Southwell and her family. Those creatures have brought her to this. If she has done anything wrong, then I believe her an innocent dupe. It is all Topcliffe.'

Shakespeare's face was set. 'You won't see it, will you?'

'I see that you still make apology for this foul and corrupt council of heretics.'

His mouth fell open. She had never said such words to him. 'Is that your considered opinion of me?'

She did not reply. Instead she continued her interrupted stitch and stabbed her finger. She winced but let out no sound. A spot of blood seeped on to the kirtle. She put the bleeding finger in her mouth.

'Well?'

Momentarily, she removed the finger from her lips. 'I have nothing further to say to you.'

'It were better you had not said as much already, mistress But, I have something to say to you.' His voice was cold and businesslike. 'I am closing down the school before the pestilence worsens. We will leave London in a few days, so prepare yourself.' He said they would take Jane, the late Mr Woode's children – Andrew and Grace – and any other members of the household who wished to accompany them to Stratford, where they would stay with his mother and father, while he returned to London. 'It will be safer for you and the children there, away from the City.'

She shook her head slowly, from side to side. 'No, I am not going to Stratford, and nor are the children.'

As he looked at her, it occurred to him that he had lost her. She had contempt for him; that was clear now. She saw him as a heretic and as an enemy to her and her faith. There was no love left. Nothing.

He turned on his heel and left the room. His head throbbed. Everything crowded in.

Chapter 17

THROUGH THE PAIN, some faint flicker of consciousness told Robert Southwell that he must be close to death. He was alone in the torture room, his hands in hard-edged fetters attached to an iron rod fastened into the wall. His legs were strapped up so that the calves met the back of the thighs. He had no idea how long he had been here. Every shallow breath was agony, his chest felt it was being crushed and blood seemed to seep from every pore of his skin. His head slumped forward against his chest, but then he could not breathe at all and, in a panic, he lifted it again.

Death would be a welcome release. He longed for it.

Elsewhere in the Gatehouse Gaol in Westminster, a woman in a black dress of velvet stood and waited. She wore a white lawn pynner about her long dark hair, its strips fastened beneath her chin. Her attire marked her out as a woman of quality.

Pickering, the Gatehouse keeper, returned to her. He was fat and out of breath from walking the short distance to Mr Topcliffe's house in the shadow of St Margaret's Church. He stopped and tried in vain to catch his breath.

'Very well, Mistress Shakespeare,' he rasped, clutching his chest as a fit of coughing burst upon him. 'I have been to Mr Topcliffe and he says I am to admit you to see the prisoner.'

'Thank you, Mr Pickering.'

'But . . .' He set about coughing again. 'But it will cost you garnish, for I have had nothing for him yet and if you want him to eat, then you will have to pay.'

'I will give you half a crown.'

Pickering spluttered some more. 'A mark. I want a mark.'

Catherine fished among her skirts for her purse and took out thirteen shillings and fourpence. 'Here is your mark, Mr Pickering. Make sure he eats well and I will bring you more . . . *garnish*.'

Pickering looked at her and smirked. 'Are you certain you wish to see him? It might be distressing for a lady of breeding.'

'Yes, I want to see exactly what you have done to him.'

Pickering shrugged his shoulders and his whole body wobbled. 'If that is what you desire, mistress, follow me.'

His fat legs rubbed together and his feet were splayed as he waddled through the dark dungeons. The stench of human ordure hung heavy in the still, unhealthy air. Groans came from cells where a dozen or more men and women were fettered in filthy straw. Catherine and Pickering arrived at the torture room. The gaoler stopped and held the handle to the thick wooden door. 'There's not many as want to come in here, mistress.'

Catherine ignored him and pushed open the door herself. The room was in darkness, even in mid-afternoon. 'Bring in your torch, Mr Pickering.'

Pickering came in with his pitch torch. The flame flickered and cast strange shadows and light around the room. Catherine could not make out what she saw, only that it seemed a vision from hell. And then she discerned his poor body, suspended against the wall, like some sack hung from a hook in a barn.

She had promised herself that whatever she found she would not break down, nor show weakness; she knew that Father Southwell would not want that, for it would be a victory to his tormentors.

'Can you let him down, Mr Pickering?'

'I cannot. It is not allowed me. He is here under warrant of the Council and Mr Topcliffe.'

Catherine stepped towards Southwell. The pitch torch was behind her now and cast her shadow over the figure on the wall. She reached up and touched his face. His eyes were closed. He did not respond; could not respond. His body was racked by spasms as it struggled for breath, independent of his soul, which had long ceased to have any desire for air or life. She turned away, her teeth clenched to stop the horror rising.

'He is almost gone, Mr Pickering. Do you think the Council and the Queen want him dead?'

Her words struck home, panicked him. Pickering hesitated, as if undecided what to do, then thrust the torch into her hands and ran from the chamber as fast as his fat legs would carry him. His last words as he went were: 'I will fetch Mr Topcliffe.'

Catherine had no means to bring Southwell down from the wall, but she put down the torch in the dead coals of a cresset and went again to him and, with all her strength, took his weight in her arms, supporting him. Keeping him alive. Easing his pain.

'Peace be with you, Father,' she whispered. '*Pax vobiscum.*'

There was no response, only thin breathing and spasms which signified some residual life. Though he was slight and not tall, he was heavy for a slender woman. Yet it seemed as nothing to her. It was a privilege to take his weight.

Topcliffe stood in the doorway, blackthorn scraping irritably against the floor, pipe stuck in his mouth, blowing thick ribbons of smoke. 'What is this?'

'He is about to die, Mr Topcliffe. Is that what you want?'

'I gave you permission to see him, not to take his weight, Mistress Shakespeare. I wanted you to see him as instruction, to show you and the other Papists what becomes of the traitors you harbour. And what will become of *you* for protecting them.'

'I say again: does the Queen and Council wish him dead? If so, they should bring him to trial and have him convicted of some imaginary charge, as is usual in such cases.'

Topcliffe strode forward and pulled Catherine away, throwing her to the dirt-strewn floor. Southwell's helpless body swung out and fell back hard against the wall, yet no more sounds came from him. Topcliffe prodded him in the belly with his silver-topped cane, then turned to the keeper. 'You're a brain-mashed bag of guts, Pickering. You should have come to me before now. Take him down and give him water.' He glanced at Catherine. 'You, come with me.'

Catherine picked herself up. 'May I not stay with him a while?'

'No.'

Pickering dragged a stool across the floor and stood on it to unhook the prisoner's gyves from the metal bar holding him against the wall. Southwell fell with a thud to the ground, his head pitched forward and blood spewed out from his mouth in a ghastly rush. He lay still.

'I fear he is dead, Mr Topcliffe,' Pickering said, a note of panic in his voice.

Topcliffe went to the fallen body and held a hand to the priest's throat. Satisfied that he had found a pulse, he stood back. 'Nothing wrong with him.' He took Catherine by the arm and pulled her from the torture room. 'Come to my house, Mistress Shakespeare, and take a cup of spiced wine with Mistress Bellamy. I am certain she would be pleased to become re-acquainted with you, for you were both Romish whores together, I do believe, though she has now seen the light. Perchance she will convert you, too, away from your lewd dealings.'

'What have you done to her?'

'Done? Nothing. Only saved her from disgrace by allowing her to lodge with me while she awaits the birth of her child. Uncle Richard looks after those who help him. I would not see her in Bridewell or spread-legged in a whorehouse, so she sups at my table and we do treat her like a princess royal. Come, mistress, come. Talk with her yourself and learn how well she is treated . . .'

Topcliffe's house was less than a furlong away, no more than a minute's walk from Gatehouse Prison, through the tidy cobbled streets of Westminster. With his hand on Catherine's arm, half pulling, half pushing, she had no option but to go. But she wanted to see Anne Bellamy again, to find out the truth of Father Southwell's capture.

Topcliffe kicked open his great oaken door and dragged her through into the gloomy hallway. A servant appeared. 'Where is Mistress Bellamy?' he bellowed.

'In her chamber, master.'

'Well, get her to the withdrawing room – and bring spiced wine.'

Topcliffe seemed almost jolly as he hustled Catherine through the dark corridors of his house. It occurred to her that the arrest of Father Southwell after six years of hunting had lightened his mood. Yet she was not deceived by his seeming affability; she knew of this notorious place; indeed, her husband had once been a prisoner here. It was a house with a dark heart – its own strongroom for torture. This was the only place in England apart from the Tower licensed to have a rack, something of which Topcliffe was inordinately proud. This was where Father Southwell had first been brought before his transfer to the Gatehouse. Catherine scented pain and murder in the air.

Topcliffe manhandled her into a surprisingly comfortable room, with settles and cushions and portraits on the wall – one of Queen Elizabeth herself, others of Topcliffe family members, she supposed. He left her there and closed the door on her.

Anne Bellamy arrived a few minutes later. The first thing Catherine noticed was how much her condition had deteriorated in the days since she had last seen her. Her pregnancy was now obvious from her swollen belly, but the rest of her was gaunt and thin, as though she had not eaten in a week. Her head was cast down and though her eyes blinked upwards and caught Catherine's, they immediately turned away and she held her head to one side, so as not to meet her gaze.

Catherine watched her a moment and saw her right hand picking at the skin on the back of her left hand, breaking it open so that blood trickled through her knuckles. Her face, too, betrayed signs of having been picked and scratched and her hair was coarse and unkempt, like a vagrant woman.

'Anne, come, let me embrace you.' Catherine stepped towards the woman, but Anne shrank into herself. She was stiff, like cold, dry putty, not warm flesh. Catherine held her shoulders, but Anne wrenched free.

'Anne, Anne, what have they done to you? What has *he* done to you?'

'Put your faith in God, you said – they all said. Trust in His providence. Where was God in *my* hour of need?' She spat the words.

'This was done to you by man, not God.'

'Where were *you*? You, my family . . . you are all the same.'

Catherine was taken aback. This woman was not the open-hearted, devout friend-in-Christ that she knew. 'No, Anne, we are not the same as Topcliffe.'

'You abandoned me to him.'

'Anne, you were arrested under the law. What could I do? What could anyone do?'

'You did not protect me. None of you.'

'Please, Anne.'

Her eyes closed tight and her lips drew back from her teeth, as though remembering something hideous. 'Where were you when . . .'

'When what, Anne?'

She turned her head sharply away. 'Nothing.'

Catherine tried to embrace her again. There was no resistance this time, but nor was there acquiescence. 'Tell me, Anne, who did this to you? Who brought you with child?'

Anne clawed at her hair with her fingers, scratching, as if at lice. 'There's no baby. I am a maiden.' She twisted the hair around her fingers.

'You must listen to me. You are going to have a baby and I must get you somewhere you can be cared for. The baby needs you to eat well; you must have good sleep.'

Anne pulled away again. She looked Catherine direct in the eye now. Her lips curled in scorn. 'He calls me his mare and says he is my stallion and now I have a canker in my belly.'

A servant, a plump woman with a beaming smile, appeared at the door with spiced wine. She looked at Anne cautiously, as if afraid of her, then put down the wine and cups on a little table. Catherine went to her and held her sleeve. 'What is happening here? What has happened to this lady?'

The servant stopped a moment, then pulled her sleeve fiercely from Catherine's grasp, the smile disappearing in an instant. 'Lady? Filthy whore, more like. A fine mother she'll make. Aye, a fine mother. Who'll tell her throes from her frenzies? If you ask me, she'd be better off dead, and her spawn. There's no hope there, mistress.'

'What have they done to her?'

'What they should do to all Papists. Tried to bring her back to the true way. It's not Mr Topcliffe's fault she's a Popish bitch harlot. Blame the Beast and all his cardinal demons for the foul contagion implanted by them in her soul. She has been ensnared by an incubus. I have fed her borage and hellebore to purge her, but she would be best shackled. Why, only yesterday Mr Topcliffe brought her to see her mother in Newgate, where she is being held for high treason. Nor was she grateful for the favour, but started ranting and kicking and spitting Romish bile. Poxy little drab.'

'I want to take her with me. She needs to be looked after.'

The serving-woman sneered. Catherine saw the plump, warm features of a motherly goodwife transform themselves into the most ugly, festering face she had ever encountered. Between this woman and the cold wreck of what once was a friend, Catherine felt herself trapped in a waking nightmare.

'For myself, you are welcome to her, mistress. But young Jones and Mr Topcliffe will have other ideas.'

Catherine turned back to Anne and felt she was looking upon a life lost. There was no way out of this. The debauchery inflicted on her by Topcliffe and Jones and his wicked father had destroyed her. It mattered little which of them was the father of her unborn child, for they were all complicit in her rape.

After the servant had gone, Catherine stayed with Anne an hour, offering her sips of wine, which she rejected. She tried to talk to her soothingly, tried to comfort her with embraces and tender words, but received only insults and cursing of God in response.

'You always were a sanctimonious cow, Kate Marvell, or Shakespeare, or whatever it is you call yourself these days. I always hated you. And now you'll really think yourself better than me, won't you?'

'Anne, I have never thought myself better than you. I always admired you and your family. You have such courage.'

'Is that so? Well, look to your own courage, for you will soon be drowning in chrism. That is what Mr Topcliffe says – you and the Shakespeares. Chrism will do for you all.'

Catherine said nothing. *Drowning in holy oil?* She had no idea what Anne meant, but the words chilled her.

'He held me down, you know. He held me down, naked, on a cold slab as if I was a side of pig at Smith Field. He was so strong. Why was God not stronger?'

Chapter 18

L E NEVE MANOR stood less than three miles from Wanstead, the palace that the Earl of Leicester had bought many years earlier from the old Lord Rich as a magnificent country estate for himself and his bride Lettice. It was still a home for Lettice, but since the death of Leicester, it was her son, the Earl of Essex, who was now effective master of the estate.

Sir Toby Le Neve's ancient pile was a great deal less impressive than Wanstead, but a sizeable building for all that. As Shakespeare approached along an overgrown dirt-track driveway, he was struck by the high chimneys that dominated the surrounding parkland and, not far away, the edge of the vast forest of Waltham. Drawing closer, he began to realise that the house was in poor repair, that the chimney stacks were devoid of mortar and liable to tumble down in a high wind. Though it had clearly been a property of grandeur, windows were now cracked and the structure leaned menacingly.

No stable hands came to greet him as he reined in on the weed-thick yard that fronted the house. He dismounted and tethered the mare to a rusty iron rail fixed into the crumbling brickwork. If ever there had been a doorknocker it had long since come adrift, so he hammered at the door with his fist. An ancient retainer, half bent and slow as a snail, eventually answered the door.

'My name is John Shakespeare. I would speak with your master.'

'He will ask me your purpose, sir.'

'Tell him it is a private matter.'

'As you wish, sir.'

The old man left Shakespeare on the doorstep and shuffled back into the house. When he reappeared, he asked him to follow. They went through to a large, wood-panelled dining hall where a man and woman sat, each in solitary splendour, at opposite ends of a long, polished table. Both had platters of food and neither of them rose at his approach. The servant bowed a little lower than his already bent body and made his painful way out of the hall. Shakespeare recognised the man at the head of the table as Sir Toby Le Neve. He sat stiffly upright. His beard was proudly trimmed beneath haystack eyebrows. He looked exactly what he was, a soldier – with all the muscle and haughty bearing that profession entailed.

The woman was a different matter. She looked twenty years younger than the man, thirty or so to his fifty, and strikingly beautiful in a world-weary way. Her hair was light and fell in a casual yet sensual manner about her face; her gown was faced with rose-red damask and welted with green velvet and had seen better days. She smiled at Shakespeare, but her husband did not.

'Well, sir?' he demanded. 'Does it please you to interrupt a gentleman's repast?'

'I merely require a few words, Sir Toby. I am more than happy to wait until you have finished.'

'A few words, sir? And what would they be about?'

'Your daughter, sir.'

Le Neve glanced down the table at his wife. Shakespeare watched the smile slowly fade from her mouth. Her husband rose from the table, knocking his chair to the floor as he did so.

He did not bother to pick it up, but marched to Shakespeare and took his arm. 'Come with me, sir. This is not a subject to be discussed in front of womenfolk.'

They went through to a side room which Shakespeare took to be an office or library of some sort, though the whole place was a chaos not just of papers and books but also of armour, swords, halberds, maces, arquebuses and other weapons of war.

'Who sent you? Why are you here? Your face is familiar.'

'My name is John Shakespeare, but I am certain we have not met. I am here on behalf of Mr Peace, the Searcher of the Dead. He believes your daughter was murdered. I am helping him inquire into this matter. I imagine you would wish to assist me, sir.'

'Do you, now? Well, you are wrong. It is a matter which does no credit to anyone. To lose a child is a terrible sadness. To lose one under these circumstances when she has taken her life, her body found most shamefully entwined with some youth, is beyond enduring for any family of honour.'

'I understand your grief, Sir Toby.'

'No, sir, I am sure that you do not.'

'But what if she did *not* take her life? What if she and the boy were, indeed, murdered? You must want the killer brought to justice.'

'You presume to know a lot about what I want, Mr Shakespeare. So I will put you right. What I want is for you to leave my house immediately and never come here again. I want to bury poor Amy and mourn in peace. That will happen as soon as the coroner releases her body to me instead of having it prodded and poked by your so-called Searcher of the Dead. Go, sir, go, whoever you are.' Le Neve was accustomed to giving orders; he barked rather than spoke. Shakespeare realised there could be no reasoning with him.

There was movement at the doorway. Shakespeare looked

across and saw that Lady Le Neve stood there. Le Neve turned and saw her, too. 'I told you, Cordelia, this is man's business.'

Cordelia Le Neve ignored her husband, instead addressing their guest. 'I believe you said your name was Mr Shakespeare. Well I am sorry that you have been berated so by my husband, but I beg you to understand how difficult these days are for us.'

'I am deeply sorry, Lady Le Neve.'

'And, of course, if there is any suggestion at all that Amy was murdered then you must make inquiries.'

Shakespeare glanced at them in turn. Le Neve's face was a mask of fury, his wife's was more difficult to read. 'It is believed they were bludgeoned. The poison was administered *after* they died, to make it seem that they took their own lives.'

'Nonsense, utter nonsense. The constable, the cunning man and the sheriff all said it was poison. They had enough to kill an ox.'

'Sir Toby, their bodies were extensively ill-used by wild animals. It would be difficult for them to discern the truth. The coroner had doubts, which is why he referred the matter to the Searcher.'

'Get out, sir, get out of my house. I will hear no more of this.' Le Neve plucked an ancient, rusty sword from its scabbard.

Cordelia Le Neve stepped forward, blocking off her husband, and took Shakespeare by the arm. 'Come, sir, let me escort you to your mount. You must take a little ale before you go, for you have clearly ridden a long way to get here.'

There was no point in staying. Shakespeare allowed himself to be led away. As he left the room, he heard the muttered words: 'I know your face, sir. I do not know from where, but I swear I know it.'

Lady Le Neve clapped her hands and the old servant appeared from the shadows. 'Fetch Mr Shakespeare some ale and make sure his horse is watered, Dodsley. He will be leaving straightway.'

'Yes, my lady.'

'Now, Mr Shakespeare, let me apologise for your poor welcome in our home.' Her voice was quiet, conspiratorial, as they walked towards the front door of the shabby old house. He noticed her scent. 'My husband has taken this very badly,' she said, 'very badly indeed. While I mourn the loss of a daughter, he mourns the loss of something less tangible, something which many people would not understand. It is honour. Nothing means more to my husband than his good name, a name that has been at the heart of England's military history since his forebears came across with the Conqueror. Le Neves were at Poitiers, at Crécy, at Agincourt, at Flodden Field, and never once disgraced themselves. He wanted a son to carry on the tradition, but he had only a daughter and now, with her shame, he feels his life is over. Murder or suicide, it makes no difference to him.'

'But . . .'

'Try to understand a little, Mr Shakespeare. Try to understand why we wish to be left in peace to mourn as we may. No good can come of delving deeper – nothing can bring back Amy or lessen our pain.'

Shakespeare would not be moved. 'One question before I go. The youth found with your daughter. Joe Jaggard. What was he to her?'

She opened the front door, just as Dodsley the servant emerged from the buttery with ale for him and a pail of water for the horse. 'Good day to you, Mr Shakespeare,' she said.

Lady Cordelia Le Neve was about to step back into the darkness of the house, but Shakespeare stayed her with his hand.

'Tell me this: did he work for a man named McGunn?'

She hesitated a beat too long. Their eyes met. She seemed to shake her head, but it was such a slight motion that he couldn't be sure. Then she pulled his hand away from her arm, retreated inside and closed the door.

Chapter 19

THE SERVANT HELD the pail for the horse while Shakespeare thirstily downed his beaker of ale. The old man looked at him like a dog that stands defiant though expecting to be whipped. Shakespeare put the empty beaker on the stone step at the front door.

'Do you have any thoughts about what happened, Mr Dodsley?'

'Put a coin in my palm and I may tell you a thing or two.'

Shakespeare dug a groat from his purse and placed it in the skeletal hand. The retainer looked at it closely, polished it and held it tight in his crabby fist. 'They haven't paid me in a twelve-month or more. All I get is my food and a palliasse with a dogswain cover. I am a serf to them and might as well be a horse for the way they treat me. Even the scraps off their table don't amount to much. But I won't be here much longer if I can find myself another position. Do you know of any gentleman seeking a serving-man, my lord?'

Shakespeare laughed. 'I am no lord, Mr Dodsley, and I know of no one to help you. But, pray, tell me about Amy. And the boy, what do you know of him?'

'Joe? I saw him around here, sneaking in like a fox after the hens. Didn't worry me. I don't blame the girl, especially knowing what they had planned for her.'

Shakespeare frowned. 'And what did they have planned for her?'

'A marriage, of course. Did they not tell you? She was wed on the day she died. Folks say my master sold her to save himself from ruin and penury, sir.'

'And who did she marry?'

'Some rich cat's bollocks of a Puritan. Mr Winterberry. Can't abide the snivelling man. But for a shilling I'll pass you the name of one who'll tell you everything you could wish to know about the whole hand-fasting business and the state of the family. Make it two and I'll fix you with a meeting, sir.'

Shakespeare sighed in resignation and made a mental note to collect these expenses from Cecil. He fetched out a florin and handed it to the old man. 'Well?'

Dodsley snatched the new coin greedily. 'Her name is Miranda Salter, sir. She is coy, but she will talk with you, for she was most fond of Mistress Amy. On the way here you will have ridden over a stone bridge across a stream. I will have her meet you there in an hour.'

The afternoon was wearing on. Shakespeare wondered whether he would be able to get home tonight, but he had to meet this girl. He rode slowly to the river, which was less than two miles away, and took the horse down to the water to drink, then allowed it to graze. She arrived promptly, walking briskly from the direction of Le Neve Manor. He guessed her to be sixteen. She lowered her head when she saw Shakespeare. Her hair and much of her face were covered by a common felt cap and she wore the simple linen smock of a housemaid.

'Mistress Miranda?'

She nodded but did not speak.

'You know who I am and why I wish to speak with you?'

She nodded again and mumbled something, which he could not hear.

'Are you worried about being seen talking to me?'

'Yes, sir.'

'I would like to see where the two bodies were found. Can you show me?'

She looked uneasy.

Shakespeare smiled reassuringly. 'Is it near here?'

'In these woods, sir, by this stream – no more than quarter of a mile from here.'

'Well, walk with me there through the trees along the river-bank and we will not be seen.'

As they strolled slowly along the dry bank where the river itself would have flowed when swollen, he could see her at last under her cap. She was a plain girl with the fat cheeks of girl-hood and a nose a little too big and bulbous to ever allow her to be pretty. He thought her grey eyes her best feature, shining bright and alert.

'Mr Dodsley must have told you my name is Shakespeare. I am inquiring into the deaths of Amy and Joe. I believe you knew Amy well?'

'I was her maidservant, sir. But I like to think she was my friend, too, though she was gentry and I was a mere servant.' She spoke cautiously and quietly.

'What sort of girl was she?'

'She was small, sir, and very pretty. Everyone looked at her, men and women. Until these past few weeks she was full of life and laughter, but she became all amort once she learned what had been decided for her. I miss her terribly, sir.'

'She was betrothed, yes?'

'Against her will. To a man named Jacob Winterberry, a wealthy merchant. I shared her dismay, sir, for Mr Winterberry was well-named. Though it is not my place to say such things, I can no longer hold my tongue, sir. Not after what has happened.'

'In what way was he well-named?'

'When he was about, it was as if a dark winter cloud was in the room, so gloomy and precise was his manner.'

'But why do you think this betrothal was arranged?'

'I do not know, sir. It does bewilder me. But perhaps it was the promise of gold. I do not know about such things.'

'And did you know the boy who died?'

'Joe, yes, of course I knew him.'

'Was he from these parts?'

Miranda laughed. 'Joe Jaggard? No, he was not born hereabouts, sir, but he has been here plenty often. Up at the big house much of the time, with his master.'

'The big house?'

'Wanstead, sir. My lord of Essex's great palace. Joe spent a lot of time there when he was collecting.'

'Collecting what, Miranda?'

'Why, money, sir, of course. That is what Amy told me, leastwise.'

'Have you heard the name McGunn?'

'No, sir.'

'Did you like Joe?'

Miranda lowered her head and seemed to redden.

'Well?'

'He was very handsome. And strong.'

'So you *did* like him?'

'I was a little frighted of him. More than a little, to tell the truth. So was Amy at first. Her parents didn't like him at all. Sir Toby used to get very angry when he came to the house. He used to wave his hagbut around, threatening to blow his head off. Said he was to stay away from his daughter. Joe just laughed. Nothing scared Joe.'

'Was he ever violent?'

'Not that I saw, but I heard tell he would cut the knee or ankle strings of any man that crossed him or failed to pay their debts. That's what they said in the village. But he never hurt Amy, sir. He wouldn't. He was mad for her, wanted to marry her and run away. That was why Sir Toby and m'lady took against him so. There was much shouting.'

'Did Mr Winterberry know of this young man?'

'I do not know, sir.'

'Were you at the wedding feast, Miranda?'

'Yes, sir. I was serving, sir.'

'And was Joe Jaggard there?'

'No, not at first. He was not supposed to be there. But then I did see him. I saw him in the shadows, beckoning to her. And then I saw him clasp her hand and pull her away from the feasting and they did run off into the long grass together. I watched them go.'

'When was it discovered she was missing?'

'Less than an hour.'

'Long enough for someone at the bridale to have followed them, clubbed them to death and returned, unseen, to the feast.'

'Yes, I suppose so. But I had thought they died of poisoning, sir. Took their own lives, so it was said.'

'Do you believe they would have done that? From what you know of them?'

She hesitated, then said. 'Amy, perhaps, not Joe. He would have just run away with her. I do believe he had gold.'

'So you were surprised when the constable said that was what happened, that they died by their own hand?'

'Yes, sir. It didn't seem to fit.'

'Now, tell me, what happened at the bridale when it was noticed she was not there.'

'At first it was just m'lady calling for her. She is her stepmother, you know; her real mother died many years since. Lady Le Neve went all around the house and garden. Then she asked me and Mr Dodsley to help find her. Then it was as if hell had torn apart the earth, Mr Shakespeare. Everyone joined in the search. A hue and cry was raised. There was much shouting for Amy, men with torches striding out into the night, but she could not be found.'

'And Winterberry?'

'He looked as cold as death. He was the only one would not join in the hunt. Him and Sir Toby, but Sir Toby had an excuse at least because he was flat-out drunk as usual. Winterberry waited at his seat of honour at the feasting table, then, of a sudden, he got up, marched to the stables, took his horse and rode off.' Her pace slowed.

Shakespeare could see the concern in her grey eyes. 'Are we near the place?'

She pointed nervously to an area a few yards away. 'Over there, through the brambles. Sir, I do think I have said enough now. Too much. This is touching on things I should not be talking of. I must go, for I will get into much trouble.'

Shakespeare took a small silver coin from his purse. 'This is for your assistance, Miranda. You are doing much good in telling me these things.'

She would not even look at the coin, kept her hands firmly clasped together in front of her. 'I could not take money. No, I could not.'

He put the coin away, then went to the little glade by the stream where Miranda indicated the bodies had been found. The dust and undergrowth had been much disturbed. The constable would have brought men here with a cart to remove the bodies. They would have scythed their way through the thicket. It seemed to him possible that Amy and Joe were killed elsewhere, then their bodies brought here and dumped. But that was surmise. There was no way of knowing, nothing to be divined from this place.

'I do not like to be here, sir. It is haunted.'

'I understand. Walk back a little way to my horse with me before you go, tell me just a bit more about Joe.'

'Please, Mr Shakespeare, I must say no more.'

'I ask you again: was McGunn his master?'

He could see she was distressed, as if it had just occurred to her what danger she might be putting herself in. She looked about her, into the trees, as if each had a spy behind the trunk, watching her and listening.

'Miranda, was it McGunn?'

She said the word so faintly that he could not hear it, but he could tell by the formation of her pink lips – and because he already guessed what the answer would be – that the word she said was 'yes'. Charlie McGunn was Joe Jaggard's master, and someone had murdered Joe. So this was the boy McGunn had used in the hunt for the lost colonist Eleanor Dare. Shakespeare breathed deeply. He put an arm around Miranda Salter's shoulder and held her to him. Even in the warmth of the evening, she was shivering.

'Miranda—'

'I have said enough, sir.'

'Did *you* love Joe Jaggard, Miranda?'

She blushed like a red bloom. 'Any maiden would have loved him, sir,' she said quietly. 'Any maiden.' She turned away, and quickly disappeared back on to the path whence she came.

Simon Forman clutched the furled chart in his sweaty palms as he stepped into Penelope Rich's lair, a high room in Essex House, and one befitting a She-wolf's daughter. He was not a happy man. He felt the sharp edge of the headsman's blade bearing down ever more keenly on his neck. This horoscope chart that he held was pure treason, for it contained the date of an approaching death that no man was allowed to foretell.

Yet Forman had not survived and prospered so long in the bear pit of London and court without knowing who must be obeyed and who might be ignored. One thing was certain: it did not pay to refuse a request from the mighty Devereux family.

As the doctor astrologer entered her black and gold chamber, the Lady Penelope Rich did not rise from her day-bed. She reclined with a book in one hand, being fanned by Henry, her black manservant, who stood at her side, his chest bare and rippling with muscles.

Forman stood awkwardly in the doorway. After a few moments, Penelope glanced up. 'Ah, Dr Forman,' she said, smiling. 'What a pleasure to see you again.'

'My lady.'

'And I see you have brought the chart. How exciting. Why do you not unfurl it on the floor here, and then you can explain it all to me.'

Forman glanced nervously at the manservant.

'Oh, don't mind Henry. I have no secrets from him.' She reached out languorously and brushed the servant's thigh with her delicate fingers.

'As you wish, my lady,' Forman said doubtfully. He approached the day-bed and knelt on a rug, where he unrolled the chart, close to the servant's naked feet. Not much in life made Simon Forman uncomfortable, but this did, painfully so.

Penelope raised herself on an elbow and looked down at the chart. There was a large circle, divided into twelve equal parts. 'It is all a fantastical mystery to me, so I think you had better explain it in plain terms, if you would, Dr Forman.'

'My lady, this chart shows the twelve houses, which represent religion, dignities, friends, enemies, life, fortune, brethren, relations, children, health, marriage . . . and death.'

'Dr Forman, do get to the point. You know what I require.

You are not a fool. Do you know she boxed my mother's ears? Do you know that, Dr Forman?'

A bead of sweat dripped from Forman's brow on to the chart. 'Well, my lady,' he said, picking his words with care. Of course he knew that the Queen had boxed the She-wolf's ears; everyone knew it, for it had been bruited about with much mirth after she was banished from court. But he was not going to acknowledge the question, for that would be to accept that he knew whose chart he had cast, and that would not do. Great houses such as this had many ears – hidden ears.

'The subject of this horoscope, whose name I do not know and will never know, is an unmarried personage in her fifty-ninth year. She will never marry, nor will she have children.'

'God's blood, Dr Forman, of course a woman of fifty-eight will not have children. That is not what I require from you. You are telling me things I know. What I want is a date. Give me the date or I will have Henry break you in two and throw you from the window.'

Forman closed his eyes and took a deep breath. 'September the . . .'

'Speak up, Dr Forman, you are muttering like a sheep.'

'It is September the eighteenth, my lady.'

'And the year?'

'This year.'

Penelope was up from her day-bed now. She pulled Forman to his feet. 'Say the words again to me, Dr Forman. Clearly, so that there can be no misapprehension.'

Forman glanced at the expressionless face of the servant, Henry, then back at Penelope, whose beautiful, flawless young face was no more than a foot from his. He was in so deep now he was limp with terror and feared he would drown in his own perspiration.

'The lady in question will die at six of the clock on September the eighteenth in this year of our Lord, fifteen hundred and ninety-two. These are her last days, the remains of one short summer.'

Penelope smiled. 'Then we have no time to lose, have we? Thank you, Dr Forman. Thank you for your diligence.'

Chapter 20

JUST AS THE bats began to fly for food in the dusk, Shakespeare found a bed for the night at the Ox and Harrow tavern in the village close by Le Neve Manor. He ate a supper of wigeon and walnut pudding, then drank two pints of ale as he talked with the landlord and tried to find out more about the Le Neve family and the death of Amy and Joe.

The landlord was a man of middle years, whose pitted face showed the ravages of the smallpox. He told Shakespeare that most local people did not believe the deaths to have been self-inflicted.

'Who do you think killed them?'

'Vagabonds? There's been enough come through here this summer, though we always drive them on after we've given them a loaf and some ale. Mind you, though, sir, something like this makes you look at your neighbours closer.'

'Do you know the family?'

'The Le Neves? Of course. Them and my lord of Essex and the Lady Lettice own everything in these parts, all the houses in the village, this tavern included. Essex and his mother own most of the land, of course, what with the forest and all the hunting that goes with it, but a goodly parcel of acres belongs to Sir Toby. Yet even *he* is beholden to the Earl and must go with him when there's wars to be fought.'

'And the boy, Joe?'

'Yes, I met him. A snout-fair lad, I'd say. He came in here for an ale once or twice. Always behaved himself proper and left a drinkpenny, so I had no complaints. But I would not have wanted to cross him.'

Shakespeare finished his ale and bade the landlord good night. Taking a candle, he climbed the rickety staircase to his first-floor chamber and quickly fell into an untroubled sleep.

He awoke in the early hours and knew he was not alone.

He could hear faint breathing. He opened his eyes. Light from a three-quarters moon streamed in through the unshuttered window and he could make out the darkness of a human figure, standing still, watching him.

Shakespeare's sword was at the side of the bed, unsheathed, ready. He knew exactly where the hilt was. He was still clothed and was not encumbered by bedding.

His left hand went for the sword hilt and in one swift movement he rolled from the bed, twisting himself back away from the intruder, then straightway rising to a crouch, close to the head of the bed. His sword arm was outstretched, pointing directly at the figure by the window.

'Fear not, Mr Shakespeare. I will not kill you.' It was a woman's voice.

'Lady Le Neve.'

'Though had I *wanted* to kill you, your throat would have been slit while you slept and you would have known nothing of it until you woke drowning in blood.' She laughed and held up a butcher's knife so that it glinted in the moonlight. 'See? I could have dealt with you as I have often done for a Christmas pig. You should have locked the door.'

Shakespeare rose to his feet, but did not relax his sword arm. 'Why are you here?'

She dropped the knife, clattering to the floorboards. 'To persuade you to leave us alone.'

'And the knife?'

'The knife was to defend myself. It cannot be safe for a lady to be out at this time of night with murderers about.'

'I ask again: why are you here?'

'The door-latch was broken.' She shrugged. 'And I wish to know who you are. You come to my house uninvited; you interrogate my maid behind my back.'

'You know who I am. You know that I was sent by the Searcher of the Dead.'

'You asked about Charlie McGunn . . . I think you are his agent, sent to avenge the death of his boy.'

Shakespeare put down his sword, still unsheathed, on the bed and took two steps towards Cordelia Le Neve. 'No,' he said.

'You are sent here to kill us, though I have done no harm to McGunn. I did not want the boy to have Amy, but neither did I cause him hurt, and I would have done nothing to harm my daughter.'

'Why do you believe McGunn wants you dead? What could make him think you killed Joe?'

'You jest with me, Mr Shakespeare. Men like McGunn do not look for evidence or proof. I have seen such men before.'

'Men like McGunn? Where would you have seen such men?'

He thought he saw the wisp of a smile in the silvery light.

'Mr Shakespeare, I have seen things you have never dreamed of. Done things that would shame you to hear. But now I wish to be left in peace, which is why I have come to you tonight, to plead with you. I had wondered about killing you while you slept, but that would not have stopped McGunn. He would have sent another and another, until the deed was done.'

'Lady Le Neve, I am no hired killer.'

'What does a killer look like? Does gentleman's attire mean

you are a gentle man?' She seemed to smile. 'No, you are *not* a hired killer. That is what saved your life when my blade touched your throat and I withdrew it. Yet I worry still, for you know McGunn.'

'Many people know McGunn.'

'He is death.'

'Lady Le Neve, the thing that will keep you safe from McGunn is finding the real murderer.'

She stepped to the bed and sat down at the end, her face half turned towards him. He saw how astonishingly beautiful she was. Her hair was wild and her complexion no longer had its youthful sheen, yet she had a raw sensuality that would make any man want to take her.

'Tell me now,' he said. 'How do *you* know McGunn?'

She sighed, but as she answered him, her voice was not desperate, nor weak. 'I might as well be plain, for I am sure Dodsley has given you some idea of our straits. We borrowed money from McGunn. A great deal of money, at usurer's terms. I believe my husband signed a note for two thousand and received fifteen hundred, to be repaid at interest of two shillings in the pound per annum. It is a common trick. Yet he had been recommended to us as a man who could help people. Of course, it became difficult to pay him, which is when the threats and demands began and when the boy came into our lives, with his razor knives and his killing smile. When he met Amy, his tone changed. I saw him climb to her chamber, night after night, and I could do nothing. It was then that I knew how deep we were in McGunn's clutches. My husband would not heed what was happening. He was either away in France fighting or he was engaged here on his other interests. I called in our lawyers and secretaries. By collecting all that was owed us in rent and leases, and by selling our lands in Suffolk, I was able to bring together enough gold to pay off McGunn in full, which I did. It left us only ruin. I cannot even afford to pay the servants. But I hoped to buy our freedom, to get McGunn and Jaggard out of our lives.'

'But you didn't.'

Cordelia Le Neve laughed. 'McGunn was not happy to have his money back. He prefers to keep control than to retrieve his money. Nor did the repayment of the debt stop that boy coming to Amy. Even on her wedding day.'

'Did you see them leave the bridale together?'

Her eyes held steady in the gloom. 'Yes,' she said at last. 'I prayed that no one else had seen them and that they would return soon, before Mr Winterberry discovered her absence. It was later, when he asked whether I had seen her – for it was time for their nuptial retiring – that I raised the hue and cry.'

'Her wedding to Mr Winterberry meant a lot to you?'

Cordelia laughed again, this time with bitterness. 'It meant the restoration of our fortunes, Mr Shakespeare. Mr Winterberry is a merchant of immense wealth. He has a wharf close by the Tower. He has riches beyond imagining. He would have given Amy the life any woman would wish for, and he pledged to help us, too. Now I have lost everything. I will probably return whence I came.'

In the semi-darkness, Shakespeare tried to look at the woman closely. There was as much unsaid as said here in this room. He needed to know more. 'Amy was your stepdaughter. Sometimes, such relationships are not easy.'

'We had differences.'

'You wanted her to make this match. She did not want it. That alone must have caused a rift.'

'Mr Shakespeare, I wanted the best for her.'

'And for yourself? You said it yourself – you had much to lose if the marriage did not proceed. If you saw her leave the bridale, you would have been enraged, would you not?'

'What are you suggesting? Her interest was paramount in this. I knew what was good for her. I would not have harmed her.'

Shakespeare tried to imagine her creeping out into the fields and woods after the young couple, taking them by surprise and killing them.

'Your maid, Miranda. Could she have harmed your daughter?'

Lady Le Neve shook her head dismissively. 'She is a plain girl. I would not be surprised if she was jealous, but I do not believe her capable of murder.'

Through the window Shakespeare saw the first light of morning. Lady Le Neve noted it, too.

'People will be about soon. I must go home. I cannot be seen here.'

'Who do *you* think killed them, and why?' Without thinking, he put his hand out and stroked her hair, smoothing down its unruly knots.

She looked up at him, unsurprised by his touch, as if she were used to such uninvited attentions. 'It occurs to me that you are that rare thing, a good man, Mr Shakespeare.' She rose from the bed, then kissed him on his lips. 'We should have met at another time and place.'

The kiss was a kind of nectar to his dry lips. His very life was dry these days. Shakespeare brought his errant thoughts back into line. 'Who killed them?'

'I wish I knew.' She picked up the knife and went to the chamber door. She opened it and turned quickly to him. 'Mr Shakespeare, I know you mean well, but please, it would be better for everyone – for me, for you, for Miranda – if you were to go now and forget us. I promise you nothing good can come of your delving.'

Chapter 21

STARLING DAY WELCOMED John Shakespeare at her house on London Bridge with her usual warm smile. She offered him unsweetened wine, salt herrings and bread, which he gladly accepted, having declined breakfast at the Ox and Harrow in his haste to depart. She also offered him a turn with her in her large bed, saying she felt the need of a man, Mr Watts being away. He thanked her, but said no.

'Have I become too fat for your taste, Mr Shakespeare?'

'You were never to my taste, fat or thin, Mistress Day. Not in that way.'

'Do you not know it is considered ill manners in society to refuse a lady?'

He laughed. 'And when did you become a lady, mistress?'

'Mr Shakespeare, you will be pleased to know that I like you very well in spite of your rudeness.'

'What I was really hoping to win from you was not swiving but information.'

'I have information, but what will you do for me in return?'

'Well, you certainly do not need my money.'

'Then you must owe me a favour.'

'And for this favour, have you *found* Eleanor Dare?'

'No, Mr Shakespeare, but I have discovered the son of her husband Ananias. The boy's name is John Dare, and he is in the care of his uncle, Foxley Dare – Ananias's brother. The boy did not go to the New World with his widowed father and his father's new young wife. Now, is *that* not good intelligence?'

'Possibly. It all depends whether Eleanor has made contact with them. Tell me what you know.'

Starling grinned broadly, delighted with her information. 'You can talk to Mr Foxley Dare yourself – he stands in the pillory less than two furlongs from here, on the corner between the Clock and St Magnus Cross.'

'His crime?'

'Wanton use of a goose. He was to have been placed in the pillory for seven hours, beginning at eight of the clock, and will be in a poor state in this heat. Take a blackjack of ale to wet his parched throat and he will surely tell you all you wish to know, including the goose's name. It seems Foxley Dare is well known among the whores of Southwark as a habitual frequenter of their services, which is how he was brought to my attention. He tries to gain credit by saying he will soon have his brother Ananias declared dead and inherit property as his nephew's legal custodian.'

The maid arrived with Shakespeare's food. He tucked into the herrings with vigour, licking the succulent juices of the fish from his fingers and tearing at the fresh white bread with his teeth.

'You seem not to have eaten in days, Mr Shakespeare.'

'Not this well, that is certain. One more thing, Mistress Day . . .'

'Yes?'

'Have you heard of a woman named Lady Le Neve – Cordelia Le Neve? I believe she has a past, and I would like to know what it is.'

'The name means nothing, Mr Shakespeare, but I shall find

out what I can for you from the stews of Southwark. And then you shall owe me another favour!'

Foxley Dare was a man of large appetites. His belly was of such prodigious girth that it made the pillory a great deal more uncomfortable and painful than it would be for a man of leaner build. He had been standing there on the plinth, his hands and neck clamped into the holes of the wooden frame, for almost four hours and still had more than three to go. His belly was pressed hard against the pillar and his feet were splayed fully six inches further back than they should have been, increasing the pressure on his neck and spine. It was his lower back and the bones in his cruelly restricted neck that caused him the greatest agony. Yet it was the fierce heat of the midday sun, blistering his face and arms, that threatened to kill him. Pinned to the pillory in front of him was a sign that read simply 'Did occupy a goose – and not even married'.

A crowd of a hundred or more people had gathered around him, enjoying his agony and humiliation, laughing at him, yelling insults and jests, pelting him with horse-shit, bad eggs and the occasional stone.

By the time Shakespeare arrived the sun was full on Foxley's face and there was a very real danger he would not survive.

A tipstaff stood at the convicted man's side, protecting him from the worst of the crowd's displeasure. 'No large rocks, please, ladies and gentlemen,' he declaimed now and then, holding up his thumb. 'If a stone is bigger than this, the thumb on my left hand, then I don't want you throwing it, for this is not a sentence of death.'

The crowd jeered all the more and pelted Foxley with a new barrage of dung.

One woman strode up carrying a live duck that she had just bought at market and held it out so that its beak was just in front of Foxley Dare's nose. 'Give us a kiss, give us a kiss,' the woman said in a voice that was meant to sound like a duck's quack. In a flurry of feathers, the duck struggled to flap its wings, defecated on its owner's kirtle and the crowd roared with laughter.

Dismayed by the scene, Shakespeare went up to the tipstaff. 'I would speak with the prisoner. I am here as an officer of the Earl of Essex.'

The tipstaff was impressed, especially when handed a six-penny coin, and allowed Shakespeare closer to the pillory. He stood face to face with Foxley Dare, though it occurred to him that he might find the back of his own head to be an interesting alternative target for the jeering mob.

'Mr Dare, my name is John Shakespeare. I need to talk with you.'

The prisoner's eyes were closed in his red-burnt and splattered face. His mouth was open, drawing in rasping, shallow breaths, almost panting like a dog. Shakespeare had a blackjack of ale with him. He poured a little into his left hand and held it to Foxley's mouth. 'Here, sup this.'

Foxley's tongue lolled out, all dry and crusted, and touched the liquid. Slowly at first, then more greedily, he lapped at it like a cat. Shakespeare kept pouring more into his hand until he felt he had had enough. 'Can you speak yet?'

'I need a hat. Please, give me your hat, or a scarf to cover me.'

Shakespeare took the felt hat from his head and perched it as well as he could on Foxley's head, covering his forehead and ears and shading his nose.

'What is the time? Has the noon bell rung?'

'Soon.'

'Three hours more. I will die here. I need dung. Coat my face and hands with dung, if you would, sir, to protect me from the sun. I shall not survive else.'

Most of the horse dung from the centre of the road had already been thrown at him and lay in splodges at the base of the pillory. Shakespeare gathered what he could and smothered it over the exposed areas of flesh, to the crowd's great amusement; they evidently thought Shakespeare's decoration of the prisoner was part of the entertainment. He gave Foxley Dare more ale from the blackjack. 'You know, Mr Dare, I have to say that she must have been a very *pretty* goose to make this worthwhile.'

Dare groaned agonisingly. 'It's all a bloody lie, sir. Those dog-wife, pox-putrid, cross-biting whores made it up when I refused to pay for the use of their lice-infested cunnies. The only goose I've ever had was roasted on a platter.'

'Well, perhaps then you should have paid the whores.'

'Why should I pay for the clap? I will do for them all when I get out of here.'

'Mr Dare, I am investigating a matter on behalf of the Earl of Essex. I believe you are the guardian of a boy called John Dare, your brother's son.'

'I can't talk. I can't even think. Give me more ale, sir, and I will talk with you when I am free of this infernal contraption.'

'Just tell me this. Is that correct, about the boy?'

'Yes, yes, and a finer nine-year-old you never met, but I will not talk more.'

The church bells of St Magnus clanged out their toll of noon.

'Four down, three to go, Mr Dare. I shall return to you anon. Don't go anywhere in the meanwhile.'

Shakespeare handed another coin to the tipstaff. 'Keep him alive, tipstaff. Make sure he is here for me when I return, and there will be yet another sixpence for you.'

It was a short distance to Dowgate. Shakespeare walked his grey mare home with some trepidation, wondering what sort of reception he would have from Catherine.

In the stable block, he handed the reins to the groom, then walked into the deserted courtyard. Two figures emerged from the shadows. McGunn and Slyguff.

'God's balls, you have kept us waiting,' McGunn said irritably.

'I cannot find Eleanor Dare sitting about at home.'

'Nor by consorting with the Searcher of the Dead, I would suggest.'

'Have you been *watching* me, McGunn?'

'What do you think, Shakespeare?'

'And what did you learn by watching me take a drink with my good friend Joshua Peace?'

'I learned that you are straying from the path, prying into matters that are no concern of yours.'

'I decide what is my concern, McGunn.'

'And why should you be concerned by a pair of deaths that have nothing to do with Roanoke or Eleanor Dare? Do you think me a coney to be caught and used at your will, Shakespeare? I want to know what game you play at my expense. I want to know why you went missing after seeing Peace, and where you went.'

'If I know of any murder, McGunn, it is merely by hearing of it in converse with Mr Peace. Our meeting was arranged long ago. And you say the deaths of Amy and Joe had nothing to do with Eleanor Dare, but I am not certain that is so.'

McGunn had a petronel slung over his shoulder. Swivelling it out, with the butt into his chest, he levelled the muzzle at Shakespeare's face. At his side, Slyguff was alert and silent.

Shakespeare looked at the barrel and turned away. He began walking towards the door of the school building.

'Do not turn your back on me, Shakespeare. Men have died for less.'

Shakespeare glanced over his shoulder. He was angry now. 'Then do not threaten me in my own home, McGunn. You think me afraid of you? You are wrong. I consider you a cheap prigger, a base roarer and bully. I have no idea what hold you have over my lord of Essex and nor does it concern me. But you have no hold over me. I will carry out my mission for the Earl in my way and in my time. And if that involves looking into the circumstances of Joe Jaggard's death, so be it. For was he not seeking Eleanor Dare when he died? If the Earl does not like my methods, then he can find another man.'

McGunn laughed, but his face showed no signs of mirth. 'I will have to teach you fear then, Shakespeare. Yes, find Joe's killer and I will reward you. But cross me and you had best look out for your pretty goodwife and your dainty child. In the meanwhile, you will keep us informed of everything you discover, as you discover it. We will not wait long.' His fleshy eyes held Shakespeare's for two or three heartbeats, then he snorted disdain and strode to the entrance gate, Slyguff at his side.

Shakespeare was still shaking with anger as he entered the school and encountered his deputy, Jerico, who appeared nervously from a side door, looking downcast. 'I thought it best to keep out of their way, Mr Shakespeare,' he said.

'You did the right thing, Mr Jerico. Are you alone here? The place seems empty.'

'Plague or no plague, the school has been closed already, sir. I had to turn the boys away this morning.'

'What?'

'The Bishop's men arrived last evening, sir, with Rumsey Blade, and brought an order for our immediate closure, citing blasphemous teaching and sedition.'

'What Bishop's men were these?'

'Pursuivants bearing the Queen's escutcheon. Their leader said his name was Topcliffe. He had a foul tongue, master. He said I must leave immediately and threatened me with torture and death. I confess he scared me half witless.'

Topcliffe and Blade. Shakespeare ground his teeth in anger. He was beyond fear. He was raging with a blood-fury he had never before experienced. He could happily kill these men.

'Where is my wife?'

'She and Jane are with the children at the Royal Exchange, for the music.'

'And Jack Butler?'

'I have not seen him, sir. But a Mr Peace came with a message. He asked me to tell you that he had released the bodies and that he believed there was to be a funeral at Wanstead. He said you would understand what it means.'

'Indeed, I do. Thank you, Mr Jerico. And fear not, we will save the school.'

Shakespeare went through to his solar. On the table in the centre of the room he spotted the bundle of papers he had brought back from Essex House. He had left them there, unread, but now, with some peace and quiet for two or three hours while waiting to return to speak with Foxley Dare at the pillory, he found himself flicking through the pages sorted for him by Arthur Gregory in the turret room.

The main document was written in the hand of John White, the father of Eleanor Dare. It was a report to Sir Francis Walsingham, written on his return to try to secure supply vessels at the end of 1587. It spoke of the hardships of the long voyage across the great ocean to the Carib Sea and, from there, up to the Virginia coast. There had been severe shortages of food and drink. Shakespeare scanned the document with interest, for it filled in gaps in the account he had already read. In particular, he noticed that one name appeared time and time again – Simon Fernandez.

Fernandez had been pilot on the earlier expeditions and was

now commander of the three small ships carrying the colonists. He was Portuguese and was, from what White had to say on the matter, more concerned about playing the pirate and preying on Spanish treasure ships than in getting the colonists safe ashore in Virginia. White spoke of constant battles with Fernandez and of his deep distrust of the man, even calling him 'malevolent'. In one margin, close to the name Fernandez, Walsingham had written, 'What are his true loyalties?' The question did not seem to have been resolved.

Shakespeare glanced briefly at the other papers. There was a deposition from Fernandez himself, dated November 1588, refuting White's allegations and calling him 'a lying dog'. It added, 'Who could trust a man who would abandon his own daughter and grandchild to save his neck?' As a final postscript it said, 'Mr White complained when we moored at Saint Croix, because there were savages there. This should tell you all you need to know about the white-livered wretch.'

There were more papers to look at, mostly of only tangential interest. He spent a few minutes studying two torn and faded drawings that he found among the documents. He assumed they had been crafted by John White, who was known as an artist. One showed a strong-muscled warrior with a breech-clout covering his waist and privies. He had markings on his skin and feathers in his hair and carried a bow as long as any English archer's, and a quiver of arrows. At his side was a woman, presumably his wife, bare-breasted with a fringed short skirt and beads about her neck. The other picture showed a native village, protected within a palisade. There were houses and barns and, at the centre, a great fire where the men of the village gathered.

Shakespeare was packing them away when a letter caught his eye. It had a broken seal. He unfolded it and smoothed it flat on the table.

The letter, a short note from Bess of Hardwick, was addressed to Walsingham and was merely signed '*Your constant friend, Bess*'. It thanked Walsingham for finding a tutor for the Lady Arbella, '*one who will teach her well in the arts of becoming a prince of the blood royal*'.

Shakespeare's jaw tightened. Whatever Walsingham did, there was always a hidden purpose. If he had found a tutor for Arbella Stuart, one thing was certain: the man – or woman – was no mere schoolteacher. He would be employed by Walsingham as an intelligencer. And he would be tasked with reporting every little detail about Arbella and her life back to Walsingham: when she sneezed, what she ate for breakfast, when she came into her time of month, the secret vices of her other tutors and lady's maids, her reading matter and passions, the attentions of putative suitors.

So Walsingham had placed a spy at the heart of Bess of Hardwick's household. And that intelligence might now be known to Essex.

Shakespeare looked again at the letter and cursed. There was no name. Bess had not mentioned the tutor by name.

His heart pounded. This was a start, but Cecil would want the name of this tutor.

One question nagged at him. It could not have been by accident that this letter had come to be here, among documents dealing with the lost colony of Roanoke, which meant that someone within Essex's household had placed it there for Shakespeare to find. The obvious name was Arthur Gregory, his old friend, who had assembled this packet of papers. But anyone with access to the turret room could have slipped this sheet in with the other documents while they were awaiting collection by Shakespeare. Francis Mills? Thomas Phelippes? Shakespeare did not really trust either of them, but nor could he discount the possibility that they had their own reasons. There were the Bacon brothers, too – Francis and Anthony – both playing delicate political games within Essex's employment in their quest for high office. And what of McGunn himself – whose side was he truly on?

Shakespeare folded the paper and thrust it safely inside his shirt. There was a knock at the open door. He looked up and was relieved to see Boltfoot Cooper standing there.

'Boltfoot, come in. What news?'

Boltfoot looked disgruntled and hot. He came in, dragging his left foot across the wooden floor. 'Nothing,' he said shortly. 'A waste of my time and yours, master. And now I cannot find Mistress Cooper.'

'Jane is at the musical concerts with Mistress Shakespeare, Boltfoot. I know you are worried, but she would not be out unless all was well.'

Boltfoot looked relieved.

'Where have you been?'

'Looking for a Portuguese gentleman. Fernandez.'

Fernandez: the sea captain whose loyalties had been questioned by Walsingham. 'Have you found him?'

'No. I was given an address in Gravesend, but he was not there. It is a tenement and they said he had most likely gone to sea again. He only ever stayed there while fitting out vessels at the docks. They had not seen him in a year and never knew when to expect him. I have wasted much time on this.'

'Who told you of him?'

'A Dutch cooper named Davy Kerk. He was on the *Lion*. It was an unhappy place to be.'

'How did you find Kerk?'

'Through a seafarer in a boozing ken. Cost me six ounces of sotweed. My *last* six ounces,' he added ruefully.

'Do you think there is anything to be gained in going back to this seafarer? What about going back to the cooper?'

On the long barge journey back from Gravesend, Boltfoot had been wondering about Davy Kerk. Had he deliberately sent him on a useless errand to find Fernandez? There was something not right about Kerk, something he couldn't nail down. He wanted to find out more about Dutch Davy. Boltfoot growled, a sign that he had made a decision. 'I will. You are right – I'm *not* happy, Mr Shakespeare. I'll go back to cooper Kerk at Hogsden Trent's.'

Shakespeare clapped Boltfoot about the shoulder. 'Don't worry about Jane. She is in good hands and will soon be out of this murrain-infested city. If we go in haste, I will leave word for you. And God speed your inquiries.'

The truth was that Shakespeare did not really expect Eleanor to be found, because he did not believe she was alive, let alone here in England. But for now, however, it was expedient to be seen going through the motions of the Roanoke inquiry; with vigour and purpose. He needed every excuse he could muster to inveigle himself into Essex's circle and stick to him like daub to wattle.

Chapter 22

THE BELL OF St Magnus struck three of the clock. Foxley Dare's ordeal was almost done. As Shakespeare arrived, the tipstaff stepped up to unlock the pillory and release the prisoner. The dung on Dare's face had baked hard like a stinking mask and he looked scarcely human.

When Foxley tried to stand, the pain in his neck and back was so severe he screamed and fell forward. Shakespeare caught him, but his weight was too much and he had to ease him down to the ground, where he lay curled like a new-born baby.

As the crowd of onlookers dispersed, a woman emerged from a house close to the church. She carried a pail of water and poured it over Foxley's face and head. 'I always do that for them,' she said to Shakespeare. 'It helps revive them, poor souls.'

'Some cloths to clean his face would help, too, mistress,' Shakespeare said. 'And herbal ointments too if you have any, for he is sore burned by the sun.'

'Bring him into my house and we will do what we can. My husbandman was an apothecary, God rest his soul, and I have lotions aplenty.'

Shakespeare turned to the tipstaff. 'Is he free to go?'

'Yes, but tell him to choose his friends more carefully. And I am not talking about the goose. This is not Mr Dare's first time in the pillory and it will not be his last if he keeps dealing with those viperous whores. The justice has said that next time he offends, he will be flogged against the post and his ears will be removed.'

An hour later, after washing and slathering of lotions and imbibing of good beer, Foxley Dare was at last in a condition to talk. The woman who had helped him was charitable and let them sit in her garden in the shade of a fig tree, a light breeze fanning their faces.

Foxley sat at the table, with his head supported by his hands. 'I am as weak as a novice's fart, sir.'

'Keep drinking, Mr Dare, but slowly.'

'Oh, every inch of me aches and burns like the hearths of hell.' Foxley groaned and rubbed and stretched his neck. He gulped his beer. 'What does my lord of Essex wish from a common man like me, Mr Shakespeare?'

'Do you know your brother's new wife, Eleanor, born White, who went with him to the colony?'

'I do. I met her twice. The first time was at their wedding. A bedazzling affair, with feasting and music, even though Ananias was turning to dull, Nonconformist ways by then. The second time was when I took John to wave them off from London in the spring of '87. What a miserable lot they did look, all praying on deck and thanking the Lord as the little ship did bear room to God knows where. I believe them now dead and have been trying to have them declared so in the courts, on my nephew's behalf. Ananias left property here, and it is young John's by right. But the courts of law are slow as earthworms in their dealings. Not so slow when they want to put you in the pillory or whip you for some imagined misdemeanour, though.'

'So you would recognise Eleanor?'

'Recognise her? Of course I would. Pretty little thing she was and from what I hear she must have already been with child when they left, for I heard tell that the baby Virginia was born that summer.'

'What would you say if I were to tell you that Eleanor Dare has been sighted, here in England, by the baiting rings of Southwark, within the past fortnight?'

Foxley tried to laugh but grimaced with pain instead. 'I would say you had a head full of bees or that you have been eating curious mushrooms, Mr Shakespeare.'

'You think it impossible any of them have returned?'

'No, not impossible. But for certain I would be the first port of call for Ananias or Eleanor – for we live in their property close by Wormwood Street, where he prepared his tiles, and they would want to see John.'

'Ananias, certainly, but what of Eleanor – where would she go? Does she have kin in London or nearby?'

'Her father, most like, for he was at the wedding, I do recall. He wore courtly attire and had fine friends. John White was his name. A letter from Sir Walter Ralegh was read out blessing the couple, and he even put in an ode for them. And Mr White had two most curious friends there that did cause a stir. Folks came out from all the houses around and about to see them and stare in wonder.'

'Did they have two heads?'

'Better than that, Mr Shakespeare, they were savages from the New World. None of us had ever seen their like. They even spoke a little English and affected English clothes to wear, though they wore their hair strangely and had no beards. I thought they were handsome men, to tell the truth, and though they were savages, they did look and act as gallant as any English gentleman. John White was a gentleman, too, though he could speak of little but the wonders of the New World, to the extent that his words seemed to infect all those that heard him, my brother included . . . which was to be his downfall.'

Dare winced once more with the pain of his ordeal. 'I did love Ananias, sir, and regretted his turning so strange. Though he never was so bawdy or lewd in his ways as me, yet we did sometimes share jests and a surfeit of ale.'

Shakespeare found himself liking the fat man. He may have been an incorrigible scoundrel, but Shakespeare was prepared to believe his denials concerning the goose.

'There was *one* thing, though, Mr Shakespeare, sir . . .' Dare seemed uncertain. 'A fortnight past, there was a woman outside our house in the vicinity of Wormwood Street. I did think she was watching us. She wore a pynner close around her hair and face and I could not make out her features. I went out to ask her what her business was, but she turned and ran away, as if the twelve demons of hell were on her tail. I gave it no more mind, sir.'

'Could it have been Eleanor?'

Dare rubbed his fingers across the blistering rawness of his forehead and bared his teeth in pain. 'It did not cross my mind at the time, but now I think about it, I suppose she was the right size and weight. I certainly couldn't say that it was *not* her.'

'If it was Eleanor, can you think of any reason she might have been scared to make herself known to you? Had there ever been problems between you?'

'No, sir, by no means.'

'Describe this woman's attire to me.'

'She looked like a goodwife. Respectable, I would say. I recall she had on a smock and kirtle, sir. She was not gentry, but neither was she of the worst sort.'

'Can you tell me any more? Was there anything unusual?'

'No, sir, nothing.'

'Well, if the woman comes back, detain her. Ask the boy if he has seen her. Come to me at the school in Dowgate with any information you have and I will give you silver. Fail to do so and

I will ensure you enjoy another spell in the pillory, with your ears sliced off for dog food. Do you understand?'

Dare nodded disconsolately.

'And listen to the tipstaff. Stay away from the whores. Nor should you leave London, for I may need to speak with you again. I wish you good day and a speedy recovery from your present ills.'

As he walked away, Shakespeare had one thought in his head: if the woman at Wormwood Street *was* Eleanor, then she definitely did not wish to have her presence in England known. That meant one of two things: she was either guilty of something, or frightened of someone.

Sir Robert Cecil was rarely agitated, but this day he could not conceal his tension. 'You must make it quick, Mr Shakespeare. You should not be here and I have much to do. Where is your messenger?'

'I have not seen Butler, Sir Robert, since I sent him to you with my confirmation about the poisoning of the Countess of Essex.'

'Then you did not receive my return message assuring you that I had acted upon it?'

'No, sir, I did not.' Where on earth was Butler?

They were in Cecil's apartments at Greenwich Palace. Shakespeare had hired a tilt-boat from the Old Swan stairs. He knew he was taking a great risk that he might be seen by Essex or one of his men, but he had no choice. As it happened, wearing common artisan's clothes and in the middle of all the bustle about the landing stage at Greenwich, Shakespeare looked like any other working man assisting the removal of the vast quantities of gowns, treasure, beds and bedding that the Queen and her entourage required wherever they went.

'You must fire him and replace him with someone you can trust. As to the Countess of Essex, I have her safe, though she is still not well. She does not know it, but her food is tried by the Queen's own tasters. She will stay with the court. The other Devereux women will be excluded, at least for the remains of this summer. Only Essex himself will be permitted at court. In truth, the Queen insists he be there, to dally and play at games with her. Now, Mr Shakespeare, why are you here?'

Shakespeare reached into his jerkin and took the letter Bess of Hardwick had written to Walsingham. Cecil read it. 'Good,' he said at last. 'Now we must find the name of Arbella's tutor. She will have several. I will make inquiries and you must discover what you can.'

'What would you have me do?'

'Stay with Essex here in London until he sets forth. Carry on with the Roanoke inquiry and when he sets out, come with him to Sudeley. Follow him. Watch his every move.'

Shakespeare bowed.

'It is possible that, knowing of his existence, Essex has taken on this tutor as his own intelligencer. If so, I would hazard a guess that he is used as a go-between for correspondence to the lady Arbella,' Cecil continued. 'So there will be written evidence. Seek it. Above all, remember that this family does not think the marriage vows as sacred as you or I might. If he does intend anything, foil him. If he weds Arbella, all is lost. On your life, you must prevent this.'

Shakespeare frowned. The way Cecil spoke, it was clear he had his own intelligence already. It might be helpful if he would divulge this, but it was clear that would never happen. Like Walsingham, Cecil was content to play the long game.

Shakespeare bowed again and prepared to leave. Cecil stayed him.

'You know, John,' he said. 'You would do well to think of removing your family from this wretched city for a few weeks. I believe you come from Stratford. Why not send them there?'

Shakespeare winced. 'It is my fervent wish, Sir Robert, but things are not well between my wife and I. She will not go.'

'Where are her own family?'

'In the far northern reaches of the realm, the North Riding of Yorkshire, sir. It would be too dangerous for them to go so far unaccompanied. I believe the road is wild, with much banditry.'

Cecil's eyes lit up. 'I might have a solution, John. Indeed, I am certain I have one – if you can move quickly. Can your family be ready by morning?'

'It is possible, sir.'

'There is a troop of militia going to the middle Marches of the border to put down a rising of freebooters and blackmailers. They leave early tomorrow – a band of thirty men. If you can get your family ready in time, I will instruct the captain to collect them and take them to their destination. They will be safe.'

Shakespeare allowed himself a smile; it was the first good news he had had in days and would remove a huge weight of worry from his overburdened shoulders. It would also, he hoped, cure his wife's melancholy and ease her hostility towards him. 'Thank you, Sir Robert. They will be ready.'

'Then that is settled. Now go.'

'There was one other thing.' Shakespeare briefly outlined the Le Neve connection – and the link between Jaggard and McGunn.

Cecil listened in silence, then nodded. 'Keep digging, John, keep digging.'

Chapter 23

Davy Kerk was not at the brewery in Gully Hole. 'He's not been in since you came here to see him, Mr Cooper,' Ralph Hogsden said. 'And he has left me in much difficulty, I can tell you. I have orders for casks which I cannot fulfil.'

'Do you know where he might be?'

'Probably gone down with the plague. It's not like him to be away. He's always been reliable.'

'How long has he been here?'

'Since Christmas of the year '90. He was in a bad way. He told me he had returned to Antwerp having had enough of the seafaring life, but then fell foul of the Inquisition. He had to escape in a hurry. I gave him a trial and saw he was a fine crafts-man. Made barrels as tight as a nun's whimsy.'

'Do you know where he lives?'

'Aye, not far from the river at Bank End. Tall, thin house, middle of a new frame with smart lozenge timbering. Must have cost him a small chest of treasure. I do reckon he did some fair privateering in his time afloat. If you see him, tell him to let me know what's going on, because I cannot keep his job open.'

Boltfoot was feeling the heat of the day as he limped haltingly along westwards through the crowded Southwark streets. He felt the weight of his caliver strung across his back and his old cutlass slapping at his thigh. His clubfoot dragged more heavily than ever.

The house was easy to spot. It was as Hogsden had described it. The exposed timbering was of finest oak. Boltfoot stepped up to the low front door and hammered with the haft of his dagger. He heard a scuffling from inside, but no one came. He knocked again. After a minute, it was opened by a fair young woman. She looked flustered and wiped her hands on her apron as if she had been preparing food.

'Yes?'

'I am looking for Davy Kerk. Is this his house?'

'Who wants to know?'

'Boltfoot Cooper. I have spoken with him already at Hogsden Trent's.'

'Well, he's not here.'

'May I come in and wait for him?'

'He doesn't live here any more. He's gone.'

Boltfoot stepped forward before she could close the door and pushed his way inside. The room was modest but well cared for. Clean rushes on the floor, a table and stools in the centre of the room. On the table was a fresh-killed cock, its fine tail feathers gleaming bright and ready for plucking. It was surrounded by an array of fresh fruits and vegetables. 'Would you have some beer, mistress, for I am feeling the heat sore bad today?'

She eyed him suspiciously. 'Is it commonplace for you to push your way into folk's houses, Mr Cooper?'

'No, but I did believe you were about to shut me out. Please, a beaker of beer and I'll be on my way.'

The young woman found a beaker and filled it from the faucet of a keg in the corner of the room. She handed it to Boltfoot. 'Here, drink it and begone.'

He sipped the beer. It was good and refreshing. He was no

expert in such things, but thought the woman well-spoken, her voice that of one from a good family, though he noted that her fingers were black like a scullery woman.

'Is this Hogsden Trent beer?'

'No, I brew it. Can't afford to be buying beer off the brewer.'

'It's good, mistress, very good.'

'Tell me what you want, then go. I'll pass on a message to him next time I see him, which won't be for quite a few days or weeks, I reckon.'

She was a good-looking, healthy young woman, well attired in a clean and pressed flaxen smock that went with the colour of her hair. 'Are you Mistress Kerk, Davy's wife?'

'Me? Married to him? He's my father, you dunderhead. Why would I be wed to an old fool like that?'

'But he lives here with you?'

He thought she looked confused, unsure how to answer the question. 'Well, he does when he's here.'

'Are you Dutch, too? You don't sound Dutch.'

'I was brought up by an aunt, here, in England, while my father was at sea. My mother is long dead.'

He glanced up at a crucifix on the wall. 'And you are of the same faith, you and your father?'

She bridled. 'What are you trying to say?'

'It was a straight question.'

'Would it make a difference if we did not share our religion? Must one family be of one mind?'

Boltfoot thought of his master, Shakespeare, a confirmed Protestant, married to a devout Catholic. Much trouble it had brought them. He shrugged his shoulders. 'No. No difference. Think nothing of it. But where is he? He has a steady job at the brewery. He should be about.'

'He has other business. Elsewhere. I look after things for him.'

'What business? Ralph Hogsden reckons he should be at work for him.'

'What's it to you?'

'I think you know.'

'Well, you're mistaken. I don't know what this is all about, and neither am I interested. So you can finish your beer and leave. Now, before I summon the watch.'

'Did he tell you about me, mistress?'

'Aye, he did. Said you were a snooping cripple. He didn't like you, and nor do I. So go. You're not welcome here.'

'Has he spoken to you about the Roanoke colony and the voyage there?'

'Go, Mr Cooper.'

'And one Eleanor Dare? Have you heard that name?'

She sighed and her shoulders slumped. 'Of course I've heard of Roanoke. Everybody in England has heard it. It has been bruited about in all the penny broadsheets and it was all the gossip in the taverns and victuallers a year or two back. You would have had to be in Peru not to have heard of all that nonsense. But just because my father was one of them as took them there doesn't mean he knows anything. And nor do I. Now I've got a fowl to pluck and other work to do, so I'd be very pleased if you would leave. I've given you beer. Other than that, I cannot help you.'

Boltfoot finished the beer and made for the door. He noticed a picture on the wall, facing the crucifix, a skilled ink drawing of a pair of guinea fowl beside a copper pot. Though austerely framed in plain wood, he could see it was an expert work. He looked again at the woman's blackened hands. 'That is a fine picture, mistress. Is it by you? Do you draw in ink?'

She did not respond, merely glared at Boltfoot.

'I will be back, mistress. Tell your father I must speak with him and that it will be to his benefit.'

Boltfoot stood outside a long while, watching the house from the shadows, expecting to see Davy Kerk appear at any moment. Even in the shade, he felt weak. At last he felt himself becoming faint; he had to get home to see Jane. He struggled through the crowds and stalls of Southwark back towards the bridge. The sweat dripped from his forehead into his eyes and he felt his shirt and breeches stick to his body with the heat and the effort of walking.

At Long Southwark he stopped. He should have searched the house, with or without her permission. He should have demanded to know where Davy Kerk had gone on his so-called business. He should have stayed there until Kerk returned, for she obviously was not preparing a chicken-fowl to eat alone.

Cursing his dragging foot and the infernal heat, he turned back westwards once more. The last thing he heard was the voice of a mother. 'Here, Bobby, give a farthing to that poor, lame soldier.' Then a boy of about eight pressed a farthing into his hand. He stared down at it, bewildered, his brow dripping sweat into his palm. He looked up and, across the road, he saw a woman's blue-grey eyes peering out at him from inside a cowl. And then, nothing.

The decision was made over supper. Catherine, Jane, the children and Jack Butler – should he return by dawn – would go to Catherine's home town, not far from York in the north of Yorkshire, with the squadron offered by Cecil.

Catherine's mood lifted immediately and she began bustling around the house, fetching the essentials for the journey and packing them in boxes and bags.

The desperate question was: where was Jack Butler? Shakespeare was now very concerned not just for his servant's safety, but because he wanted the family to travel with at least one trusted man in attendance. He ruffled young Andrew

Woode's hair. 'Well, lad, if Mr Butler does not appear, you will be the man of the family.'

'Yes, sir.'

The thought of Catherine leaving for a journey of more than two hundred miles with Jane, little Mary and their wards Andrew, now eleven, and nine-year-old Grace, somehow made their recent disagreements over religion and Father Southwell seem insignificant.

'I shall miss you, Catherine,' Shakespeare said.

'Join us then, John.'

He smiled without conviction. 'Yes. As soon as I can.'

'I saw Father Southwell in the Gatehouse,' Catherine said quietly. 'Topcliffe allowed me in. He wished to gloat.' She looked closely at her husband for his reaction.

A few days earlier, Shakespeare would have exploded in a fury at such news. Now it seemed pointless. She was going away now, beyond the reach of Topcliffe and the plague and all other sources of harm.

'I had thought you would go there. How does Southwell fare?'

'Not well. He had been left hanging against the wall, his legs strapped back. He was close to death.'

'It was the course he chose, Catherine. I believe he has longed for martyrdom.'

She was about to say something sharp by way of reply, but held her tongue. 'John, let us talk of that another time. I have much to do before the soldiers arrive for us. One thing, though, I must tell you. I also met Anne Bellamy, who is changed beyond recognition. I know it is caused by the horror of what she and her family have come to, but I confess I found her hard to like. She said something curious to me, though. A warning or a threat, I know not which: she said we will all be drowning in chrism. The Shakespeares, she said, as if it included all of us.

I know not why, but it even occurred to me that she meant your brother, too. How would she know of Will?'

Shakespeare saw the connection at once. 'She must have been with Father Southwell at Southampton House. William would have been there oftentimes; he has the patronage of the Earl of Southampton. What her warning could mean, though, I cannot say. Why should we drown in holy oil?'

'She was very confused, full of hatred for God and the world – and me.'

Shakespeare was silent a moment. It sounded like yet another filthy attempt at intimidation by Richard Topcliffe. Either that or the meaningless ranting of a poor Bess o'Bedlam; anyone taken into custody by Topcliffe might be turned mad by his brutality. 'Pay it no heed, Catherine. Here, take another glass of wine with me and be merry at the thought of seeing your mother and father.'

Later, they spoke in quiet tones and sat with wine in the candlelight. Both had much to say to each other which they could not say, and though they slept in the same bed for the first time in days, they did not make love. The distance between them was still unbridged, but perhaps it was not quite a chasm. Nonetheless, it was a bad way to part.

In the early hours of the morning, Shakespeare rose from the bed, unable to sleep. He looked at Catherine lying there and touched her face. She was so still and quiet, he wondered whether she, too, were awake. But she did not respond to his touch. Treading barefoot, he walked in silence to the solar and lit a candle. He looked again through the papers he had brought from the turret room.

He studied the Roanoke documents once more. One of them was a sheet he had dismissed earlier as being of no consequence. It was dated 1589, the year before it was discovered that the colonists were missing. At the top were the words *SWR's new*

Virginia Corporation, and below were a list of the names of the investors. Shakespeare ran a finger down the names. They were all great merchants of the City, with plenty of spare gold to put into such a risky venture. His finger stopped at one of the names and he went cold. Jacob Winterberry – the Puritan bridegroom of the murdered girl Amy Le Neve.

So Jacob Winterberry was an investor in Sir Walter Ralegh's Roanoke colony. At this befuddling hour of the morning, Shakespeare could make no sense of it. Was it mere coincidence? Everything he had learned from Walsingham had taught him that such things were never coincidence. He felt suddenly tired. Perhaps he would see Winterberry on the morrow. He would find out then. He went back to the bedroom and slipped once more into the marital bed, beside the still, warm body of his wife.

They rose at first light as the cocks crowed. The troop of thirty mounted soldiers came by in a clatter of hooves and bucklers while the family was still at breakfast. The children were all agape to see them in their helmets, with their mass of armour and armaments borne aboard thirty more packhorses behind them, ready to fight the feared Scots raiders on the northern Marches. Jane and Catherine gave ale to the soldiers. They then loaded up their sumpters, tying the baggage securely with maling cords, and stood in the courtyard waiting for the order to mount up and depart. Shakespeare hugged the children and kissed them, and made them promise to be good and God-fearing. Two lieutenants lifted Andrew and Grace into the saddle with them.

Shakespeare gave a last hug to Mary, the only one of the three children who was of his own blood. He smiled at her. 'Look after your mother,' he said.

Finally it came time for Shakespeare and Catherine to take their leave. They stood bashfully before each other. He moved forward to kiss her, but her face turned from him at the last moment, and his lips only brushed her cheek. 'God speed, Catherine,' he said, trying hard to smile.

'We will be fine with these troopers, John. Do not worry for us.'

Catherine mounted and Shakespeare handed up Mary to sit with her. Next to her, side-saddle on a bay palfrey, sat Jane, her swollen belly very evident.

'I will send Boltfoot to you post-haste, Jane. And Jack Butler will follow.' He turned to the commander of the troop. 'Look out for them, Captain.'

The captain saluted Shakespeare, then turned his horse and led the way out of the courtyard on to the streets of London, heading for the dusty, perilous road north.

Chapter 24

As SHAKESPEARE RODE slowly the last mile to the church at Wanstead, the mortbell knelled clear across the meadows. It rang just one note again and again, a deep, dread clang that could only mean a body was to be laid to rest in the cold earth.

The mourners were gathered in the graveyard close by the Le Neve house and on their land. So few were there, a mere ten or so, that a passer-by might have thought it a pauper's bleak interment.

Shakespeare reined in his mare a hundred yards outside the churchyard wall, and watched as the little band began walking through the porch into the church. Sir Toby and Cordelia Le Neve were there, attired all in black. So were the maid, Miranda, and the sour and ancient retainer, Dodsley. A minister was speaking the plain new funeral service as they walked. On his right was another man, a wide-brimmed black felt hat held against the chest of his dark, broadcloth coat. He looked straight ahead, his face stern, as though cast from iron.

At their head, four men in workmen's leather jerkins carried the simple coffin into the church.

Cordelia Le Neve turned and saw Shakespeare. Shock crossed her features, then anger. She touched her husband's arm and he looked across at the intruder, too.

Miranda Salter also saw him but immediately looked away, as if ashamed for ever having spoken to him, or perhaps from shame at having betrayed their conversation to her mistress. Shakespeare dismounted and walked the mare to the church wall, where he tied her to a ring by the wrought-iron gate beside some other horses. In the yard, outside the church, there were new crosses and several fresh-dug graves, and he wondered, briefly, whether the plague had begun its dread work in these parts.

He followed the mourners into the church. A hole had been dug at the eastern end of the chancel and mounds of earth piled up on either side. Sir Toby strode towards him, fury in his eyes. 'You are not welcome here,' he said. 'You intrude on private grief, sir, and I will not have it.'

'Sir Toby, I am inquiring into a murder. I must talk with you again. And with others.'

Le Neve's hand was on the hilt of his sword, though he did not draw it from its scabbard. 'Go, sir, go. Or I shall cut you down like a Frenchie, even in this, the Lord's house.'

Shakespeare looked across to the man with the hat and the dark, broadcloth coat. 'Is that Mr Winterberry, your daughter's bridegroom?'

'It is no business of yours, sir. Go.'

Shakespeare ignored his entreaties and threats and walked on along the nave towards the mourning party.

'Mr Winterberry?'

'Yes.'

The two men stood face to face, both tall, though Winterberry was older and his sombre clothes did not hang well on his angular frame. His face was sallow and serious.

'I would speak with you, sir, about the death of your wife.'

'She was not my wife.'

'I had believed you were wed, Mr Winterberry.'

'In church, but not in the bedchamber. In the eyes of man, but not of God, who sees all things. Now, may I ask who *you* are?'

'My name is Shakespeare. I am inquiring into the murder of Amy and the boy, Joe Jaggard.'

'And do you think this to be the meet and proper time to talk of such things?'

'It is a most heinous crime. I would have thought you would wish it solved.'

'She was frail, Mr Shakespeare. She had the frailty and vanity of woman. The profane enemy, the minister of darkness, took her to his abominable breast. Look to the instruments of the devil if you would know more of this death, sir.'

'I insist on talking with you, Mr Winterberry, unless you wish me to fetch a mittimus from the justice to take you into custody for questioning.'

Winterberry stared at him hard. Whatever else he was, he was a merchant, and merchants were practical men who did deals every day. 'Come to Indies Wharf by the Tower this afternoon and I will answer your questions, Mr Shakespeare, though I can think of none that pertain to me. Now go, sir, as Sir Toby has demanded of you.'

Lady Le Neve came to Shakespeare and took his elbow and pulled him away firmly but without force. 'Our daughter is being buried here alongside her forefathers and mother, Mr Shakespeare. Have you no shame?'

'And what of the boy?'

'He took his life. He took Amy's life. He has been buried at the crossroads. Now go.'

Shakespeare looked around at the little gathering and saw nothing but hostility. There was no more to be gained in this place today. He bowed in acknowledgement of their grief and to honour the dead girl about to be lowered into the earth, then walked slowly out of the little church and back through the churchyard towards the gate, where his mare waited patiently.

On the brow of the incline to the west, he saw a horseman, stock still beneath a sycamore tree. It was impossible to make out his features from this distance, but something in the way he sat, thin and wiry like a stoat, told Shakespeare the watcher was Slyguff.

Shakespeare mounted his horse, pulled the reins southerly and spurred her into a light trot.

And still the mortbell tolled.

Shakespeare spoke to Perkin Sidesman and told him that if anyone were to ask, he was to say the school would be closed down for the summer but would reopen in October. If anyone wished to speak with him, they were to leave a note or spoken message. 'I badly want to hear word of Jack and Boltfoot.'

'I understand, master,' the groom said without enthusiasm. He did not look happy about the extra responsibility loaded on his shoulders, but then he rarely looked happy about anything.

Shakespeare took a wherry from the green and slimy waterstairs at the Steelyard and headed downstream. On the south bank, as he passed, he watched fishermen pulling in draughtnets of salmon. The tide was with the wherry, but would soon be turning; the narrow race between the struts of London Bridge was a hazardous affair, and one which, when the current was strong, many preferred to avoid by disembarking and walking to the other side of the bridge. Shakespeare did not have time for such delicacy. He held his breath as the watermen steered the craft at speed through the churning white water.

Glad to be through and alive, he breathed again, only to catch a lungful of the stink that blew from the Billingsgate fish market. Further downriver, Smart's and Morris's quays were thick with shipping, all moored alongside each other in a profusion of spars, rigging and furled sails. The whole of the Thames here was a chaotic mass of proud-masted vessels; a hundred or more ships of all sizes riding at anchor in midstream, lying on their sides on the muddy banks for careening of barnacles and weeds, or standing at the wharves for discharge and loading of cargoes.

Past Customs House on the north bank, then the Tower and St Katharine's Dock, finally, the watermen guided the little vessel in among the tangle of carracks, barks and flyboats that encumbered the frontage of Indies Wharf.

Shakespeare paid the men fourpence, then stepped ashore on to the long quayside, hemmed in on one side by ships and on the other by warehouses. Gantries and tall cranes of oak and elm stretched out across the quay and river, creating a cacophony of creaking timbers.

A family of brown rats scurried along the edge of the wharf, unafraid. Shakespeare strode among them and went through an arched entrance into the largest of the warehouses. He found a foreman docker, who directed him to the counting house on the landward side of the warehouse.

Jacob Winterberry stood at the end of a long, well-polished table in a rich room; intricate plasterwork on the ceiling and ornate oak wainscotting on the lower portions of the walls seemed to tell much about his wealth. He still wore his funeral clothes; perhaps, thought Shakespeare, such sombre dress was his daily attire.

A clerk was reading from a bill of lading. 'Guinea coast, St George del Mina, aboard the *Tempest*, carrack of six hundred tons, outward bound: two hundred pounds linen, two hundred pounds kersey, five hundred axe heads, same number hammer heads, one thousand English arrows, five hundred French bolts, one hundred fifty Flemish brass basins, assorted hats of felt, pins, trinkets and beads to fill two casks, two hundred each of daggers and swords . . .'

The clerk stopped, as if noticing for the first time that there was another man in the room.

Winterberry looked up and met the newcomer's eye. 'Ah yes, Mr Shakespeare.' He said the words in a businesslike fashion, no welcoming smile or greeting hand proffered. He met his clerk's eyes. The clerk quickly gathered together his quills, documents and ledgers and hurried from the room, bowing low as he went. 'Now, what would you ask me?'

Shakespeare noticed that a large book lay before Winterberry on the table. Winterberry followed his eyes and put his right hand squarely down on the book. 'Yes, Mr Shakespeare, it is the Holy Bible, which informs everything I do and everything I say. Every portion of my trade with the wider world is done in Christ's name, to bring the word of God to those benighted savages still cloaked in darkness.'

'Would you like to swear on it now, that you will answer my questions truthfully?'

'I live by the Book every day of my life, Mr Shakespeare. I do not need to prove to some lowly officer of the Searcher that I speak the truth.'

'You are a proud man, Mr Winterberry.'

'If I am, then I do repent it and beg the Lord's forgiveness, for pride is a deadly sin.'

Shakespeare thought he had never seen such a stern, closed face. He did not know this man, but he knew he did not like him. 'You had reason to murder Amy Le Neve and Joe Jaggard.' He said the words as a statement, not a question, hoping for some reaction, some fissure in the rock of Winterberry's features.

'You were at the funeral, Mr Shakespeare. You heard what Sir Toby Le Neve said. The Jaggard boy murdered Amy with poison and then took his own life in like manner. That is the Sheriff's verdict and the matter is closed.'

'That is not the belief of the Coroner, I understand, nor of the Searcher of the Dead.'

'Well then, they must take up the case with the Sheriff and try to have it reopened. As for me, I consider the matter now to be between those two young people and their maker. I pray they can find salvation, though the Lord will have to be very forgiving.'

'She was your wife, Mr Winterberry. Can you dismiss her death – her murder – so lightly?'

'She was a purple strumpet, Mr Shakespeare. She chose the World, the Devil and the Flesh, and she was struck down as all such idolatrous harlots will be struck down.' Winterberry spoke with barely a pause between words. The words were angry, but the voice was quiet and cold. 'With her painted face, she was too vain to realise that she would, within the blink of an eye, be screaming for all eternity in the fire.'

Winterberry's face was still a mask of stone, but Shakespeare noted that the veins on his hand were raised and white as he pressed down hard on the Bible.

'Then why marry her?'

Winterberry raised his hand from the book. He crossed his arms. His voluble voice became quieter. 'I wanted a wife, Mr Shakespeare. Someone to manage my domestic affairs and home and bear my children under God's divine order. Do you have a wife?'

Shakespeare thought of Catherine and Mary, at present somewhere a few miles to the north of here on the first stage of their long journey through the heart of England to the little market town of Masham, in the desolate shire of York.

'I had never had time for such things, being precluded by my business and my calling. Where to find one unsullied by the world? All around me I saw the ensigns of lust, sloth and gluttony. I saw foul abuses – women daubed like butterflies. Observe the butterfly, sir, how she flutters all pretty about the garden, then alights on a dog turd.'

'You thought her young and untouched?'

For the first time, Shakespeare imagined he saw a human emotion behind the mask, a crushed sadness about the eyes. 'Indeed, I did hope her to be a virtuous woman. I have known Sir Toby many years. I thought a daughter of his would be pure and young enough to bear me children, and I wished to help Sir Toby, whom I knew to be in difficult straits. Even in the tents of the unclean, I thought our match would mock the malice of the enemy. I was wrong. Satan had already sunk his bladed nails into her.'

'So it was not her pretty face, her young flesh or the proud name she bore that attracted you to her?'

'You accuse me of lust and avarice. Why should I listen to this?'

'Then it is untrue?'

'It was what I took to be her purity, sir.'

'And when you discovered she was not pure?'

'This is intolerable, Mr Shakespeare. You berate me like the Antichrist.'

'Why did you ride away without looking for Amy that night?'

He did not answer.

'Could it be that you knew what had happened to her, that she already lay bloodied and murdered? You had followed her and bludgeoned her and Joe. Is that how it was?'

'No, Mr Shakespeare, that is not what happened. I did not search for her because I knew that she had gone with *him*. I knew then what she was, what foul vice she was about. Why should I look when I expected them to return, flushed and sated?'

'You observed her leaving the bridale with Jaggard?' Shakespeare saw dour fury in Winterberry's eyes, very close to the surface. Could it be triggered to violence, or was he in control?

'Yes,' Winterberry said, spitting the word. 'Yes, I saw them moving as the chariot wheels of Satan to their damnable, abominable bed of grass and their vile carnality. I saw them go where they might rut like the beasts of the field. Why would I search for her, Mr Shakespeare? I would rather pluck out my eyes than let them fall on such a vision of hell.'

'What did you do then, Mr Winterberry?'

'Do? What should I do?'

'Most men would have stood up there and then and ridden off into the night. You stayed, though.'

Winterberry hesitated. 'I was confused. I could not comprehend what I was seeing. We had been married in her father's church a mere two or three hours earlier! Now she is buried there, beneath the ground where we stood and made our vows.'

'It seems extraordinary to me that you neither followed them nor left the bridale.'

Winterberry bowed his head as if crushed. 'Yes. I see that now. But then . . . Mr Shakespeare, I did not know of such things. I still do not.'

'Did you leave the bridale at any time?'

'No.'

'Could anyone who was there testify to that?'

Winterberry regained his composure. 'There was dancing and music and merriment. There were venal sins, horrible in their abomination: gluttony, greed, lust such as you might find in the circles of hell. I saw bottle ale, Satan's device to keep us from the narrow path, and fumes belching from the dark chasms of their bodies. How would they note me or my movements through such a cloud of mist and error?'

Shakespeare closed his eyes for a moment. 'How many were at the bridale?'

'Twenty, fifty, I know not and care less. It was something to be endured. I have had enough of these questions. Begone, Mr Shakespeare, before I have you marched from here.'

The darkness was brewing, but Shakespeare carried on regardless. He had already goaded him to doubt; could he now provoke the man to thunderous rage? 'I have but a few questions more, Mr Winterberry. When the hue and cry went up, you could have told someone what you had seen.'

'And trumpet my shame to the world?'

Shakespeare almost felt sympathy for this strange, cold man. He was severe, almost frantic, in his religion, and yet he was a man, too. And what man would know how to deal with the adultery of his bride?

'What of the lad, Joe Jaggard. Did you know him?'

Winterberry scowled and paused, considering his reply. 'Jaggard? I may have met him, but I paid him no heed. I took him for a vulgar, godless youth.'

'What were the circumstances of your meeting?'

He hesitated again. 'I am not sure I recall. I was at Wanstead frequently, you understand, treating with Sir Toby. I took him for an estate hand.'

Shakespeare was not convinced. Winterberry would have been well aware of Jaggard; a man will always know his rival in matters of love.

'Mr Winterberry, you said you wished to help Sir Toby in return for the hand of his daughter?'

'We were friends of old. He had fallen on hard times. I was able to help him.'

'What was the portion you were to bring to the marriage?'

'That is between Sir Toby and me. It is not something either of us would wish bruited about. Anyway, it is done with now. The transaction will not happen.'

'You are withholding the settlement?'

'Why should I not?'

Why indeed, thought Shakespeare. Winterberry was a merchant, this marriage was a deal like any other as far as he was concerned, and the goods were not only soiled but had not even been delivered to his bed. It was a sour logic, but it fitted. Shakespeare changed tack.

'Tell me about your business interests, sir. With whom do you trade?'

'I trade with the world. I send trinkets and I send the word of the Lord into the Africas and the Levant and the Spanish Indies. I send light into their darkness, and the Lord has seen that it is good and has allowed me to prosper, providing yet more means to do His work.'

'These are difficult days, Mr Winterberry. The war with Spain is never-ending. Venturing great fortunes on expeditions of trade is fraught with danger, is it not?'

'Indeed, which is why I say prayers of thanksgiving every day for the blessings He has bestowed upon me.'

'I heard the list of commodities you send out, Mr Winterberry. What goods do you hope in return?'

'Silver, gold, spices and souls. Now if you are done with me, I have much work to be doing.'

'One last question.' It was the question Shakespeare most wanted to ask – and he looked closely for any reaction in the long, stony face that confronted him. 'Do you, Mr Winterberry, know aught of the Roanoke colony in Virginia?'

Winterberry's head jerked slightly backwards, as if thrown by the question. 'Roanoke?' he said, frowning. 'What has Roanoke to do with your inquiries, Mr Shakespeare?'

Shakespeare was firm. 'I cannot say, but I *would* like to hear whether or not you know of the place and the colony founded there.'

'I do know of it, of course, for I am one of Sir Walter Ralegh's investors. I was happy to lend my name and my gold to the venture, for I know the colonists to be unspotted lambs of the Lord. It is only meet that such folk should be in the vanguard of this brave world of Virginia. I am certain, too, that they will be found well and thriving in time, for the Lord will care for these His servants.'

'Do you know any of the colonists?'

'I know Mr White, but he is now in Ireland, I do believe.'

'And his daughter, Eleanor Dare?'

'I know of her. Why do you ask these strange questions, Mr Shakespeare? What possible interest can you have in the colony?'

'I have been making inquiries on behalf of my lord of Essex, who has an interest in the matter. Mr Winterberry, do you think it possible that this same Eleanor Dare, born White, could now be in England?'

'Mr Shakespeare, I do not know what madness you are engaged in, but I know that Eleanor Dare could not be in England. If any had returned, the corporation would have been the first to know. Do you think the searchers at the ports would not have informed us? They send postriders to me whenever a ship arrives at any port from Sandwich to Falmouth. Now I have answered all your questions with plain and honest speaking, and I must ask you to leave. Let me accompany you to the water-stairs.'

Winterberry walked with ponderous purpose towards the door. He had picked up the Bible from the table and now held it in both hands behind his back, in the way another man might carry a concealed weapon.

The air in the large central warehouse fronting Indies Wharf was thick with the exotic aroma of spices, all ranged in great casks along the walls. England could not get enough of them to flavour the foodstuffs on its tables.

'Do you enjoy the scent of spices, Mr Shakespeare?'

'Who could not, Mr Winterberry?'

'They are God's most wondrous gift to us: nutmeg, cinnamon, cumin, mace, coriander, hot spices, ginger and the greatest of them all, sugar.' They came to the arched entrance to the landing stage where barrels were being loaded by hand and by crane on to a huge carrack. The name emblazoned on its bow was *Tempest*.

'God speed, Mr Shakespeare. I am sorry you have had these wasted journeys today.' Once more, he did not proffer a hand to be shaken.

The jib of the crane above them swung out from the vessel, pushed by a docker standing on the deck. The man in the wheel cabin worked hard at the pedals, raising the pulleys by a system of cogs. Shakespeare looked up and saw the barrel directly above them. Suddenly it was released from the boom. It was coming down, dropping towards them, falling. Shakespeare thrust his arm at Winterberry's chest and threw him to the ground.

The cask fell to the quay with explosive force, cracking open in a shower of staves, splinters and a clattering array of metal goods. A copper platter flew up and struck Shakespeare hard on his lower back, but the barrel itself had missed him. He realised he was lying over Winterberry's prostrate form and quickly rose, dusting himself down as he did so. He rubbed his back where it had been hit.

He looked to the man in the crane cabin; he had an expression of pure astonishment and horror. Then Shakespeare looked to the deck of the ship where the docker had pushed out the jib. There was no one to be seen.

As Winterberry struggled to his feet, Shakespeare tore across the landing board and leapt on to the deck of the *Tempest*. A man was sitting inside the bulkhead, idly smoking a pipe.

'Where did that docker go? The one pushing the jib.'

'He should be here on the main deck, working. He's a day labourer. Never saw him before today.'

Shakespeare loped to the bows and looked down into the grey, lapping depths of the Thames. He ran back to the stern-castle. There was no sign of the man. At the larboard side, there was another ship lashed to the *Tempest*, and another beyond that. The docker could easily have leapt across from deck to deck. Angrily, Shakespeare walked back to the quayside.

'Did you see him?'

Winterberry said nothing. His face was grave. He signalled to the crane driver to lower the ropes and then examined the frayed ends where the barrel had come away. The strands were sheared. Winterberry ran a finger over the frayed end.

'This was cut.'

'Who wants to kill you?'

'I would ask the same of *you*, Mr Shakespeare. It seems to me you delve in murky, ungodly waters. I can think of no man who would do me harm. Now, good day to you. My wherry-man will take you back upstream, if you wish. You will find no hire boats here.'

Shakespeare met Winterberry's eyes. He had one more question for him. 'Did you know that the boy Joe Jaggard was also interested in Roanoke, Mr Winterberry – that he was searching for Eleanor Dare?'

Winterberry's humourless expression did not change. 'Good day, Mr Shakespeare,' he said, and turned away.

As he was rowed out into midstream, Shakespeare gazed back at Indies Wharf. A dark figure stood in the archway to the spice warehouse. Jacob Winterberry was watching him go.

Chapter 25

Boltfoot woke with a pounding head pain. He tried to look up, but could not focus. He seemed to see beams and an unfamiliar ceiling. Strange sounds all around only made the throbbing of his skull the worse. He was too weak to move.

A woman clothed in a simple gown, with a long white apron and a crisp white coif, like a nun's wimple, floated across his field of vision. She peered down at him, two warm brown eyes looking into his with concern.

'Where am I?' he managed to say. 'What has happened to me?'

'You are in the Hospital of St Thomas, sir.'

He reached up to his head and found it was bandaged. He winced at the mere touch of his hand. 'Why?'

'You have been injured. But it is good to see you have awakened, sir, for we had feared for your life.'

He closed his eyes and it began to come back to him.

'And the day?'

The nurse laughed lightly. She was dumpy, but made pretty by her smile and evident kindness. 'You have been here more than twenty hours. A young woman saw you, all bloody in the street, and came here to ask the beadles to fetch you. You were fortunate, for many would have left you there to die, so poor was your health. If you have more questions, the hospitaller will walk through the ward within the hour, and you may ask him.'

Boltfoot held up a hand from the coverlet. He needed to get out of here. He felt dizzy. He tried to move up on to his elbows, but immediately fell back, fighting for breath. His head felt as though it had been struck by the edge of a halberd. 'Please, get word to Dowgate for me,' he said weakly. 'Tell my goodwife who is big with child that I am here, and my master.'

She smiled. 'Do not fret yourself, sir. I will come and talk with you later. If you are good and quiet, I shall try to find you a bed of feathers. And if you are not good, I must tell you that there is a whipping post and stocks in the yard. You will be excused chapel in the morning, though not again.'

She bustled off about the ward, examining bandages, taking away fouled bedding to be laundered. Through the haze of his pulsating head, Boltfoot tried to remember what had happened to him.

He had been in one of the small streets to the west of Long Southwark on the way back to the house of Davy Kerk. He remembered how faint he felt, how his clothes dripped with sweat. Across the narrow road he had noticed a woman, all covered in a hood, watching him and then, from behind, a shadow and then the blow. And that was all.

If only Jane would come to him.

He drifted off to sleep again, this time proper sleep, not the loss of consciousness, the simulacrum of death, that comes with a crushing blow to the head.

When Shakespeare got back to Dowgate, Sidesman was washing down a horse on the cobbles by the stables. He shook his dour head slowly. He had seen neither Boltfoot nor Jack. Shakespeare felt a gnawing, churning terror in his stomach. Neither man would have been out of contact this long.

'But you will find that a lady has arrived to see you, sir,' the groom said.

Cordelia Le Neve was in the anteroom. She was looking through a Latin primer, but put it down on a coffer when Shakespeare entered.

'You are very welcome, Lady Le Neve,' he said, 'although your custom of entering people's rooms without being invited is a little unnerving. I trust this time you come unarmed?' he added wryly.

She was dishevelled and dusty from the ride. Her hair was windswept and tangled about her shoulders. She wore a linen kirtle and a close-fitted chemise, open at the neck, where her skin glowed. She might have passed for a serving-wench except there was something about her bearing, the tilt of her head and her fine looks that said otherwise.

'You may search me if you wish.'

He smiled. 'I shall leave it to trust, Lady Le Neve.'

'As you will. Do you have refreshment, Mr Shakespeare? I fear I will perish without a little ale to ease my poor, parched throat.'

He went to the buttery where the keg was kept. She followed him.

'This is a fine school, Mr Shakespeare. I would say it is new built.'

'The main part is but five years old, originally built as a home for the merchant Thomas Woode, the Lord rest him. I am afraid the Bishop has now closed it down, however.'

'I am sorry.'

'Fear not, I am sure we will reopen come All Hallows.'

'It is curious that you run errands for the Searcher of the Dead as well as being High Master of a school.'

Shakespeare pulled two pints of ale, handing one to Cordelia. 'I have spent many years as an intelligencer and investigator of certain crimes for the late Mr Secretary. The Searcher is a friend of mine.'

'Why do I feel there is something you are not telling me?'

'I could ask the same of you, Lady Le Neve. Your connection with McGunn, my lord Essex and Mr Winterberry is most intriguing. Tell me: why have you come here?'

'I have come here to answer your questions.'

'That is good.' He waited.

'And . . . there are things . . . things that someone – you – should know.'

'Such as?'

'Let us talk awhile.'

Shakespeare shrugged his shoulders. 'As you wish. Start by telling me how much Winterberry was going to pay you for your daughter's hand.'

'Five thousand pounds, I believe, though such details are men's business. We have seen none of it, and never will.'

'What did he hope for in return? Did he believe your daughter loved him? He is an austere man.'

'All men are the same when you strip away the attire, be it Puritan broadcloth or courtly taffeta. It is lechery and vanity. He wanted a pretty maiden for his bed and he wanted connection to our family name. He had already been to the College of Arms to see how he might adopt my husband's armorial bearings. But then he did not know of Amy's feelings for the boy Jaggard, and nor did we at first.'

'Now he lies buried at the crossroads, for taking his own life and another's, though the truth is very different.'

'He does not lie at the crossroads. McGunn has now taken his body and given him a burial by the church on Essex's estate of Wanstead.'

Shakespeare paused. The silence hung between them. Then, abruptly, 'This marriage, Lady Le Neve, did it not trouble you that you were selling your stepdaughter like a . . .?' He stopped.

'A *whore*, Mr Shakespeare?'

If she was offended, Lady Le Neve did not show it. 'Winterberry is not a young man, and in time she would have been left one of the wealthiest widows in the realm, to pursue whatever fancies she desired. I know what poverty is like, and I can tell you that it is a great deal worse than the fumbling attentions of an ageing man.'

Shakespeare watched her closely. There was something not right here. The last time he had seen this woman, she had wanted rid of him. 'I ask you again, Lady Le Neve, why have you come here?'

She breathed deeply, as if summoning up some inner fortitude. The silence drifted on until, at last, she spoke.

'I have no one else to turn to. I thought you might be that rare thing, an honest man. I am scared, Mr Shakespeare.'

'You know the name of the killer?'

'I must tell you in my own way. It is a long story.'

'Come. Let us go to my solar. We will be more comfortable.'

They proceeded to the room where Shakespeare most liked to work. Through the west window he saw that the sun was low in the sky. Lady Le Neve, so unlike Catherine in her looks and manner, sat on a settle and he stood by the cold hearth.

'We are impoverished because my husband likes to gamble,' she said. 'He plays cent, primero and tables. He will hazard money on the fighting skills of a cock or the speed of a horse. He plays with my lord of Essex's friends: Southampton, Rutland, Danvers, Gelli Meyrick, his brother-in-arms Roger Williams. They all wager more money than is sensible, huge sums. And Sir Toby is the maddest of them all, for his inheritance was poor.'

'And McGunn?' Shakespeare persisted, eager to get to the point, the name.

'Essex told my husband that if ever he needed money, McGunn was the man. There could be no higher recommendation than that. Sir Toby is intensely loyal; he comes from a long feudal line and regards Essex as his liege lord.'

'And why, pray, does Essex keep the company of a man like McGunn?'

Cordelia's mouth was set. 'Gold. Essex lives like a sultan of Turkey with his vast houses, his legions of retainers, his army of knights all liveried in tangerine. Where does he find the money to maintain these men at his command? The Queen keeps him stretched like a bowstring. McGunn keeps Essex afloat, for he has such a burden of debt, he could sink to the depths of the northern seas.'

'And what does McGunn get in return?'

'Power, Mr Shakespeare. Control. Overlordship. The same as he exercised over us. But how would I or anyone else know what desires lie hidden in the cold, dark shadows of Charlie McGunn's mind. Watch his impudent boldness with great men – you would not think that Essex was the premier Earl and that McGunn was the lowly kern from the boglands of Ireland. You would think McGunn the chief of the two.'

'And how has McGunn come into so much treasure, Lady Le Neve?'

'Usury, violence, debauchery. He is as cold-blooded as a snake. He would kill and his heart would beat no faster.'

'You said you had seen such men before?'

She stood up abruptly. 'I have said enough.' She turned to go. The sun was close to the roofs towards the west of the City. The sky was darkening.

Shakespeare put up his hand. 'No. I want the name.'

'It is late. I should not have come here.'

'You say you are scared. Well, you are safe here. You cannot ride back alone to Wanstead this evening.'

'Do you think I have not been out alone in the darkest of nights?' She laughed.

'There is the Swan nearby.' He closed his eyes. 'Or there is this house. There are empty beds this night. You may make use of one, but you will give me the information I require.'

Her eyes, unabashed, met his. 'Yes,' she said. 'I will tell you the killer's name.' She sat down again.

'Let me tell you my story, if you have the stomach for it. I am of the notorious Kett family from Norwich in Norfolk. Have you heard of us, Mr Shakespeare?'

'Indeed.'

'It is a name tainted with treason, but I wear it with pride. Robert Kett was my grandfather and a landowner of wealth. Our family lived well, with landholdings around Norwich and Wymondham. My grandfather's rebellion, though he would not have called it such, ended all that. When he was hanged in chains from the battlements of Blanche Fleur, all his lands were attainted and given by King Edward to Lord Audley, his captor. My father and his brothers, who had thought they would inherit lands, were brought to impoverishment.'

Shakespeare refilled their goblets.

'By the time I was born in the first year of Her Majesty's reign, we lived in a small cottage not far from Wymondham. My father worked for Audley's estate as a common farm-hand, a serf, and my mother took in weaver's work. It was a modest enough life, but we had enough to eat and my parents ensured we were all educated in reading and some writing. They taught us, too, that we were better than the place to which we had been brought by fate. There were three of us, all girls, and I was the eldest. The others in the village thought we were above ourselves; they did not like to see maidens with books and mocked us for it. At the age of eight, we had to work on the farm, milking, churning, reaping, feeding the stock and collecting the eggs. Then, when I was twelve, we were brought yet lower.' She stopped for a moment, unable properly to find a voice to speak. 'Forgive me, Mr Shakespeare.'

'Drink a little wine.'

'The sickness came. The sweat. It pains me grievously to recall it, even now. It took mother and father and my youngest sister, all in the space of a fortnight. That left just Matilda and me. We had no help from our neighbours. Even the almoner called me a dirty maunderer, spat in my face and said he would not give me so much as a farthing.'

'So what did you do?'

'We took the road to London, as I thought. But it was no such thing. We joined a band of vagabonds for protection and became runagates ourselves. That is no life. You can have no idea of the cold, Mr Shakespeare. In mid-winter the frost bites so deep that the elders and babes amongst us froze where they slept.' She held a hand to her bare throat, as if overcome by the recollection. 'There were men there, and women too, that would kill for half a loaf. I saw them fight until the blood ran freely into the mud over the ownership of a dead hare. We scavenged for anything and everything. Nettles, insects, all the fruits of the forest and hedgerow, cats and dogs and rats, too. Whatever we could find. I don't doubt there were some that gnawed on human flesh. There were fifty of us in our roving camp and we were unwelcome wherever we went. If we went near towns, the men would drive us away with whips and mastiffs. If the headborough or foreign officer caught a vagabond man, he would be accused of every crime committed within the year and be hanged that day without trial. If they could catch a dell they would treat her no better than a whore, even though she might be a maiden. And we were flogged without mercy. I have the stripes still.'

'I believe you.'

'We stayed in the open air. But there was always a hamlet nearby, so they would gather all the farm-hands to drive us away. Some were Christian folk, a few, and would give us loaves and ale, but they always told us we must be on our way after our repast. There was no money to be had and we slept beneath hedgerows or in byres if we could.'

'How long were you on the road?'

'Two years. Two years that aged me a hundred. I have not even told you the worst.' Her voice broke again. She tried to regain her composure. Tears streamed down her cheeks; yet she did not sob. 'My sister . . .'

'You do not need to tell me this.'

'My little sister, Mr Shakespeare. Poor Matilda. Eleven years. They took her in the night.'

'The vagabonds?'

'No. Men from a town. It was in the shire of Cambridge. I do not even know the name of the town. They came in the night while we slept. They came with bats and pole-axes and torches to light the way for their foul designs. We rose from our slumber and gathered our few belongings and ran and ran, as we had done many times before. But there was a fog and the night was dark, and I lost Matilda. I lost her, then heard her voice cry out. I think she had stumbled and fallen and the men were on her like ravening animals. I ran in the direction of her voice, but I became tangled in thorns and could not find a path. In the distance, growing fainter, I heard her as they carried her away. She was pleading, screaming "No, please no, in God's name no." Nothing else, just that, over and over. And I could not get to her. We found her body in the morning.'

'I am so sorry.'

She wiped the tears from her face, but still they came. 'They had taken all her clothes and left her naked. She was impaled on the prongs of a dung fork. Its handle was buried into the earth like a fence pole, and she was on the other end, five feet off the ground, face down. One of the two prongs had pierced her breastbone, the other her belly. It was clear to one and all how they had used her before killing her.' She closed her eyes.

Shakespeare watched her in silence. There was nothing to say.

'There,' she said at last, looking up. 'That is my story. It is the first time I have told it, Mr Shakespeare. It is how I know about men like Charlie McGunn. It is why I know that the slavering and pawing of an evil-smelling Puritan is better than poverty.'

'It is a tale of monstrous cruelty.'

She touched his hand as if trying to break the dark spell she had woven. 'Gentle townsfolk do not know what is done in their name. Go to Bridewell one day and see how the vagabonds are treated there.'

'I know Bridewell. I know how they flog the prisoners every Friday for the entertainment of any who would pay to watch. It is not something I like.' He looked at her bowed head. He wanted to reach out and touch her. Instead, with an effort, he asked, 'Are you recovered a little, Lady Le Neve? Can I find you a kerchief?'

'It is not important.'

'Your story is not quite finished, is it? You have not told me how you came to your present pass as the lady of a great knight.'

'It was pure chance, nothing more than that. Pure chance, or perhaps an act of God, who decided I had been punished enough for one lifetime. We were by the roadside in Kent, a few weeks after Matilda's death. The camp had broken up and there were no more than a dozen of us, looking to pick in the orchards. I was sitting alone at the side of the Canterbury road when a troop of a dozen cavalry soldiers came riding our way. In the past, we would have run ten miles at the sight of the soldiers, for we knew what they might do to the women. But I no longer cared whether I lived or died or who used my flesh. And so I sat there and watched them ride along in their shining armour and mail, their pistols and swords flashing in the sun. They rode past and then the officer called them to a halt. He trotted back and leant from his saddle to me and asked me what I was doing. I suppose there was something in my looks that caught his eye, or in my voice, which was of a more refined timbre than others on the road. He asked me what my family was and I told him I was a Kett. He knew of the history of my family, for it is a famed story. He asked me whether I could read the Holy Book and play music and dance, which I could. Then he said, "Climb up here behind me, mistress."' She smiled. 'And so I did, for what did I have to fear? When you have nothing, you have nothing to lose.'

Shakespeare was not certain he believed this part of her tale; but it was of no consequence and he let it pass. More than anything, he wanted a name. 'And now?'

'Now I will tell you the name of Amy's murderer.'

Shakespeare looked at her expectantly, his face set.

'It was my husband, Mr Shakespeare. Sir Toby killed his daughter Amy and the boy Joe Jaggard. He beat them about the head with his war mace. I know this for certain, for I found the weapon in his armoury, and it was stained with the blood of his own poor daughter.'

Chapter 26

SHAKESPEARE COULD NOT sleep. He lay in his bed, eyes open, staring into the darkness. Two rooms away, Cordelia Le Neve lay in the single bed usually occupied by Andrew Woode. He wondered whether she, too, was awake.

He thought back to what she had said.

'It was a matter of honour, Mr Shakespeare. Sir Toby felt she had brought shame on his great name.'

'You think he planned it, the murder?'

'No. On the night of the feast, Winterberry got wind of the state of things and refused to pay the bride price for soiled goods. And so my husband destroyed those goods – his own daughter. He had been angry a long while, but I believe the deed itself was an impulse. He followed them with his mace and bludgeoned them when he saw them naked in the wood. He must have returned later with the poison, thinking to cover his tracks.'

'And why have you not mentioned this before?'

She had finished her wine. Slowly, she put down the goblet. 'Fear, Mr Shakespeare. I feared losing my wealth and standing – and being cast out once again into this bleak land where the nobility and gentry live in splendour, while others sleep in the ice and mud and must forage, starve and die unmourned. But most of all I feared McGunn. I know he will take vengeance for the death of Joe. If he knows my husband is the killer, he will kill us both. I thought at first that that was what you were sent for.'

Shakespeare thought back to his last meeting with McGunn. 'Find Joe's killer and I will reward you,' he had said.

'And why have you now come to me?'

'I could not live with myself,' she whispered. 'Inside I was raging, for Amy, for Matilda, for every murdered soul whose death goes unheeded, unmourned, unavenged.'

'Where is this mace, the murder weapon?'

'Still among his armaments. Still stained with gore.'

There had been no more to discuss; this was no time for small talk. 'We will go there at first light,' he said. 'Let me show you to your room.'

He had led the way. At the doorway to Andrew's room he handed her a lighted candle. For a moment their fingers touched as the candle passed between them, then he withdrew.

'Good night, Lady Le Neve,' he said, and bowed. Time hung between them like that indefinable moment when you chance upon a turning tide and are not quite sure whether it is about to ebb or flow.

She had reached out and touched his hand, held it, as if she would pull him in. But then she withdrew and smiled. 'Good night, John.'

As he turned and left her, he thought he heard her say, 'Come to me if you wish.' But he carried on walking to his own room, without looking back.

In the morning he would have to go with her to Wanstead to bring in Sir Toby for hard questioning, but now, here, naked in his solitary bed, he was wide awake and doubted he would ever sleep this night. Soundlessly, he rose and padded across towards the door of his chamber. The candle was snuffed, but he knew this room so well that he did not need light. A loose floorboard creaked beneath his bare foot as he reached the fine oak door.

He stood there, listening. He fancied he could hear breathing on the other side. His hand went to the latch and hesitated, as if he would lift it. But he pulled back and reached, instead, for the bolt. Gently he slid the bolt into its slot, sealing the door. He stood there a few moments longer, before returning to the cheerless comfort of his bed. 'Come to me,' she had said. He would not. But what if she were to come to him?

They said few words as they broke fast together on ale, three-day-old bread and some cold hard-boiled eggs. The air was charged between them, like the sky before a dry, summer storm.

As they rode out from the stables, he spotted a watcher on horseback a little way along Dowgate. Well, he would just have to follow them, for it would be impossible to evade detection while riding with Cordelia Le Neve at his side. Anyway, such matters were the least of his concerns. What worried him most was what he was going to do about Sir Toby. He had to be arrested and arraigned for murder, of course, but how was that to be effected while maintaining his relationship with Essex? McGunn, too, would have his own ideas about how justice should be dispensed on Joe's killer.

In the event, the problem of Sir Toby was taken out of his hands, for he was not at home when they arrived at Le Neve Manor.

'I am afraid I do not know where he has gone, my lady,' said Dodsley. 'He asked for his horse to be saddled up and rode off an hour since. He had a sumpter with his court attire and other accoutrements. He was riding with a purpose, as if he had a journey to make. I am certain it was not a morning's hunting.'

'Well, Mr Shakespeare,' Cordelia said. 'What will you do now?'

'Show me the mace.'

A hundred or so yards away, the horseman who had followed

them sat impassively on his horse. Shakespeare stood watching him a moment and then turned to follow Lady Le Neve into the house.

They went to Sir Toby's private office, where Shakespeare had already seen his clutter of weapons. 'Many of these armaments have been in the Le Neve family for generations.' She pointed to a cabinet against a side wall. 'It is in there.'

Shakespeare opened the cabinet. Inside, it was dark and dusty. It was packed with old iron – chain mail, a helmet covered in dents, the rusting heads of old halberds and pikes and pole-axes. To the left, barely visible, was a mace. He picked it up by the handle. It was heavy and deadly. The wooden haft was long and ornately carved, the sort used by cavalrymen, who needed longer-handled weapons than the infantry. The head was round and decorated with knobs.

'My husband has told me in the past that a Le Neve man-at-arms used that at Agincourt.'

'It seems old enough. How did you discover it?'

'I looked for it. I had my suspicions after what you had told me of the manner of their deaths.'

The iron head of the mace was coated with dried blood and strands of hair. There was an eerie silence in the room and a sense of unreality.

'I will need to take this with me. I want the Searcher of the Dead to look at it. He should be able to tell me whether this could have been the weapon that killed your daughter.'

'Take it. I cannot bear to have it in the house.'

'And your husband?'

'I do not know where he has gone or when he will be back. He goes off for days, weeks, even months at time. Much of his time is spent with Essex or at court, where wives are not welcome. No one must eclipse the sun Queen.'

'Well, get word to me if he appears. If the Searcher tells me the mace is the weapon, your husband will be apprehended. I must take my leave. There is much to do.' He looked away from her as he spoke.

'You might have come to me last night,' she said in a low voice. 'I wanted you.'

Yes, he thought, he might well have gone to her. Any man would have done. He said nothing.

'You are a rare man, Mr Shakespeare. I see the passions within you, yet you hold back where other men would not. You lead a mysterious life which I do not understand, for I am certain you are no schoolmaster.'

Shakespeare laughed, breaking the frost between them. 'But you have seen my school.'

'The school is closed down. Your family is gone. Why are you still here?'

'You ask too many questions.'

'And you give too few answers. God speed, Mr Shakespeare.' She looked at him wistfully for a fleeting moment.

Outside, his mare was watered and ready and the mace wrapped in jute sacking, bound with string. Shakespeare tied it securely at the side of his saddlebag and then mounted. Dodsley handed him the reins. Cordelia Le Neve stood on her doorstep. Shakespeare bowed his head to her, then spurred his mount forward. Further along the path, the watching horseman still sat motionless in the saddle. It was of no significance, for he had learned nothing new by watching them; Shakespeare knew, too, that he would soon lose the watcher on the way back into London.

Shakespeare kicked his mare into a gallop. He would get the mace to Peace without delay and turn his attention to the whereabouts of Boltfoot and Jack. Both were well able to take care of themselves, but it was troubling that they had not yet reported back.

Chapter 27

JOSHUA PEACE UNWRAPPED the mace and held it in his arms, mentally weighing it and estimating its killing force. He examined the round iron head and gently picked strands of hair from the coagulated blood. Carefully, he put them aside, on the central slab where he did his work.

'Yes,' he said. 'This could well be the weapon, John.'

'But you cannot be certain?'

The Searcher of the Dead smiled. 'Well, in truth, I *can* be sure. Wait just a moment.' He went through to his cool, inner room, where he kept the tools of his trade and bodies awaiting his examinations. He reappeared a few moments later with two curious-shaped pieces of hard-dried plaster.

'I took clay moulds of the regions of their heads which were injured, then cast these plaster likenesses, showing the true nature of the injuries. You can clearly see the indentations caused by the weapon, for I shaved away their matted hair.'

Shakespeare studied the plaster casts, fascinated by the detail. They had the curve of a human head and then, in the middle, a caved-in area of about four inches across, where they had been struck with great force. Inside this central indentation were multiple smaller dents where the knobs on the head of the mace would have made their mark.

'It certainly seems to be the weapon that did these injuries, Joshua.'

'But let us be certain, as I said we would.' He took the ancient mace and held the round head into each of the casts in turn. 'A perfect fit. You have your weapon, John.' From his apron pocket, he produced two little wooden boxes. One was inscribed 'ALN, female', the other 'JJ, male'. He opened them in turn and showed them to Shakespeare. 'These are locks of the hair of Amy Le Neve and her lover, Joe Jaggard. Look at their hair and compare them to the strands I just took from the head of the mace. It is impossible to say for certain that they are the same, but it is fair to say that they are similar, would you not agree?'

'Indeed.' Even with his high-born connections Sir Toby would not wriggle free of this. The evidence was plain for all to see. He had the motive, he had the weapon. 'Thank you for your diligent work, Joshua.'

The Searcher of the Dead carried the casts, the mace and the samples of hair from the crypt into the side room. Shakespeare followed him. The room was full of shelves with boxes and jars and items taken from the scenes of crimes. There were three trestle benches, with a small wooden wheel at the end of each leg, so that they might be wheeled between rooms with ease. On one of the trestles a body was laid out, covered in a shroud: a prodigiously large man, well over six feet.

Shakespeare's heart skipped a beat. 'Joshua, who is that?'

Peace began pulling back the shroud. 'I do not know his name, but he has been most foully treated. Tortured, then murdered. His body was found in the Thames, near Greenwich.'

'May I see his face?'

Peace unwound the shroud until the face was visible. The wide-open eyes, blank and dead, were brown, the hair was black and curly. He had a long, ragged beard and a dark-tanned face, stained with much blood. A wooden peg-leg was strapped to his thigh and projected downwards from just below the knee. His forearm was distinguished by a long and vivid red scar.

Shakespeare let out a long sigh of relief. It was not Jack Butler. From his size and shape, Shakespeare had thought it might have been his manservant. Instinctively he crossed himself as, so often, he saw Catherine make the sign.

'Look at these injuries, John. Most curious. He was killed in a manner I have not seen except on the battlefield when I was in the Netherlands back in '85. Hewing and punching they call it. It is an English military thing. With your sword you first slash down on the side of the neck – the hew. Then you immediately stab upwards into the stomach, which is the punch. Hew and punch – a quick and methodical way to despatch an enemy. In the heat of a battle, a man may effectively do this time and again as the foe come at him: hew and punch, hew and punch, hew and punch. Into soft flesh and away from bone, so that the blade is not blunted so soon. No one survives it.'

'So you think a soldier inflicted these injuries.'

'Most probably. But first, they inflicted a foul and vicious torture. Using some sort of tool, his tormenter cut the webbing flesh between each of his fingers. It was done to both hands – eight savage cuts in all – leaving the hands looking like a bird's crooked talons. It would have been most horribly painful. And his tongue was cut out for good measure. If they wanted him to reveal information, that seems a strange way to get him to talk. It's not the first one like this, either. I was brought another a week ago with the exact same injuries. That body was found on the mudflats on the Isle of Dogs, close to the river where this one was found.'

'One week? Not more recent?'

'No. And he was a much smaller man.'

Shakespeare was relieved. This corpse could not then have been Jack Butler or Boltfoot; it had already been found dead before they went missing.

Peace went on: 'Given the area they were found in and the nature of their bodies – weathered faces and coarse, callused hands used to hauling on ropes day after day – I would hazard a guess that they were both mariners. And fighting ones, too. Look at this fellow, see his scars.'

Shakespeare noted the man's livid red scar across his forearm. 'Well, good luck with your inquiry, Joshua.'

The Searcher of the Dead laughed mirthlessly. 'My inquiry? What inquiry? The coroner sent me the bodies, but no one will look into the deaths of two unknown seafarers – however monstrous their torments. The constable feigns concern, but he is more interested in clearing vagabonds into Bridewell than investigating the murder of a pair of unmourned souls. That is what Londoners want – streets clear of sturdy beggars. No one will notice a couple less mariners; there are plenty more to be pressed where they came from.'

'I have never heard you so bitter, Joshua.'

'Put it down to the heat, John. That and the prospect of the pestilence taking us all in the next few weeks.' Peace laughed again, this time with a smile and a semblance of mirth. 'Look after yourself, my friend.'

'I will – and I am certain, at least, to take the killer of Amy and Joe. They will have justice.'

'Good. Do you know the killer's name?'

'I do.'

'Just a word of caution. Ask yourself this: why did the murderer not dispose of the weapon where it would never be found? Even more to the point, why did he – or she – not at least clean the telltale gore and hair from the mace?'

'Because he did not need to,' Shakespeare said. 'As far as he was concerned, no one was ever going to suspect murder – until *you* delved into the affair.'

Boltfoot woke from his long sleep. It was night-time. The only light came from a small candle somewhere near the door. The pain was still heavy, though not as intense as it had been. All around him he heard the sound of snoring, groaning and creaking beds. How long was it since first he woke in this hospital? He had no idea. With great effort, he managed to slide from the bed on to the floor.

He felt faint, but he had to get out of here. He had to get to the house of Davy Kerk, he had to get back to Jane. Where were his own clothes? And where were his cutlass and caliver and purse? He took two steps forward, stumbled and fell across another bed, his legs buckling beneath him. The inhabitant of the bed kicked out and cursed.

Boltfoot tried to push himself up again, but he was as feeble as a baby. Two gentle hands tucked themselves under his arms. 'Oh dear, sir, you really are in a very poor way.' It was the voice of the nurse again. With practised strength and tenderness she helped him up from the bed and gently guided him back to his own.

He allowed her to lay him down, for he did not have the fight to resist.

'I must leave this place . . . my caliver . . . my cutlass.'

'Do not concern yourself with such things. They are safely kept by the hospitaller and will be returned to you when it is time to leave. Now, if you wish, I could bring you a little broth to build up your strength.'

He nodded slowly. Yes, he needed strength.

The nurse fetched a bowl and fed him with a wood spoon. His mother had died of childbed fever and his father had raised him alone. He supposed there must have been a wet-nurse for some months, but he had no recollection of her. It was soothing, this feeding by a woman.

'Your head has been badly injured. The surgeon says the skullbone has been broken on the temple. He said it was lucky you had such a hard head. He also said you need rest.'

'I do not have time.' He had never known his mother, but in his dreams she would have been like this woman, this nurse, with her kind hands and plump, warm face. He thought he saw his mother once, in the southern Pacific Ocean when the sea raged for days without end and he believed they must all go to a watery grave together; he thought he saw her face, serene and inviting in the heart of the storm. She was beckoning him in and saying that all would be well. Yet he knew that that face was no more than a spirit, a siren; this woman, here in this hospital, was soft flesh and warm blood.

'At the very least, you will have to stay here a few days.'

Boltfoot groaned.

'A woman has called for you, sir. I had thought she was the woman who found you and had you brought here. She said your name was Mr Cooper. Am I right in thinking that it is you?'

'Yes, I am Boltfoot Cooper. What manner of woman was it? Was it my wife, perchance? Was she with child?'

'No, not with child.'

'Then she was not my wife.'

'She called herself a friend and asked after your welfare. She is not here now but she will come again in the morning to check that you still breathe. She was very concerned.'

'Tell me, what was her appearance?'

'Well, I would say she was fair of hair with blue eyes. Pretty, most would call her. Yet she did seem nervous, frightened even. She was very worried about you.'

It sounded like the woman in Davy Kerk's house, the one that claimed to be his daughter. But why would she be worried about him? Was it Kerk that hammered him to the ground? There was only one way to find out. Sleep more – this night at least – regain his strength and his weapons, then watch and wait for her.

Chapter 28

FROM DOWNRIVER, a volley of gunfire suddenly burst forth in the early morning air, then a great peal of church bells commenced. As Shakespeare was about to step into a tilt-boat at the Steelyard stairs, the gunfire increased and drew closer. Churches all along the route of the river took up the peal.

'She's off,' one of the watermen said. 'We must hasten or we'll be pushed aside and waiting forever while she passes.'

'We have missed our chance,' Shakespeare said brusquely, stepping back from the boat. 'I will ride instead.'

After a night of troubled sleep, followed by a solitary breakfast foraged from the buttery, he was brittle and on edge.

The Queen's summer progress had reached London from its starting point of Greenwich. It would make the first part of its long journey westward by river, then the bargeloads of luggage and furniture – including her own great bed – would be transferred to wagons for the road.

Shakespeare had business at the Tower, but waited a short while to watch the river spectacle.

The royal vessels drew ever closer. The advance guard was already forging ahead, clearing river traffic for the Queen's barge. At the banks of the river, moored boats were slapped back and forth by the wash from the royal traffic.

In the vanguard was a vessel full of noise and fury: a dozen drummers beating as one, flutes singing, trumpets blaring and gunfire exploding. Then came the Queen herself. She sat in state, alone in the front cabin of her fabulous vessel with its gleaming windows of glass, the frames painted with gold. Above her, a red satin canopy billowed against the sun and the river breeze. Ten or more royal pennants streamed behind the dazzling boat. This barge was tugged by ropes attached to another, slightly smaller, vessel, in which twenty-one of the strongest oarsmen in England pulled hard to maintain the craft's astonishing speed. This was no leisurely summer outing on the Thames; the Queen wanted to get well upriver by day's end.

Shakespeare had seen inside the Queen's barge on other occasions and was familiar with its lines; in a cabin adorned with coats of arms, she would be seated on a cloth-of-gold cushion and her feet would be rested on a crimson rug. All about her would be fragrant blossoms and petals and garlands of eglantine roses.

Now, as he gazed, he thought he made out Sir Robert Cecil and his father, old Burghley, in the second cabin. Was Essex there too? If Essex was gone on the progress, he would have to follow straightway to keep him observed. Nothing – not lost colonists nor murders – could come before that.

As the gilt prow of the royal barge cut smoothly through the water, the Queen waved to her people. Crowds had massed along the riverside to wave back to her. There were shouts and cheers, too, from mariners, dockers, ship workers and fishermen aboard their little scutes. Hats were thrown into the air.

The whole river was alive with colour, cheering, music and the noise and smoke of exploding gunpowder. All the bells of London and Southwark rang with frenzied joy, as if knowing that this would be the last time for many months that they would toll; after this day they would be silenced as a mark of respect to the victims of the plague. It was, thought Shakespeare, the unacknowledged spectre that hung like a limp black flag over this pomp and pageant.

Behind the royal barge came a host of other vessels. Fireworks flew from some, gunfire erupted from muskets and cannons in others. And more drums beat out their frantic noise. Courtiers, retainers, clergy, officers of state, the royal guard – all were part of the display. One man, however, was certainly not there: the man Shakespeare wished to see this morning. The man behind the Roanoke colony, a man disgraced and under arrest for an altogether separate matter. His crime? Marriage without the Queen's permission.

In his cell, high in the impregnable battlements of the Tower, Sir Walter Ralegh watched the royal progress along the river in full and awful awareness of his fall from grace. He was shunned by his Gloriana, his soul's heart, his joy, his bitch queen, the mother cow from whose teats all the treasures of the world flowed into his ever-gaping maw.

This prison was now Ralegh's home. He had committed the crime of secretly marrying Bess Throckmorton, one of the Queen's maids-of-honour, and was paying the price. Bess was here in the Tower, too, though they were separated. Their new-born child, a son called Damerei, was elsewhere with a wet-nurse.

In a fit of dramatic pique, worthy of some playhouse production, Ralegh had set upon his keeper, demanding a boat and oars to row himself to the Queen's barge, where he might beg her forgiveness. Daggers were drawn, but the whole ill-considered act fizzled and died out like a squib dropped into the Thames.

Ralegh, so tall and handsome despite his forty years, sat despondent like some grandfather at the hearth awaiting comfortable death. He could no longer bear to look from the little window. He could not shut out the noise, though: the crowds cheering, the drums beating, the bells chiming, the great roar of gunshot. How he loved her; how he loathed her. He wished himself away from the rotten, festering court forever. He would rather live obscurely in the wild, untarnished innocence of the West Country, with his wife and their boy.

John Shakespeare presented himself at the gatehouse with his letter-patent signed by Essex.

'Swisser-Swatter? I wouldn't wager on him wanting to see you, Mr Shakespeare,' the guard said. 'I hear tell he's in a temper most foul and wishes death and torment to the whole world.'

'I shall take my chances.'

'As you wish. It's your death.' The guard trundled off to make inquiries.

Shakespeare smiled. Everyone in London knew of the provenance of Sir Walter Ralegh's nickname. He had been debauching a young lady of the court against a tree, so the tale went, and she, being maidenly, cried, 'Sweet Sir Walter. No, sweet Sir Walter . . . sweet Sir Walter . . . sweet Sir Walter' until, rising to uncontrollable ecstasies of pleasure, she was heard to mumble and moan, then cry out *'Swisser Swatter, Swisser Swatter!'* over and over, as she clutched him to her and crumpled at the knees.

The guard reappeared. 'He says he will see you, sir. He wishes to kill someone this day, so you will serve his purpose.'

'Very droll, guard.'

The guard laughed. 'You think I jest, Mr Shakespeare, but blood has already been shed up there in his little eagle's nest this day. I wish you well of your visit – and if not a long life, then a painlessly quick death.'

Shakespeare was escorted up to the high cell, where he was

kept waiting in a little anteroom until the keeper ushered him in.

At six foot, Ralegh was no taller than Shakespeare, yet he dominated his comfortable gaol. He filled his jewel-encrusted white satin doublet with lean muscle. His face had a natural backward tilt so that his sharp little beard thrust forward. Each finger of his hand was adorned with diamonds, and in one ear he affected a single pearl earring. At his waist was a dagger with a hilt of gems. On a settle, beneath the window, another man in rich attire sat with his feet up, lounging against a gold-threaded green bolster. He was nursing his hand, which was swathed in a blood-stained bandage. Shakespeare recognised him as the poet Arthur Gorges; clearly it had been his blood that had been shed.

Shakespeare bowed to Ralegh and glanced at Gorges in acknowledgement of his presence.

In response, Ralegh looked Shakespeare up and down as he might assess a horse. 'And you are?' he said at length, in a voice dripping with languor, as if this whole day were all too much effort.

'John Shakespeare, Sir Walter. I am an agent of my lord of Essex.'

'And what, pray, does Essex want from me? Has he sent you to twist the knife in the wound, to gloat at my undoing?'

'No, Sir Walter, nothing of the kind.'

'Well, have your say, and I shall be the judge of his motive. His *true* motive.'

A servant appeared with a tray of small silver goblets and a silver flask and poured a healthy measure of dry wine into three of the goblets. While the man served them, Shakespeare told of his commission to find Eleanor Dare. 'And that is why I am come to you, Sir Walter,' he concluded, 'for you must know more about the lost colony than any man.'

'The colony is *not* lost, Mr Shakespeare,' Ralegh said emphatically. 'The City of Ralegh in the colony of Virginia is a flourishing town, a splendid city to rival and better anything the Spaniard can do in the southern estates of the New World. There are great buildings there in my city – schools, government houses, a magnificent church and markets – every bit as fine as those to be found in London itself. And yes, Mistress Dare is most certainly alive, and a fine wife to Mr Dare, I am sure, and mother to their little daughter, Virginia, a healthy five-year-old. There is no reason to think otherwise.'

'But when Governor White and the supply ships returned to Roanoke—'

'The colonists were never meant to stay on Roanoke. They had moved. Do you know *nothing* of the affair?'

'Indeed, I do, Sir Walter. But there is this report of Eleanor Dare in London.'

'Lies. Lies intended to undo me. Lies intended to have my royal patent revoked. I will hear no more. If your filthy blood were not likely to befoul my cell, I would slit you open. When I am released, I shall take ships to Virginia and I shall bring back the fruits of this majestic enterprise. There will be great carracks laden with sugar, with gold, with tobacco and silver and spices and pearls. I have faith in my goodmen and women every one. I know in my heart that they are not only alive but thriving.'

'I pray you are right, Sir Walter.'

From the settle, Gorges joined the talk. 'What about the man White, Walter?'

'John White is a fool and a coward. I should never have put him in command. And then to just leave the colonists like that, with no leader . . . but they are doubtless better off without him.'

'Where is he now?'

'Ireland. Best place for him. Land of bogs and barbarous

mongrels. The savages of the New World are gentlemen by comparison. I am glad White has left. As to the rest, there is no evidence that anything untoward has become of them. I am certain they are living at peace with the savages, and soon I shall prove it to the world. That will do for the doubters and gloaters like Cecil and Essex.'

'Sir Walter, we know for certain that the colonists were no longer at Roanoke when White took the supply ships back there. So where do you think they have gone?'

'First to the Croatoans, for help to get them over that winter, then up the coast to the great bay where it was intended all along that they should go. It is there that they have built this City of Ralegh. There is no cause for doubt about this, none at all.'

Shakespeare had been sipping the sack and now finished it in one gulp. It was pointless arguing with Ralegh's fantasy; to do so would merely bait him to violence.

'Thank you for your time, Sir Walter,' he said. 'And you, Mr Gorges.'

Gorges grinned. 'Ask yourself, Mr Shakespeare, who might have bruited about this mad tale of a woman flying the ocean – and to what purpose? There is some mischief here. Do you not agree, Walter?'

Suddenly Ralegh fell into a rage. 'God damn their black hearts to hell! They wish me away from her presence forever. Yet they will both pay for this. Cecil and Essex – Satan and Beelzebub. Go to, Mr Shakespeare. Begone with you.'

Yes, Shakespeare thought wryly, you liken Cecil and Essex to the devil – yet all the while men call *you* the Great Lucifer and the Beautiful Demon . . .

'Before I depart, Sir Walter, I would ask you one last thing. The corporation – your investors – are they still confident?'

For a moment, Shakespeare truly believed he would be set

upon and stabbed to death, so dark a fury crossed Ralegh's brow. 'The corporation?'

'Men such as Jacob Winterberry.'

'Winterberry and the corporation? They are less than dogs, they are beneath the snakes that crawl upon their bellies and eat dust. Talk not to me of corporations and Winterberrys. I will have none of them.'

'But have they not put in all the money necessary?'

'Aye, and some do try and sue for it. I know not what Winterberry has to do with this visit of yours today, Mr Shakespeare, but I wish only evil to him. He risks his money, but would he ever hazard his life? Never did I meet a man of such small parts – his character, his form. I thank the guiding spirit when I hear that his ships do not come in. The devil's canker on him and all his benighted ilk.'

Chapter 29

As SHAKESPEARE RODE back through the narrow city streets, the sound of the river fanfare receded to a distant hum. He was frustrated; the visit to Ralegh had yielded little reward. Nor was he looking forward to his next visit, to Essex House, but he had to discover Essex's movements.

Outside the entrance, the usual band of Irish beggars clamoured around demanding money. They threw obscenities and profanities at him when he ignored them. Inside the courtyard, the halberdier guards gave his letter-patent a cursory glance and waved him through.

Up in the turret room, he found his former colleagues. Francis Mills gave him a look of disdain and continued to eat the hunk of bread and cheese that he had on a trencher before him, Phelippes barely looked up from a paper he was reading. Only Arthur Gregory stammered a welcome.

Shakespeare touched his arm. 'A word if I may, Mr Gregory.'

'Of course, Mr Sh-Shakespeare.'

They went through to the side room.

'How may I help you?'

'The matter is this, Mr Gregory: do you know whether the Earl is leaving with Her Majesty? What are his plans?'

Gregory put a finger to his lips. 'He is in the most monstrous s-s-sulk, Mr Sh-Shakespeare,' he whispered, 'though you did not hear that from me.'

'Does that mean he is still here at Essex House?'

'For the moment. He is furious at being passed over for the chancellorship of Oxford and believes C-C-Cecil did for his chances. He had set great store by it and blames him – and her. But she *will* s-s-send for him, and then he will have to go to her, like an obedient puppy. Yet he will s-s-seethe inside.'

'Then he could leave at any moment.'

They went back into the main room. Phelippes looked up through his thick, heavily scratched glasses and gave a smile that only served to make his pox-ridden face more grotesque. 'Mr Shakespeare, I have a puzzle for you. I remember of old that you were a fine intelligencer with a wit that could solve any manner of mysteries.' He pushed a paper towards him. It was written in code. A code very like the book code he had used to communicate with Sir Robert Cecil. A chill of ice slid through Shakespeare's blood. It was not *his* hand – but was it Cecil's?

'Tell me, pray, what in God's world this piece of correspondence might mean.'

Shakespeare had an awful sense of foreboding as he examined the message. Never once in all their years working together for Walsingham had Phelippes ever asked him for assistance.

'You are the code-breaker, Mr Phelippes.'

'Indeed, I am, and I have never been bested yet. This looks like a book code, don't you think? You know what a book code is, do you not, Mr Shakespeare?'

'How could I not, having worked for Mr Secretary so long?' Shakespeare kept his face impassive. He knew Phelippes was scrutinising him for a reaction.

'So we need to find the book. What sort of book would you use?'

'Whatever came to hand. There must be thousands of books. You could work a lifetime on it, Mr Phelippes. What is the context? How did you come by it? Do you think it Spanish?'

Phelippes's lips curled into an oily smile. 'A man in the street brought it to me. Ah well, I thought you might have an idea. Fear not, I shall find the answer soon enough. But perhaps *you* have lost your edge, Mr Shakespeare.'

'Perhaps I have.'

Shakespeare looked away. His eyes drifted to the shelves behind the great code-breaker, and he wondered whether *The Profitable Art of Gardening* was among the books piled there.

Phelippes smiled his unctuous version of a smile once more. 'No, it was none of those. I shall just have to keep looking.'

Shakespeare's heart sank. Had Butler brought this message here – or had it been wrested from him? Did Essex and his intelligencers have doubts about him? He was at the heart of their headquarters and must be vulnerable, yet found himself angry, not scared. Did Phelippes, Mills and Gregory know what they were engaged in? Did they have an inkling of the plot against the crown?

McGunn appeared in the turret-room doorway, his hand gripping the hilt of his sword, still sheathed. 'Shakespeare, where in death's name have you been?'

Shakespeare did not recoil at the grinding, murderous voice. He met McGunn's stare full on and gathered himself in. He would show no fear to this man. 'Finding Eleanor Dare for your lord and master.'

McGunn gazed at him with scorn, his gold earring catching the sunlight. 'I have no lord, nor any master. I say again, where have you been? Meddling in matters that are none of your concern. Come with me, Shakespeare.'

McGunn led him down from the turret room to a private study on the floor below. The two men stood facing each other like a pair of dogs about to be unleashed.

'So have you found her? That is all I want.'

Shakespeare was stiff with rage. 'This day I have been with Ralegh, who is much discomfited but can shed no light on the question of the lost colony. He seems to think it not lost at all, but is a thriving city, rich in gold and tobacco.'

McGunn scoffed. 'He thinks nothing of the sort; he wants to keep his patent.'

'But I believe I have another sighting of Eleanor Dare, by her brother-in-law, Foxley.'

'Ah, so you have found *him*, have you? Well, that is a start. Where is he?'

Shakespeare lied without hesitation. 'I believe he is in a house at St Dunstan's Hill, called Tiler's Cottage. Though that is not where I found him.'

'And where did you find him?'

'In the St Magnus Cross pillory.'

McGunn smiled at last. 'Well done, Shakespeare, though I am sure a blind infant could have done as much. Bring him to me. I will question him.'

'No, I will do the questioning. I do things my way, McGunn.'

McGunn laughed. 'Is that what you think?'

'And I am certain, too, that my man Cooper is on to something, or he would be home by now.'

'Where was he last?'

'Gone to Southwark to seek out a man who was on the *Lion*. Also to find Simon Fernandez, the commander of the ships that took the colonists.'

McGunn studied Shakespeare as a physician might examine a stool for evidence of evil humours. 'You do not know where he is, do you? Your own man is lost and you are alone. But I know where he is, Shakespeare. I have people who tell me things.'

Shakespeare felt the frozen fingers of fear claw into his heart. 'What do you know of Boltfoot, McGunn? What have you done?'

'The world is full of hungry maggots. Men who will do my bidding in return for morsels to gnaw on. Your Cooper has served his purpose.'

'McGunn, if you are a man, tell me what you know.'

'Stow it, Shakespeare. I will tell you nothing. But you tell me: have you found Joe's killer – or are you merely swiving the girl's mother? Is your bed become so barren and cold that you must warm it with the soft flesh of another man's wife? Would you like Mistress Shakespeare to hear of your wanton midnight ramblings?'

'I care nothing for your threats, McGunn. And if I knew the killer of your base hireling, why would I tell you?' Shakespeare moved a step closer to McGunn. The Irishman's fist came up and would have cracked Shakespeare's nose and teeth, but he was expecting the blow and stepped sideways. The punch hit nothing but air. McGunn's fleshy, pulpy face was suffused with rage and he lunged forward as if he would throttle Shakespeare. But he was not quick enough.

Shakespeare had his poniard from his belt, its needle-sharp tip at McGunn's throat. McGunn stood a moment, his face so close to Shakespeare's that their breath mingled. Then he pulled back and laughed.

'I would kill you for talking about Joe like that, Shakespeare. He was no base hireling, but a good lad, a prizefighter and mine own.'

'Your son?'

McGunn was silent.

'If he was your boy, I should have thought you would wish

the matter resolved. Give me Boltfoot and I will bring the killer to justice.'

McGunn snorted derision. 'I do not need you for that. I will avenge Joe without the aid of a mewling English girl-boy.' McGunn raised his hand and gently eased the poniard away from his throat. 'Put up your little dagger, Shakespeare. I would kill you, for you and Boltfoot Cooper have served your purpose and are dead men waiting to happen, but Essex seems to think you still have something to offer him. You are fortunate.'

'I want to see him. Now.'

'He will see no one. But the idle wench will. Lady Rich wants to see you this afternoon at three of the clock. Perchance she has heard of your adulterous ways and wishes for some jack-saucery herself. I shall enjoy telling your wife about your lewd excursions.'

'I have no idea what manner of man you are, McGunn, but I tell you again, you do not scare me.'

McGunn shrugged his shoulders nonchalantly. 'Well, I shall have to teach you some fear then. Remember this: I know where your family has gone. That groom in your stables is talkative. I do not think he likes you well. And did I tell you about my man Slyguff? He has a nice way with the tanner's shears, for he used to work in the leather trade back in Ireland. For all I know he may already be on his way to a little town in the middle of nowhere in the far north, taking his sharp shears with him.'

Shakespeare moved hurriedly through the high halls and narrow passages of Essex House, out towards the warmth of the sun to gather his thoughts. He did not fear McGunn for himself, but the mention of his family – and his knowledge of where they had gone – filled him with dread.

At the front steps of the great mansion, Shakespeare almost walked straight past his brother.

'John, are you here again?'

He turned at the familiar voice and embraced his younger brother, then held him at arm's length so that he could look into his fresh, laughing face. 'God, but it is good to see you, Will,' he said. Someone in this mad, dissembling world he could trust.

Chapter 30

THE MERMAID IN Bread Street boomed with singing and shouting and reeked of ale, sweat and tobacco smoke. They ordered a pitcher of muscatel wine from the pot-boy, then went outside to the slightly more savoury air of the teeming street.

They leaned against the tavern wall, beneath the garish, painted sign of a fair-haired sea siren.

'Are you well, John?'

'Well enough. And you?'

'They have closed the theatres. Some foolish brawl near the Rose gave the Council the excuse they wanted.'

'I am sorry to hear that, Will. I am sure they will open again soon.'

'I fear the worst. This coming plague will close them for longer. I am told the mort bills rise week by week. That is why I slime around the houses of Essex and Southampton like a hungry serpent. I accept patronage where I can get it, for I must eat. And you, John, what takes you to Essex House?'

Shakespeare had been wondering how much to tell his brother; he did not wish to burden him with dangerous knowledge.

'It is complex.'

'John, I do believe you are at your old tricks again.'

The pot-boy arrived with their pitcher and two beakers. After he had poured the liquor, Shakespeare gave him threepence for the muscatel and a drinkpenny for himself.

'This is difficult, Will,' Shakespeare said at last, after they had both taken a good draft of the powerful, spicy wine. 'I would tell you everything I know, for I trust you with my life, but I do not think it in your best interests.'

'I do not wish to know anything. Your life is not for me, John,' Will said, but suddenly his manner changed. He looked around the passers-by and the carters in the street and the other drinkers crowding around the Mermaid door. He lowered his voice and spoke close to his brother's ear. 'Because I love you, John, I must tell you things that might change your mind about Essex and those around him. All is not as it seems.'

'Will, I was there at the summer revel. I saw the masque, as did you.'

'Indeed. But that is not the worst of it, brother. I must confess to you that I have traded most perilously in pursuit of preferment.'

Shakespeare tensed. 'Was it *you* that wrote the masque?'

'No, no. I told you, Robert Greene was the coter. I hope I am not *that* foolish.' He stopped. 'You should know, John, by the by, that Greene has died, having been taken ill after a dish of pickled herrings.'

'Perhaps they were soused in poison. He always lived dangerously. But what, pray, are *your* concerns, William?'

His voice lowered again. 'I have composed certain odes of love and correspondence of the heart.'

'Yes? And does Anne know of this?'

'Do not jest, brother. This is not about me. It was a serious error. At first I had thought I was merely pandering to the whims of noble men. A game of love, if you like. I penned the odes in good faith, believing them to be for the wooing of some young lady's maid of the court whom my lord of Essex wished to take and ravish.'

Shakespeare saw the way this was going. 'But something happened to make you change your mind.'

His brother nodded. 'By chance, I discovered for whom they were intended. I was in the picture gallery at Essex House with my lord of Southampton. There were others about, including my lady Rich. She had with her one of my odes, sealed and ready to despatch. She waved the paper in front of my face and said mischievously that my honeyed words would lure any maid to a man's bed, but when her messenger appeared and took the missive he said to her, "Another one for Mr Morley at Shrewsbury House, is it, my lady?" She looked at him as though she would happily cut the pizzle from his person and thrust it down his throat to silence him. I affected not to have heard a thing.'

Shakespeare was thunderstruck.

'Have you nothing to say, John? You must realise which young lady resides at Shrewsbury House?' Will lowered his voice yet more, to an urgent whisper, and moved closer to his brother's ear. 'A young lady with royal pretensions, even named by some as first in line.'

'I am quite aware who lives at Shrewsbury House, Will. I cannot believe you have got involved in such a thing as this.'

'I told you, I thought it but bawdy sauce.'

'You have no idea how perilous this is.' Shakespeare was angry now, and desperately concerned for his brother's safety. He had written verses for Essex to woo Lady Arbella Stuart. It was tantamount to treason. It did not seem too great a leap to believe this Morley might be the spy that Walsingham had put in Arbella's company to watch her. If so, then he had now transferred his allegiance to Essex's intelligence group, and was passing his letters of passion to the impressionable girl.

'Of course I know the danger,' Will said, sounding as

annoyed. 'That is why I have told you of it. You must extricate yourself from this circle, as I am doing. And I must tell you that I know this Christopher Morley who receives the letters from Essex. He has been at Southampton House, making cow eyes at my lord there. John, this man Morley is poison. Pure poison. He fancies himself a poet, but he is less than that. Every instinct tells me he is not to be trusted. You would never know which side he was on.'

Shakespeare gritted his teeth. He had met many such men in his years with Walsingham. They were staple fare in the intelligencers' world; men who sold secrets to both sides and owed loyalty to none. But what had Will got into here, treating with such people? He was not equipped to be embroiled with double-dealers. 'God's blood,' was all he said.

'John?'

'Will, do not fret for me, think of yourself. You do not know this world. What if Mr Morley has your verses? What if he decides to use them to his own ends? Worse – what if Arbella is found in possession of them? These loving words of yours could bring you to the scaffold. *You* are the one in danger. You must tell no one else of this. Nor must you let anyone of Essex's circle realise that you understood what was said. Affect ignorance. Your life may well depend on it.'

Jack Butler was a strong man, yet the bonds that held him to the chair were stronger. In the distance he heard the call of seabirds and the barking of dogs, but no human voices to comfort him. He had no notion of how long he had been here in this forlorn, forgotten place. The hours had drifted into days and the pain into a numb nothingness.

He looked down at the bloody, throbbing mounds that had once been his hands. As he gazed at them, they seemed to be no longer part of him.

When the men had seized him, not far from Dowgate, on his return from Sir Robert Cecil, they had asked him one thing only. 'Who gave you the letter?' Nothing else. They had said it once and never again. Then they had brought him here, tightly bound in the back of a cart, and started their diabolical work.

How long, he wondered, before they came to him again – Slyguff with his shears and McGunn with his sword of Spanish steel? 'Your twinkly toes next, Butler,' McGunn had said, laughing.

Butler shuddered. His throat was parched. He could not even shout out.

How long before he told them what they wanted to know, that the encrypted message he was bringing to Shakespeare had come from Sir Robert Cecil? Only his silence had kept him alive this long. He knew he would die here and he wished he could endure the pain. But he could not. No man could. He would tell them what they wished to hear, even though the telling would hasten his own death.

Shakespeare ran through the streets down to the river, where he pushed to the front of the queue for a wherry with the call, 'Queen's business! Queen's business here!'

The watermen who took his fare were a sour-tempered pair of middle-aged men who went about their rowing like reluctant donkeys at the turn-mill.

'Row faster, wherryman,' Shakespeare demanded of the senior of the two, a grey-haired curmudgeon with a mouth that turned down as if eternal winter had arrived.

'If you want faster, it'll cost you double. What's the hurry? We'll all be dead of the pestilence by summer's end.'

'Aye,' said his mate. 'All but the nobility and gentry and merchants, God curse their lily-white livers. They're all off to their country estates and palaces to dine on dainty dishes and finger each other's wives.'

It was the best part of three-quarters of an hour, accompanied by a dunghill of complaints about the plight of London and the deceit of foreigners, before the grand edifice of Shrewsbury House finally emerged from the heat haze on the north side of the river.

He noted immediately that all the great windows that fronted the Thames were shuttered. Shakespeare gave the watermen their due but no tip – which caused yet more grumbling – then strode around to the postern gate where he had entered before. The guard recognised him. 'Ah, good day, Mr Marvell,' he said. 'I am afraid you have missed her ladyship. She departed in haste at midday yesterday.'

'Gone where?'

'To Derbyshire, sir. Hardwick Hall.'

'And is the Lady Arbella with her?'

'Indeed, yes, master.'

'And the countess's staff and tutors?'

'Why, yes, most everyone. The train follows piecemeal. They will go by stages.'

'Is Mr Morley with them? Christopher Morley, one of her tutors.'

The guard turned to a sheaf of papers and ran his finger down a list with scores of names, reading them out loud with difficulty. 'Jas. P, Tom. L, Matt. P . . . here you are, Mr Marvell.' He handed the manifest to Shakespeare. 'Chris. M, tutor.'

Something jangled in Shakespeare's brain. Chris M? And then it clicked into place, like a key into a lock. The warning Catherine told him about, the one from Anne Bellamy, the embittered woman who had connived in the trap set for Father Southwell: *You will all drown in chrism.* It had meant nothing at the time, but then that was perhaps the intent.

Was it just a grotesque little riddle, the sort of crass humour Richard Topcliffe delighted in? If so, it meant Topcliffe knew something: something, perhaps, that he had learned from an informer inside Southampton House.

Shakespeare walked away. It was clear his brother was hopelessly compromised. Shakespeare breathed deeply. He must steel himself and return to Essex House. He had an appointment with Lady Rich. It was a meeting that filled him with trepidation, for he knew he would have to lie, conceal, and lie yet more to delve into the corrupt heart of the Essex circle so that he might watch the magnificently flawed earl as closely as one of Sir Robert Cecil's hawks. And somehow find some kind of evidence against Essex – evidence that would *not* implicate his own brother and take him to the scaffold.

Chapter 31

PENELOPE RICH WAS at her ablutions in her private chamber. She stood naked in front of a copper bowl that rested on a small table, attended by two maids.

As Shakespeare entered the room, the maids were rubbing her arms and legs with a cloth and a soap ball. Her breasts were still well formed despite the birth of six children and she made no attempt to cover them. She looked up, unashamed. 'Come in, Mr Shakespeare, come in.'

Though the day was hot, a fire of ash wood and sweet-smelling herbs roared in the hearth. 'The herbs are to keep the pestilence at bay, Mr Shakespeare. Dr Forman tells me I must burn rosemary, bay and juniper. He gives me much more advice besides, some of which is not so pleasant. I do not mind sniffing and sucking oranges and lemons to ward off the evil contagion, but I cannot abide the flavour of wormwood in wine vinegar, nor the chewing of garlic and gentian root. In truth, I would rather die than partake of such things.'

Shakespeare stood awkwardly a few feet inside the door. He had never seen anything quite like this room. Her bedchamber was completely draped in black and gold. Even the bedding was black, as were the cypress-guarded curtains that hung from the four carved oak posts around it.

'Water,' she shouted suddenly. A footman came scuttling in

with a bowl of clean water, which he exchanged for the bowl of dirty, soapy water. Penelope's maids immediately proceeded to rinse the soap from her body, splashing water all over the wood floor, then dabbing at her with a large, dry sheet of linen. She was, thought Shakespeare, a magnificent specimen of womanhood.

'Bring me a gown.'

A maid hastened through an inner doorway and returned immediately with a long linen jacket, embroidered in silver and black, which she held out to her lady. Penelope slipped it on and tied it loosely at the front, so that the soft mounds of her breasts were still visible.

One of the maids began to comb her lady's fair hair, while the other set to painting her face with powders and brushes. Penelope stood regally between them accepting their ministrations.

'Now, then, Mr Shakespeare, my brother has asked me to knock some sense into your head. He would have you as his chief intelligencer, but he is told by Mr McGunn that you are fluttering about like a silly girl who cannot decide whether to allow a handsome knight to deflower her.'

Shakespeare was sweating, both from the heat of the fire and from a deep feeling of unease. 'My lady, I am greatly honoured by your brother's offer.'

'Then may I tell him you are agreed?'

Shakespeare hesitated. 'I had thought,' he said, meeting her piercing gaze, 'that my lord of Essex employed Mr Anthony Bacon in that position.'

'Indeed, he does work for my brother, and you would be required to cooperate fully with him. But your roles will be very different. Mr Bacon has spent many years on the continent, where he has built up an unparalleled group of contacts. But he does not have your experience in the day-to-day running of an intelligence-gathering network here on home soil. The Spanish will try to come at us again, Mr Shakespeare – both at sea and secretly, with dag and blade. So we must strike out and destroy them first. No one knows the ways of these Spanish intrigants better than you. You have smelled them out before; find their stink for us again.'

'My lady, you overstate my worth.'

'Mr Shakespeare, I believe I know you better than you know yourself. There are those who would sue for peace. Men who would lick the Spanish king's boots. I know you are not of that ilk, for you were of a mind with Mr Secretary.'

'Those days are gone.'

'We need men such as you. We have heard much about you and we all admire you greatly. My brother gathers together the best minds in the land to carry on the work of the late Mr Secretary and wishes you to be part of it. One day he will be Principal Secretary, and those loyal to him will be ministers of the crown. In the meantime, the Spaniard beats at our door, Mr Shakespeare. He plots to snatch our throne and rule us as once he did with Bloody Mary. He would impose his vile inquisition on us and burn us all as heretics. Is that not worth fighting against?'

'Of course, my lady.'

She waved her maids away and they scuttled from the room like mice discovered in the cheese cratch.

'Mr Shakespeare,' she said once the maids had shut the door. 'There are those governing this country who feign friendship towards my brother, all the while twisting the knife into his back. They pretend strength against the Spanish, all the while treating with Parma for peace. They speak out for England, all the while offering the crown to James of Scotland. You are no fool, you know of whom I speak.'

She was talking of Sir Robert Cecil and his father, Lord Burghley. Shakespeare inclined his head. He was not about to acknowledge that he understood the gist of what she said.

Penelope sighed, a long weary sigh such as a mother might produce when her little boy fails once again to do his chores. Her voice softened. 'Mr Shakespeare, you are an exceeding handsome man.' She took his right hand in both hers and held it to her breast, his fingers within the lapel of her gown against her skin. 'Do you feel my heart beat in here? Is this not a heart of England, beating *for* England?'

As once before in the garden of this stately house, he caught the heady whiff of her scent. She tilted her head up until their lips were but an inch apart. She seemed to hover there before him, like a ripe red plum ready to be plucked from the bough. Her black eyes never wavered from his own.

Her lips touched his and their mouths opened and kissed. His right hand stayed on her breast while his other arm encircled her and pulled her soft belly towards him. She moved her body forward at his bidding, with no resistance.

All the pent-up frustrations of these last days and weeks seemed ready to burst forth, but then she removed her lips from his mouth and held his face gently between her hands and smiled at him. 'John Shakespeare,' she said softly, 'there is time enough for this. But we have things to talk on.' She stood back.

His yard was hard in his breeches and all too obvious. She touched him there briefly with her perfectly manicured hand. 'Well, sir, I see you are, indeed, a man of stout English oak. We must look after you well.'

'My lady—' he began.

'Say nothing. Listen to me, and listen well. Think on this: our beloved Queen is old and declining. She does not have long to live – and then what? She will not name a successor. Would you have a Spanish infanta in her place, or James the son of Mary Queen of Scots as your sovereign? These are stark choices and imminent.'

'I did not believe the Queen so diminished.'

Penelope went to a console table beside one of the tall windows and, from a drawer, took out a rolled parchment. She handed it to Shakespeare.

He unfurled it slowly. As soon as it was laid out he saw that it was an astrological chart.

'It is a chart, a life chart,' she said softly, looking at him all the while. 'It displays the exact span of a life and reveals the star-divined moment of impending death. The date of this death is September the eighteenth, which is almost upon us.'

'Whose chart is this?' he asked, though he knew very well. At the top of the page he read the words *At what date will a certain person pass from this life.*

'Whose do you think it is?'

'I would rather not say. I think the mere sighting of such a piece of work could lead to the scaffold.'

She laughed. 'I had thought you a man of oak, hard and strong, Mr Shakespeare.'

'But this is treasonable, my lady. This is like a razor in the hands of an infant that will surely cut. Do you not know how dangerous this is?'

'And now you have seen it, what will you do as a loyal Englishman and subject of the crown? Will you have my head chopped off?' Penelope Rich looked at him. 'I know you under-stand the power of these things – that they are not to be treated lightly. That is why this chart is important. It is the wherewithal to save us all. It is telling us the date so that we know there is no time to lose. It is a gift from God, instructing us to act without delay to ensure the English succession. And to do so, we need every man of oak. This is your duty.'

Shakespeare could not take his gaze from the horoscope. She called it a gift from God, but he thought it more like a death warrant from the devil.

She read his thoughts and shrugged her delicate shoulders. 'I see this unnerves you.' Casually she tossed the parchment into the fragrant fire of herbs. The flames leapt up and devoured it. 'There, it is gone.'

'It is better thus,' he said. But within his heart he was cursing. He could have used that chart; it would have been the evidence Cecil sought and might have saved his brother.

'But we still know what it said. And that brings us back to you – for I now need to know your answer, John Shakespeare. Are you with us or are you against us? She is about to enter her sixtieth year. What few teeth she has are blackened stumps. Her face is held together by paint and her body is a trillibub that the slaughterman would not rate fit for pies. She cannot live long. Everyone knows that, the whole world. The chart but proves it. Would you have a strong English king or a stranger on the throne? Would you have a man who would fight the Spanish with every last drop of his blood, or be ruled by a Scotch toad and a craven cripple who would faint at a cut finger?'

'An English king?'

'My brother, Mr Shakespeare.' She looked at him searchingly. One of her fine eyebrows lifted and the corners of her mouth turned up. 'Are you really so shocked? Can you think of a finer monarch for this great realm?'

'Your brother is noble, but he is not of the blood royal.'

'Is he not? Do you not think Great Henry's blood runs through our veins?' Penelope laughed and touched the front of his breeches again. 'You seem quite deflated. Do not worry about my brother's entitlement. All will become clear. Now decide: for us, or against us. There is no middle way.'

He went down on one knee and bowed his head low in obeisance. Then he raised his face, took her hand in his and kissed it. 'I am with you, my lady. I humbly accept the position you have so graciously offered me.'

She bent and took his face between her soft white hands again and kissed him, long and deep. He wanted very much to put his hands inside her long embroidered gown, to slip his fingers between her legs, to throw her on the great black-draped bed and take her with more urgency than he had ever known, but he could not do it. His mind was willing, so was his body – almost more than he could bear – yet his soul held him back, as sure as an iron fetter keeps a man chained to a wall.

Playfully, she pushed him away. 'You are a married man and I am a married woman, John Shakespeare. Do you wish to ruin me?'

He bowed his head.

'I jest. It is the forbidden spice that makes love so piquant. Devotion without lust is like wine without sugar. Come to me in Staffordshire. My mother and I go to Blithfield and Chartley on the morrow. You will find us there until autumn, idling the days away in the gardens. Come to me by night, John, and we will instruct each other in country matters. I will show you pleasures you have never dreamed of. For the present, you must follow my brother, who is gone to court. There is much to be done.'

Chapter 32

SIMON FORMAN KNEW for a certainty that he had the plague. But he knew, too, that it was the so-called red pest, which he believed to be not quite as deadly as the black disease.

It had come on the previous day. He had lacked energy as he *haleked* a rich mercer's mistress and she had complained mightily over his poor performance.

'I come to you because my master is otherwise engaged, Dr Forman, and you can scarce keep your prick hard for me, nor attend to my needs. I had expected better of you, sir.'

'Forgive me, I am not myself this morning, mistress.'

She saw how distressed he was and softened towards him. 'No matter, Dr Forman. I am sure it is a passing thing, for I know your instrument to be like a broom handle.'

'I fear I may have some little summer sweat, mistress.' But even as he said the words, he knew the truth. He had the pestilence. He knew, too, that the cause was twofold – firstly the adverse position of Mars and, secondly, retribution for all his manifold sins, not least of which was lust. But he was not downhearted, for he had devised a cure, and who better to try it on than himself?

He bade her good day and promised to make certain of her satisfaction the next time she came, then returned to his rumpled bed.

The first appearance of the pestilence was already there by afternoon: swellings in the pits of his arms and lower down, close to his member and stones. When these swellings increased, with great purple boils, then the red lumps, it would be time for him to act. He must take a clean, sharp kitchen knife, or a dagger honed and tempered in the flame, then cut into the pustules, releasing the evil humours. The resulting raw wounds would have to be washed with boiled water, then dressed with clean muslin, tied firmly into place and changed every day. It would help, too, he was sure, to indulge in a little blood-letting. It would be an uncomfortable few days for him with none of the customary fleshly pleasures in which he delighted, but he did not fear he would die, for he was in robust health.

He heard a hammering at the door downstairs and his spirits rose. It would be Mistress Annis Noke. She would nurse him through this, bringing him broth and electuaries as and when he required.

Shakespeare was in a hurry. This was to be his last task before collecting his court attire and riding west towards the castle of Sudeley in the county of Gloucestershire, where the Queen was also heading for the fourth anniversary celebration of England's victory over the Spanish Armada.

His impatient hammering at Simon Forman's door went unanswered. At last he turned the latch and pushed. It was unlocked.

He heard a distant voice.

'Mistress Noke. I am in bed with the sweat. Will you not bring me a little spiced wine?'

Shakespeare ascended the stairs of Stone House to the first floor. In the front chamber he found the astrologer physician stretched out naked on his mess of a bed.

'Simon Forman?'

The man opened his eyes with a start at Shakespeare's voice. He sat upright and pulled his bedding around him as though it would protect him from the stab of a blade.

'I am not here to hurt you, Dr Forman. My name is Marvell. John Marvell. I am here about an astrological chart.'

Forman's shock subsided. 'Do you just walk into a gentleman's bedchamber?'

Shakespeare looked about him nonchalantly. It was a comfortable room in a sizeable house; clearly Forman must be doing well from his potions and charts. 'The door was open. No one answered. Do I find you unwell?'

'A slight summer sweat. Nothing of consequence.'

Shakespeare kept his distance. 'Well, I am sure you will cure yourself.'

Forman bridled at Shakespeare's tone. 'You sound the sceptic, Mr Marvell. Fear not. I *shall* cure myself. I can cure cankers and consumptions, sir, and a hundred other evils besides.'

'I care nothing for your physic. It is your casting of horoscopes that concerns me.'

'Mr Marvell, look at me. I am a sick man. I cannot go about casting charts for you at present. Come back to me in a fortnight, sir, and I shall see what I may do for you.'

'I am here as an agent of the Privy Council, in particular Sir Robert Cecil. It has come to the Council's attention that you did recently cast a chart requested of you by a great lady.'

The look on Forman's face could not have undergone a greater transformation if he had been hit dead centre by a crossbow bolt. The blood drained. For a man who a moment ago was laughing at the reaper's meagre efforts to kill him off with his filthy pestilence, he suddenly seemed to realise he was staring into the gaping jaws of death itself.

'You appear to have lost your power of speech, Dr Forman. I am here with orders to seize copies of this chart. If you refuse, you will be taken to Newgate and will be arraigned in the Court of Oyer and Terminer. Do you understand?'

'Mr Marvell, forgive me, I know not what you say. I am a humble physician. I can help you with the ague, I can even divine a chart to help you find the woman you should marry and tell you the best date and time to conceive a child. But who is this great lady you speak of – and what is this chart?'

Shakespeare eyed his quarry and saw he had him. 'You know very well what chart I speak of, Forman. I have seen it. It is a chart that will sever your head from your body and your entrails from their housing if you do not cooperate with me as fully as required by law. I know you understand this.'

He saw real fear in Forman's eyes. He could also tell that he was ill. Very ill. Most probably the plague.

'Mr Marvell, please, I beg of you. Have mercy for I have been slandered. I know the law and I have drawn up no chart that might be considered unlawful.'

Shakespeare did not speak for a few moments. Then he turned on his heel and strode to the door, only stopping momentarily to look at the hairy, stumpy, scared figure cowering behind his blankets.

'I shall find it myself then, Dr Forman.'

There was a door from the chamber. He went through it into another room and from there into the hall, where he found the stuff of Forman's work: his jars and vials of herbs and unspeakable alchemical substances, his charts and books and scratched papers with drawings and coded Latin notes.

Forman was close behind him, having dragged his aching body from the sickbed. 'Please, Mr Marvell, do not rummage here. This is my life's work, sir.'

Shakespeare picked up a horoscope and examined it. 'Tell me what this is.'

'It is the chart of a goodwife from East Cheap, sir. It tells her she must have her husband occupy her on the fifteenth day of her month, following the onset of the flowers, and that she will conceive a healthy boy-child. It is innocent enough, Mr Marvell, as are all my charts.'

Shakespeare tossed it carelessly to the floor. He picked up another chart. 'And this?'

'That tells a young courtier when he might find a suitable wife, sir.'

'And how much faith do your customers place in these charts, Dr Forman?'

'They have complete faith, Mr Marvell.' Suddenly, Forman's voice strengthened. 'Why should they not? Why, even the worthless College of Physicians understands that the silent movement of the stars is not to be mocked, sir. The stars are never wrong, Mr Marvell – never. Any fault must lie in man's interpretation of them. And I am not a man to make mistakes, which is why the wealthiest of merchants, the greatest of the gentry and nobility come to my humble abode and rely on me. I am, sir, the foremost exponent of this science in the modern world.'

Shakespeare screwed the chart into a ball and dropped it behind him, then moved on. He took a vial from a shelf. He read the label. 'Ash of little green frogs, Dr Forman? What is this?'

'It is as it says, sir. I beg you to be careful with it, for it is most valuable for the easing of pain in the teeth.'

Shakespeare took out the glass stopper and tipped the ash upon the carpeted floor.

Forman clutched his chest, then sank on to a settle, his mouth open and breathing heavily, his eyes closed.

'So where is the chart I require, Dr Forman? Produce it for me and I vouch that I will not use it against you. I pledge, likewise, that if you do not give it to me, then I most certainly will hold you responsible for it. What have we here?' He picked up another vial. 'Italian theriac, devil's venom for the falling sickness . . .'

Forman was gasping for breath. 'Mr Marvell, that did cost me three sovereigns to bring from the city of Milan, sir.'

Shakespeare took out the stopper and began to pour out the thick treacle. Forman tried to stay his hand, but Shakespeare pulled away from his contagious touch. 'Please, Mr Marvell,' Forman managed to say. 'I will do as you wish. But I need time. A few days, for I must redraw the chart for you and I am not well.'

'Then I will send the plague men around. This house should be closed up and crossed so that none enter.'

'I beg of you, I plead with you, sir. I will do whatever you require, but keep the plague men away. It is naught but a summer sweat. I am a physician, sir, I know these things. And I will do what you require. Just a little time.'

Shakespeare put the stopper back in the vial. Although he knew he had Forman on the rack, he knew, too, that this man was as slippery as a water serpent. 'I will be back, Dr Forman. You have this one chance to save your miserable skin. If you are alive when I return, and if you do not have that which I require, I will summon pursuivants to break this house apart, destroy all your love philtres, burn all your books and hoist you off to the lowest dungeon in Newgate. If you fail to cooperate, it will be the worst move ever you make, for you will create an enemy of Sir Robert Cecil, the one man who might take your part against the College of Physicians.'

Whether it was the word *Newgate* or *Cecil* that made Forman falter, Shakespeare was not sure, but suddenly his attitude changed. 'Mr Marvell, sir,' he began, his voice unctuous and cajoling. 'Mr Marvell, there is one other matter it is my duty to tell you, a matter which I believe might be of great interest to Sir Robert.'

Forman folded his arms across his chest and shivered though his face and forehead dripped with sweat.

'You really are not a well man, Dr Forman.'

'No, indeed, sir, I am not. But you were correct when you said in jest that I would cure myself, for I do know the way . . .'

'I wish you fortune. Now tell me, what is this other matter of which you speak?'

'The matter is this,' he said with a resigned air. 'I was asked to cast a second chart, sir. By the same great lady.'

'Another death chart?'

'No, sir, a nuptial chart, to find the most propitious date for a wedding. It is for a man born on November the tenth in the year 1567 and a young lady brought into this world on October the fifteenth 1575.'

The birth dates of twenty-four-year-old Robert Devereux, Earl of Essex, and the sixteen-year-old Lady Arbella Stuart. So Cecil was right. There was to be a wedding, and one that could only be construed as rebellion and high treason. It could end only one way: open warfare and bloodshed in the snatching of a crown.

'I will need a copy of that chart, too, Dr Forman. But tell me this: what date did the stars decide on for this wedding?'

'September the fourteenth, sir. Four days from now.'

The date, so close, hit him with the force of a gale. He did not wait to hear Forman's whimpered pleadings a moment longer but ran from the house and drove his grey mare hard through the stifling streets to Dowgate. He had to fetch his court attire and ride west to find Essex – and inform Cecil – with not a moment's delay. Four days. He had just four days to prevent a wedding that could bring England to insurrection.

But in his worst nightmares, nothing could have prepared him for what he was about to find.

Chapter 33

THE BODY OF Jack Butler was stretched out, macabre and obscene, in the school courtyard where, until recently, boys had played in their recesses from class and where they had suffered the birch when the fancy took Rumsey Blade.

Butler had been a big man and somehow his height and great barrel of a chest added outrage to the dreadful things that had been done to him.

His injuries matched those inflicted on the murder victim Shakespeare had seen in the Searcher of the Dead's crypt at St Paul's, except worse. Butler's face was coated in rust-dried blood, his hands were like talons, red and bloody and sliced with some vicious implement. His toes, too, had been mutilated. A tanner's shears? Was that what had done this? His head was near severed and his abdomen had a gaping wound. *Hew and punch.* Those were the words the Searcher, Joshua Peace, used. Hew and punch – a military method of despatching an enemy in quick order without blunting the blade or leaving any margin for error. First a slash at the neck, then the sword driven hard into the abdomen.

But there was nothing military about this death. This killing had not been done in the heat of battle. This was murder in cold blood. And not just murder but torture, for Butler's hands and feet had been sliced along the crucial web-like muscle between the digits. By the look of the coat of blood that masked the face around the mouth, the tongue had been sliced out, too.

There was something else. Cecil's code book, *The Profitable Art of Gardening*, lay on Jack's chest, pinned to him by a long thin dagger thrust through the centre of the cover and pages and through his flesh, deep into his dead heart.

Shakespeare sank to his knees before the body of his servant. He wanted to weep for him, for he had been a good man. A quiet man, but stout and loyal. He had given five years of dutiful service without a word of complaint. Shakespeare put his hands together, closed his eyes and said the Lord's Prayer. *Our Father . . .*

He touched Jack Butler's cold face and rose again to his feet. What was McGunn's true purpose in all this? Shakespeare did not believe for a moment that McGunn was protecting the Earl of Essex. The Irishman looked out for one man alone – himself.

He walked out to the stables. The groom was there. Shakespeare was in no mood for explanations. 'Get the constable here straightway, Sidesman.'

'Yes, Mr Shakespeare.' Perkin Sidesman scurried away. Shakespeare went back to the school. He found a blanket and put it over Butler's body, then went to collect his court clothes and some gold coin. By the time he returned to the yard, the constable was there. The groom held back.

Shakespeare showed the body to the law officer. 'Inform the sheriff and the coroner and get this body to the Searcher of the Dead at St Paul's. Is that clear?'

The constable, a dullard with thin hair and a distended belly, looked doubtful.

'He has been murdered, constable. His name is Jack Butler. He has been murdered in exactly the same manner as at least two other men. Tell the Searcher John Shakespeare sent you and he will explain all you need to know. Tell him a name: McGunn. Charlie McGunn. If he can be found, arrest him and hold him for questioning. He is a dangerous man. He has an accomplice, known only as Slyguff. Take him, too, and hold him.'

Shakespeare could have added that a good place to start the hunt for the two men was Essex House in the Strand, but clearly no law officer in the land would dare ask for a warrant to enter the Earl's premises. In the back of his mind, he realised this was a matter he would have to deal with himself. No one else would bring these two men to justice.

He turned to the groom. 'What did you see, Sidesman?'

'Nothing, Mr Shakespeare, nothing at all.'

Shakespeare was sure he was lying, but there was no time now to pursue it. 'We will talk in due course,' he said coldly. 'I could have you in custody this very day for I believe you may have information that will prove useful to a prosecution, but I fear the horses would not get fed and watered. Stay here. Help the constable, tell the sheriff all you know and I will see you presently. Do this and I pledge that your work here will be safe.'

Sidesman bowed his head. 'Thank you, Mr Shakespeare.'

'Now feed and water the mare, for this day I must ride harder and faster than I have ever ridden.'

At ten o'clock in the morning a reluctant Boltfoot Cooper went to the hospital chapel with the other walking-wounded patients. Sister Bridget, the nurse, had told him he must do this if he was to retrieve his weapons and purse from the hospitaller.

The preacher delivered a hectoring tirade on the price that man must pay for his manifold sins – and that price was sickness. Boltfoot listened but did not hear, for his mind was elsewhere. He wanted to be back in Long Southwark in case the unknown woman came to ask after him again.

As they left the chapel, Sister Bridget turned to him with angry eyes. 'He was saying the people of London have brought the plague on themselves, yet I know of good people who have fallen ill and died of it – godly people who never did harm to any man and kept true to His commandments. Why should He scourge the Godly and ungodly alike?'

Boltfoot grunted in agreement. The fate of Jane and their unborn child was much on his mind. He was sure she, Catherine and the children would have left London and the plague far behind by now, but he was anxious for news.

'It gets harder day by day,' the nurse continued. 'Every day we turn away more people who have the plague and send them on to the Lock Hospital in Kent Street. I cannot believe they are all the worst of sinners.' She shook her head sadly. 'It is pitiful to see their faces, for they know that the Lock Hospital is a sentence of death. Few come from there alive.'

Although Boltfoot's head was still swathed in bandages, he was in less pain and he had regained much of his strength from the beef, bread and copious ale the nurse had brought him.

'Will you take me to the hospitaller now, Sister?'

'Mr Cooper, I should be setting you to doing some carpentry today. That is the rule for those not confined to bed. The women must launder as drudges and the men must help with their craft.' She gave him one of her motherly looks, but nonetheless led the way to the hospitaller's office.

The hospitaller was a solemn man of advanced years and heard Boltfoot out. 'Indeed, Mr Cooper,' he said. 'A most unlikely tale if I might say so.' But he handed Boltfoot back his weapons, his powder horn and his pouch of balls.

Boltfoot examined them carefully. They were undamaged. He fixed his belt and cutlass about his middle, then slung his caliver over his back. Though the weapons were heavy and he was still weak, it felt good to be armed once again. He looked in his purse for gold. He had two marks and a few pence. He offered them to the hospitaller, who waved them away.

'I will not leave you impoverished, Mr Cooper. Return with money for us when you have some to spare. All gifts are gratefully received from those who can afford it.'

Boltfoot bowed. 'Thank you, Mr Hospitaller. I believe you and your establishment have saved my life. Indeed, I know it to be true.'

With the nurse by his side, he walked out through the front gate into Long Southwark, where she bade him farewell with a shake of the hand. The gateway was narrow and clogged with the stalls of butchers and other market men. The noise and stench of the place brought Boltfoot back to the jarring reality of city life after the tranquillity of the hospital. He dragged his foot behind him across the dusty road and waited in a doorway. It was, he realised, near to the spot where he had been bludgeoned. The question was, would the woman who sought him come by here this day on her way to St Thomas'?

He did not have to wait long for an answer. The fair young woman from the house in Bank End, the home of Davy Kerk, arrived carrying a basket of bread.

Boltfoot followed her as she walked around to the back gate in St Thomas' Street, where patients were usually admitted to the hospital. He observed her as she spoke to the gatekeeper. The man shook his head and she turned away, disappointed, and made her way back in the direction of the river and westwards towards her home.

Boltfoot's energy was low. His club foot slowed him more than usual. He was out of breath and his head throbbed. The woman walked briskly and it was all he could do to trail her.

He battled to go faster and had just managed to get close behind her when she reached her door. She turned, and came face to face with him. She recoiled and he put a hand to her mouth, stifling her cry.

'Open the door,' he ordered, taking his hand away from her face.

She hesitated, then removed a key from the bread basket and pushed it into the lock.

Before the lock could be turned and the latch lifted, Boltfoot heard a sound from within; the sound of a groan, a thud, a sharp cry, another thud and a muffled scream. He stayed the woman's hand, then unslung the caliver from his back and quickly primed it with powder and ball. His fingers were steady and practised. If, in the heat of battle, a man could not pour powder without spilling it, he was of no use to his captain-general or his copesmates. Boltfoot's hands had never trembled in conflict, however hot the fire.

With a nod, he signalled the woman to open the door, slowly. She was clearly frightened, but she did as bidden.

Boltfoot went in first, the light wheel-lock musket in front of him with its ornate octagonal muzzle pointing deep into the room. His cutlass swung at his hip, ready to be drawn in a second.

At the far end of the room, in a doorway, he saw the shadow of a figure, the eyes glinting at him from the gloom. For a moment it seemed as if the figure would spring to attack, but then the eyes lighted on Boltfoot's deadly firearm and the man vanished.

In the centre of the front room, draped over the table where the woman had been plucking a fowl when last Boltfoot had been here, was a body, dead but not yet still. The legs and arms dangled over the edges of the flat surface, twitching in their death throes.

Boltfoot took in the scene with sweeping glances. Behind him, the woman gasped and buckled at the legs.

There was blood everywhere. Boltfoot slipped and slid in the gore as he hurled himself at the doorway where the figure had disappeared. He found himself in a large storeroom with grain and beans and other foodstuffs. A beplumed turkey cock hung by its neck from a hook. Not far from the bird was a thick hempen rope with a hangman's noose at its end, hanging from a high rafter, swaying in the light breeze from the open back door.

Boltfoot pushed through the back door, his caliver tightly gripped in his right hand. He looked both ways down the narrow alleyway, but could see no one. The figure had gone.

He returned to the scene of carnage. The woman cowered in a corner, trying to shield her eyes from the body of Davy Kerk lying across the table. The twitching of arms and legs had all but ceased. The injuries that caused the death were evident. His head was half severed, the left side of his neck slashed with a downward sweep of a sharp blade, and there was a bloody gash to the belly.

Boltfoot put down his caliver and lifted the body from the table. The head flopped pitifully. With great effort, he laid the corpse on the floor at the edge of the room, away from the woman. He brought a blanket from the storeroom and covered the carcass as best he could. Then he picked up his weapon again.

Of a sudden, the woman stood up and dashed for the door. Boltfoot moved fast to hold her. Even in his weakened state he held her firm.

He turned her around so that she had to face him. 'I need answers. Who are you?'

'There is no time. He will kill me, and you too.'

'Who are you?'

'You know who I am.'

'Eleanor Dare?'

She nodded frantically. 'Now, please, I cannot stay here. You see what he did to Davy. He will do the same to you and he will hang me.'

The noose in the storeroom. She had not even seen it, yet she knew that she was to be hanged.

She tried again to break free. Her terror was giving way to fury. 'You led him here! You brought him to us.'

Boltfoot ignored her, slung the caliver over his back and pulled the woman into the storeroom, binding her around the waist with a length of thick-knotted cord. She looked at him with a curious mixture of resignation and contempt.

'You think you can beat him, don't you, Mr Cooper? No one can. You are wasting your time.'

He wrapped the other end of the cord around his own left wrist. He used sailors' knots. There was no more than eighteen inches of cord between them. It was not going to come loose.

He pushed the woman from the front door and out into the dusty street. She stumbled and almost fell, but he held her up by her elbow, then marched her a quarter of a mile eastwards, past the Clink prison. She cried out for help to an apprentice, but he laughed.

'You got your hands full there, mister,' he called back to Boltfoot. 'I'd trade her in if I were you. Plenty of willing whores hereabouts.'

A couple of women sitting on the doorstep of a bawdy-house scratching their sores cackled with laughter as he pushed Eleanor ever onwards. They reached the water-stairs at St Mary Overy. The only people there were two stern-looking wives, who glanced disapprovingly at the heavily armed Boltfoot and the woman with him, now covered in dust and grime, her fair hair awry like a hedge of twigs.

Boltfoot hailed a tilt-boat and hauled his captive into the back. The boat rocked violently as she struggled against him. One of the watermen eyed the pair suspiciously.

'He is holding me against my will.'

'I am taking the dirty callet home to feed the children and stop her whoring,' Boltfoot said.

'I'd leave her on the game if I were you. Nice-looking lass like that will earn a groat or two, put good English beef on your table.'

The watermen chuckled and set to rowing across the river to Dowgate. Boltfoot sat back in the boat, beneath the canopy. He was exhausted. The woman beside him said nothing more, but sat defeated, looking eastwards down the river as if there might be some succour or escape along there.

Boltfoot had but one thing in mind. To get to his wife, Jane, and keep her safe until their child was born, healthy and sound. First, though, he had to fetch this woman Eleanor Dare – this so-called lost colonist – to Essex House in the Strand and deliver her into the hands of those who had commissioned the search for her, the Earl of Essex himself, or his agent Charlie McGunn.

And the body of Davy Kerk in the house at Bank End? Mr Shakespeare would know how to deal with that.

Chapter 34

SUDELEY CASTLE ROSE from the late morning haze like a fantastical palace. John Shakespeare reined in his weary grey mare and gazed down on the magnificent vision nestling below him, deep in the folds of Gloucestershire.

A mass of flags fluttered idly from the battlements and towers of this great house. Its royal connections went back to the days when Great Henry brought Elizabeth's mother, Anne Boleyn, here in 1535, the year before he relieved her of her head.

From churches all around, the joyful peal of bells filled the air. But it was the long train of carriages and horses, stretching into the distance further than a man could see, that really stirred the blood. At its head were Elizabeth's servants, resplendent in their royal livery, followed by a troop of guards, banners held proudly aloft. Then came thirty of her equerries and chamberlains, followed by half a dozen privy councillors, among whom were Sir Robert Cecil, watchful and alert despite the exhausting day's ride; the great Sir Thomas Heneage, Chancellor of the Duchy of Lancaster and the Queen's truest friend; white haired Howard of Effingham, Lord Admiral of the Fleet and the man who, with Drake, destroyed the Armada four years earlier.

With these was the Archbishop of Canterbury, John Whitgift – ferocious enemy of Puritans and Catholics alike – riding with fifty of his own horsemen. And last, immediately preceding the royal carriage, came the Lord Treasurer, old Burghley, afflicted by the gout and suffering in the heat of the day.

Elizabeth sat alone in splendour, waving to the adoring throng of peasants and townsfolk that lined her route with cheering and waving of little flags. They had left their looms and their mills and their shepherding to come here, never having seen such pageantry and magnificence in all their lives. It was a sight they would talk of for years to come, regaling their children and grandchildren with tales of the day they saw Elizabeth, Gloriana, come with her court to their little town of Winchcombe to stay at Sudeley Castle and celebrate the Armada victory. The family who lived here – Giles, the third Lord Chandos, and his wife Frances Clinton – had spent six gruelling months preparing for this visit, to offer their sovereign three days of unparalleled feasting and merriment.

Behind the Queen rode Essex, Master of the Horse. No one sat taller in the saddle. He was followed by more privy councillors, then two dozen maids of honour in fine gowns, riding side-saddle on white palfreys, and a hundred more of the royal guard. And so the progress went on; scores of nobles and knights, courtiers and their retainers, hundreds of horsemen and women, receding into the distance. Among those closest to the fabulous royal carriage, Shakespeare spotted the squat, feral figure of Richard Topcliffe. Even at this distance, two hundred yards or more, he exuded a raw malice that would frighten children and dogs.

Shakespeare was exhausted. He had pushed on hard westwards and a little north across England. He had ridden through the night until he was almost asleep in the saddle. Even now, with this remarkable sight below him, he could happily fall from his horse and sleep in the open field.

Yet though he was driven in his desperation to meet up with the royal train, he had not been able to ignore the state of the country he passed through along the way. The England he had encountered had been very different to the glittering spectacle of the Queen and her train now entering Sudeley. He had ridden through a land of desperate poverty, dry fields of tares, pathetic beggars with outstretched hands, gibbets of bones at every crossroads, even the occasional unburied victim of starvation and disease left at the roadside as carrion for the magpies and crows to peck at. The sights had filled him with gloom.

He would have to find lodgings. Every spare room and bed in the town would be full. He shook the rein and spurred his weary mount gently forward. First, he had to try to find Essex. Clearly McGunn had discovered Shakespeare's links to Cecil – but had he told Essex?

He also needed to speak secretly with Cecil. There was much to tell him, but one thing he could not reveal: his brother's part in all this. Somehow, Shakespeare thought through the smoke of his tired mind, he had to protect Will from the deadly foolishness that had enmeshed him in this web of intrigue.

Eleanor Dare sat on the green and slippery water-stairs at Dowgate and refused to move. The brackish incoming tide lapped at her feet, soaking her shoes. Boltfoot did not have the strength to drag her and, besides, a mass of people thronged the landing stage; he did not want one of them to intervene or call the constable.

He squatted down beside her and tried to reassure her. He could see that she was terrified and stricken with horror at the fate of Davy Kerk.

'Was he your husband, Ananias?'

She shook her head.

'Who did it? Who killed him?'

She put her hands to her mouth and gasped for breath.

Boltfoot tried again to put a comforting arm around her but she pushed him away and hunched into herself.

'I am not here to hurt you, Mistress Dare. I was sent to find you by my master, John Shakespeare, on behalf of the Earl of Essex. Will you not come with me now to Essex House? You will be safe there.'

Her breathing was panicky and shallow. She clenched her hands into fists. In anguish, she began to hit her head at both temples, screwed her eyes closed and bared her teeth in a silent scream.

On an impulse, Boltfoot withdrew his dagger from his belt and cut the rope that had bound them together. 'There,' he said. 'Go. You are free to go.'

But she made no move to get up or escape; merely sat and beat herself in her torment.

Boltfoot stood up. 'Come with me, or go. If you come with me, I will protect you.' He said the words quietly; they were for the woman alone, not the crowd waiting for wherries across the Thames. Two or three people glanced at them, but shrugged it off; whatever was happening between this man and woman looked no more than a domestic dispute between husbandman and goodwife.

He thought she was close to madness. Three years at sea circumnavigating the globe with Drake had taught him to deal with Spaniards, scurvy and storms, but they had not shown him a way to cope with a distraught woman. On the rare occasions Jane had a weeping fit, he could do naught but stand and watch her, wishing himself anywhere else in the world. Now he felt just like that.

'At least come with me to my home near here where we may talk. I vouchsafe, I will do you no harm.'

She shook her head again, violently. Her hands twisted and turned and she tugged at a ring that bejewelled her slender forefinger.

'I swear before God you can trust me. Could I not have killed you back there, at the house? Or delivered you into the hands of the murderer?'

Eleanor turned and looked at him, her startling blue eyes with the strange grey ring ablaze. 'Davy wanted you dead. He said you would lead him to us, and you did. I should have left you on the street to die.' Her voice was clear; she was beside herself with anger.

'I led no one to you. Who are you talking about?'

'McGunn, of course! McGunn. The devil himself.'

McGunn? The Irishman who had come to bring Mr Shakespeare to the Earl of Essex. As Boltfoot put the pieces together in his mind, he realised the true import of what he had done: he had found this woman for McGunn and the Earl of Essex. She was right: he *had* indeed led them to her.

He hung his head. 'I am sorry. I did not know.'

'How could you? How could anyone know how far McGunn would go to find me? I am a dead woman. And you have killed me just as surely as if you had put my neck into the halter.'

They could not go to Essex House or home to Dowgate: McGunn could be watching at either place. The only thing that had stopped him killing Eleanor at Bank End had been Boltfoot's loaded caliver. Next time, Boltfoot knew, McGunn would be better armed.

Eleanor stood up and grasped Boltfoot's hand. 'Come with me. But be quick. There is a place we may find sanctuary.'

She loped through the narrow streets. Boltfoot struggled to keep up with her. The weight of his caliver and his cutlass and the pounding of his head made him sluggish. He could scarcely focus on the road ahead, yet still he stumbled on, his clubfoot scraping the dust of the road into a snail's track behind him.

In a quiet alleyway, she stopped. He slumped down against the daub wall of an overhanging house and fought to draw breath.

'We are going to the house of someone I believe will help us,' she said in a whisper. 'He does not know of my existence here in this town, yet I believe we may trust him.'

Boltfoot tried to untangle the cobweb of his mind. The woman had survived this long, somehow, so there seemed a good chance she knew what she was about. He had a plan of his own: leave London with her as quickly as possible and join Jane and Mistress Shakespeare. They must be well away from the city by now, probably in Stratford. Eleanor would be safe there, too. He would go to the groom, Sidesman, to be certain.

Yet McGunn would be watching the stables at Dowgate. He could not go there with this woman. He needed to leave her somewhere, if only for a short period, while he found out more.

'Yes,' he said. 'Let us go to your friend.'

They went slower now, walking northwards up Broad Street towards the city wall near Bishop's Gate. Here were the immense buildings of the Dutch church and Winchester House, on the right Gresham College and, as they turned into the wide sweep of Wormwood Street, Tylers' Hall, one of the great livery companies on which the wealth of the City was based.

Eleanor glanced around, walked a little further eastwards past the gaping gateway out of the City, then ducked into a short alleyway. Boltfoot struggled on in her wake.

The woman hesitated at the modest doorway to a small dwelling. She raised her hand, but before she could knock, the door opened and a monstrous face confronted them, scarlet with flakes of white dead skin over all its bulbous surfaces. Eleanor fell back in shock, as did the monstrous figure itself.

'Eleanor?' the bulky figure in the doorway demanded tentatively.

'Foxley?'

'God's blood, it *is* you, Eleanor.'

'Foxley, your face . . .'

'Oh, that. Scorched by the sun.' He did not elaborate. 'Eleanor, how are you here?' He stepped back into the house, allowing his sister-in-law in.

With trepidation she walked forward into the darkness. Boltfoot followed, his hand firmly gripped about the hilt of his cutlass.

Foxley Dare held Eleanor to his enormous body, enveloping her in his burnt and blistered arms. She submitted to his embrace without returning it in any way. Sensing her distance, he stood away from her. 'And my brother?' he asked. 'What of Ananias? Are you both home? The world had thought you dead.'

She shook her head quickly.

'Ananias is dead?'

She said nothing but held her arms about her tight.

Foxley nodded. 'I am sorry, for I loved him. Yet I had expected it.' He turned to Boltfoot. 'And who might you be, Mr Pirate?'

'Cooper. Boltfoot Cooper. I take it you are her husband's brother?'

'Yes.'

'She is in great danger. There is a man called McGunn who would do for her. I do not know why. But I know that if he discovers she is here, your own life will be in peril.'

'What manner of man is this?' Foxley asked.

'From across the sea in Ireland,' Boltfoot said. 'A brutish fellow with a face like a dog, yet given to wearing fine courtly clothes.'

'He is not the only one that seeks you, Eleanor,' Foxley said.

'Then we are not safe here. It must be one of McGunn's men.'

'He gave his name as Shakespeare. I thought him an honest man.'

Boltfoot smiled at last. 'He is my master.'

From an inner doorway, a boy appeared. Foxley clasped a fat arm around his young shoulders. 'And this is my nephew John. John, say good day to your stepmama.'

The boy was slender, though strong, with dark, tousled hair and clever eyes. He was about nine years of age.

'Good day, mistress,' the boy said.

She shook his hand. 'Good day, young John. Do you recall me?'

He shook his head.

'How could you? It is five years since last you saw me.' She looked at him closely and smiled sadly. 'You are the very image of your father, my husband. God rest his soul.'

'I cannot remember him.'

'He spoke of you often, though. I know he would have been very proud to see what a fine boy you have become.'

Chapter 35

THE MASTIFF SNARLED, its teeth bared, saliva dripping from its gums into the dust. Crouching low, it inched nearer the bull, then dashed in from the side and snapped at the bull's hindlegs. Despite its immense strength and size, the bull was quick and nimble and span round, its head lowered. The beast met the dog full on. One of its horns thrust upwards into the smaller animal's soft underbelly and tossed it into the air.

The dog yelped in pain as it flew upwards, a deep gash in its belly raining blood, before smacking down clumsily on to the ground. Snorting and trampling the dog under its hooves, the bull spiked it once more on its horns and tossed it again. The bull tried another charge, but was brought up short by the eight-foot rope that tethered it to a post in the centre of the dusty ring. The crowd roared approval, and another mastiff was brought in to try its luck.

All eyes were on the bloody spectacle. All eyes but those of John Shakespeare. He was watching Essex, who was just taking his leave of Her Majesty in the royal viewing box, bowing low to her before strolling off to meet up with a group of a dozen or so spectators. Among them were the Earl's closest associates, Henry Danvers, Gelli Meyrick, the Earls of Southampton and Rutland.

The word *conspirators* came to Shakespeare's mind. Were

these men all in on the deadly game on which Essex was embarked? There could be little doubt of it. He took a deep breath and strode towards them.

It was a muggy afternoon. For the first time in weeks there were dark clouds on the horizon. There would be rain before the three-day celebration was done.

The ageing Queen fanned herself as she watched the entertainment beneath a canopy of green and gold stripes. She was as enthusiastic as any of her subjects in her applause. After the bulls, there would be bears, horses and monkeys to delight her with their flowing blood. As he studied her animated face, it occurred to Shakespeare that the Queen looked mighty healthy and spirited for a woman supposedly destined to die within a few days.

A beautiful black woman in fanciful Roman battledress – gold breastplate and helmet and short fringed war-skirt – strolled past, her hands straining to contain chain-link leashes with a large spotted wild cat at the end of each. Shakespeare stepped aside.

All around, refreshments were to be had. A fountain rained Rhenish wine, a hogshead hidden in a bush of roses had a tap to dispense claret. Waiters offered trays of little delicacies – pastries with the breasts of peewits, sugar cakes with saffron, salted potato from the New World. Shakespeare helped himself to a portion of finest tobacco leaves and placed them in a pouch.

At the welcoming pageant, dozens of the most artful jesters and tumblers of England had clowned and bounded about. In the fields all around there were fairground stalls with oxen roasting and casks of free ale for the commoners and townsfolk.

It was a perfect setting. This castle, Sudeley, had been Elizabeth's own home when, as a girl in her teen years, she was cared for by her stepmother, Katherine Parr, the last of Great Henry's six wives. Elizabeth had memories of happy days in these gardens with her young cousin, Jane Grey. But those days were too short-lived, for Katherine Parr had died soon afterwards, in childbirth, and Sudeley had passed into other hands. Poor Lady Jane's own fate had been no happier, ending on the block at the age of sixteen after ambitious men had thrust her unwillingly on to the throne in a vain attempt to keep it from Catholic Mary.

Shakespeare bowed to Essex. 'My lord.'

'Mr Shakespeare, you have arrived.'

'Your sister was most persuasive, my lord.'

Essex laughed loud and waved away his companions. 'The idle wench is irresistible, is she not? She can certainly rule me and I am her own little brother.'

Shakespeare breathed a sigh of relief. His welcome indicated that Essex — at least for now — knew nothing of Shakespeare's secret dealings. 'I am delighted to be of service to you.'

'And that you shall.' His voice lowered a tone or two. 'Did my sister give you an inkling of the great matter on which we are engaged, Mr Shakespeare?'

'An inkling, sir, yes.'

'And were you daunted by the enormity of our momentous task?'

'No, my lord. I was not daunted.'

'Then we must set you to work, Mr Shakespeare, for there is naught more vital than the safety of our realm. It is by winning the war of secrets that we shall be kept safe.'

'That is why I am here.'

'Do you have lodgings? I fear there is little space at Sudeley.'

'I will look around.'

'Be patient. I will call on you soon enough. Know that when you perform a task for me, you do it as a true and loyal Englishman. Do you see that proud bull in the ring, how mastiff after mastiff launches itself at the beast, and yet it impales them all? I am that bull. I shall repel the Spaniard and the Scotchman and every other foreign potentate that covets the throne of England. Be ready, John, for I shall call on you at a moment's notice. We must seize the day – *carpe diem*!'

'And the case of Eleanor Dare, my lord?'

Essex brushed the topic aside. 'Think no more of Roanoke for the moment, John, we have great affairs of state at hand.' He patted Shakespeare's arms and was gone with a sweep of his white, gold and tangerine cape, a group of friends and followers trailing in his wake.

Shakespeare watched them a moment, then his eyes strayed across the bull-ring to the royal box, where he saw that Elizabeth's eyes were following the perambulations of her handsome favourite. Essex made her feel a girl again with his flattery and fluttering and swooning. Did she have any idea what treachery he was embarked upon? At her side now was the small, insignificant figure of Sir Robert Cecil. He caught Shakespeare's eye and acknowledged him with an almost imperceptible nod of the head.

Starling Day hove into view on the arm of John Watts, London's richest merchant. Watts was weighed down with jewellery and gold: diamond earrings, brooches, neck-chains and enormous pearls. Starling's attire was magnificent in its awfulness, a vast and garish confection of silver and blue satin and silk, with a ruff the size of an October moon. Her hair was piled on her head beneath a silver-thread caul that almost obscured her face. She continually pulled the caul away from her face with her plump, heavily ringed fingers so that she could look about her properly.

'Mr Shakespeare, see, I am at court! And at the finest merriment the world has ever seen. For lunch I ate cygnet and snipe, subtleties of jelly dressed as great roaring lions, oyster pies, dotterels, godwits and every manner of songbird, marchpane meats, figs and little sweet things from the far lands of Turkey. I really don't know what else, Mr Shakespeare. There were foods the like of which I have never seen. Am I not come a long way, sir?'

'Indeed, you have taken a remarkable journey, Mistress Day.'

She introduced him to Watts, who nodded in bored acknowledgement, then took advantage of Shakespeare's presence to leave his mistress and go off in search of better entertainment.

'Have you found good rooms, Mr Shakespeare?'

'I shall sleep beneath a hedgerow, Mistress Day.'

'Mr Watts has procured one of the best apartments for us, here in the castle itself. Can you imagine, Starling Day will sleep in a royal castle this night? Of course, that assumes Mr Watts allows me any sleep. But you cannot sleep beneath a hedge! There is a room with our luggage a little way from our bedchamber that would suit you well. It overlooks the main courtyard and is in a prime spot.'

'That is very gracious of you, mistress.'

'Then that is settled.'

Boltfoot limped through the streets of London down towards the Thames and Dowgate. He had his caliver primed and loaded, slung loosely in his arms.

He slowed to a crawl, looking about him all the while as he neared the school. There was a man, in leather jerkin and leather cap, on watch, close to the main entrance. He was gazing elsewhere and did not spot Boltfoot, who immediately stepped back and went around to the rear of the house to the stables, where he found the groom, Sidesman, bringing nosebags to the horses.

Sidesman looked as if he had seen an apparition. He stood

back from Boltfoot and stared at him, his gaze shifting uneasily towards the house, then back to Boltfoot and his caliver.

Boltfoot lunged forward and put the muzzle of the weapon to the groom's throat. 'Where is Jane?' he whispered in a raw, low voice. 'Is she here or gone?'

'She's gone, Mr Cooper. With a troop of militia to the north. A place called Masham, to the family of Mistress Shakespeare, by York.'

'Someone is watching for me, yes?'

Sidesman froze and did not speak.

'Is it McGunn?' Boltfoot demanded. 'Tell me, Mr Sidesman, or die now.'

The groom's eyes slid sideways. His body was rigid with fear. An explosion rang out and Sidesman fell, half his face ripped off by a volley of balls. Boltfoot ducked down and scrabbled on hands and knees from the stable forecourt. He looked back at the bloody pulp that had been Sidesman's head. Something told Boltfoot the shot had hit its intended target. He, Boltfoot, was wanted alive. He was the route to Eleanor Dare.

Another shot rent the air close to Boltfoot's body. He was up now, caliver in hand, shielded by the edge of the wall. He loosed off a shot of his own, but it was unaimed and without hope of hitting home.

Boltfoot scuttled off up Dowgate. He was not the fastest of movers at the best of times, but now he was weaker than usual. His heavy foot scraped through the dust as he ran. As he crossed over the road eastwards, he stumbled in the stinking sewage kennel that ran down the centre of the thoroughfare. Scrabbling clumsily to his feet, he heard the sound of running footsteps behind him. He stopped and knelt down on one knee, quickly reloading the caliver with expert speed, dropping none of the powder corns he poured from the horn that hung at his belt. McGunn was no more than thirty yards away from him, coming on fast. Boltfoot lifted the caliver and pointed its intricately engraved octagonal muzzle directly at the oncoming pursuer.

McGunn stopped and dived to the left, behind a cart.

Boltfoot cursed his luck. Too slow. He did not fire, but rose to both feet and backed away, his weapon trained on the cart. A young woman in a barley-coloured dress walked by with two small children, one at each hand. When she saw Boltfoot with the weapon clutched in front of him, backing past her, she screamed and huddled down, cradling the children close to her breast. There was a puff of smoke from the side of the cart, then balls tore past Boltfoot's ear and slammed into the brick wall of the long hall that fronted the road. Boltfoot dodged into a small alleyway at the side of the northern end building; he could hear the woman still screaming, accompanied by the wailing of her children.

He turned and lurched on down the alley into Cousin Lane, then heard another sound behind him. Looking over his left shoulder, he saw McGunn and another man, the one in the leather jerkin and cap from outside the school. They each had a pair of heavy petronell pistols, slung on straps about their chests, with one held out in front like a monstrous funnel of fire. He was hopelessly outgunned.

Boltfoot stopped in a doorway and dropped again to his knee. McGunn was the man. He lined up his caliver on McGunn. They were twenty yards from him now and he knew he could get McGunn, even if the other one took him.

'We don't want to kill you, Cooper.'

'Then put up your weapons.'

'We want the woman. Give us the whore's arse of a woman and you're a free man.'

Boltfoot ignored them and kept his caliver trained on McGunn.

'There's no way out for you, Cooper. Drop your weapon and I pledge you will be safe. We can follow you all day, if needs must.'

The door behind Boltfoot swung open. A woman with an empty basket, all done up in her pynner and light worsted cape as if she was going to market, stepped out and stopped, looking with astonishment at Boltfoot.

He struggled up and, bent double, pushed past her into the house. A shot exploded behind him and took the basket clean from the woman's hand, tossing it thirty feet along the street. She stood frozen, mouth agape. Behind her, the door was slammed shut by Boltfoot. He pushed home the heavy bolt, locking her outside.

Boltfoot found himself in the spacious, stone-flagged ante-room of a solidly built new-brick merchant's house. He took in his options at a glance. There were two doors leading further into the building. Take the wrong one and he might be trapped. He took the one on the left and found himself in a kitchen. A young, scar-faced malkin dropped the copper pot she was scouring and it clattered to the floor at her feet. Boltfoot side-stepped past her.

'Is there a postern door?'

Wide-eyed, she pointed behind her to another door from the kitchen. Boltfoot went towards it. From the front of the building, he could hear the smashing of glass. They were stoving in a window to get into the house.

He pushed on through the door into a buttery. There were shelves of preserved fruits, baskets of eggs, kegs of ale and a churn for butter. There was another door, wide open, leading to a large backyard. He plunged through it without hesitation.

The yard was enclosed by a brick wall. At one end there was a chicken coop, where half a dozen fowl clucked and pecked at seeds. A goat was tethered in the middle of a grassy area in the centre of the yard; it looked up at Boltfoot with soulful, disinterested eyes, then returned to munching grass. It seemed to Boltfoot he was trapped.

He went back inside. The malkin cowered in terror, holding the copper pot in front of her as a weapon of defence.

'Is there a way out?'

He heard a loud crash from the front of the house. Through the open doorway to the anteroom, he could see that they had a mallet and were beating down the mullion and transom of the window.

The malkin could not – or would not – speak. With the copper pot, she gestured once more to the yard, as though desperate to get this man out of her kitchen at any cost. Boltfoot went out into the yard once more. His eyes lighted on the chicken coop again. It might just take his weight.

He slung his caliver across his back, then dragged himself over the low picket fence that kept the birds enclosed. They scattered in a wild panic of feathers and clucking. Awkwardly, he clambered on to the roof of the coop. It was rickety and certainly not built to take a man's weight, but it held and gave him enough height to reach the top of the brick wall. Sweat poured from his bandaged head into his eyes. His hands were slippery, yet he managed to get a grip at the top of the wall and, with every remaining ounce of strength, pulled himself up and swung his good leg, his right leg, over the top. For a moment he hung there precariously, trying to get back his breath. Then with a mighty effort, he pulled his left foot up and over and fell in a clatter of weapons on the far side of the wall, suppressing a yelp of pain as the hilt of his sheathed cutlass dug into his hip-bone.

He was in the great court of the Steelyard Hall. Above him, a hundred feet or more high, was the stone-built tower where a constant watch was kept for returning trade ships as they made their slow tack up the Thames from all the distant shores of the world, bringing with them fortunes or disappointment.

'Here, you!' an artisan called out to him, anger in his voice.

Boltfoot rose painfully to his feet, unslung his caliver and levelled it at the man in warning. The man took one look at it and hurried away, around the side of the hall. Boltfoot limped on across the court, past the great watchtower and towards the Windgoose Lane gateway. He heard a noise and turned to see that his pursuers were clambering over the wall from the hen coop, the man from outside the school first. Boltfoot loosed off a shot from his caliver. The man screamed and fell, clutching at his shattered shinbone.

Smoke rose lazily from the weapon. Boltfoot slung it over his back and slipped through the gateway, looking about him. At the northern end of the street, he saw her at the prearranged spot: Eleanor Dare, mounted on a bay gelding, holding the reins of a second horse at her side. Boltfoot called to her and she saw him and urged the horses into a trot towards him.

'Quick,' he said. 'He is right behind me.'

With supreme effort he launched himself at his mount and pulled himself into the saddle. They wheeled, kicked their heels into the animals' sides and broke into a canter northwards. A volley of shots broke the silence behind them, but by then they were beyond the range of McGunn's petronells and were gone, into the maze of alleyways that crowded this part of London City.

In the early evening lull, Shakespeare retired to the room that Starling had offered him. It was small but convenient, being in the main part of the house – at great expense to Mr Watts, no doubt – where Shakespeare would not be far from Essex, and could monitor his movements closely.

On his way to the room, he had tried to see Sir Robert Cecil, but Clarkson had told him the meeting would have to wait; Sir Robert was in a session of Privy Council and would then attend upon the Queen.

In Shakespeare's little chamber, which was cluttered with luggage boxes and rails of gowns, Starling had had a mattress and blankets put out for him on the floor beneath the window. He lay down, intending to steal an hour's rest before the evening madness began, but fell into a deep sleep.

It was dark when he awoke. From below the window came the roar of laughter, the din of loud music, wild cheering and stamping of feet. Quickly, he dressed in his ancient court attire and made his way down to the teeming central courtyard, which was alight with pitch torches and blazing cressets of oil against all the walls. More light, from hundreds of candles, spilled out through the tall windows of the great hall, where revellers drank heavily and danced the volta with abandon.

Weaving his way through the crowd and into the hall, he felt a tap on his shoulder and turned to see the smiling face of Frances, Countess of Essex. 'Mr Shakespeare, I thought that was you. I saw you at the baiting this afternoon.'

He bowed. 'My lady.'

'Oh don't be so formal, Mr Shakespeare. And before you ask, I am feeling quite myself again, thank you. The Queen's own physicians have been treating me for my little illness. They are so attentive to me. I believe Sir Robert Cecil has even forbidden me to depart from court, so careful is he of my health.'

'I am delighted to hear it.' More delighted, Shakespeare thought, than she would ever know. 'And have the tiny flying things gone?'

She frowned. 'What flying things, Mr Shakespeare?'

He laughed. 'Pay me no heed, my lady. I have supped too much claret.'

As he spoke, his gaze drifted off across the hall to where her husband, Essex, was talking to McGunn's man Slyguff. As he watched, Slyguff took a paper from his doublet and showed it to Essex. The Earl broke the seal and read it, then looked up. Slyguff indicated Shakespeare with an incline of his thin face. Essex followed his gaze.

Shakespeare felt a chill in his bones.

'Ah, look, there is my husband,' the Countess said, as if spotting an old friend she had not seen in months. Her voice turned more melancholy. 'You know, Mr Shakespeare, although Sir Robert keeps me at court, still my lord of Essex seems very distant. He has not spoken more than ten words to me these past days.'

Shakespeare did not know what to say; he could think of no crumb of comfort to offer this woman, who had wed two of the greatest heroes of England – first the tragic warrior-poet Sir Philip Sidney and now Essex – but had never won either of their hearts. The world knew that Sidney's great love had been Penelope Rich – the Stella of his poem *Astrophil and Stella* – and that, on Sidney's death, Essex had married Frances merely for the heroic associations in taking on a brother officer's widow.

'He is with Mr Slyguff,' she continued. 'Do you not think that Irishman a most curious, cold fellow, Mr Shakespeare? He never seems to speak a word. Perchance he is dumb.'

The Countess drifted off into the throng, then a drum roll, like distant thunder, silenced the talk and laughter in the hall. The Master of the Revels took to the stage and clapped hands for attention. Shakespeare saw that the Queen had taken the prime seat up in the gallery. She was surrounded by her favourites – Heneage, old Burghley, Drake, Howard of Effingham. Essex walked away from Slyguff and ascended the gallery steps to join the royal party, kissing the Queen's hand with an excessive show of ardour. He took the seat on her right. Sir Robert Cecil was on the other side, at the far end of the row, small and unassuming in his dark and sober attire. The contrast between him and the flamboyant, domineering Essex could not have been more marked.

On stage, an entertainment with mock ships-of-war reconstructed the sinking of the Armada and made jest of King Philip of Spain. At one point, Sir Francis Drake himself jumped on to the platform and grabbed a wooden sword from one of the players and made much ado about running the king through, to great applause.

John Dowland, the lutenist, played a ballad about a shepherd and his sheep. Players dressed in shepherds' smocks entered the stage, driving a flock of six Cotswold sheep before them. The Master of the Revels then introduced Lord Chandos, the owner of Sudeley Castle, who bowed and offered the sheep as a gift to Her Majesty, describing them as the finest wool-bearers in the county.

The Queen accepted the gift with good grace and said she would take care to protect her new pets from she-wolves, at which the audience roared with laughter. As if on cue, a player dressed as a huntsman came on stage, with a wolf straining at a leash. The wolf had been put into fine lady's clothes, with gold and silver threads, emeralds and sapphires. It also bore a fine ruff around its collar and a lawn coif about its narrow grey head, with its ears pointing up through two slits. It panted and drooled heavily, revealing its long teeth.

The crowd gasped. Shakespeare looked towards Essex. How would he react to this undisguised mockery of his mother? Everyone in the room knew it to be a calculated insult.

His face was as dark as a storm-laden sky. He seemed to hesitate a moment, then made his decision. Without taking his leave or even bowing to his sovereign, he rose to his feet and stalked from the royal gallery. The Queen feigned indifference and continued talking with Lord Burghley on her left, but none present could have failed to note the disrespect, even contempt, that Essex had shown her by turning his back and walking away from her so. If anyone else had done such a thing they would have been despatched to the Tower without delay. Only Essex, with his tempestuous, hot and cold relationship with the monarch, could get away with such insolence.

'Well, well, well.'

Shakespeare swung around and found himself face to face with Richard Topcliffe.

'That should sort the sheep from the wolves.'

'Have you run short of women, children and priests to persecute, Topcliffe?'

Topcliffe was in court clothes: a black doublet with slashed arms, showing a gold inlay, yellow-gold breeches and black netherstocks. He exuded an unholy stink.

He sneered at Shakespeare. 'And whose side are you on? Whom do you favour in the battle that lies ahead?'

'What battle, Topcliffe?'

'You are more the mooncalf than ever I had imagined.'

Topcliffe eyed him a moment with overt loathing, then pushed him in the chest, forcefully, with the palm of his right hand. Shakespeare reeled but kept his feet.

'I look forward to the day that I drain your blood, you son of a Papist. And I will see your dog-daughter drab of a wife and her runt in the grave before the year is out. You can all join your good friend Father Southwell at Paddington Green.'

Shakespeare was unarmed – no side arms were allowed here, so close to the Queen – or he might well have killed Topcliffe. Instead he turned away, with Topcliffe's foul laughter ringing in his ears.

He was still shaking with fury ten minutes later when Clarkson found him. The old retainer quietly ushered him towards the White Garden beneath the royal apartments, where a covered passage extended from the private chambers of the castle to the chapel. It was in this concealed space that they found Sir Robert Cecil, standing in the shadows, lit only by a single candle in a wall sconce.

Clarkson retreated to the entrance to make sure none should enter and disturb them. Shakespeare bowed. 'I bring you grave news, Sir Robert,' he said. He told him of Forman's horoscopes – the death chart that claimed Elizabeth would die on September the eighteenth and the wedding chart that suggested a suitable date for the wedding of Essex and the Lady Arbella Stuart to be on the fourteenth, less than three days from now.

'Then you must stay close to Essex. Do you have his trust?'

Shakespeare thought of the look Essex had given him when he read Slyguff's missive. McGunn and the intelligencers in the turret room must have learned all they needed to know of Shakespeare's loyalties when Jack Butler broke under torture. He shook his head. 'I think not, Sir Robert. I am no longer sure what game he plays with me.'

'What of the correspondence between the Earl and the Lady Arbella?'

Shakespeare spoke carefully. 'I have discovered that there was, indeed, correspondence. Love letters and odes from the Earl to the lady.'

'And who composed these verses? Essex is no Sidney or Ralegh. He is not a poet.'

'I cannot say, Sir Robert.'

'Cannot – or *will* not?'

Shakespeare ignored the question. 'I *can* tell you, however, that the go-between is one Morley, Christopher Morley, tutor to the Lady Arbella. I believe he was placed there as an intelligencer by Mr Secretary Walsingham, but has now passed into the hands of Essex.'

Cecil continued as though Shakespeare had not spoken.

'Because you do understand why I ask you this, I hope. It is because we *must* find the evidence. We must have it to hold over the parties to this illegal marriage even though we stop the wedding. Essex and those who sponsor him must know that we have the wherewithal to put their heads on the block. Bring me the verses. I will settle for nothing less.'

Shakespeare understood that all too well. Most of all, he understood that it was his own brother's neck that was in danger. He bowed to Cecil. 'Indeed, Sir Robert, I will bring you evidence.'

But how, he wondered, as he walked slowly back to the celebrations, would he do that *and* save Will? He wondered, too, why Cecil had not displayed more interest in the name Morley.

The sky was suddenly lit up by a dazzling display of fireworks, bursting above the castle like the onset of war between gods. Shakespeare stopped and looked up in awe and wonder; he had never seen their like before – specks of red and gold and silver fire, exploding like flowers in bloom, then fading and dying as they fell to earth. He shivered and wrapped his arms tight around his body. For the first time in many weeks, he felt a chill in the night air.

Out in the fields where the common people had their fairground stalls, bonfires were lit for miles around and minstrel music was played, all mixing in the night air with the finer melodies played here at the castle.

More fireworks flared up and lit the castle with their brilliance. They also lit the face of Slyguff twenty yards away, watching him unblinking with his one good eye, the other, the left one, dead and opaque.

Shakespeare did not sleep. He paced his room, glancing every few moments from the window, not knowing what to expect, but certain something must happen this night.

The room was bathed in shadows from the single candle he burned, casting eerie glimmers on the boxes and chests that belonged to Starling Day and the merchant venturer John Watts. For a long time he was alert, every muscle and fibre tensed for the noise or sight that would propel him into action. But by three of the clock he was weary and sat down on the mattress with his back to the sill. He began to feel drowsy, his eyes heavy-lidded. At first he thought the noise he heard was part of a dream, but then he was suddenly wide awake. Somewhere, not far away, he could hear the sound of hooves and horses whinnying. He looked out of the window. It was raining, for the first time in God knew how many weeks. Cool rain, at last.

Shakespeare picked up his sword and dagger and slipped from the room and down the side staircase to the courtyard. A guard stiffened at his approach.

'Can't sleep. Need a walk.'

The guard eyed his sword.

'There are a lot of common revellers and vagabonds out there, guardsman.'

The guard nodded sullenly, hunched against the rain, hood pulled over his head, rubbing his hands before his brazier.

Shakespeare walked quickly through the main yard towards the lesser court. He could hear what sounded like a large group of horsemen to the west, somewhere in the direction of the little Isbourne river and the town of Winchcombe. Halberdiers, wearing tangerine tabards that denoted them as Essex men, were on guard at the gatehouse. They blocked his way, but he could see past them. A band of twenty or more horsemen was saddled up, ready to ride. Their mounts trampled the ground. The rain came down in torrents.

At their head was Essex, tall and arrogant on a black stallion. He was surrounded by his closest supporters and retainers

– Southampton, Danvers, Meyrick and the rest. They carried a deadly array of armaments: wheel-locks, swords, lances, pole-axes, all glittering wet in the light of burning pitch cressets and torches. Sir Toby Le Neve was there, too; Le Neve, wanted for the murder of his own daughter and Joe Jaggard. Well, there would be no way of plucking him from this group tonight.

Essex saw Shakespeare and their eyes met through the teeming rain. The Earl held the intelligencer's gaze for no more than two seconds, then tugged sharply at the reins and spun his mount. All his men turned their horses, too, lining up beside or behind him. Then, at a hand signal from Essex, they spurred their animals and trotted forward in a disciplined knot, kicking up splashes of mud and quickly disappearing into the darkness of the night.

Shakespeare watched until they had gone. They were heading vaguely north. So this was it; the plot was under way. Shakespeare ran back towards the state apartments. He had to get a message to Cecil, then take a horse and pray he reached Derbyshire – and Arbella – first.

Something caught his eye. Through the downpour, he saw a movement by a doorway into a side staircase of the state apartments. Even in the darkness of night, lit only by the guard's sizzling brazier, he recognised Slyguff. He would know that cruel-hearted, unblinking stoat of a man anywhere. Where in God's name was he going? Of course. Clarkson had told him all he needed to know about who among the nobility had the prime living quarters. Lady Frances, the Countess of Essex, was billeted in these apartments, on the first floor. A killing to legitimise a wedding.

In the shadows of the banqueting hall Shakespeare could just make out Slyguff as he handed something to the guard. He had a curled length of rope slung over his shoulder. As the Irishman slipped in through the doorway, Shakespeare emerged from the shadows and followed him. The guard moved away from the brazier to bar his path.

'I saw the bribe you took,' Shakespeare said in a low, hard voice. 'I am an officer of Sir Robert Cecil, and if you do not let me pass, you will hang before dawn.'

The guard scuttled out of his path.

Shakespeare went on through the door. He listened for the sound of footfalls, but he knew how softly he trod from his encounter with Slyguff in the turret room at Essex House on the night of the summer revel. He could hear nothing.

He waited a few moments. Then, silently, he stepped forward and walked up the circular stone stairway. His way was lit by beeswax candles in wall sconces, guttering in the cool, rainy draught. Drawing his sword from its scabbard, he held it in front of him. He reached the top step and looked along the corridor. There was no one there.

The rope came out of nowhere. A noose around his neck, the moment he stepped out from the stairwell. His assailant was behind him, twisting the rope with unreasoning ferocity, pushing him down towards the ground with a foot in his lower back. It would be a quick kill.

Shakespeare kept his footing, just, and swung around, desperately trying to stay upright. He was a tall man, but Slyguff's wiry body had the tight, ungiving strength of twisted cable. Shakespeare shouldered his attacker into a wall, pulling a tapestry down about his head. Slyguff's grasp slipped for a moment, just long enough for Shakespeare to push two fingers of his left hand under the noose to save his windpipe from being crushed.

But he was already choking for air and knew he had little time left. Dimly, he saw a figure in a doorway further along the hall, in the light of a sconce. It was Topcliffe. Richard Topcliffe, standing there, pipe in his mouth exhaling fumes, a smile on his wicked face as he watched Shakespeare going down to his death.

Shakespeare could not die, *would* not die. It was not merely his own life that counted now. Death was nothing. The thought of Topcliffe's satisfied smirk gave Shakespeare the rage he needed. Like a wounded animal just as the predator closes in for the kill, he found Slyguff's balls with his right hand and crushed them as if squeezing every drop of juice from a lemon.

A guttural sound came from the back of Slyguff's throat; but he wrenched frantically at the rope even as he curled into himself. Shakespeare knew this was his last hope. He slid his fingers out from under the rope constricting his neck. He barely noticed they were rubbed raw by the rough hemp, or the injuries inflicted on his throat that threatened to do for him. He needed this arm free. With a stab of desperation, he elbowed back into Slyguff's face. Again and again, beating his temple against the wall, he elbowed the man, bearing down on him with all his remaining power and weight.

At last the rope loosened. Shakespeare fell away, panting. He picked up his sword. Topcliffe was coming his way, his blackthorn in his right hand. The grin had not left his face all the while. Shakespeare pointed the sword in Topcliffe's direction, but he did not have the energy to rise and run him through. Topcliffe pushed the blade away with the silver tip of his blackthorn, then knelt down beside Shakespeare and the silent, writhing figure of Slyguff. He put his left hand over Slyguff's face and pushed him down into the ground. Carefully, he put the blackthorn to one side and picked up the discarded rope, twisting it once, twice, around the Irishman's neck, then turned the ends in his fist, so that the rope creaked. Shakespeare heard a sudden crack as Topcliffe pulled Slyguff's head back by his hair, snapping his neck.

The body went limp, save for the occasional jerking of the

legs and arms. Slyguff was dead. Topcliffe released the rope, then picked up his stick and held it to the raised weal circling Shakespeare's throat.

'I was enjoying that,' he said, deliberately blowing smoke into Shakespeare's eyes. 'Better than the bull-baiting, I fancy.'

Shakespeare expected to be killed at any moment. The blackthorn had a heavy head, like a cudgel, and one blow to the temple would do for him. Yet he had no strength left to defend himself; he had expended all against Slyguff. All he could do was put his hands to his own bruised throat and gasp for breath. He was coughing, choking, his lungs were heaving and his head was pounding as if he had been struck with a six-pound hammer, but he no longer cared.

Topcliffe withdrew the stick. 'You're soaked through, Shakespeare. Mustn't go out in weather like this without a cape and hat or you'll catch your death.' Topcliffe laughed at his own black humour. 'Come on, you Papist-loving milksop turd, I need your help to carry this dead weight.'

Shakespeare's breathing began to ease.

'I'm protecting her, you slow-witted worm,' Topcliffe said, as if reading Shakespeare's thoughts. 'You don't think Cecil would have left the Countess's safety in *your* hands?'

Shakespeare struggled to his feet and twisted his head from side to side, all the while rubbing his neck. He knew how near he had come to death.

'Take the legs,' Topcliffe ordered, sliding his hands under Slyguff's shoulders. 'Come on.'

'Why did you kill him?' Shakespeare demanded, his voice rasping and sore. 'We could have questioned him.'

Topcliffe snorted scornfully and blew a cloud of smoke from between his lips. He dropped the body and wrenched open the dead man's mouth. 'Look in there,' he said.

Shakespeare looked into a gaping, tongueless hole.

'Cut out at the root. You could have questioned him, but he would never have answered you. His silence was assured. Come, Shakespeare, you snivelling boy, pick him up and get him away from here. Sir Robert will not want her ladyship's peace disturbed by the discovery of a dead Irishman outside her chamber.'

Chapter 36

THEY DRAGGED THE body from the house under the terrified eyes of the guard. Topcliffe ordered the man to fetch a handcart and a tarpaulin. The guard dropped his pike clattering to the stone-flagged ground and scurried like a beaten dog into a workshop.

When he re-emerged, they hauled the corpse into the cart, covering it in a heavy sheet of canvas.

'Haul away, Shakespeare,' jeered Topcliffe. 'Put your back into it.'

Topcliffe and Shakespeare took one handle of the cart each and pulled it through a side passageway. It was hard going in the rain over the rough, muddy grass and tree roots as they pulled their burden down through the woods to the west of the castle towards the river. Their clothes were soaking, rain pouring down their necks beneath their flattened ruffs.

'These people piss me off,' Topcliffe growled to no one in particular as they reached the river and hoisted the body out of the cart and dropped it unceremoniously on to the slippery bank.

Shakespeare saw the pair of black shears hooked on the dead man's belt and shuddered as he thought of Jack Butler. And Boltfoot Cooper? Had they also shorn that loyal man of his fingers?

Topcliffe kicked at the body like a football, pushing it with his foot into the edge of the slow-running waters of the stream. 'Traitors. Agents of the Antichrist, every one of them. What sort of man orders the murder of his own wife?'

What sort of man, thought Shakespeare, has a torture chamber in his own house and laughs and jests as he tears men apart? But all he said was, 'An ambitious man.'

'He was going to hang her, make it look as though she had taken her own life in her madness. Lucky I was there, eh, boy?'

The body floated out into centre-stream, caught the current and began to drift away. They watched it for a few moments until an arm became tangled in some roots protruding from the far bank, and twisted around.

'They're all the same. Essex and his mewling, dissembling ilk. Noble blood? I'd stick their ancestry up their treacherous arses. Southampton is the worst. Thought he could keep the vile Southwell from my pretty chamber of iron and fire.' Topcliffe barked a laugh. 'No one bests Richard Topcliffe – and certainly not girl-boys like Southampton and Southwell. Who'll fondle the Earl's little pizzle now Southwell is in my grasp? Your brother, I fancy. He'll rub him up and down, up and down with a handful of sweet chrism, I shouldn't wonder.'

Shakespeare stiffened with contained fury. Now the carcass was dumped, he just wanted to get back to the castle as quickly as possible and talk with Cecil. He was breathing easier, but his throat was bruised and he would have a neck as rough as birch-bark for days. He started marching back up the bank into the trees.

'You next, Shakespeare,' Topcliffe spat after him through the rain. 'You and your Papist dog-wife and Romish puppies. I'll have you all swimming like Mr Slyguff here. I'll be dancing when your severed parts are parboiling merrily in the Tyburn cauldron.'

Shakespeare turned back, half sliding, half stepping down the muddy incline. Taking the powerfully built Topcliffe by surprise, he swung a wild punch at him, catching him on the side of the head. Topcliffe stumbled and sprawled into the mud.

'Your threats have never scared me, Topcliffe, but no one calls my wife a bitch. Learn some manners as you grovel.'

Topcliffe floundered and slid, grasping at nettles and briars as he tried to rise. Shakespeare turned on his heel. Topcliffe lashed out with his arm to trip or catch his retreating foot, but he kicked free and ascended the bank once more into the trees, then strode back towards the dim, flickering lights of Sudeley Castle through the rain-drenched night.

Cecil was awake, pacing his bedchamber in his nightclothes. Clarkson had brought him news of Essex's departure.

'There is no time to lose, John,' he said when Shakespeare entered the room. 'You must be gone to Hardwick straightway.'

Shakespeare told him of Slyguff's intent on the life of the Countess of Essex. 'He now floats down the river Isbourne, the air choked out of him and his neck cracked by Topcliffe.'

'Good.'

'I confess, Sir Robert, I was surprised by Topcliffe's role in this.'

Cecil shrugged off the implied criticism of his secret dealings with the brutal torturer. 'Suffice it to say that whatever you think of him, no one is more loyal to his sovereign. He is the Queen's servant: his only loyalty is to his Protestant God and his monarch. And he has assisted me in keeping the Countess of Essex alive. We will talk more of it later; there is no time now. But I thank you for *your* work – you have confirmed all my fears.' He handed Shakespeare a letter, with his seal of office as privy councillor. 'Now carry this letter to the Countess of Shrewsbury at Hardwick. Ride like the wind.'

Shakespeare's brow furrowed. 'Do you not think I need to take men with me, Sir Robert? Essex's band is twenty strong – men-at-arms.'

Cecil did not smile. 'Do you think I want another Battle of Bosworth Field, Mr Shakespeare? What would happen if I sent you with twenty men, a hundred men? You would start a civil war. Subtlety is required here, sir, subtlety. That is why I want you and not Topcliffe. Arrive before Essex and you can spirit the girl away to a place of safety, which would be the best solution for all concerned. Ride fast. You must stop a wedding.'

Penelope Rich stirred in her black sheets and looked at the man on the bed-cushions beside her. She ran her elegant fingers through the dark curls that flowed across the pillow. She loved him and wanted more of his children.

The man beside her on the bed at Blithfield Hall in Staffordshire was Sir Charles Blount, a kinsman of her mother's husband Christopher Blount. Charles had been her lover for two years, their passion all-consuming. At the age of twenty-nine, she had already done her duty by the husband forced upon her by her family and her sovereign, bearing him five children; now, in her prime, she had had her first with Charles.

She smiled in the early evening light and thought of the other man in her life: her younger brother, Robert. She wanted the world for him. His heart was strong but he was so easily – so infuriatingly – distracted. He needed her steel to drive him on to the goal he deserved. It was her life's work, her great project. One day he would be king, and she would guide his hand.

Three years earlier, she had made an error; she had courted the Scots king, James, with sweet letters and flattery, hoping for preferment if they could raise him to the English throne on Elizabeth's death. She had nearly come unstuck when word of that emerged. But the close call made her think: why hand the throne to James Stuart? Why not *this* family? Her great-grand-mother was Mary Boleyn, beloved of a king. Could anyone doubt that Great Henry himself was her great-grandfather? That his royal blood flowed in their veins?

Elizabeth knew it. That was why she scorned them. Penelope's mother had been banished from court, so had her sister. And was Robert chosen as the Queen's toy-dog for any reason other than to rub their noses in the Queen's shit?

The Devereux women had seethed at the injustice of it – every slight, every snub, every humiliating plea for money that her brother had to issue. Why, he had to woo the old hag like a girl to win preferment; it was worse than any degradation endured by a common whore.

And then Penelope had seen a way to repay her; a way to raise the Devereux family to the position that was rightfully theirs. It was the arrival at court of a rather plain, lonely girl, who would not be noticed in any room were it not for one thing: her undoubted claim to the succession.

Her name was Arbella Stuart, and many believed her right to the crown to be greater than that of her cousin James Stuart.

Penelope had observed her. She saw the way the awkward young girl looked at her brother, gazing on him adoringly, like a hound-pup stares up at its master – wide-eyed, waggy-tailed and longing to submit. That was when the plan took shape in Penelope's clever head. If Robert were to marry Arbella, the union of their blood-lines would be too powerful for any to gainsay, even the Cecils.

But wooing the girl under the watchful gaze of her guardians alone was difficult, so Penelope had had another idea. Robert must court her from afar, with words. And she knew just the poet to pen those words: young William Shakespeare. His verses dripped passion, and he was desperate for patronage.

It had worked. This night, the girl would be lying awake in

her bedchamber at Hardwick Hall, her mind full of Robert Devereux, her bold Earl of Essex, her love; wet for him, breathless in her desire to be taken.

A wedding was but the start. It had to be followed through with conviction or it would merely consign both Robert and Arbella to the Tower, just as Ralegh now languished there with his new bride.

They needed a protective circle of men. A round table of the greatest in the land; men to stand with them. Southampton and Rutland for their nobility; McGunn for his endless stream of gold; Thomas Phelippes, Francis Mills, Arthur Gregory, Anthony Bacon for their secret ways; Francis Bacon for his political instincts; Meyrick, Danvers, Williams and Le Neve for their military prowess.

With meticulous care, wiles and flattery, she had drawn them in. At last, the group was complete: twenty or thirty of the most formidable men in the kingdom, all utterly loyal to her brother. Men whom even the Cecils could not resist.

There would be no arrest warrant issued while these noble warriors, along with their host of retainers and knights, stood together. And if there was resistance, if the issue was forced . . . well, the throne would come to Robert all the quicker.

There had been one minor hurdle to overcome: Robert's wife Frances. Though she was dull, Penelope had always rather liked her. Her instinct was merely to ignore the marriage, have it annulled as unlawful at a later date. That would be easy enough, especially once the crown was theirs. But others felt it might be better if she were out of the way *before* the wedding.

The last part of the puzzle had been John Shakespeare. Mr Mills had been insistent that there was no better man in England to organise the vital work of intelligence-gathering. With his brother so deeply involved, it was better that he stand with them, too. And such skills as he possessed would be critical once the crown was theirs. If anyone could protect the fledgling regime from usurpers and rebels, it was a man of his anxious diligence – a man who, like Walsingham, had worked so tirelessly to protect his Queen for so many years. Shakespeare was such a man. Shakespeare would be their Walsingham.

Her brother had not been sure of John Shakespeare; he told her that McGunn had doubts. She had her own doubts, though: doubts about McGunn. Though they had needed his riches, she understood the danger of selling him their souls. McGunn would want much in return; yet the nature of that reckoning had never been clear.

Penelope turned towards Charles and curled her body around his. He was warm. She wrapped her arms around his waist and her hands found his yard, which stirred at her touch. She would like him to take her now, but it hardly seemed fair when he slept so peacefully after their long afternoon of love-making.

The rain beat against the walls.

She fancied she heard horses in the distance, but she had imagined that all day long. They *would* come, she was sure of it. This night, they would come to her on the first leg of their momentous journey.

She sat up. Even through the howling rain, she could hear the trample of hooves on heavy ground. Suddenly there was a clatter as the first horses came through on to the cobbles in the courtyard. Penelope nudged her beloved. 'Charles, they are here.'

He turned to her. His face was severe in the cloud-darkened light. As a soldier, he was used to waking to instant alertness without the groggy interlude of ordinary mortals. 'I am not coming. I will not see them.'

'But Charles . . .'

'No. I shall smoke my pipe and read a few verses until they are gone.'

He would not countenance her plans. It had been a running

battle between them, the only point of disagreement in an otherwise intense and devoted relationship. She had explained her thinking: the absolute certainty that the Queen must soon die – 'We are all mortal, Charles, and she is old and fading fast' – and the need for a strong man to take the crown, not Scottish, nor Spanish, but English.

Even when she had shown him Dr Forman's astrological charts, he had refused. 'You may well be right, my alderliefest, but I will err on the side of caution in such matters,' he had insisted. Yet, while he would not join them, she knew that he would not betray them either.

She rose and kissed his face, then stepped to the window to see the four-man vanguard sitting astride their steaming horses, drenched and muddy. She rang a bell to summon her maidservant, who assisted her to dress in a gown of black satin with gold edging.

Penelope arrived in the courtyard just as her brother cantered in at the head of the main body of horsemen. Their mother stood on the steps of the great hall, regally attired in a French gown of cloth of silver, embroidered with little scarlet wolves, with small cuts to the arms revealing gold threads. Her bodice descended in dramatic fashion to a sharp-pointed stomacher and, to protect her from the rain, she wore a black taffeta cloak and hat. The effect, in the darkening sky and against the mellow brickwork, was quite dazzling. She looked every inch the queen she believed herself to be.

Lettice opened wide her arms to greet her beloved son. He walked his black stallion forward to the steps until he was beside his mother, then leant over and kissed her proffered hand. All his companions, still high in the saddle, roared their approval.

Penelope purred with pleasure. It occurred to her that anyone who did not know better might have thought these men were hailing their God-ordained king.

She looked around the group and saw all the familiar faces: louche Southampton, still managing to look elegant in the saddle, despite being mud-caked, with his hair all in rat's tails; Rutland, a wicked glint in his eye; Le Neve, stiff and soldierly as ever; Danvers, sneaky and thin; Meyrick, staying close to his master, for whom he would happily sacrifice his own life if need be.

Servants carried trays with silver goblets of wine and brandy to the assembled horsemen now crowding out the court-yard. When all had their cups filled, Lettice held up her own goblet and the horsemen went silent. 'A toast,' she said, 'to a wedding.'

'To a wedding,' they all shouted in unison, then downed their drinks in one, tossing their empty cups down to the cobbled stones.

Penelope held up her hand to silence the group, then spoke quietly to her brother, though all could hear. 'And where, pray, is Frances?' she asked, in a voice of beguiling innocence.

'She is indisposed, madam,' came the reply, and the horse-men all erupted in laughter. 'Now, let us take supper. We ride again with fresh horses in one hour.'

And I shall ride with you, thought Penelope, *for I do love a fine wedding*.

Chapter 37

As JOHN SHAKESPEARE rode, thoughts crowded his mind. It was clear now how Cecil was able to promise to protect him. It was because he controlled Topcliffe – or, at least, as much as any man could control a rabid dog.

His thoughts turned to poor Jack Butler. He must have withstood agonies to protect his master. In the end he had succumbed, as any man would, yet his courage had not been totally in vain, for it had bought Shakespeare valuable time – time in which he learned what he needed to know from Penelope Rich.

Having finally discovered where Shakespeare's true loyalties lay, Slyguff had been despatched to Sudeley Castle to kill him, along with the Countess of Essex, but Shakespeare was one step ahead. The question now was whether he could maintain his advantage and reach Hardwick Hall in time.

His grey mare made good progress. Shakespeare felt certain that he, a horseman alone, must soon overhaul a band of twenty or more men.

A little way south and west of Nottingham he took a wrong turning. It was easy to do; the rain was lashing his face, the road was turning into a pot-holed bog, he could find no milestones to guide him and there was no one on the road to direct him.

Four hours later, when he arrived at the market town of

Grantham, he realised his error. He cursed. Angrily, he handed the reins of his mare to an ostler to be watered, washed down and fed, then strode into the post tavern for ale and food. It was late at night and dark; he should have been at Hardwick by now.

Hurriedly he ate his fill, then asked directions from the amused tavern keeper.

The landlord laughed heartily. 'You'll have a day's ride ahead of you.'

Shakespeare groaned. 'How far is it?'

'More than fifty miles, I would reckon.' He turned to a drinker. 'What say you, Gilbert? You're a travelled man. Fifty miles to Chesterfield?'

'A day, I'd say, if you keep your horse about its business.'

Shakespeare departed as soon as he could. As he rode on through dark woodland along drenched, muddy tracks, the rain got to him. His skin was cold with the wet and he knew his mission was now hopeless; he could not possibly reach Hardwick before the Earl of Essex.

At least the mare was sound and held strong. She never faltered nor stumbled. It was a slog, a desperate slog, and he had to stop frequently to give her fodder and water, but they eventually reached their destination at about six of the clock the following afternoon.

Hardwick Hall was magnificent. It was not one house but two, one of which was still under construction not fifty yards from the older hall, which had been Bess's childhood home and which was still occupied by her. The new property had already risen to four soaring storeys of dazzling golden-brown sandstone. The builder's art ran through Bess of Hardwick's very veins.

Shakespeare saw immediately that he was too late. From some distance away he could see Essex's men-at-arms practising their fencing and marksmanship in the gardens, oblivious of the rain. Unseen, he watched them for a few minutes, then wheeled his horse and rode wearily back to the village he had just passed.

At the Woodcutters, a well-kept hostelry, Shakespeare asked the landlord if there was a trustworthy man who could take an important message for him to Hardwick Hall. The landlord fetched his own son and Shakespeare handed him the sealed letter from Sir Robert Cecil. A waxed pouch had kept it dry. It was, thought Shakespeare ruefully, the only thing that *had* stayed dry on his long, arse-chafing journey from Sudeley.

'This,' he said, 'is a letter from a privy councillor, one of the greatest men in the land, answerable directly to Queen Elizabeth herself. Do you understand?'

'Yes, master.' The lad clasped his cap tight in his hands. He was broad-chested and held his shoulders back confidently.

'It is to be placed in the hands of the Countess of Shrewsbury at Hardwick Hall. You must hand it to no one else, neither noble nor gentleman, nor commoner or servant. Her hands alone. If she is unavailable, you must bring it back to me. If someone offers to take it to her, you will decline, however senior that person might be. This is Queen's business.'

'I do understand, sir. I will hand it to no one but Bess – the Countess of Shrewsbury.'

'Good lad. Go then, and you shall receive reward on your swift return. Tell no one what you are about and bring me her reply straightway. Wake me if I sleep.'

Somewhere on the great south–north road, in a forest, Boltfoot Cooper and Eleanor Dare slid from their horses and fell asleep on the earth beneath a dripping canopy of oak and ash.

For more than two days they had ridden hard from London, stopping only for food and rest when absolutely necessary and striking on without delay. There was no talk between them, only a shared need to get to the far north as quickly as possible. Boltfoot was driven by the thought that Jane's time must be almost upon her; Eleanor by the certain knowledge that McGunn would hunt her down with relentless purpose – and that nowhere in the world would she ever be safe from him.

The boy arrived back at the Woodcutters two hours later, in the company of the Countess and two of her retainers. Bess wore a cowl to cover her face, but nothing could disguise the fine quality of the clothes she wore and everyone in these parts knew her well. All the drinkers in the taproom went silent and bowed to her as she entered. Never had they expected to see this greatest of ladies in their drinking hole.

Shakespeare bowed low to her. 'My lady,' he said.

'Mr Marvell? How curious. I was told I was to meet a Mr Shakespeare here.'

He ushered her to a private booth. Her retainers took position outside.

'The name is, indeed, Shakespeare, my lady. John Shakespeare. I could not reveal my true identity before.'

'And are you the John Shakespeare that saved Sir Francis Drake from a Spaniard's sword?'

'I am.'

'And I suppose you are come here to warn me of Spanish intrigues?'

'My lady?'

'Well, I can tell you that you are too late. For my lord of Essex has already arrived with a band of men-at-arms to protect us from the intrigants. We are quite well looked after.'

Shakespeare was silent for a long few moments. He knew the contents of the message from Cecil. It was addressed directly to Bess and told her but one thing: that she must listen to

Shakespeare. It committed nothing to paper which might be used as evidence, either against Cecil or Essex.

'My lady,' he said at length. 'I have to tell you that things are not as they seem with my lord of Essex.'

'Mr Shakespeare, he tells me they have uncovered a Catholic plot to snatch my granddaughter away, take her to Flanders and then on to Spain, where she will be introduced to the world as England's queen-in-waiting, ready to be placed on the throne when a new armada is launched against these shores. Is that not your understanding?'

'No, my lady,' Shakespeare said grimly. 'That is *not* my understanding.'

Bess clapped her hands and one of her retainers came in. 'We could do with a little refreshment, Mr Jolyon. Some canary wine with a pinch of sugar would suit me. What would you like, Mr Shakespeare?'

'That would suit me well, my lady.'

The retainer bowed low and backed out of the booth.

Bess smiled. 'Well, Mr Shakespeare, you will be pleased to hear that I did not believe a word that my lord of Essex said to me. I suspect the danger is not from Madrid, but from here at home.'

'Then we are of one mind.'

'I fear my house has been taken over, that I am almost a prisoner in my own home. Now, tell me what this is all about, if you will.'

Oswald Finningley, the vicar of St John the Baptist Church, finished his seventh pint of strong ale and wiped his sleeve across his dripping-wet beard. Rising unsteadily to his feet, he waddled to the low door that led from the Woodcutters. He had seen Bess of Hardwick making her entrance but thought it best not to let her see him, for she would not approve.

Outside, in the rain, he lifted his cassock, which was stained with drips of beer and pork fat, and let out a long sigh of satisfaction as he pissed against the wall. His belly hung so low that he could not see his pizzle; in truth, the only person who *had* seen it these past fifteen years was the widow Bailey, and even she seemed to find it an unfulfilling chore to have aught to do with the little worm-like creature nowadays.

He splashed the last few drops of piss over his feet and dropped his cassock. He pushed himself away from the wall and lurched up the path towards her house. The rain was cutting rivulets in the muddy track that passed as a road in this village. It is God's blessing, he thought dully, for at least it washes away the accumulated dung. Even as the thought came to him, he stumbled and fell, face down, into the drainage kennel. He spluttered, then tried, clumsily, to push himself up.

Of a sudden, help was at hand. Strong arms lifted him from all sides and he wondered, for a moment, if angels had come to raise him up to heaven.

But instead of floating on Elysian clouds, he came down with a crack of the head, thrown unceremoniously into the back of a farm cart. And he heard a voice, which was decidedly not the voice of God.

'Come on, reverend, you've got to get yourself sober. There's a job of work to be done in the morning.'

Bess listened to Shakespeare intently. She did not interrupt him, until finally he said, 'So, I believe we must somehow remove the Lady Arbella to a place of safety.'

'You know, Mr Shakespeare,' she said with great deliberation, 'I have never made any secret of my ambitions for my granddaughter. I have raised her as a royal princess, believing – *hoping* – that she would one day, in the fullness of time, ascend to the throne of England, for I consider her to be first in line. This has not always been appreciated by the Queen, who does not care to dwell on her own mortality. I confess that we have not always seen eye to eye on the matter. But never did I think to do such a thing – such a treasonable thing – as is now being proposed by my lord of Essex. We must prevent it, Mr Shakespeare, or we will all lose our heads.'

'Can she be spirited away?'

Shakespeare could not imagine Bess losing her composure, yet now he saw real anxiety in her eyes. Her small hands were clenched into balls.

'First we will have to find her.'

'My lady?'

'I went to her chamber not two hours since. She was not there. Her lady's maid was most flustered and said she had gone off with a group of young gentlemen, she knew not where. I looked for her in vain. I asked my lord of Essex where she was and he said he had not seen here. His men feigned ignorance, too, and made a great show of looking for her. Even her tutors could not tell me where she was.'

Shakespeare felt his whole body tightening. Bess's demeanour told him that she, too, was fully aware of the extreme danger of the situation. 'Your tutors – I believe one is called Morley?'

'Indeed, Mr Shakespeare. You seem to know a great deal about my arrangements.'

'He conspires with Essex, my lady. He is one of them. It seems clear they already have the lady Arbella in their keeping. I fear we may be too late . . .'

Chapter 38

THE ANCIENT CHURCH of St John dominated the fields like a spectre in the grey morning light. Its stone walls, five or six hundred years old and first built before the Conqueror came to England, were weather-worn and strangely welcoming. The bells in the square tower were silent this day.

At the head of the wedding procession that traipsed slowly on horseback across the meadow towards the yew-planted church-yard were Essex and his best man, Southampton, richly attired and mounted on caparisoned war stallions.

The rain had gone, but the clouds remained heavy and threatening. A lone ploughman gazed over at the wedding party but did not stop his work. He lashed the ox pulling the plough and carried on carving a deep furrow for winter wheat.

Inside the church, Oswald Finningley stood at the altar, a shaking hand clasped to the communion railing to support himself. He could not hold himself still, his head ached and he was desperate for ale or brandy to take away the shaking and the nausea. Last night was a blur. He had been abducted and locked away in some strange room and this morning two men had come for him and woken him with a pail of cold water over his face. They had given him a good breakfast, most of which he had puked up, and had then brought a clean cassock and new-laundered, bright white surplice and ruff. It was only as they set off for the church that he realised that he had been held within the servants' quarters at Hardwick Hall.

The two men had jogged him along mercilessly on the back of a rattling farm cart, which served only to make him feel more sick. He now stood silently, a man at either side to prevent escape.

Essex and his guests entered the church: twenty hard-edged but finely dressed men. The Reverend Finningley looked at them as if they were strange creatures from some far-flung land. He had no idea who they were, nor what they wanted of him. Yet from their apparel and demeanour he could tell that they were of noble blood, and his knees began to buckle.

The two men guarding him thrust their hands under his armpits to keep him from falling. 'Just say the wedding words, minister, and you will be back at the tavern pouring ale down your throat in no time,' one of the men whispered in his ear. 'Make a commotion and I'll pour boiling tallow down your miserable gullet instead.'

Essex's men found places to sit or pillars to lean against, hands on sword hilts. Essex paced about like a caged leopard, waiting for his bride to appear. He did not have long to wait.

Heralds at the doorway trumpeted her arrival. Two ushers escorted her into the building and indicated the altar where Finningley fought back an overwhelming desire to bring up the last remnants of his breakfast.

A man in scarlet and gold velvet escorted the Lady Arbella along the aisle. He was slender and languid, scarce bearded with a thin, dark moustache.

Arbella was almost skipping with excitement. She wore ivory satin and gold thread, her face covered by a lace net. As she reached the Earl of Essex, she looked up at him from beneath her veil with adoring, besotted eyes. He looked at her distractedly, then, as if remembering that this was to be his wife, he smiled at her.

'Now, Mr Finningley,' one of the men at his side said. 'Do your business, sir. And remember the hot tallow.'

Finningley recognised Arbella and was horrified. He wanted to say that the banns had not been called, that this was most irregular, but he was convulsed by fear. He took a deep breath and began to intone the words of the service in a weak, spindly voice that belied his great bulk.

'Dearly beloved friends, we are gathered together here in the sight of God, and in the face of his congregation, to join together this man and woman in holy matrimony . . .'

He droned on through the service as laid down in the Book of Common Prayer introduced during the first year of Elizabeth's long reign. All the while, Essex glared at him impatiently.

'. . . and therefore is not to be enterprised, nor taken in hand unadvisedly, lightly or wantonly, to satisfy men's carnal lusts and appetites, like brute beasts that have no understanding . . .'

'I know all that. Get on with it, man.'

'It is the form of solemnisation of matrimony, sir . . . my lord.'

'Yes, yes.'

The congregation of his friends and supporters mumbled their approval. One or two applauded with clapping of hands.

Finningley sighed. What did it matter? He couldn't imagine any of this was legal anyway, not without the banns. And so he omitted the next part and got on to the nub. 'Will you have this woman to your wedded wife, to live together after God's ordinance, in the holy estate of matrimony? Will you love her, comfort her, honour, and keep her, in sickness, and in health? And forsaking all other, keep you only to her, so long as you both shall live?'

'Yes, yes, of course.'

'You must say "I will", my lord . . .'

'I will. I will. Is that it? Are we married?'

'Almost, my lord, almost . . .'

In the trees, unseen, John Shakespeare had watched the wedding party proceed towards the church. He knew the bride must come eventually and so he waited for her. At last she came with Penelope Rich and a man he did not know, apparelled in scarlet velvet, a sword at his waist. His head moved this way and that, slowly, like an adder. Shakespeare found himself half expecting the man's tongue to flick out and be forked. Some instinct told him the man was Morley.

The ivory bride dismounted. She moved her veil aside momentarily to look about her and Shakespeare recognised the sad face he had seen at the window in Shrewsbury House, Chelsea. Her eyes were blue and a little too big; her mouth was too severe and her nose large. Now she smiled and her eyes darted. Yet even the smile did not suit her and nor did it disguise her loneliness and unease; she cut a poignant figure, here with these people who wanted everything from her, but nothing for her.

The men at the door helped her from her horse and then Penelope and the man in scarlet took her inside the church. As soon as they had gone in, Shakespeare entered the porch, hesitating at the door as long as he dared. From inside, he heard the words of the minister as the service got under way. He looked about him before turning the latch on the strong old oak door. As he pushed it, the iron hinges creaked loudly, then the iron edge of the door clanged as it swung inwards against the stone wall.

Shakespeare stepped inside. Heads swivelled in his direction; eyes bore down upon him as if seeing some apparition.

At first there was surprise and curiosity in their expressions, then a gathering rage. The vicar's mouth hung agape, in mid-sentence.

'In the Queen's name, I say this wedding cannot proceed,' Shakespeare bellowed in a voice of surprising power and confidence. He was unarmed, for what use would one poor sword or pistol be against twenty war-hardened men? He walked forward along the nave, between the ranks of Essex's supporters, their fingers suddenly tightening on the hilts of their swords.

Penelope Rich rose from her seat and stepped forward to bar his path. 'I am afraid you are too late, Mr Shakespeare. The ceremony is completed. My brother and the lady Arbella now stand before you as man and wife.'

Shakespeare stopped. He did not believe it; there had not been sufficient time. He turned to the minister, who was quivering like an ash leaf in the breeze. 'Is this true?'

Even through the haze of his muddled, befuddled and panicking mind, Oswald Finningley knew he was caught up in something very bad; this man, whoever he was, had invoked the authority of the Queen herself. To talk to these nobles in such wise must, at the very least, make him a senior officer in her government. Though hopelessly outnumbered and at the mercy of these armed men, he understood that to stand *with* them might very well result in a traitor's death, with everything that entailed. He shook his head.

'No,' he said, his voice no more than a whimper.

'They are not married?'

Finningley shook his head again.

'Then I say, this wedding will not take place. It is forbidden under the law, not only because it is unlicensed by Her Majesty, but also because the bridegroom already has a wife.'

The gangling figure of Essex moved away from his bride towards the source of interruption. His handsome head was angled forward from his awkward, sloping shoulders. '*Had* a wife, Shakespeare,' he said, spitting the words. 'I am recently bereaved and am, sadly, a widower. She died of her madness. God's blood, sir,' he suddenly shouted, 'what is all this to you?'

Shakespeare suddenly realised what loathing he felt for this man who would sacrifice his wife, the mother of his child, to self-serving ambition. A man who would turn on the very monarch who had raised him to such great power and public esteem.

'My lord,' Shakespeare said coldly. 'It is not long since I left Sudeley Castle, and I can tell you your wife was in perfect health, quite recovered from her sickness of mind and body. Your friend Slyguff does not fare so well. He floats down the river Isbourne, feeding the water voles and rats.' He turned to the bride and spoke sharply and with all the authority he could muster. 'The Lady Arbella Stuart will come with me now, back to the protection of her grandmother. This wedding has not been sanctioned and will not take place.'

Shakespeare brushed past Lady Rich, took two steps towards the chancel, knocked elbows with Essex, then reached out and grasped the arm of the young claimant to the throne. Arbella sobbed, but did not resist. He began to drag her away, back along the nave towards the porch.

Essex was thunderstruck, frozen in indecision. And then he acted. He strode towards one of his heavily armed band and seized a flail that hung loose from his belt. The weapon had a three-foot haft, then a short chain of four or five links, attached to which was a heavy metal ball with six spikes protruding like a bursting sun. As Shakespeare pulled the bride through the centre of the church towards the door, he did not see Essex pursuing him like a man possessed, the haft of the flail clasped in both hands as if he would bring it down in a man-killing blow.

Shakespeare pushed on towards the open door, but then his exit was closed off. Half a dozen men-at-arms barred his way, among them Sir Toby Le Neve and the swordsman in scarlet velvet.

Le Neve put up the flat of his hand at Shakespeare's chest. 'Mr Shakespeare, you have an unpleasant habit of appearing where you are not wanted. Now, hold fast. You will not leave this church.'

Shakespeare pushed the hand aside. 'I take no orders from murderers.' He had lost all fear now. 'This is Queen's business, Le Neve. Move aside. I have enough on you to hang you twice over and will deal with you later.'

A three-pound ball of solid black iron, encrusted with short, deadly spikes, came down through the air towards Shakespeare's head. He had no way to get clear of the blow. All he saw was the look in Le Neve's eyes – a look of horror and dismay.

Le Neve flung him sideways to the stone-flagged floor of the church, and Shakespeare felt a whisper of pain as a spike of the flail skimmed his temple on its downward trajectory. Behind him, Arbella sprawled forwards, tripping over her skirts and collapsing in a sobbing heap at the edge of the aisle.

It was Le Neve who took the blow. The dead weight of the ball and the malevolent spikes crushed through the bottom half of his face, destroying his chin and carrying on through into his throat, where it dug through his windpipe, pummelling his Adam's apple into a mush of gore and gristle. He crumpled at the knees and was thrown backwards to the ground, the spikes embedded in his upper body. Blood gurgled in the remains of his throat and spurted from his demolished mouth. His upper lip moved as though he were trying to say something, but no coherent sounds emanated from him.

Shakespeare should have scrabbled away, for out of the corner of his eye he could see the flail being raised again, but instead he rose to his knees and knelt beside Le Neve. He saw cloudy resignation in the warrior's eyes, followed quickly by the opacity of death. Feeling a curious pang of sorrow, he was about to close the dead man's eyes when he looked up to see Essex about to bring down the flail once more and knew that he, too, was about to die.

'Enough!'

Bess of Hardwick was not tall, scarce over five foot, and yet her voice boomed through the echoing chambers of the church like a serjeant-at-arms.

The arc of the ball's swing hovered at its zenith. Essex stared down at this diminutive woman and Shakespeare rolled sideways, out of reach of Essex's blood-dripping flail.

Bess looked at the Earl with disdain, then stepped forward, past the body of Sir Toby Le Neve, and roughly grabbed the forearm of her young ward.

'Come with me, you foolish girl,' she commanded, dragging Arbella to her feet with astonishing strength. Ignoring the sharp steel that surrounded her on all sides, she turned to the man in the scarlet velvet suit of clothes and gazed on him with stern majesty. 'Do you think it wise to pull a sword on your mistress, Mr Morley? Look outside the church door, if you will.'

Morley, Essex and everyone else within the church turned to look through the gaping doorway. The churchyard was full of men.

Bess smacked the man called Morley across the cheek. 'Return to your classroom, sir. I will have words with you later.' She nodded to two men who had followed her into the church, and they each grasped one of Morley's arms and dragged him out. She then pulled Arbella with an angry tug of her arm, and marched her from the church. Shakespeare rose and followed her.

Men of every size and shape thronged the churchyard: working men with hoes, hammers, hayforks, picks, trowels and shovels, but also with longbows, crossbows, halberds, axes and rust-bitten arquebuses. Perhaps five hundred in all, maybe more. They looked like an army ready to do battle and not give an inch.

Some were mounted on farm horses and oxen; some had arrows laid across fully drawn bowstaves, ready to strike a man dead within the blink of an eye. They wore the leather jerkins and aprons of builders and carpenters, stonemasons and farm-hands. They were a rag-tag bunch, but they were a fearsome sight – and they outnumbered Essex's men twenty-five to one.

Bess smiled with satisfaction at the sight of all her builders and estate workers, hastily assembled by her retainers this morning. She knew they were all loyal, would kill and die for her, for she had brought prosperity to them and their families with her great building works and with her well-husbanded farmlands and industries. She turned back to Essex, who had followed her to the door. 'Well, my lord,' she asked. 'Do you have any argument with me now?'

Essex scowled as he gazed upon the unexpected army that confronted him and upon the slight figure of the woman who dared defy him.

He dropped the flail, drew his sword and seemed about to lunge at her, but suddenly two long-handled weapons – an old pike and a dungfork – came across his path forming a cross that barred his way. An archer stepped forward, close to Bess's side and pulled his bowstring taut, the arrow pointing directly at the Earl's heart.

Penelope Rich touched her brother's arm. 'Come, Robert,' she said softly. 'Do not die here at the hands of peasants. Live – and prepare for another day.'

*

In the confusion, no one noticed the minister, Oswald Finningley, waddling into the vestry, his skirts clutched about his knees for ease of movement. With shaking hand, he opened a little cupboard and took out a pint-flagon of communion wine, which he uncorked and drank in one draught.

Chapter 39

IT WAS OVER. There would be no pitched battle between men-at-arms and common men, no civil war on a muddy field in Derbyshire beneath lead-grey skies. Where Essex saw only a mist of blood, his elder sister saw things with sun-bright clarity. She knew that Bess would say nothing of this and nor would John Shakespeare. She understood the workings of their minds. She left the church with her head held high. With fortune, there would be another day for the Devereux clan. She would consult Dr Forman.

In the porch, John Shakespeare stood face to face with Essex. 'My lord, you will disband and hasten from this place, for if you do not, I vow that a royal militia will be raised against you that will hunt you and your band down to all your deaths.'

Essex ignored him. He looked down at the flail where it lay in the mud, its round head covered in the thick, coagulating blood of Sir Toby Le Neve. He seemed to study it, as if he would find some answers there, in its unforgiving iron. He shook his head slightly, perhaps suddenly realising what he had done. 'Toby . . .'

Shakespeare gazed on the strange, poignant tableau with a mixture of feelings. Le Neve had saved his life, had deliberately put himself in harm's way and had taken the lethal blow intended for his foe. It was a difficult thing to comprehend, that a man guilty of such a heinous crime should sacrifice his own life for a near stranger; perhaps there was a conscience in that heart, a need to find redemption. 'He died in honour, my lord. Take him and bury him with military honours.'

If Essex had words, he did not utter them. He looked at Shakespeare for a moment without expression, then strode away, across the face of Bess's army, followed in dribs and drabs by his supporters. Four of them lifted up the body of Sir Toby Le Neve and bore him on their shoulders; they would take him away from here and bury him in their own way.

Their horses were tethered in the trees at the edge of the churchyard. Essex threw himself into the saddle of his black charger and kicked it into motion with unnecessary ferocity, galloping off southwards in the direction of Hardwick Hall, his disorganised contingent trailing in his wake.

Shakespeare watched them go until only Lady Rich was left.

'What will you do now, Mr Shakespeare?'

'That is not for me to decide.'

'The Cecil crookback has snared you.'

Shakespeare was silent.

'But you can do nothing, can you? You cannot touch us without condemning your own brother. And I know you, Mr Shakespeare – I know that you would never do that. Nor can Bess say a thing. If one word of this ever reached the Queen's ears she would bar Arbella from the succession – writ in law – and would likely demand her head.' Penelope touched his arm with something akin to affection. 'You have been grievously in error this day, sir. You have handed the throne of England to a malodorous Scotch garboil – or perchance a simpering Spaniard. You have seen the chart. The Queen will die within days and the Cecils will arrange everything to their own gain and England's loss.'

Shakespeare said nothing. The matter of the succession was not his to decide; nor was the fate of Essex and his sister and the rest. His task was the defence of the realm and the life of the monarch.

Penelope laughed lightly. 'McGunn was right to distrust you. Your silence tells me everything. You have sold your soul.'

Shakespeare still said nothing. Essex and Lady Rich had thought to play him like a fish, knowing that if he did not swim with them he would end up fried on their platter.

'Well, Mr Shakespeare, it seems you have chosen your path. And it is a path of burning coals. You have made powerful enemies this day. My mother has the towering rage of the Tudors and she will want your blood. Do you think your choice will have been worth it? Does the crookback pay you well?'

At last he spoke, his voice clipped and expressionless. 'I have been loyal to my sovereign.'

Peneloped laughed. 'Today's sovereign. What of tomorrow's? What will become of you when the sovereign dies and the crookback's star wanes and falls?'

'As you say, my lady, I have chosen my path. I will live with it.'

'Or die . . .'

Shakespeare began to walk away, behind Bess's great artisan army, now proceeding at a steady pace towards Hardwick Hall. Bess was with them, marching her deflated granddaughter home.

Penelope took the reins of her horse and rose into the saddle. She trotted up towards Shakespeare. 'Wait,' she said, her voice softening

He stopped. His head had survived the glancing blow of the flail but his neck was still mighty sore from Slyguff's rope. 'My lady?'

'There was something between us, was there not? For a while, for a moment, I did wish . . . our timing was crossed.'

He shrugged. 'Perhaps. But I am a married man, and you are wed to your brother's cause.'

'Take care, Mr Shakespeare. I wish you no ill.'

She turned her horse and, without another look back, spurred on and rode south.

In the library of Hardwick Hall, Bess scolded her granddaughter as though she were a kitchen maid. The girl sat on a plain, three-legged stool, her wedding dress askew and muddy from the mile-long walk back to the hall. She alternately sulked and sobbed, but did not utter a word.

Shakespeare looked on as Bess paced the room, cuffing the girl's head or boxing her ears with hard blows each time she passed her. Arbella let out a cry of pain each time she was hit, for Bess struck her with venom.

'You behave like a common drudge, so you will be treated like one. From this day forward, you will stay indoors unless accompanied by me. You will sleep in my room by night. You have no idea what you have done. Everything I planned for you might now be brought to ruin by your foolishness. Did you not once ask yourself why the Earl of Essex should wish to marry you? Did you really think you had the womanly charms to lure a man from his wife? You knew he was married – and, more importantly, you knew that a woman of the blood royal could never wed without her sovereign's consent. You might still end your days in the Tower for what you have done this day. Have you learned nothing from the fate of your cousins Jane Grey and Mary Stuart? Are you grown so tall that you would wish to be a head shorter?'

She hit her again. Arbella cried out but said not a word.

'Now go. Get out of my sight. Your meals will be brought to you in the classroom every day for the next month. You will not venture out.'

Bess clapped her hands and a governess in Puritan black appeared. 'Take her to the classroom, Mistress Beacon. Keep her at her studies until dusk. Then begin again at dawn, without respite.'

When her granddaughter had gone, Bess at last sat down. She sighed heavily and shook her head. 'Come, Mr Shakespeare, let us drink some sweet wine and talk a little and see how we may all survive this.'

'First I would speak with the tutor, Morley. Would you allow that?'

'Very well, but I pledge that he will not be a tutor here by this day's end.'

Christopher Morley was not about to be cowed by Bess of Hardwick or John Shakespeare. He felt sure of the power he wielded. He stood in the centre of the room seeming to take more interest in the cut of his ink-stained fingernails than in the other people present.

'Do not think for a moment that Essex will protect you, even if he could,' Shakespeare said, bridling at his lack of concern.

Morley looked up nonchalantly. 'I do not need Essex, Mr Shakespeare. I can fend for myself in this matter, for I have the letters and verses, safe in a place where you will never find them. And I will use them – believe me, I will use them.'

'For what? To put a noose around your own neck, Morley?'

Morley snorted his derision. 'Sir Robert Cecil will thank me for bringing them to him, for they will be just the proof he needs. He will give me a pension.'

'Cecil already knows you work for Essex.'

Morley surveyed Shakespeare with disdain. 'I had thought you an *intelligencer*, Mr Shakespeare. It is a curious word for one of such inferior wit. Yet it will be a great sadness to see your brother carved like pork belly at Tyburn. His *Henry the Sixth* afforded me much pleasure at the Rose this spring last.'

'If I kill you now, Mr Morley, Sir Robert will thank me for disposing of a traitor.'

Morley laughed. 'You do not have the stomach, Mr Shakespeare. More pertinently, you do not have the letters and odes your brother wrote in his fine hand. Nor will you find them, for they are not here. Do you think I would leave such stuff lying about?'

Bess was having none of it. She clapped her hands again and a liveried butler entered the room, bowing low. 'Mr Jolyon, you will take two footmen and search Mr Morley's quarters – every inch and beneath every floorboard. Bring all papers, correspondence and documents to me within the hour. You will have two more men do the same in the chamber of the Lady Arbella. And see that they are thorough.'

'Yes, my lady.'

'So, then,' Bess said, looking first at Shakespeare and then at Morley. 'We shall wait here and see what turns up.'

Shakespeare looked at Morley's yawning, reptilian face. He was a strange creature. His expression betrayed nothing. Why had Walsingham sent him here to coach a royal heiress? Shakespeare wondered. Such a position was offered to only the most outstanding scholars. This was the sort of man Mr Secretary used, but never trusted. It had been a most curious misjudgement.

'I know the way Walsingham worked. He paid you to spy on the Lady Arbella,' Shakespeare said.

Morley affected a careless shrug of his rather sloping shoulders. 'I may have passed him the odd titbit of interest.'

'And then, on his death, you transferred your allegiance to the Earl of Essex.'

'He was the coming man. Why should I not assist him? No

one is closer to Her Majesty and I know that he is carrying on Mr Secretary's excellent work in the war of secrets. Is it treason to make oneself of use to the Queen's most trusted courtier?'

Shakespeare's anger erupted. 'If you knew what Essex was about, you are guilty of treason – if you did not, you are a swill-witted fool. Why did you not think to approach the Privy Council for approval? There is more to this, Morley. You had another motive.'

Morley kept his silky composure. 'I was doing Walsingham's bidding, nothing more. He put me here. When he died, I became Essex's man because he took on Walsingham's duties.'

'But you went much further. Passing secret love poems to the Lady Arbella – do you think Mr Secretary would have approved of that?'

'Who knows? Who could ever tell the workings of Mr Secretary's labyrinthine mind?'

'What did Essex offer you? A knighthood? He likes to hand out knighthoods, I do believe. Or gold?'

Morley was silent. He glared at Shakespeare through narrow eyes. Bess of Hardwick looked on, intrigued.

'Or perchance it was silence.'

Morley almost seemed to hiss. His teeth rubbed together and made an unpleasant scratching sound. Shakespeare pushed the palm of his right hand hard into the tutor's sneering mouth, then gripped his throat with his left hand. Blood seeped from Morley's torn lip on to Shakespeare's hand.

He held Morley against the wall. Their eyes met and held, Morley's not quite so assured now. Shakespeare punched him in the guts, then kneed him. Morley groaned and crumpled.

Shakespeare let him fall. He lay on the ground, whimpering.

'Well, Mr Morley?'

Morley said nothing.

Shakespeare unsheathed his sword. He pulled Morley's hair up and wrenched his head to one side, then gently slid the sword's sharp edge against his neck.

Morley was shaking. 'I have nothing to say. Kill me.'

Shakespeare laughed. 'Oh no, Mr Morley, I won't kill you. I will leave that to Skevington's irons. You will be taken to the Tower, where Mr Skevington's engine will bend you double, so contorting your body that blood will spurt from every hole in your miserable carcass until you talk – or die. My lady . . .'

Taking the cue, Bess clapped her hands. A servant appeared. 'Have Mr Morley taken away under guard. He is to be held in close confinement until arrangements are made to transfer him to the Tower.'

Shakespeare pulled his sword away and resheathed it. 'Thank you, my lady.'

The servant was a powerfully built man. He took Morley by the collar and dragged him to his feet.

'Wait,' Morley said, scrabbling against the footman's grip.

'Take him away.'

'No, I'll talk.'

Bess nodded to the servant, who dropped Morley, then retreated from the room.

'Well, Mr Morley?' Shakespeare demanded again.

'A plague of Satan's vomit and ten thousand hells on you, Shakespeare. I think you know *exactly* why I had to do their bidding.'

'McGunn.'

'Of course, McGunn. And his demon acolytes Jaggard and Slyguff. They lure you in and trap you.'

'You have secrets . . .'

'Here is Mr Smith, they say. Is he not a fine lad? And he was a fine lad, the most golden boy I ever saw. And then comes Mr Abel, a slender eleven years with the knowing ways of one twice his age. He is an even finer lad, with Moorish tricks to please you, they say. On and on they come – three, four, five, six of them to my chamber over days and weeks and I am in very heaven.' He sighed and shook his head. 'They were beautiful, oh, they were beautiful. But they were rotten, every one. Decayed to the core – like apples that are juicy red on the outside but corrupt within, all eaten by worms.' He uttered a dry, sardonic laugh. 'And the law was the least of their threats. McGunn is the devil. He sees men's weaknesses and buys their souls. Once bought, you are his forever.'

There was a knock at the library door. The butler entered, a jewel-encrusted box held across his outstretched arms. He placed it on the table in front of Bess, then bowed and retreated.

'I wonder what we have here,' she said, lifting the hinged lid.

Chapter 40

SHAKESPEARE RECOGNISED HIS brother's hand straight away. He was aghast as he looked at the array of verses and letters; in the wrong hands it amounted to a death sentence for Will.

'Where did you find these, Mr Jolyon?'

'In a little-used closet in the music room, my lady. The chest was concealed under jute sacking behind a box of viol strings.'

'Fetch a lighted taper, Mr Jolyon.'

He bowed low and left the room.

Bess laid the papers out over the floor. There were at least twenty letters and a dozen odes. And though they were signed off with the mark of Robert Devereux, Earl of Essex, each one bore the indelible imprint of Will's quill.

The three people in this light, airy room, with its soaring shelves of volumes of priceless books, many of them hand-scribed on vellum, stood in a triangle around the parchments. Sir Robert Cecil wanted these verses and letters. They would give him power over Essex, but both Shakespeare and Bess had another thought: these papers must be destroyed. Whatever their differences, they shared this common cause.

Jolyon returned with the flame. Bess took it and dismissed him from their presence. Shakespeare was already busy screwing the papers into balls and throwing them into the fire-grate.

Bess touched them with the tip of the taper and the dry papers went up in a brilliant conflagration, the flames leaping into the chimney flue. Within two minutes they were all gone, turned to black ash. Will was safe.

'Mr Morley,' Shakespeare said, 'remove your doublet.'

Morley folded his arms across his chest.

'Or would you wish me to do it for you?' Shakespeare unsheathed his dagger.

Morley unhooked the front of his doublet and threw it wide open. Papers fell out on to the floor. Shakespeare scooped them up and placed them in the fire.

'You still cannot harm me. I still have the testimony of my voice,' the tutor said.

'We will take our chances on that.'

Morley was silent.

'What were you planning to do with these papers? Sell them?'

'There are those that would pay good money for them. Essex, Cecil . . .'

'Topcliffe?'

'Oh yes, Mr Topcliffe would pay very well to do for you and your brother. He would happily take you on a hurdle to the scaffold, Mr Shakespeare. Perhaps he already has some of the verses . . .'

Bess shook her head. 'I have heard quite enough, Mr Morley. You are dismissed from my service, without pension or recommendation. Nor do Mr Shakespeare or I have the slightest interest in your boys. That is between you and God. Good day to you, sir.' She summoned her butler once more. 'Mr Jolyon, see that Mr Morley is gone from this house within the half-hour. First strip off his clothes and search him thoroughly, then give him new attire and a horse, one fit for the knacker. Do not let him take any belongings, not even a book. They will be sent on later when they have been thoroughly searched. He is never to be admitted again.'

'One last thing, my lady,' Shakespeare said once Morley had been marched from the room. 'I must send a message to Sir Robert Cecil. He is most likely on his way to Oxford by now. Might I use the services of two or three of your most trusted retainers to deliver it safely?'

Bess looked doubtful. 'What exactly were you thinking of saying in this message?'

Shakespeare held up his right hand. 'Nothing that would in any way reflect ill on your ladyship or the Lady Arbella. I merely wish to tell him that there will be no wedding. All else is clear to him. You may read it before I seal it.'

'Why not take it yourself, Mr Shakespeare?'

'Because, my lady, I have urgent business in the north.'

The rain had stopped but the September sky was still a dark grey. Shakespeare reined in his mount at the crossroads where the long track from Hardwick Hall intersected the great south–north road. There was nothing more he could do. Cecil would put a ring of impenetrable iron and steel around the Queen. If she were to die on September the eighteenth, as predicted by Dr Forman's death chart, it would have to be by God's hand, not man's.

He looked both ways, then turned left. Duty could wait.

The journey north, a hundred miles, might be possible in a day if ridden hard. But the grey mare had already suffered harsh treatment on the way to Hardwick from Sudeley, and so he took it more easily, stopping the night at a comfortable wayside tavern where he and the horse received good accommodation and fine food – oats and water for her, roast beef, fieldfare puddings and ale for him.

He left at dawn. By mid-afternoon he was drawing near to

Masham in Wensley Dale, a lush valley in the north of the vast county of Yorkshire. He could scarcely move his horse along for sheep. Great flocks of them crowded the road and the grass banks on either side, all being driven in the same direction. An ancient shepherd laughed and said they were all going to the town's sheep fair. 'Seventy thousand sheep,' he said. 'Count that if you please, master. That'll get you off to sleep.'

Black sheep, filthy, mud-arsed sheep, shorn sheep, milk-heavy ewes and ragged rams. Everywhere you looked there was a sea of sheep. The old shepherd told him there used to be a lot more, perhaps a hundred thousand head in the old days before Henry tore down the great abbeys of Jervaulx and Fountains. 'My father used to shepherd them for the silent white monks at Jervaulx. When he and I brought the sheep to the fair it was proper mayhem, like all the clouds had fallen from the sky and landed on the grass.'

Shakespeare left the road, looking to find a better way through the meadows running parallel to the main path. He was apprehensive at the prospect of meeting Catherine's family for the first time. He knew that her father, James, had developed a shaking palsy and was grown too frail to teach, so they now lived quietly near Masham, with a small pension from the grammar school and the dowry that Catherine's mother, Mary, had brought to the marriage many years ago. Catherine's brother was gone up to Cambridge on a scholarship, concealing his Catholicism as best he could.

The market square in Masham was heaving with sheep, many of them penned off but many more on the margins, being moved about in quest of a berth. In a side alley Shakespeare saw a big lamb held down having its throat slit ready for the butcher. Further along, a boy was sitting by a pot of boiling sheep fat, repeatedly dipping in a wick to make tallow candles. All around there was a mass of movement and the din of human and animal noise. The inns that opened out on to the large square were packed with smock-wearing shepherds and farmers, all quenching their thirst with great jugs of ale. Shakespeare went in the taproom of the first inn and asked a cheerful-looking ale-wench the whereabouts of the Marvell family.

She called out to the landlord. 'Jeremiah, where did you say the Marvells lived?'

'Out on the Jervaulx road. Old farmhouse without a farm, on your right. Just past the milestone.'

'There you go then, master. North-west is the way. You're the second stranger today looking for them. Must be a right royal revel out there. Is it christening, wedding or funeral?'

She was about to turn away to serve another customer, but Shakespeare stayed her with his hand. 'This other stranger – what was he like?'

'I don't know. Square-shaped, strong. Looked more like a pirate than a farmer with his pistol and sword. Not from these parts neither, from the sound of his voice.'

'A Devonshire man?'

She laughed. 'Now, how would I know that? I wouldn't know a Devon man from a Turkey man. I've never been out of Yoredale.'

'Well, did he have a limp, a club foot?'

'Can't say as I looked. There's hundreds here for the sheep fair, and I'm not going to spend my time staring at their feet. All I can tell you is that he had a face like a dog and gave me a drinkpenny for my trouble. Now, are you after some ale, or can I move along?'

Shakespeare thanked her and left the inn, quickly mounting his mare and kicking on through the dense crowd. He prayed it really was Boltfoot arrived here.

He found the farmhouse easily. Mary, Andrew and Grace were playing in the pathway at the front. Mary was chasing, and the older two were laughing as they dodged her outstretched arms. Mary saw him first and her little face creased into smiles as she ran up to his grey horse.

As he slid from the saddle and scooped her up in his arms, he felt the tension in his neck muscles ease a little and the anguish and terror of the past few days begin to recede.

The house was a scene of quiet domesticity. Boltfoot was holding his new baby, John, as if the little thing would break at his touch. Jane was enjoying five minutes of respite, sitting on the settle in the parlour beside her husband. She looked at him and their baby with undisguised adoration.

'Well done, Jane,' Shakespeare said. 'And you, Boltfoot. It is good fortune that Little John takes after his mother, not you, for indeed he is a handsome lad.'

Boltfoot took the insult as a well-meant jest and grunted. 'He has perfect little feet. Perfect.'

Shakespeare, still carrying little Mary in his arms, smiled and touched his friend's shoulder. 'That is good, Boltfoot.'

'I was frighted about his feet.'

Shakespeare smiled. He handed his assistant a small pouch of tobacco. 'I think I owe you that, Boltfoot.'

Boltfoot's eyes lit up. He had not had a pipe of sotweed in many days.

'He's brought someone with him, Mr Shakespeare,' Jane said. 'A woman called Eleanor Dare.'

The words brought Shakespeare up with a jolt. 'You found her?'

Boltfoot grunted again. He handed the baby to Jane and began packing a pipe with his new tobacco.

Shakespeare noticed Boltfoot's head was injured, his hair on one side cut close to reveal the scab of a healing wound. 'Boltfoot, your head.'

'That cooper I told you about. He was Mistress Dare's man. Clubbed me to the ground. But I have a hard head, so the barber-surgeon said at St Thomas' Hospital.'

Shakespeare frowned. 'Is it truly her? How did she get here?'

'I brought her. It was not safe in London. McGunn wants her dead. I had a shooting match with him, master, and we did ride away in great haste.' Boltfoot proceeded to fill in the details: the shooting of the groom, Perkin Sidesman; the intention to do for Eleanor; the killing of Davy Kerk. 'McGunn did for him like an English trooper might, Mr Shakespeare. Hewed him and punched him with a short sword. And he meant to string up the woman.'

Hew and punch. Those words again. Shakespeare shuddered. 'Where is she now?'

'Out walking with Mistress Shakespeare and her mother, master.'

Shakespeare's blood was running cold in his veins. 'Boltfoot, how long have you been here in Masham?'

'Over a day and a half, master. It was a long journey, could have taken a week over it, but we made good speed – got here in time for the birth, thank the Lord.' His weather-beaten face crinkled into a smile of affection.

So it had not been Boltfoot who had asked the bar-wench for directions earlier this day. 'Boltfoot,' Shakespeare said, his tone grim. 'McGunn is here. Where did you say Catherine and the women have gone?'

Boltfoot was already putting away his pipe and rising to his feet as Shakespeare spoke. 'Sidesman must have told him.'

Charlie McGunn walked his bay gelding to the livery stable behind the square. The horse was lame. The ostler shook his head and told McGunn the stables were full.

'Don't worry. He's yours. Look after him well, for he's a fine horse and will repay you well if you can mend him. Here, there's half a crown to help you along.'

The young ostler took the coin and unsaddled the horse. It was not every day a man brought money and a free gelding.

'Thank you, master.'

McGunn patted the horse farewell. 'But I'll be needing another one, a fresh horse, your fleetest and strongest. I will pay you four sovereigns in gold.'

'Indeed, I have just the fellow. A black stallion, fast but gentle. Very sound.'

'Good. Saddle him up for me and I'll collect him within the hour. Just do what you're told and you'll be a richer man by the time I leave.'

McGunn smiled at the lad, who had clearly never been offered so much money in his life and would be wondering who this brutish-looking man might be. A man with a foreign voice and an assortment of deadly armaments adorning his body: two decorated pistols thrust into his belt, a jewel-hilted Spanish sword – given him by King Philip of Spain – daggers, rope slung around his shoulder. The boy reminded McGunn of Joe. He handed him another half-crown. 'Find a girl and spend that on her – and I vouch she'll let you have your way with her out in the fields where the clover grows. Good luck to you, lad.'

He had taken his time riding here. There had been no hurry, never had been. Twelve years now, but it could go on another twelve years and twelve beyond that. As he walked away from the stables, he ran his fingers down the strong, hempen rope. Strong enough to take a woman's dead weight. He knew the limping cooper had brought the Roanoke woman here. He would take her out into a barn or some woods to string her up. Blood. There had to be more blood. The world would have to drown in blood to assuage his thirst.

The only hurdle was the crippled cooper. Shakespeare was dead, snuffed out by Slyguff, along with the little rope job he was doing down there at Sudeley, a wedding gift for Essex – *his* man Essex. The way things were going, he, Charlie McGunn, would soon have this whole pissing country in his purse. He laughed to himself; he didn't even want the stinking place.

The church bells rang six of the clock. It would be darkening soon. Just time to gather the others to refresh themselves with some food. The old farmhouse on the Jervaulx road was already watched. Tonight, they would make their move.

Chapter 41

SHAKESPEARE STOOD AT the back door to the farmhouse, looking out across the lush fields. He understood why Boltfoot had thought to bring the woman here, yet he was angry that he had brought McGunn after them and endangered their families.

In the distance he could see the three women, walking his way, carrying baskets laden with berries. In the centre was Catherine. He shivered at the sight of her, the most beautiful woman ever made by God. He watched her walking slowly through the long damp grass as in a dream.

On her right was the woman he took to be her mother. Smaller, her hair greying, but unmistakably her mother, Mary, for whom their own child was named.

And the fair, pretty woman on the left, was that really Eleanor Dare, one of the lost settlers of Roanoke? What strange story would this woman have to tell?

At the back of the house there was a vegetable garden with a chicken run, a pig shed, three beehives and a little area of lawn. Beyond it, to the left of an orchard, heavy with red apples, there was a low stone wall with a gate, a little over fifty yards from the house. As the three women came through the gate, Catherine saw him for the first time.

Her pace quickened. She moved away from the other women,

walking towards him. He had thought of this moment so often during the long saddle-sore hours, wondering how she would receive him.

She took his hands in hers and smiled. For a few moments they looked into each other's eyes. At last she spoke, laughter in her beautiful voice. 'I can't get away from you, can I, Mr Shakespeare? You follow me to the ends of the earth.'

He tried to laugh, too. 'I thought to do some business here, Mistress Shakespeare. As a wool factor, perchance, if I can find a sheep or two.'

'There are none in these parts, sir.'

'More than enough shepherds, though – and most of them being fleeced in the inns and ordinaries.'

'Will you bleat nonsense all day long, sir, or will you kiss your wife?'

He kissed her. Though they were observed, he kissed her lips and her mouth long and deep. He closed his eyes and wished fervently that the world and everyone in it would simply vanish for an hour or two, so that he might raise her skirts, here and now in this commonplace yard, and enter her.

He pulled back from her and gazed upon her face. It was wet with salt tears. Were they hers or his? It did not matter. What mattered now was that they were in grave danger, all of them. McGunn was here – and it was not likely he would be alone.

'It is good to see you, John. We have missed you greatly.'

'We have been absent from each other too long. But I bring grim tidings.' He turned towards the women accompanying her. 'Mistress Dare,' he bowed, 'you and Mr Boltfoot Cooper have been followed. I have information that the man who would kill you is in the town.'

Eleanor Dare's face was drained of colour and expression. Her eyes darted, as though looking for the bolt or arrow or ball that would cut her down. 'Then I have to get away,' was all she said.

'I agree.' He turned now to Catherine's mother. 'Mistress Marvell,' he bowed again, 'can you think of any place where we might safely go? The killer knows of this house.'

Catherine's parents would not leave their home, but everyone else in the house had to go. They travelled in separate directions in the late evening light. The three children went with Jane and the baby to the home of the constable, a friend of long standing, who had two strong lads. Jane would ask the constable to go to the town elders to see what could be done to raise an armed force to take on McGunn and his men. It occurred to Shakespeare, though, that a small, remote town like Masham would be unlikely to have anyone who could deal with a heavily armed mercenary such as McGunn.

The others – Shakespeare, Boltfoot, Catherine and Eleanor Dare – saddled up and rode along the Jervaulx road. The roads were full of livestock, farm workers and horsemen, some bound for the sheep fair, others heading home.

Shakespeare had not wanted his wife to ride with them. 'The children need you,' he had said, but she refused.

'How will you know where you are going without me?'

He had shrugged his shoulders. She was, of course, right.

Along the way, he told Boltfoot of Jack Butler's fate.

'The hew and punch,' said Boltfoot, shaking his head. 'I have seen it done before by trained men in battle.'

'But McGunn is not an English man-at-arms.'

Boltfoot rode on in silence for a few hundred yards before speaking. 'I have also heard of it used as a method of despatch under other circumstances: summary execution of captive enemies not worth ransoming. It is bloody, but effective and quick.'

By the time they neared their destination, three or four miles distant, scarcely a soul was on the road. The last of the grey daylight was turning to black.

Catherine slowed to a halt and her husband reined in sharply. The skeletal remains of the old abbey stood gaunt against the darkening northern sky. The rain was coming again and the wind was blowing up. God, but this was a bleak place. At their coming, a band of vagabonds scuttled away into the night like a family of squat rats. Shakespeare paid them no heed.

Catherine indicated somewhere in the dark fields and woods beyond the ruins of the abbey. 'Just yonder, on the edge of the river. The shepherd's cottage. It has been used by our cousins for many years. No one will disturb us there and he will never find us. We can make other plans on the morrow.'

Shakespeare kicked on slowly. They were away from the road now and it was almost impossible to see their way, for though they had pitch torches, it would be too dangerous to light them. All they could do was walk their horses as cautiously as possible in the moonlight, which gave a thin glow to the clouds; any sudden inclines or potholes could cause them to stumble. The scattered abbey stones, those that had not been stolen away after the dissolution, were the greatest hazard.

Catherine rode up beside her husband, picking her way between the ruins. 'It is all vanity and power, my husband, here in these stones.'

Shakespeare breathed deeply but said nothing.

'This place was dedicated to the Virgin, the mother of God's only begotten son, but it was destroyed by a devil masquerading as a man, a devil who thought nothing of relieving his own wives of their heads and who tore down God's houses as if they were children's castles of mud.'

'I understand your feelings, Catherine. And I am truly sorry for all that came between us these past days.'

'I know, John. I am sorry, too.'

The house was pitch dark. Catherine dismounted first and walked to the door. It was unlocked and she pushed it open, hesitating a moment before stepping inside. She had spent happy summers here in her childhood. She and her cousins had played in these fields and in the ruins of the abbey, splashing in the river, climbing the perilous walls and hiding in old hearths among the weeds and undergrowth that ran riot through the ancient stones where once Cistercian monks had spent their lives in worship and work.

Boltfoot was close behind her, lighting one of the pitch torches they had brought with them. He looked around. It was cold, damp and empty, a two-room house with bare stone walls and no hiding places. Each room had a single window, but neither of them had glass, so they were exposed to the wind and rain; all the building provided was a roof over their heads.

They had loaded their pack-saddles with meats, cheese, bread, ale, water and blankets. Soon they had a fire going in one of the rooms and ate their fill in silence, wondering where they might seek a more permanent shelter on the morrow. Outside, the wind hammered against the door. The torch and candles inside guttered in the draught and threw strange shadows across the walls.

Shakespeare stood up. 'We are sitting here like targets, Boltfoot.'

Boltfoot nodded his head and growled. He knew what to do. He rose, unslung his caliver, took the dry powder horn from beneath his hide jerkin and handed it and the firearm to Shakespeare. Then he thrust his cutlass into his belt and stepped out into the squally darkness.

The rain and wind blew in at the opening of the door, extinguishing the candles. The torch stayed alight.

At last Shakespeare turned to Eleanor Dare. 'This is a

most curious way to meet, mistress,' he said. 'I must confess that when my lord of Essex asked me to find you, I had never thought that this day would come.'

'Thank you for helping me.'

'I confess, too, that I was not happy when I discovered you were here, for it seemed you had brought evil with you. Men are dying because of this curious quest to find you.'

Catherine put an arm around the woman. 'Do not be hard, John. Eleanor has told me a little of what she knows. There is a story within her that burns her like a fever. Perhaps she will tell it, while we sit and wait for morning . . .'

'As you wish. Tell it as best you may and I will listen.'

Chapter 42

HER VOICE WAS quiet, scarce more than a whisper. 'We were on this shore,' she said. 'Watching the boats depart, waving God speed.'

That had been her last sight of her father. 'Tears streamed down my cheeks. Ananias, my husband, was at my side. I held Virginia tight to my breast, where she was suckling. I pointed at my father as he grew ever more distant. "There is your grandfather," I whispered to her. "He will return to us soon."'

It had been a forlorn hope for the darkness of war hung over England and no English ships would reach Roanoke again until three years later. And so they had to make the best of their new homeland. She described the island in disparaging terms, with loathing even. Yes, she said, it was sheltered and wooded, but it had little in the way of food for foraging or hunting and they had arrived too late for planting.

Worse than that, though, was the feeling that it was somehow haunted, that eyes watched them wherever they went, that they were not welcome and never would be. And their fear was not mere imagination, for most of the native Indian tribes in the area had come to loathe the settlers from across the sea. There had been clashes. A local chieftain had been killed. The danger of reprisals was always present – and the Indians could no longer be relied on to help when the colonists were short of food.

'Our home was a small, wood-built cottage with wattle-and-daub panels,' Eleanor said. 'The first colonists had put it up and it was serviceable, though it was ill-equipped for the winters, when the wind rattled through the gaping holes and thatch. We were outside the main fort, but nearby in case of attack. We all wished, though, that the houses had been *within* the palisade, for we would have slept more soundly.'

That late summer and autumn of 1587, after the ships had gone, the settlers began to realise that it was going to be bad. If the men went fishing or deer hunting, they had to go in numbers, with arms, for fear that the savages would pick them off. Just going to the midden, away from the palisade, filled them with terrors.

One of the assistant governors, George Howe, had been murdered even before John White left with the ships. Eleanor reeled off the names of others who soon fell victim. 'Thomas Stevens was the next, filled with arrows and his eyes taken. Then Agnes Wood and Jane Jones vanished together one day while foraging for nuts. They were never found, neither dead nor alive.'

Eleanor Dare paused, her eyes closed as if remembering something, a face of a long-dead friend, perhaps. Catherine Shakespeare reached out and took her hand. 'What had made you go there, Mistress Dare?'

Eleanor sighed. Outside the stone cottage, the wind gusted and the rain beat down. 'I never did want to be on that heathen shore, but Ananias was full of zeal. "We'll be able to worship free, Ellie," he would say, "as God intended for us. We will never be free in England." Ralegh had promised us five hundred acres of virgin land. My father and the others – Harriot, Hakluyt, Sir Walter and the corporation – they said it was a land of untold riches. The men believed every word, but not me. My mother, God rest her soul, did always call me Doubting Ellie, for my suspicions; whenever others cheered I always held my counsel.'

She spoke then of the long journey there, when she was already with child, and how she had become increasingly wary. The voyage had been full of sickness. Two and a half months long from early May, through the summer, 'in weather so hot the ship's bilges threw up a stink, like the bowels of hell'. The mariners did not like them and gave them the worst of the food – salt pork with maggots, biscuit that had turned blue-grey with mould. But Eleanor, at least, found some kindness. Perhaps it was her prettiness or the fact that her belly was swelling with each passing day, but one of the crewmen had looked out for her, bringing her the best of the meats and butter, cheese and ale. He made certain that she was as comfortable as could be, despite the sour looks of Ananias, who did not like the attentions the man paid his wife. 'I am sorry if Ananias was unhappy, but in truth I doubt I would have seen my baby to term without that man's help.'

Eleanor shivered and folded her arms about her chest. She paused, summoning up the memories so long suppressed. The first winter had been terrible, she said. They had been told it would be warm and mild all year round, being so far south, but that was not how it was. Winter there was more bitter than any they had encountered in England. The wind cut in from the sea like a knife forged from ice and steel.

Ananias, her husband, was killed on Christmas morning. He had gone out from the palisade alone to check on the traps and bring in some firewood. When he did not return by noon, some of the men went out after him, but all knew there was no hope. They found him stretched out on the ground, tied by his ankles and wrists to four stakes. A fifth stake had been driven through his belly and he had been left there to die. He must have screamed in pain, but they did not hear him. Or if they did, they took it for the howling of the wind. The men went out to avenge him, but that brought no comfort.

The rift was so deep then that none of the tribes would trade with them, not even those that had held back from open hostility. When the settlers approached their villages, the Indians fled for the woods.

'Thomas Topan was next to die, then Mark Bennett. Horribly murdered and mutilated, both of them. There was sickness, too, and by spring a half-dozen were gone with the bloody flux, including Margery Harvey's baby, who had been born soon after my Virginia. Our only hope then was that my father would return with supplies. But the summer came and went and there was no sign of him.'

The words Eleanor spoke and the lashing of the rain were the only sounds in that shepherd's cottage next to the ruins of Jervaulx. Suddenly, Shakespeare put up a hand to hush her. 'Listen,' he whispered. For a minute the three of them sat in silence, imagining voices in the wind or footsteps among the raindrops. Was that how it had been night after night in the New World? 'Nothing,' Shakespeare said at last, though he was less than certain. 'Nothing . . . I'm sorry. Carry on, Mistress Dare.'

The second winter came, she said. Their crops had failed. They had so little food they ate seaweed from the shore and bark from the trees. 'Every little animal trapped, even a mouse, was like a gift from God to our shrunken stomachs.' Their livestock died one by one. John Borden and Joan Warren were taken by the flux.

Yet still the colony survived and spring came again. The spring of 1589, then summer. And then, at last, in early July of that year, ships came. With English ensigns bravely flying, they waved to the settlers as they rowed ashore in their ship's boats. 'Never before or since have I seen a sight to so gladden the heart,' Eleanor said with a bitter laugh.

There were four ships, two of them fighting galleons and two barks. Eleanor's voice became slower as she recalled that fateful day. 'Thirty or more men came ashore with shouts of welcome and we did instantly recognise two of them from the voyage to Roanoke: there was Davy Bramer and Mr Slyguff. There was also the man that I now know to be Charles McGunn, smiling broadly and booming a loud greeting.'

Unarmed, the men, women and children all ran towards them. But Eleanor held back. 'I could not tell you why, except that I have these feelings. When others do seem keen, I begin to have doubts.' And so she slunk back towards the palisade and waited there in silence in one of the storehouses, holding Virginia, who was nearly two by then.

She knew something was wrong as soon as she heard shouting and orders. 'Soon, I did not hear the voices of my fellows any more, only those of the mariners that had come for us. Nor were they all English voices, but Spanish, too. The reason I am alive today is that Davy Bramer looked for me and found me before anyone else.'

It had been Davy Bramer who brought her food on the voyage out. Now, in the coolness of the storehouse, where their paltry provisions were kept in sacks of jute, he put a finger to his lips, then gestured for her to follow him out from the palisade into the woods. No one saw them go. At times, she said, she wished they had, so that she might never have had to live through what was to follow.

As if divining what Eleanor was about to say, Catherine squeezed her hands. 'You don't need to go on . . .'

Eleanor shook her head. 'I must tell you this. Oh, the horror is with me still. I cannot look upon a child but I do think of that day. He took Virginia from my arms and bade me kiss her. She was shaking, even at her tender years, she was in fear. Gently, he lay her down upon the ground, her head upon a flat rock. I watched, though I knew what he would do and why, and I did nothing to save her, because I could not. Davy brought up a boulder of half a hundredweight by my reckoning, and, with all his force, drove it into her head, killing her without a sound, except for the crack of stone on bone, like a hammer.'

'I cannot tell you what happened next. I was gasping for air. My smock and kirtle were covered in my baby's blood. I know that we did bury her beneath some leaves and I know that somehow Davy did get me aboard the galleon, but I do not know how he did it.' Her body was moving, she said, but her mind was dead. Davy put her in a jute sack and told her to be still, as still as death. Somehow he carried her aboard as though she was a bag of carrots or some other produce. All she could recall was that she was manhandled, that she heard voices and smelt the sea and the tar and the bilges.

At one time she was dropped heavily on to a deck, but even then she did not cry out, nor move. 'Somehow he did get me aboard that rotten ship of death, and he did conceal me in the nethermost region, among the ballast and bilge water and cable rolls and barrels of tar, where few men tarried except when they needed to collect stores. It was dark there and smelt like the devil's jakes, but there were nooks for me to hide in when a mariner came down in the long weeks that followed.'

She lived there like a rat, scuttling at the slightest footfall, crouching behind a cask or reclining silently along the bilge-keel, listening to her heart and hoping it would not be heard. Davy brought her scraps of food and ale. But he could never stay long. It was weeks before she asked him what had become of the others. At first he seemed reluctant to tell her and she could scarcely bear to know, for she knew there was horror. She knew the reason he had killed Virginia was that they were all destined for death and because he could never have brought her to safety. 'I knew he had done it to save me and to save her from a worse fate, and that he had much courage, for he was hazarding his own life. But I often wished he had killed me with her.'

He told her the others had been taken aboard ship at the point of gun and sword. The Irishmen took great delight in carving the letters *CRO* on a tree, and the word *Croatoan* on a gate of our palisade. They also dismantled the houses and carried them away so that nothing should be left.

The truth, of course, was that the ships were Spanish, bearing false flags. The crew was more than half Spanish, along with many Irish and a few Netherlanders, including Davy. Mostly, they were military men, sailors or kerns. Davy told her it was Slyguff who had somehow got copies of the rutters from Fernandez on the earlier voyage aboard the *Lion* – and that was how they had navigated their way to the island. As Davy understood it, the mission was funded by Philip of Spain, but it was McGunn who lay behind it.

'What did they do to the colonists?' Shakespeare asked.

'Davy told me it happened in the first hours out from Roanoke, within four or five leagues of shore. McGunn killed the colonists himself. Each and every one. He killed all the women by hanging and the men with swords. Each woman was hanged from the yards, and the men forced to watch. Then he did for the men. One slash to the neck, one in the belly. As each died, McGunn kicked him into the Western Sea. And as one sword blunted, so he took another and another, until all the men were dead and the decks were thick with gore. His own clothes were drenched in the blood of a hundred poor innocent souls.'

The Spanish and the others had looked on in silence. As far as they were concerned, it was done for King Philip, to avenge the Armada, but Eleanor never believed that and nor did Davy. It was all done for McGunn, who seemed to carry a dark hatred in his heart.

'Now I am the only one left and now McGunn knows I

am alive, he will pursue me until I am hanged like the other women. I must be hanged, I know that much, though I know not why. He will kill me no other way.'

There was a sound outside the cottage somewhere. Shakespeare put a finger to his lips and peered out. For a moment he thought he saw a light among the trees, but then it was gone. A gap in the clouds, a trick of the moon, perhaps. He picked up Boltfoot's caliver; it was primed with powder and loaded with ball-shot. He held it close to his body, aimed at the door. They waited a minute, two minutes, in silence.

'It could be a deer. Perhaps a wild dog,' Catherine said at last, though she did not believe it.

'I must finish my story.'

Shakespeare nodded his assent. 'Whisper it.'

After six weeks, she said, the vessel moored at the port of Angra on the south side of the island of Terceira, to take on supplies. The island was Portuguese, though ruled by Spain, and there were peoples of many different hues and languages there. It was among those islands called the Azores, and was a place where the treasure fleets from the New World put in. It was a busy port, with many ships jostling at anchor in the harbour.

With Davy's help, it was a simple thing for her to get off the ship at night, when all the crew were ashore drinking and wenching. He had found a lodging among the narrow streets, a small room on the second storey of an old Portuguese white-painted house that looked out over the harbour. The landlord was an honest and holy man, a Papist Fleming, who took a fair rent and fed them well.

They did not leave that room until they saw that McGunn's ships had sailed from the harbour. Even then, they waited a week before venturing out, for fear that it was a ruse and that they would return to find Davy.

'Those were strange days. We came to know each other, Davy and me. He had risked his life for me, and I grew to love him, though never forgive him. He told me that when he had embarked with McGunn, he did not know what was planned. It was only when he was told that they must get all the colonists aboard without alarming them that he became worried. He could think of no other reason for their deception than that they meant to kill us. He thought they probably planned to kill him, too, before the voyage ended.'

They spent the autumn and winter on Angra. 'I found much kindness there. The quayside was full of the smell of good fresh fish cooking over red-hot coals.' But they knew they could not stay on the island. One of the Spaniards or Irishmen might return at any time and spot them. Shipping came in and out every week, so it would never be safe. Two years ago, in the spring of 1590, Davy heard of a merchantman from the Spanish Lowlands, and made inquiries of the master. He agreed to take them to Antwerp, where he was headed, for twenty gold ducats.

'Davy always had coin, so he paid our fare. The voyage was uneventful at first with fair weather and brisk winds.' But they were set upon by English privateers as they neared the western approaches of the Channel, and their ship's master surrendered without a fight.

Eleanor and Davy were taken into Plymouth and set at liberty. Davy had told Eleanor they must never reveal the truth of who they were, so they told the customs officials that she was the widow of an English merchant venturer in Lisbon, returning home by way of Antwerp, and that Davy was her manservant.

Davy understood that his life would be forfeit if ever it was known he had been involved in the capture and slaughter of the colonists. They knew, too, that Eleanor would be condemned as a traitor and a harlot for surviving as she did. 'But most of all, we knew that the devil McGunn, wherever he was in the world, would pursue me to his last dying breath if he knew I was alive.'

Davy changed his name from Bramer to Kerk and they hoped to live quietly. They had no idea that McGunn would come to England. They thought him wedded to the Spanish and Catholic cause, like so many Irishmen, and so they made their way to London, where they believed they might go undiscovered. And so it turned out for a year or more. She came with child twice, but lost them both times, which she took to be God's judgement for the death of Virginia.

'Then Agnes Hardy saw me by the baiting pits. I was meeting Davy there from his work. I heard her and saw her, and did make away as best I could and prayed she would think she was mistaken.

'I have no idea what ill chance brought news of it to McGunn. When Mr Cooper turned up at Hogsden Trent's that day, Davy was horrified. We did not know what to do for the best, nor did we know, then, of McGunn's involvement. Should we stay in London, or go elsewhere? And if we should go, where should we go to? It felt to us then that there was no place in the world that we would be safe. Davy said that the City was the best, because a man could vanish and bury his past in a great place like London.'

That was when Boltfoot became more insistent, however. 'So, Davy said he would fix him. I begged him to do him no harm; I said there had already been too much blood, but Davy was beyond reason, and did try to kill him.' Eleanor had followed Davy and saw it happen. Davy was about to hit him again, but she pulled him off.

'I thank God we were so near the hospital, and that they could save Mr Cooper's life. He is a fine man. By then, though, it was too late for us. Mr Cooper did not know it, but he had led McGunn to us. He killed Davy just as he killed all the colonists, with a slash of his sword to the neck and a stab to the belly. I was to be next, strung up by the neck in the buttery. Yet Mr Cooper did save me, and here I am. I have walked through the valley of the shadow of death, Mr Shakespeare, but I fear my days are drawing to a close. I fear the devil will find us here. Soon, very soon, I will hang by the neck and join my Virginia in the hereafter. I pray with all my heart, that you good people here with me will go unharmed . . .'

Chapter 43

SHAKESPEARE LISTENED TO the tale with half an ear to the wind outside. It was told simply, without embellishment. At last he said, 'It was Agnes Hardy's master, the portraitist William Segar, who told Essex and McGunn of you. When I set Boltfoot to find you, I had no reason to believe anyone intended you harm.'

'It is no fault of yours, sir. I accept that.'

Shakespeare yawned with fatigue from his long hours riding, yet he knew he must stay awake and alert. 'Try to sleep,' he said to his wife and Eleanor. 'I will keep watch, and with Boltfoot outside, watching in the woods, we will be safe. No man will find us here.'

They had eaten some of the food they had brought and had sipped from the flagon of ale. Shakespeare took very little liquor, for he had to keep his wits sharp. Though he was as certain as he could be that this place was secure, he also understood that McGunn was a man of cunning and unnatural persistence.

Outside the old shepherd's cottage, the wind lashed the rain into a frenzy. Inside, the two women huddled into their blankets and sat on the floor against a wall.

At the edge of the wood, thirty yards from the cottage, Boltfoot lay in the undergrowth. He was not far from the river, as still as stone. Every ounce of his being was concentrated on the area in front of the house and beyond, towards the ruined abbey. Anyone coming from the highway must cross his path.

Being soaked through was nothing new to him. Many times in the raging gales of the southern oceans, there had not been a thing left dry aboard ship. For days and weeks on end his clothes had been sodden and his skin cold.

He lay on a carpet of leaves and twigs and mud, his eyes keen in the darkness, sensing movement as a nocturnal animal might. A badger scurried into view, caught his scent and hastened away. Boltfoot thought of the caliver he had left with Shakespeare. It would have been pointless bringing it out here in this rain. He could have kept the powder dry for some time, but lying prostrate on the earth, with the rain tumbling in torrents, the damp would have seeped through the horn's lid and rendered it useless.

The rain came and came. Boltfoot did not share his master's fond belief that they were safe here. Everything he knew, all his experience, told him that McGunn would come for them this night. He was right.

The attack came with terrifying speed and deadly purpose.

The two women had not slept, yet they were heavy-lidded and their senses had slowed. They sat side by side against the wall, out of sight of the gaping window, as Shakespeare had insisted. The way they huddled, Catherine and Eleanor might have been old friends or sisters.

He heard a noise outside. A figure sloshing through the mud. Coming their way.

There was a scream and then an explosion, then moaning.

The two women both jumped to their feet at the sound of the discharge. Shakespeare put his finger to his lips; then patted the palm of his hand downwards to indicate they should stay low. He extinguished the candle and doused the little fire. Better to equalise the darkness than allow the light to be used against them.

He picked up Boltfoot's caliver once more. It was still primed and loaded. He held it in front of him, pointing it at the closed door.

Boltfoot had sensed the man in the darkness even before he began his move for the house. He was coming at a crouch across the mud-slide of open ground. Boltfoot crawled on his belly, then lifted himself a few inches on one elbow and knee. He swung back his right arm and with his razor-edged cutlass cut like a farm-hand scything barley at the man's legs.

As steel struck bone, the intruder screamed and crumpled. Instinctively, his finger clenched the trigger of his wheel-lock, firing a ball harmlessly into the ground.

Boltfoot rose to both knees, took his long dagger from his belt and thrust upwards with his left hand. The narrow blade slid through flesh, up into the man's belly, up under his ribs, until the point cut the heart to bring death. Boltfoot pulled the dying body to him, as a shield, and crouched down behind it. The man moaned – more an outrush of air than a cry – and his body twitched.

Crouching behind the body, Boltfoot knew the attack had been nothing but a foray. The dead man had been a sacrifice to draw him out into the open. Boltfoot was exposed now, and vulnerable. How many more men did McGunn have out there?

There was little light, just enough to make movement visible. He had to get away from the body, slowly. Flat to the ground, he tried to edge away towards the copse where he had been hiding. A musket shot rent the air and a ball struck the ground where he had been a moment earlier. He let out a scream, to make them think he had been hit. Another shot. This time the ball hit the dead body of the assailant with a sickening whump.

Boltfoot did not halt. He had to move away or the next shot would do for him. But how could he move in open ground when McGunn had his range? As he inched away, Boltfoot resigned himself to death.

Shakespeare peered out of the empty window. He could make out two dark humps on the ground in front of the house. One was moving, one was not. Boltfoot was either dead or in trouble. Shakespeare pointed the caliver in the general direction of the dark-shadowed abbey ruins and loosed off a ball, with no idea where he was shooting.

The recoil knocked him back into the room, just as another shot whipped over his head and struck the far wall, gouging out an uneven wedge of mortar and stone.

He scrabbled up into a crouching position. It was darker inside the room than out. 'Catherine,' he whispered. 'Catherine, keep down. Lie flat.'

'John, she's gone.' Her voice was urgent and low.

'What are you saying?'

'It's so dark. I think Eleanor slid out of the other window into the night.'

'She will die out there.'

'She said something, "Futile, futile". Then she was no longer at my side.'

They were trapped like magpies in a cage and the bird they had been trying to save had flown. Another musket-ball struck nearby, dislodging a six-inch splinter of rotting wood from the empty window frame.

Shakespeare raised his head, looked out and saw a light. A pitch torch cast an eerie glow on the broken walls and archways of the long-dead abbey. A figure crossed in front of the torch. How many men were there? Two? Three? Four? Twenty?

Another musket-ball exploded in the night.

'Catherine,' he whispered, reloading the caliver as best he could. 'I am going out there. We must both get out from this house. It is a death-trap. You make for the woods, away from the abbey.'

'I know this land, John. Do not fret for me. You do what you must do.'

'Go first. Slip from the window, then run as fast as you are able. Do not go straight, but weave from side to side. Foil their aim. Crouch low.'

'Mr Shakespeare, I see you are as overbearing as ever. But for once, I shall forget my pride and obey you.'

He could scarcely see her in the gloom, but he could smell her musky scent and feel her close presence. Quickly he took her in his arms and kissed her. Her arms encircled him as she arched her body into his. It was as if there had never been any distance between them.

They moved away, their hands clasping each other's until it was just the tips of their fingers touching. 'Go, Mistress Shakespeare. Go and survive and I pledge that I will never attempt to command you again.'

Catherine was small and slight. She slid over the sill and ran. She knew every inch of this ground and headed with all speed through the teeming rain towards the copse to the right of the house. She thought she saw two bodies to her side, but she paid them no heed. She could do nothing for them, whoever they were.

One musket-ball, two, clipped past her, slapping into the wet ground somewhere beyond her. And then she was in the dripping trees. She went on, catching her dress on brambles, battling through thorny undergrowth until she was sure she was clear of the killing ground.

She sat a few moments on the wet leaves, caught her breath, then moved on towards the abbey and McGunn. Even without light, she would be able to navigate her way through its stones. She had obeyed her husband against her better judgement once before; she had no intention of doing so again. Someone had to see what sort of foe they were up against, and no one was better qualified on this terrain than she.

The sight that greeted her was awful in its horror. When she had encountered Father Robert Southwell, bundled in agony against the wall of the Gatehouse Prison, she had thought there could be nothing more hideous in the world, that she would be haunted by his torment for the remainder of her days. But this . . . the awfulness of this lay in the very familiarity of the surroundings, this place of happiness from her childhood days, now turned into a scene of unspeakable barbarity.

Covered lanterns had been lit, casting a hellish light on the old, rain-wet stones of the monks' dorter, where the Cistercian brothers had once slept. From the high wall of this dormitory, a rope had been slung over a projecting beam. It hung down malevolently, with a noose at its end around the slim neck of Eleanor Dare.

A long ladder had been placed against the wall. Eleanor was halfway up the steps, forlorn and drenched, her arms bound behind her back, waiting to be hanged. A man behind her was pushing her ever upwards and she scarce seemed to put up any resistance, as though she were resigned to her fate.

Beneath her, two more men stood watching, both of them heavily armed. One of them held the loose end of the hanging rope, tightening it as Eleanor ascended the ladder.

'Come out, Shakespeare!'

Catherine, crouching behind a block of sandstone in the old

cloister, did not know the voice but guessed it to be Charlie McGunn's. It was rough and taunting.

'Come out, Shakespeare. Come and see the show. We'll do your wife next; make a night of it. Your man Cooper is already dead. Here you are, come and get him . . .'

With immense strength, the man dragged a short, squat body from the ground and held it aloft over his head. He spun it around, then flung it away as casually as a farmer would toss a sack of turnips into a cart.

The other men with him laughed.

Boltfoot dead! Oh, Jane, poor Jane. Catherine felt utter despair. She had no way of saving this poor woman, any more than she had been able to save Southwell or Anne Bellamy from the foul Topcliffe. John had been right all along. Be wary. Place your trust in cold caution, not faith. While God slept, the powerful held sway and the good died.

Chapter 44

SHAKESPEARE HAD FOLLOWED Catherine through the window but ran away from her to divide McGunn's fire.

He had barely gone five yards when the musket-ball hit him. He fell heavily to the ground, grunting with shock. His right hand went to his left shoulder. The ball had sheared a groove of flesh, on the outside of the upper arm, just beneath the shoulder blade.

Ignoring the injury as best he could, he dived for cover behind a broken old wain. The ancient wagon sat on its overgrown undercarriage, its four wheels fallen away and splayed out. He heard horses whinnying away to his right. He touched his shoulder again. It was sticky with blood and rain. He still clutched the caliver in his left hand. He tried to cover it beneath his cape. If he could loose off one shot at close range, it might be crucial.

He heard a voice, not more than thirty yards away. McGunn. Taunting him. Threatening to kill his wife. Gloating that Boltfoot was dead.

Shakespeare crawled away to his left. No musket-balls followed him. There was a low dry-stone wall, and he sped the last three steps until he was behind it. For a moment, he caught his breath. Hunching low so that only the curve of his back was visible above the wall, he began running – away from McGunn, but also around him. He would come at him from the other side, to the south of the abbey ruins.

He stopped and peered over the wall. He had a clear view now. The area in front of the abbey was lit by torches. He saw the rope slung high and he saw Eleanor Dare about to die. The man behind her pushed her roughly and she climbed another rung up the ladder. Apart from him and a man who looked from behind very like McGunn, there was one other visible. But there could be any number of armed men concealed.

In the darkness behind the high wall with the noose, he saw a movement in the stones. He peered closer and saw, with horror, that it was Catherine. Shakespeare had to do something, and fast. He took aim with the caliver, pointing at the back of the man he took to be McGunn, and fired.

Nothing happened. The powder was damp. He looked at the weapon in dismay, flung it down and picked up a rock, the size of a small cannon ball, and hurled it at the man by the abbey wall.

It caught the man's heel. He jumped and swivelled around, glaring in Shakespeare's direction.

It was McGunn. Shakespeare ducked down below the wall. 'Get him!'

McGunn had a short sword drawn. He advanced on the wall with the man closest to him, leaving the hangman halfway up the ladder behind Eleanor.

Shakespeare crouched down and began to lope away southwards in the darkness, hoping to draw the men away from Catherine. His approach scattered a group of startled sheep, then he stumbled on a rock and fell awkwardly on his injured shoulder in the muddy grass. He stifled a cry of pain.

He pushed himself up on to his hands and knees and tried to stand. But he was too slow. McGunn's man had his arms in a grip as tight as a torturer's screw and wrenched him up and backwards.

'Well, well, Mr Shakespeare,' McGunn said, striding up to him, the naked Toledo steel blade of his sword slung nonchalantly over his right shoulder. 'You're just in time for the hangings.'

The man laughed as he marched Shakespeare back towards the abbey. Shakespeare looked at the body on the ground. His captor kicked it as he walked past. Shakespeare looked more closely. It wasn't Boltfoot.

'On with the show, Mr O'Regan,' McGunn shouted to the man on the ladder. 'Kick her away and let her swing.'

Shakespeare watched in horror as the man on the ladder looped the end of the rope around a jutting rock, and then knotted it so that the rope was tight.

He pushed Eleanor off the ladder, then leapt down, pulling the ladder away, leaving her unbound legs scrabbling for a foothold that was no longer there. The rope lurched tight around her neck, choking the life from her. For a few moments time seemed to stand still as Shakespeare and the three men watched her hanging there, struggling for life.

'See how she dances, Mr Sh—' McGunn began. He was cut short by an explosion. The hangman fell forward, the top of his head sheared away. A mist of blood seemed to hang in the air, then fell with the rain.

McGunn held his sword in front of him. With his other hand, he reached into his belt and pulled out a loaded wheel-lock.

With every bit of power at his command, Shakespeare pitched himself backwards, knocking his captor into the rocky ground. The man screamed as he fell against a boulder, cracking the centre of his spine against the sharp stone. Shakespeare, winded, pulled himself away from the man's arms. He turned and, reaching out behind him, closed his hand round a large stone, battering at the man's head.

The rain-soaked night was lit by the flickering flames of

three covered pitch torches. McGunn was looking from left to right, his mastiff-like face eerily brutish in the weird light and rain. He could not see where the shot had come from, so he aimed the wheel-lock at Shakespeare and fired. The ball hit the writhing figure of his own man in the side of the chest. A stream of thick blood washed over Shakespeare and he felt the man go limp.

As Shakespeare rolled away, he saw Boltfoot stride out from the darkness like some monster from the depths of the dripping forest, his left foot dragging behind him. He had a pistol in his left hand, and in his right he held his cutlass, the bright blade glistening.

Dropping his expended wheel-lock, McGunn pulled another one from his belt. As he raised it to aim at Boltfoot, Shakespeare launched himself at the Irishman. McGunn tried to twist around to shoot Shakespeare instead, but the ball flew harmlessly between the two men.

McGunn tried slashing down at Shakespeare's neck with his sword, but he stepped away easily, then McGunn thrust forward at his stomach. Once more, he slid aside but felt the blade cutting into his doublet.

'You are going to hell in pain, Shakespeare,' McGunn growled as he pulled the sword back and tried to thrust again. From behind him, Boltfoot hacked down with his cutlass and McGunn's sword clattered from his hand on to the sodden earth and rocks.

Boltfoot had him now. He was shorter than the bull-muscled McGunn but he was strong. He grasped the scalp above the nape of the Irishman's neck and pulled back his head, while Shakespeare tried to wrestle him to the ground.

McGunn emitted a low roar, like a wildcat at bay, but he could not stand under this onslaught and slid and collapsed to the ground. Shakespeare pinioned his left arm, while Boltfoot struggled to control the right hand, which had grasped the jewelled hilt of a dagger and was attempting to pull the long blade from its sheath.

Twisting, Boltfoot dug his elbow hard into McGunn's mouth, then pulled his dagger hand back and cracked the man's forearm down against his knee. The force was so great it was like breaking a dry, dead branch over a farm gate. The forearm snapped. McGunn did not cry out, but just growled deeper. He was practically helpless now, yet still he fought on as Shakespeare and Boltfoot struggled to turn him over on to his face.

'For pity's sake, one of you help me!'

Shakespeare looked up startled at the sound of Catherine's anguished voice. She had the ladder against the wall and was almost at the top of it, holding the body of Eleanor Dare, taking her weight.

Shakespeare heaved himself to his feet and ran to the ladder. He shinned up, first encircling his arms around Catherine, then pulling himself higher and taking the weight of Eleanor, whose body hung as limp as a slaughtered pig.

'Ease yourself down,' he commanded Catherine. 'And reach for my knife.'

Releasing her grip on Eleanor, Catherine slid down under her husband's body. She found his dagger in its sheath and handed it to him. Taking Eleanor's full weight in his right arm, he reached up with his left hand and sliced and slashed at the hemp rope. Fibre by agonising fibre, he cut through the taut cable until suddenly she slumped away from it, the noose and a foot of rope still about her neck. Clumsily, he slipped down the rungs holding her over his shoulder.

He laid her out on the ground and fought to loosen the rough noose from about her neck. Finally it was free. He put his ear to her chest. A heartbeat. He was sure he could hear a heartbeat.

Pulling her lean young body up into his arms so that she sat upright against him, her head over his shoulder, he smacked her back as he would a baby that needed winding.

Of a sudden, she was coughing, her ribcage beating against his chest in spasms. She was sucking in air, gasping. She was alive.

Catherine watched Eleanor return to life and crossed herself. Her thoughts had been in the Gatehouse Prison, where she had held Father Southwell's limp, dead-weight body, tormented against Topcliffe's wall. Please let me save this woman where I could do nothing to save Robert, she had prayed as she held Eleanor's hanging weight at the top of the ladder. O Lord, show your mercy.

'Thank God,' she said now. 'Thank you, God.'

Shakespeare and Boltfoot bound McGunn hand and foot with the length of rope used to hang Eleanor. They knew it must cause him immense pain to have his broken arm so restrained, but they did not care much. While life still flickered in this man's breast, he was a danger.

They examined the three dead bodies. Shakespeare thought they might be among the Irish beggars that congregated around Essex House. He recalled the words McGunn had used when first they saw them: 'They may be only beggars, but they are *our* beggars.' Men he paid so that he might call on them whenever he had some dirty work to be done. They were his men, and now they had died for him. But who was the squat one whose body McGunn had held aloft in triumph, mistaking him for Boltfoot? They studied his face closely. 'All I can think is that he was one of those vagabonds we encountered as we turned from the road, come scavenging for food,' Shakespeare suggested.

Boltfoot nodded towards the woods. 'There's another one in

there. I clubbed him and took the pistol from him. He might be still alive. We'd better get him. The one who came first, in front of the cottage, is dead, though. I'm certain of that.'

They dragged McGunn to the little house while Catherine tended to Eleanor. In the larger of the two rooms, they tethered the wrist of his uninjured arm to a ring embedded into the wall and made a rough splint, which they fixed to the broken forearm. He sat there sullenly, his eyes full of malice and no remorse.

Boltfoot went out to find his caliver and take the firearms, swords and daggers of the dead men. In the woods he found the man he had clubbed. He was still breathing but unconscious. Boltfoot tied his inert body to a tree and left him there to soak in the unceasing rain. As to the dead men, they would deal with them in the morning.

Helped by Shakespeare, Catherine had brought Eleanor to the shepherd's cottage. She had her hand to her fiercely swollen throat, and though she was weak and faltering, she was conscious and able to walk slowly. They sat her down in the other room and gave her sips of ale to try to soothe her. Catherine gathered up capes and blankets and made a palliasse for her to lie on.

'Sleep, if you can,' Catherine said gently. 'You are safe now. I will stay with you.'

In the other room, Boltfoot had his caliver, now dried and primed with fresh gunpowder, trained on McGunn. Shakespeare ignored the blood seeping from his own wounded shoulder and took over. 'It were best if you ride for Masham, Boltfoot, to the constable.'

Boltfoot nodded obediently and handed the weapon to his master.

McGunn looked at his captor with eyes that seemed

strangely resigned. 'Would you have a sup of ale for me, Mr Shakespeare?'

Shakespeare had a flagon at his side. He held it to McGunn's lips. He drank thirstily.

'Thank you,' he said. 'You can stop pointing that thing at me, you know. I'm not going anywhere.' He nodded his close-shaved, pulpy head at the caliver.

Warily, Shakespeare placed the caliver on the dirt floor, well away from his captive but close enough to his own right hand.

'I will be dead soon. I wanted to tell you a thing or two. Explain, perhaps, though I don't expect anything from you in return. I have no remorse and I seek no redemption. But some-one should know what this was about. You might think I am going to hell, but I know that hell is here, in this world.'

'Tell it to the justice.'

'No. I'm going to tell you. It was the autumn of 1580. I was a farrier in those days. I had never picked up anything more lethal than a hammer and never struck anything but an iron shoe on the anvil in anger. I had a wife and was about to have a child. My wife – my beautiful fine girl – was called Maggie Maeve and I loved her more than life itself. You'd know about that, Shakespeare. You have a beautiful fine girl yourself.

'We lived a little inland, in a farm village. Maggie Maeve's widowed mother lived at the coast, at Smerwick or St Mary Wick – well, that's its English name. It is a lovely harbour vil-lage, a little way north of Dingle Bay on the south-west coast of Ireland. Maggie Maeve was heavy with child when she went to visit her mother that October. She had no idea – how could we? – that a Catholic force of a few hundred Spaniards and Italians had landed and that the English were coming for them, in force. Four thousand blood-hungry savages from this mon-strous island, who had no cause to be in my country.

'Maggie Maeve found herself trapped, along with the

Spanish and Italian soldiers and two hundred Irish men and women who had joined them to fight the English. She had no way back to me, for the English laid siege to their makeshift fort with artillery. All escape was blocked off. After three days of bombardment, it was clear the situation was hopeless and so the besieged Spaniards and their Irish allies hung out the white flag of *misericordia*. They then surrendered, believing their lives were to be spared.'

'What happened?'

'What do you think happened, Mr Shakespeare? The English slaughtered them. Every man – excepting the few Spanish nobles that might raise a ransom – was disarmed, bound and cut to pieces one by one by the English soldiery. Butchered like oxen: a hack of the sword to the neck, sometimes severing the head, sometimes not, then a thrust to the stomach to make certain. Hew and punch. That was what they did to the men. First, though, they saw to the few women that they had caught. Nor was Maggie Maeve the only one with child. They hanged them by the neck until they were dead. They strung up Maggie Maeve like a common criminal, though she was nothing of the sort. She was a beautiful fine girl with a smile and laugh that would light a room brighter than a thousand beeswax candles. They strung her up and killed her and my unborn child. She looked a lot like your wife, Shakespeare. Long dark hair, blue eyes.'

'I'm sorry,' Shakespeare said.

'Well, it's a grand thing to be sorry. But I didn't want your apology or your pity. I wanted your blood, and your wife's blood, and I wanted it to flow and flow until the whole world was washed red. Because nothing you can do or say can bring Maggie Maeve back to me. Mr Slyguff was the same as I, an honest tanner, until the English took his tongue and cut it from him with his own shears, then set about snipping his brother's fingers as if they were manicuring his nails.'

Shakespeare's stomach turned. 'But what had the Roanoke colonists to do with all this? I recognise King Philip's thirst for vengeance for the defeat of his armada. But what were those people to *you*?'

'Ah, now, that's the story, isn't it. Let me tell you this. The English force was commanded by one Arthur Grey of Wilton. I care nothing for him. He is a mere stain on the world. The one I wanted was the one that oversaw the killing field, who took delight in kicking away the ladder from beneath Maggie Maeve's feet and who watched her die, though she was heavy with child. The man who waded in the blood of men who had surrendered in good faith that they would be shown English mercy. He is the man I have pursued all these years. He is a man revered by your stinking nation, Mr Shakespeare, and you know him.'

Chapter 45

'RALEGH?'

'Of course, Ralegh. He was the butcher, and I have dogged his steps ever since. I have piled treasure upon treasure on Robert Devereux of Essex to increase his favour and reduce Ralegh's. I have gone to the ends of the earth to destroy his ambitions and plans for a New World colony. I have killed his soldiers and his mariners, one by one. I made sure Essex dripped word in the ears of your sovereign when I heard of Ralegh's new marriage so that he now languishes in the Tower. And I have told him about it all. He knows what happened at Roanoke. Oh, he knows it, for I wrote it for him plain. Everything I have done has been done to hurt Ralegh. Bit by bit, piece by little piece, I have cut the flesh from his reputation, bringing him ever closer to ruin and despair.'

'Why not simply kill him?'

'That would be but a moment's pleasure. I wanted him to live long and be haunted until the end of his days. I wanted him to be married so I could destroy his wife and his child. He had to know that I would traverse the world to destroy him and all that was his. Vengeance without end.'

Shakespeare felt sick in his stomach. Could a man pursue vengeance with such relentless persistence down through the years? 'But how do you know it was Ralegh? Were there survivors?'

McGunn laughed bitterly. 'No, there were no survivors. But there was one there unseen: Maggie Maeve's young brother was hidden behind a rock. He saw it all and described the man to me, though he was but six years old at the time. And later, years later, in the year 1585 when first we came to England, he pointed him out to me wide-eyed with horror and there was no doubt. I saw the terror and revulsion in his eyes and I knew for certain that it was Ralegh who had done this thing to my wife. It was as certain as if it had been printed on his eyes with a press. My vengeance burns now as bright as it did the day I learned what the English had done at Smerwick.'

'And Essex?'

'I was in England making my fortune, for I had a great need of gold. I gave your filthy people what they wanted and exacted my price. When I learned of the enmity between Essex and Ralegh, I knew that Essex must be my friend. And a good friend I have been to him, giving him gold a-plenty. I asked nothing in return, for I knew that, enriched, he would give me what I needed: humiliation for Ralegh. It was a simple trade, though I doubt Essex ever had the wit to understand its workings.'

'But you speak of Ralegh's wife and child, as though you would even take vengeance on them . . .'

McGunn's lips curled down in the humourless likeness of a smile. 'His child is already dead, Mr Shakespeare. Poor little Damerei Ralegh, damned and dead in the night.'

'This cannot be so.'

'Oh, can it not? Well, you shall see. And you shall know who has done it.'

'Well, McGunn, it is over now. There will be no more killing by you.'

'Just the one more . . .' He nodded to the flagon of ale and Shakespeare put it once again to his lips.

'No. No more.'

'You must surely have deduced the name of Maggie Maeve's brother, Mr Shakespeare?'

'Joe Jaggard.'

'I had him brought up here in England, with a cousin, but he was always my boy. Do you think I could die with *his* death unpunished?'

'His killer is dead. He took a blow intended for me. He was a murderer, but he died honourably saving my life.'

McGunn's brow creased. 'Do you still think Sir Toby Le Neve killed Joe and Amy?'

'I know it to be so, McGunn. There can be no doubt.'

'Then you know nothing. If you want the killer – go to London Town, to a house on the corner of Beer Lane and Thames Street, by the gun foundry, and there you shall find your murderer.' McGunn burst out laughing, even though it hurt him greatly.

As he laughed, his eyes strayed past Shakespeare, but the humour never left his face, even as Eleanor Dare stepped silently into the room, picked up Boltfoot Cooper's loaded caliver wheel-lock from the floor where Shakespeare had placed it, reached forward with the octagonal muzzle full in McGunn's thick-set, fighting-dog face, and fired.

Eleanor had waited and watched as Catherine's eyes grew heavy. Finally, when Mr Shakespeare's wife could no longer stay awake, she rose quietly from the makeshift palliasse of blankets. Her throat was agony. A dark-bruised weal ringed her tender skin and her windpipe was so constricted that her rattling breathing was shallow and strained. She struggled to contain the noise as she walked barefoot from the little room to the other room, where she saw Shakespeare and McGunn and the wheel-lock on the floor.

She knew how to use a pistol as well as any man. All the

women at Roanoke had been trained in their use. As she came into the room, her eye caught McGunn's. He was laughing at something. That was good, because it distracted Shakespeare long enough for her to pick up the pistol. McGunn was still laughing at the point of death, as she thrust the infernal weapon close to his face and fired.

The recoil knocked her back. The ball gouged out the centre of McGunn's face, throwing him back against the wall.

As Shakespeare grabbed the smoking weapon from Eleanor's hand, she was shaking. Tears were flowing from her eyes like the rain that battered the land outside. Through the fog of her tears, she gazed upon the gaping red cavern that had appeared in the triangle between McGunn's eyes and the bridge of his nose, leading deep into the remains of his brain.

'That was for Virginia,' she whispered, her hoarse voice barely audible. 'And for Davy and all the others.'

Chapter 46

THE SOUND OF children's laughter drifted up from the garden to the open window of the first-floor chamber where Shakespeare lay naked beneath the sheets on an old oaken bed.

He opened his eyes and gazed up at the canopy above him. It was threadbare, but had once been a fine hand-woven fabric patterned with roses, all entangled like lovers' limbs.

The light that streamed in at the edges of the curtains told him it was daytime; other than that he had no idea whether it was morning or afternoon, nor which day. All he knew was that he was back at the home of Catherine's parents, and had collapsed, exhausted, on this bed, falling straightway into a deep slumber.

His shoulder, now cleaned and bandaged, throbbed where he had been skimmed by the musket-ball. He breathed deeply and caught a heady, musky scent. He reached out his right arm; she was there, beside him. His hand lingered on the soft warm skin just beneath her left breast. His fingers traced her ribs. She did not shy away from him.

Without a word, she nestled closer to him in the warm pit of this comfortable cot. She wrapped her legs around his and her hand went to his yard and caressed it with exquisite tenderness. It needed little encouragement.

She kissed his neck. 'Hello, husband,' she said in a quiet voice. 'I have missed you.'

He lay still on his back, stretched out, enjoying her touch and willing it not to stop. She was pushing herself against his side as her hand stroked him and teased him. He turned half towards her and his hand caressed the base of her spine and the curves of her buttocks.

'I swear you have the finest arse in Christendom, Mistress Shakespeare.'

'Have you sampled them all, sir?'

She kissed his mouth, deep with longing. Her legs parted more and she moved across his body and her hand guided him into her. They gasped together at his entry and filling of her.

'Mistress,' Shakespeare whispered, aware that the house was full and sound travelled. 'You part your legs like a wanton.'

'And you prance up like a satyr, sir,' she breathed into his mouth. 'Now, if it please you, stop your talking and get about your business.'

They rose to ecstasy together, then lay joined for half an hour, holding each other, saying not a word, until he began to rise again inside her and moved his body once more, turning her and twisting her. She responded with eager abandon and they took their fill of joy. And so the afternoon wore on, to the accompaniment of birdsong, the rustling of leaves in trees and the hopeful notes of children's laughter.

He left the next morning for London, leaving Boltfoot to bring them all down south to him when he sent word that the plague had eased.

On his return to Masham, Shakespeare had spoken at length to the constable and coroner and had sent a sealed note to the lieutenant of the county. No word of this was to come out until Sir Robert Cecil had been consulted and decreed what was to be done. In the meantime, Eleanor Dare was to stay in the house of the Marvells on pain of arrest if she tried to leave. Catherine and her mother would bring her soothing broths and lotions for her injured neck. There was no question of any charges against her at present; Shakespeare had removed the bindings from McGunn's corpse before the constable arrived with Boltfoot at the shepherd's cottage. It was clear, he said, that McGunn had been killed in self-defence. The sole survivor of his band of mercenaries, a sallow, taciturn forty-year-old of little wit, was charged with attempted murder and had no defence. He would be hanged for his crimes by week's end.

Shakespeare and his wife had talked and made love all afternoon and most of the evening, only rising from their chamber for a cup of wine and some pigeon pie to replenish their strength and to give some supper to the children. She understood that her husband had to see Cecil, but she was loath to let him go.

'I fear I have been a poor wife to you, John,' she said as he prepared to mount his grey mare and ride south.

'There were faults on both sides. Let us put it behind us.'

'I had thought there was no crossing our religious divide. It seemed to me you did not understand that there are worse things than dying, that you can starve from spiritual hunger, that Anne Bellamy's fate is more wretched than anything Topcliffe could devise for his torture room.'

'You must think me a man of little faith.'

'No, not that. I knew all along that your only thoughts were for my welfare. But you asked too much of me.'

'I am sorry.'

'Do not be. You did your duty, trying to protect those you loved. Yet, I must confess to you that before I came here I had decided to ask you to grant me a separation. It seemed to me that we could never live together in peace.'

'And now?'

'Now I cannot bear to be without you.'

He had tried to smile and say he loved her, but emotion constricted his throat and mouth and rendered him speechless. He averted his eyes and patted his horse's neck rather than meet his wife's gaze.

'The same old John Shakespeare,' Catherine said, laughing lightly. 'Too sentimental for his own good; too sentimental to be an intelligencer, that is certain.'

'But that is what I am.'

'I know. You have been a schoolmaster too long. Leave it to Mr Jerico. He will make a fine job of it. Work for Cecil.'

Shakespeare nodded.

'And John, when you are in London, find out what you may concerning Father Southwell. I pray for him every day, but I fear his suffering must be truly terrible.'

'I will ask Sir Robert what may be done.'

The ride south took four days – days of intermittent rain, grey skies and brisk winds. He arrived at Theobalds to be told by Cecil's manservant Clarkson that his master had departed for the West Country on urgent royal business. A Portuguese carrack named the *Madre de Dios* had been taken off the Azores and brought in triumph to the port of Dartmouth. It was said that the vessel was the richest ever seized by English privateers, heavy laden with spices from the East Indies, along with chests flowing over with gold, silver, silks and gems. But triumph was quickly turning to disaster as mariners and merchants plundered the cargo. The Queen was in a rage, for a large portion of treasure should have been hers by right. Cecil's task was to protect what was left and recover what had been taken.

'It is said that mariners in the ports of Devon are all drunk, night and day, and are easily known for they all stink of rare Orient perfumes. They sell pearls and amber for the price of a tankard of ale, Mr Shakespeare. The roads west are packed with merchants, hurrying to buy the treasures from the pillagers. Sir Robert is so concerned that he has summoned Sir Walter Ralegh from his cell in the Tower, to go west to help him in his task of bringing order to the region; the Navy's treasurer, Sir John Hawkins, believes that if the men will listen to anyone, it is Ralegh.'

'Sir Walter is a free man, then?' So much, thought Shakespeare, for McGunn's vengeance.

'Not exactly. He is kept under the guard of keepers all the while and will return to the Tower when his mission is done. As for his wife, Bess Throckmorton, she remains in the Tower at the Queen's will.'

'What of their baby?'

Clarkson shook his head sadly. 'The boy Damerei? He has died. The child was born sickly.'

Shakespeare shivered. 'Was there any suggestion of foul play, Mr Clarkson?'

'Not that I have heard, sir.'

Shakespeare arched his aching back and winced. It seemed to him that he had spent two weeks on horseback. His shoulder was healing well but his saddle-sore inner thighs were as ill-used as a Southwark whore's. Now another ride beckoned.

'If I may prevail upon you, Mr Clarkson, I would be grateful for food, a bed and a fresh horse for the ride west. My grey mare has done more than enough these past days.'

Clarkson stopped him with his outstretched palm. 'Do not think of going down there, Mr Shakespeare. Sir Robert received your message from Hardwick Hall and commanded me to tell you that he will see you on his return.'

'Did he say anything else?'

'He says that he trusts you have the evidence. That is all.'

*

The streets of London were overgrown with weeds. Flies buzzed around the dogs that lay dead on every corner. Rats scuttled unhindered along the clogged drainage kennels. Rosemary and other herbs had been scattered about in a pathetic attempt to cleanse the air of the plague miasma. The pestilence was doing its foul work regardless. People still went about their daily business, but in fewer numbers. Those who did not have to leave their homes didn't. Those who had enough gold had left for their country estates long ago. And each day the plague men dragged more cartloads of corpses to the mass graves.

Shakespeare found Simon Forman in remarkably good spirits at Stone House in Fylpot Street. He seemed tired, but otherwise healthy. The astrologer physician welcomed his visitor with a warm shake of the hand.

'It is good to see someone who does not have the pestilence, Mr Marvell. I spend all day every day tending to them and dispensing my miraculous tinctures.'

'Indeed, Dr Forman. I trust they are more miraculous than your charts, for you were certainly wrong about the death of a certain person of high rank – and you could not have chosen a more inauspicious day for a wedding.'

Forman grinned broadly, his generous red lips creasing apart in the small gap between his bushy golden-red beard and moustache. 'And I am the happiest man in England that my chart erred concerning the great lady, but nor am I surprised – for is she not the sun itself, and do not the very stars trace their paths about her elegant and stately progress?'

'Admit it, Forman. Your charts are as worthless as your potions and ointments. Ash of little green frogs? You prey on gulls, sir.'

Forman shrugged his wide shoulders, still grinning. 'I had taken you to be a sceptic, Mr Marvell. But I tell you this: I was right about my plague cure – for, see, I am hale and my heart is strong. Not only that, but the French welcome is gone, too.' In truth, he felt himself not only healthy but never happier; women flocked to him for *haleking*, deciding they must make the most of this world today, for tomorrow they might be in the hereafter. He was also proving himself a real physician who could bring comfort and the occasional cure to the sick. 'I am not like those coney-hunters at the College of Physicians who have hounded me without mercy for so many years and are nowhere to be seen now that the people need them. I cured myself and now I take my electuaries to the sick and suffering, be they drabs or gong farmers and, with God's grace, I heal many. Only one in five survives, they say, but I do better than that.'

'I am pleased to hear it. I will be even more pleased when you give me what I have come for. And my name is not Marvell but Shakespeare. Strange, is it not, that your charts were unable to reveal that? Now, give me the charts I require and I promise you that you will have immunity from prosecution and all the protection you need from the College of Physicians.'

Forman hesitated. 'I wonder,' he asked tentatively, 'would you be able to supply me with a letter of patent from Sir Robert? He is not the only powerful man in the land and nor is he immune to the ravages of disease or accidental death. If I take his part in this, I will surely be most unpopular with others. I must think of the future and what would become of me if anything were to happen to him, Mr Shakespeare.'

'You will have no such letter. But I say again – if you do not supply the charts, you will be in Newgate before this day is done. And the pursuivants I send will destroy every last book, vial and instrument that you own.'

'Mr Shakespeare, please . . .'

'And I will require an affidavit with your mark upon it to show that *you* did cast these charts, and for whom you cast them.'

'No, you cannot ask me to do that!'

'Then good day to you, Dr Forman. Mr Topcliffe will be here with a squadron before day's end.' Much as he loathed Topcliffe, Shakespeare knew the power of his name. Where once men spoke of the rack or the manacles or the branding iron, now they simply referred to *Topcliffean practices*.

Shakespeare saw the fear burning bright in Forman's eyes. 'I wonder, Dr Forman, about the tinctures you supplied for the sickness lately endured by my lord of Essex's wife, the lady Frances? She said you supplied her with potions to rid her of the little flying things she saw. What, exactly, were they? Wing of sparrow, toe of faerie?'

'Mr Shakespeare, please. I beg you . . .'

'Or were they, perhaps, essence of wolfsbane, Dr Forman?'

Forman held his hand to his chest as though his heart would seize. 'Never, sir. Never. I would never be party to such a thing. My mission is to heal, not kill.'

'What then? We know of your alliance with enemies who tried to poison her, Dr Forman. You dabble in alchemy – you had the means to acquire whatever they desired. And that thing was wolfsbane. I do believe she was being poisoned with the foul root and you gave it to her.'

Forman sat down. 'Mr Shakespeare,' he said, his voice hoarse and riven with panic. 'This is all wicked fancy. I promise you by God's holy name, I have done no such thing, nor ever would. I talked to the lady and quickly realised she had an affliction of the mind, some languishing sickness. I gave her nothing but a hypocon water of *Hypericum perforatum* – commonly called St John's Wort – which I know will cure the sadness in some melancholics.'

'It is too much of a coincidence. No court in England would believe the tinctures weren't poisoned.'

Dr Forman nodded his head, his shoulders slumped in

defeat. 'I will do everything you ask, sir. I have the charts pre-pared already, and you shall have your affidavit before you go.'

Shakespeare smiled and clapped Forman about the back. 'Good man. Then we shall be the best of friends and I vouch-safe that Sir Robert Cecil will look after your interests and save you from the dread attentions of the College of Physicians.'

'And I swear to you that I have never supplied poisons, nor used them, though I have been asked.'

On the way out, with the charts and affidavit tucked safely within his doublet, it felt to Shakespeare as though a hundred-weight burden had fallen off his back. At last he had evidence which, he prayed, would satisfy Cecil and save his brother Will.

His thoughts now turned to McGunn's last words, and his pace quickened as he hurried through the echoing, half-deserted streets of London . . .

Chapter 47

THE HOUSE AT the corner of Beer Lane and Thames Street was boarded and nailed shut. A cross was painted on the door. It was a plague house. Anyone incarcerated there must stay until death took them.

Shakespeare looked about him. Across the street, two men in tattered jerkins sat on a hay bale, tankards of ale and pipes of tobacco in their hands, playing cards. They wore herb-filled plague masks – pointed, beak-like protuberances that made them look like hellish birds of prey.

'Who lives there?' Shakespeare demanded, as he approached them, gesturing towards the plague house.

The men looked at each other and laughed. The taller of the two, a rangy, balding fellow, stood up from the hay bale and pulled off his mask to reveal a sour, gaunt face.

'Who wants to know?'

'My name is Shakespeare. I am here on Queen's business.'

'Well, no one lives there. It's a plague house. They'll all be dead.'

Shakespeare noted the man's voice. His accent was Irish, like McGunn's.

The men were laughing again.

'Though I did hear a little scratching sound coming from

within this morning, Tom,' the seated one said. 'Perhaps it was a mouse.'

The large one drew on his pipe and blew a cloud of smoke towards Shakespeare. 'At least the rodents will be feeding well in there,' he said. 'So long as they can stomach plague pudding with Puritan sauce.'

'Is Winterberry in there? The merchant Jacob Winterberry?'

'Aye, that he is. Now aren't you the clever fellow, Mr Shakespeare. And we're here to see that he don't come out. We don't want him spreading the plague about, do we? That would be most unchristian of the man.'

Shakespeare bridled. 'And by what authority do you keep watch on this house?'

'Why, sir, the authority of the City of London corporation, which has appointed us plague men and pays us each eight pennies a day for our pains. That and the plague masks they gives us. We brought Mr Winterberry from his home especially to lodge with this plague family in his last days.'

'There is a family in there with him?'

'Aye, sir, a husbandman and goodwife and their two children. All grievous sickly they were when Mr Winterberry arrived. I have to say that Mr Winterberry himself looked in prime good health at the time. No sign of no buboes nor other marks of the pestilence.'

'So you placed a man in perfect health in a house with a contagious family, then nailed him in?'

The tall one took a long draught of ale, then wiped his grubby sleeve across his straggly beard. 'Aye, sir, we did. He was not at all pleased to be brought here, mind. Begging like a little child he was, pleading not to be put in there, crying. But we knew what was good for him.'

'He was still a-whimpering as the carpenter hammered the boards across the door and windows.'

'Then you have committed murder!'

The shorter one, still sitting on the bale, nonchalantly tapped out the ashes of his clay pipe against the heel of his shoe and began stuffing in more tobacco. 'Now that is not the way we see it, sir. We see it as saving Her Majesty and the Council the cost of a trial and a hanging, for we know Mr Winterberry to have been a felon of the worst sort. I am certain there is none more worthy of a painful and unpleasant death.'

Shakespeare pulled the man from the bale, knocking his pipe from his hand and dragging the beak-mask from his head. 'Get this house opened straightway or you will answer for it, I promise you. You should know that McGunn is dead. He is dead, a ball through his face and into the depths of his brain. He now rots in a pauper's grave in the northern wilds of England with worms for company. Now open that house or I will kill you where you stand.'

The men looked at Shakespeare with new respect, even fear. They were no longer sure of themselves. They glanced at Shakespeare's hand on the hilt of his still-sheathed sword.

'He told us to stay here until there had been no sound from within for at least forty-eight hours,' the taller one began. 'They were his orders.' His eyes flickered back and forth between Shakespeare and his companion.

Both men suddenly dropped their tankards and turned on their heels. They dashed as well as they could northwards up Beer Lane, stumbling through the shit and kitchen waste that lay uncollected all along their escape route. Shakespeare let them go.

He walked to the boarded-up house and banged on the solidly barred door. From within, he heard a sound, almost like tiny footsteps on the stairs. He hammered again and called out, 'Is anyone alive in there?'

Shakespeare thought he heard a small voice from within. 'Hold firm,' he said. 'I will have this door unbarred.'

He looked about. At the nearby gun foundry he found an apprentice smoothing the rough surfaces of a new-forged cannonball. Shakespeare ordered him to bring his tools.

Ten minutes later they had jemmied off the three-inch thick planks and pulled out the heavy nails that kept the door so firmly closed. Shakespeare lifted the latch and the door opened. He stumbled back, as did the apprentice, assailed by the most awful stench of rotting flesh and disease.

Clutching his kerchief to his face, Shakespeare gave the boy a coin and told him to go back to the foundry, but the boy stayed, close behind him, peering down the dark entrance hall of the plague house. A body lay close to the door, blocking the way. It was Jacob Winterberry.

With the kerchief held close to his nose and mouth, Shakespeare touched him and knew he was dead. The body, clothed in Puritan-black broadcloth streaked with vomit and dust, was cold and still. The exposed skin was blue, blotchy and bloated.

Shakespeare turned again to the apprentice. 'Go back to your work. This place is not safe for you.'

Reluctantly, the boy shuffled away. Shakespeare tied the kerchief around his face and stepped into the hall, over Winterberry's corpse. A cloud of flies rose from the putrefying mass of pustules that had once been the merchant's face.

'Is anyone here? Come forth,' he called into the echoing hall.

Half a dozen yards down the way, there was a staircase.

'Come to me and you will be safe.'

From the shadowed recesses of the hall, a figure appeared. A child, Shakespeare thought, or some sort of wraith. The figure stepped forward tentatively, shielding its eyes from the light of day. It was a girl, thin and shivering, clothed in a dark linen smock.

'Come, child. Come to me.'

He guessed she was ten or eleven, but it was difficult to be sure. Her long fair hair was matted with filth, and yet he could see that her skin was clear of the dread buboes. One in five survived, Forman had said. Well, she must be blessed.

She held back from him. 'You will die if you touch me, sir,' she said in a quiet voice.

'No. You are well, child. Your skin is clear.'

'I saw death, but the Lord turned me away.'

'Are there any others alive here?'

She shook her head.

'Then the Lord wants you to live. Come to me. Come from this place.'

She stepped closer to him. He reached out his hand. She stared at it from beneath the sun-shield of her right palm, then looked up at him, her eyes creased against the light. Their eyes met. Shakespeare smiled at her. 'Come, child,' he said again, reaching out further and taking her left hand. 'All will be well.' She allowed him to take her hand. It felt tiny to him. Gently, he led her from the front door out into the daylight.

The apprentice had returned. 'I heard you talking. Here . . .' He held out a flagon and a crust of bread. 'She'll need food and drink.'

'Thank you,' Shakespeare said. 'You are a good boy.'

As the boy went back to the foundry, Shakespeare led the girl across the road to the hay bale from where McGunn's men had been watching the house, and sat her down. 'Take a drink, child.'

She gnawed at the bread and sipped ale from the flagon. 'They left food and water for us, but the food did run out.'

'How long were you there?'

'I do not know, sir. Perhaps eight days, nine . . . night and day were the same, for the windows were all boarded. And I do not know how long I had the fever. The Lord took my sister and mother and father.'

The girl did not weep for her family. Shakespeare realised she was still too full of horror.

'What is your name, child?'

'Matilda, sir. I will be eleven years of age on Christmas Day.'

'Matilda, there was another man in there with you. The man who lies dead in the hall. Did you know him?'

'His name was Mr Winterberry. He was nailed in with us, sir. We did not know him until then. They brought him here, bound and struggling. They wore bird masks and were laughing as they threw him down, then closed the door on us. We were all sick at that time, but we unbound him. He seemed untouched by the pestilence and said he should not be there, that it was murder. He was sore troubled, but I think he was a good man.'

'Why do you say that?'

'When I became more sick, he did nurse me through my fever. Brought water to cool my brow when I was burning hot, and fed me when the fever passed. Then he became sick, too.'

'You said he was sore troubled?'

'He wept and said he was a vile sinner and that he deserved to die. He prayed and prayed. I did not understand all he said. Things like corruption of the flesh, guilt without end. He begged forgiveness and beat his fist against his forehead.' She lifted her gaze to Shakespeare. 'Did you know him, sir? Was he a good man?'

'I did know him, Matilda. But I do not know if he was a good man.' He thought back to the incident on the quayside at Indies Wharf, when the cask fell and nearly killed him. Perhaps Winterberry had wanted him dead, to put an end to his investigations. His Puritan coldness hid deep passions. Sir Walter

Ralegh had hinted at ships lost at sea. Certainly, Winterberry's investment in Roanoke had come to nothing. It was possible he was not so wealthy.

Yet it was not financial ruin but the jealousy and rage of the cuckold – a story as old as man – that had finally done for him and brought tragedy on the Le Neves. 'God will judge.' He smiled at the girl. 'Now,' he said, 'what are we to do with you? Do you have relatives who might take you in?'

She shook her head. 'No, sir.'

His thoughts suddenly turned to Cordelia Le Neve, who had once had a sister named Matilda. She was all alone now. Perhaps . . .

'I think I might know just the place for you, Matilda. Just the place.'

Chapter 48

THE DAY WAS bright and autumnal. There were no church bells, but there was hope in the air; hope that the chillier weather would bring an end to the plague, or at least slow down its ravages.

John Shakespeare and his wife walked side by side along the leaf-strewn streets of Greenwich. They were going to a wedding. Shakespeare did not wish to go to it, but his wife, although apprehensive, had insisted. He had shrugged his shoulders and agreed. His marriage was strong and loving once more; he did not want to threaten its stability by gainsaying Catherine over something as trifling as a wedding.

As they arrived at the church porch, all bedecked with autumn flowers and foliage, Shakespeare stayed his wife. 'Wait. See who is there.'

He raised his head. Across the way he could see Justice Young, the magistrate of London, and Newall, the chief pursuivant, both close associates of Topcliffe.

Catherine's mouth turned down in distaste. She knew those faces well. She knew that, like Topcliffe, they would happily hang her and every other Catholic.

'We should go,' Shakespeare said. 'This was a bad idea. I want no part of it.'

'No, John, we must stay.'

'Are you sure?'

She nodded firmly. 'I am sure.'

They walked into the plain church. Twenty or thirty people, mostly men, sat on wooden chairs. Briefly, they turned around to see the newcomers. Shakespeare recognised Thomas Fitzherbert, a pursuivant. Catherine spotted Pickering, the lumbering Gatehouse gaoler. He was mopping the sweat from his brow, though the day was not hot.

'This is not a church of God but of the devil,' Shakespeare said, dismayed.

'Sit down, John. We must stay, though it break my heart.'

They sat towards the rear of the little church. In place of the altar, there was a bare table. The coloured windows had all been smashed and replaced by clear panes. The place was bleak, without hope or joy.

A murmur disturbed the stillness. The bridegroom was coming in. His wedding finery could do nothing to disguise the fact that he was a thick-set ruffian with slimed hair, thin beard and leering smile; Topcliffe's apprentice Nicholas Jones, now to be a married man. He smirked at John Shakespeare.

'Poor Anne,' Catherine said, shaking her head sadly as Jones and his bent and watery-eyed father, Basforde Jones, walked up the aisle to await the bride. She had been driven mad through ill-usage by Topcliffe and Jones, scarce able to admit to herself the enormity of what she had done to her family and Father Robert Southwell, who now languished in solitary confinement in the Tower, almost forgotten.

The first Shakespeare and Catherine saw of Anne Bellamy was her swollen belly. She was heavy with child and waddled in, head bowed, shoulders slumped. She had put on a lot of weight since Catherine last saw her, much of it due to her appetite rather than the child. Her voluminous dress, with slashed sleeves and protruding stomacher, was brown and murrey and studded with gemstones at the wrists. In the absence of her father, she was on the arm of Richard Topcliffe. He was dressed in black with silver-thread trimmings to his velvet doublet. He strode in, proud and pugnacious, swinging his silver-tipped blackthorn.

Together, Topcliffe and the bride walked to the front of the church, where she stopped beside her intended and smiled at him. Topcliffe looked around at the gathered congregation. It seemed for a moment as though he would take a bow, like a player on stage. Then he grinned at Shakespeare and Catherine and turned to face the front, where the parson waited to perform the ceremony.

Catherine tried to stand up, to stop this mockery of a wedding, but her husband motioned her to sit down. 'There is nothing to be done, Catherine. She came here of her own accord. I saw her smile at Jones. There is no impediment to this match.'

'But it is a travesty, John.'

'Yes, I fear it is.'

Like groundlings at a tragedy, Shakespeare and his wife witnessed the wedding. When the parson declared Nicholas Jones and Anne man and wife, it was too much to bear. Catherine stood and walked to the door. Shakespeare followed her.

'How can such a thing be allowed, John?'

'Who is to stop a man and woman marrying, if they both so desire it? She said "I will" with a clear, strong voice.'

'She did, did she not? A most fortunate young woman, she is.' Topcliffe was at their side, striding along with them, unbidden and unwanted. 'A lucky slattern to have found a man like my Nick to make an honest woman of her.'

Shakespeare tried to keep his wife walking, but she stopped and squared up to Topcliffe. 'She is a victim of *your* cruelty, Mr Topcliffe. You have used her ill and brought her to this state. She knows not what she does.'

Topcliffe leered. 'Oh, but she does. She can't get enough of him. He scratches her itch. But she will bring my boy a fine dowry. Her family does not know it, but they will give Preston Manor and all its lands and farm-holdings to my lad Nick, whether they like it or not. Sixty-six pounds a year, that will be worth to him. He will be a wealthy young gentleman, which is no more than he deserves for his loyalty to his master and his monarch. And in return, she will no longer be thought the dirty, prick-hungry Popish whore that we know her to be, but Mrs Nicholas Jones, gentlewoman and Protestant. Now is that not a fine trade-off?'

'And where are her family today, Mr Topcliffe?' Catherine demanded as Shakespeare tried to pull her away. 'Have you killed them all yet?'

Topcliffe gave her a look of pure scorn. 'Her family will learn soon enough. They will learn what it means to harbour lewd priests. They will find what it means to cross Topcliffe. As will you. Soon enough. You and your stinking pups, dog-mother whore.' He turned to Shakespeare. 'And you – you and your brother – you are both fortunate to be alive, for you have been slithering with toothed serpents and greased priests, oiled and slippery in a tub of the purple demon's chrism . . .'

Shakespeare lingered a long moment with his hand on the hilt of his dagger. He had no sword with him. He did not take swords to weddings. He looked coldly down into Topcliffe's eyes and came as close as ever he had to killing a man in hot blood.

Instead he turned his back on the Queen's servant. 'Come, Mistress Shakespeare,' he said to her. 'Let us go home where the air is clean.'

Chapter 49

WHEN, AT LAST, Sir Robert Cecil returned from the West Country, having salvaged what he could of the *Madre de Dios* treasure, Shakespeare made haste to see him. There was much to be settled.

Shakespeare handed the privy councillor a list of the names of all Essex's supporters at the abortive wedding to Arbella Stuart in the church by Hardwick Hall.

Cecil glanced at the names, then filed them away with other papers. 'Thank you, John. We shall deal with this quietly.'

Shakespeare raised an eyebrow in disbelief. Cecil saw his reaction. 'John, would you wish to be the man who told the Queen that the thing she loves above all else, her golden warrior, is naught but base metal? Can you imagine her rage? I care nothing for Essex's head; it is his to lose as he wishes. But the child Arbella? Should she be another Jane Grey? What of the others? I must tell you I fear the blood-letting would go as far as your brother.'

Shakespeare was shocked. 'My brother?'

'Did you think I was unaware of his role in this?'

Shakespeare was silent. Of course he knew. Topcliffe . . .

'Which leaves us with the question of the evidence you promised me, John.'

Shakespeare stiffened. Cecil was expecting a bundle of letters and verses, signed by Essex but penned by Will. From his doublet, he took the charts supplied by Forman, a death chart for Elizabeth, and a nuptial chart for Essex and Arbella, and Forman's affidavit.

Cecil studied them in silence, then nodded. 'Very well. I think you have given me enough. I have my lord of Essex where I want him.' He filed the charts away with the list of names.

Shakespeare bowed.

'And I can now tell you something else, John: Francis Mills is *my* man. It was he that told Essex and McGunn that they must have you – that you could be their Walsingham. And it was Mr Mills that helped you from within Essex House and protected you when they became suspicious. I trust your past differences will now be at an end, for he is discovered, too, and has hurriedly left Essex House. He will work with us.'

Shakespeare frowned. Work with Mills? Stranger things had happened. Nothing was certain in this intelligencers' war. Cecil against Essex. Circles within circles. All that could be said was that the opening shots had been fired in a war of secrets between the two greatest young men of the age.

'The Earl, meanwhile, will remain the Queen's pet,' Cecil continued. 'But his progress will always be impeded. He no longer has McGunn's gold to fund him and must crawl on his belly once more for favours from his sovereign.'

'Is he back at court already?'

'Shamelessly. Closeted all night with her, playing tables and primero, paying her sweet compliments, dancing until dawn. He keeps her amused. The years roll off her shoulders and England is the better for it. But he knows he is found out and will forever be watched. His coven can stir their cauldron as they wish, but they are figures of jest. The She-wolf paces in lonely exile in the Midlands. Penelope cavorts with her amour in her black-draped chamber. As to Southampton and the others, they sleep at night with aching necks thinking how close they came to the axe.'

Shakespeare took a sip of wine. 'And what of Sir Walter?'

'He is back in the Tower. I am sure he would not be content to have the massacre of the Roanoke colony bruited about, for it would leave him in a yet more parlous state, his patent from the Queen turned to ashes.'

'Do *you* wish it advertised, Sir Robert?'

'You know me better than that, John.'

Indeed, Shakespeare had been reflecting on how like Sir Francis Walsingham his new employer was. Both men shared an extreme, almost cold, level of caution. In their world of intelligencing, knowledge was all, and to be guarded jealously. Cecil would not want word of the Roanoke slaughter to see the light. Ralegh must be freed and his rivalry with Essex nurtured. That way both men would be weakened, leaving the course free for Cecil. To that end, Eleanor Dare must be silenced.

'She will stay in the North Country,' Shakespeare assured him. 'She is living with my wife's mother and contents herself with her inks and quills and parchments. I do believe she wishes naught but peace and solitude.'

'And we shall wink at the death of Mr McGunn. What of the brother-in-law?'

'Foxley Dare continues to pursue a claim that his brother be declared dead so that he and the boy may inherit the property. He would not wish a counter-claim. Anyway, who would believe a man with a reputation for swiving geese?'

Cecil did not smile. 'The important thing is that McGunn is dead. It is now clear how widespread and malign was his influence. In Mr Secretary's day such an insect would have been squashed under foot long since. You will ensure such men never hold sway in this realm again, John.'

Shakespeare had considered McGunn's role. He had been

the hub of an infernal wheel, whose spokes touched lives in terrible ways: the tragedy of the Roanoke colonists; his funding of the Essex treachery; the corruption of Christopher Morley, Winterberry and the Le Neves. All spokes led back to McGunn. But Shakespeare also found himself wondering about the event that lay behind it all – the pitiless killing of his wife at a small, rocky outcrop of Ireland known as Smerwick. He asked Cecil about it – was there truth in the claim that Ralegh had blood on his hands?

'I do believe so,' Cecil said. 'My father told me that Ralegh carried out the killings with grim efficiency, watching his soldiers hewing and punching six hundred unarmed and bound men, and hanging pregnant women. They were cruel days. Ralegh's half-brother, Humphrey Gilbert, had a row of Irish heads lining the path to his tent. I heard also that when Ralegh caught an Irishman stealing willow branches from an English camp, he demanded to know what they were for. "To hang English churls," the man said. Ralegh had him strung up there and then, saying the branches would serve as well for an insolent Irishman. I cannot stomach such things, which is why I strive for peace, not war. That is what you sign up to, John, when you agree to assist me. You understand that?'

'We are as one, Sir Robert. Except . . .'

'Except my use of Mr Topcliffe. I believe you had the same problem when you worked for Mr Secretary Walsingham.'

The anger rose in Shakespeare's gullet. 'I have to speak plain, Sir Robert. The man tried to ensnare my wife. He takes pleasure in torture. He has raped the young Bellamy woman. He conspired with the poisonous Morley. I say that Topcliffe is worse than any of England's enemies.'

'Sit down, John,' Cecil ordered. 'Let me tell you that I share your feelings. And yet . . .'

'There is no *and yet*, Sir Robert.'

'And yet I need Mr Topcliffe, just as Mr Secretary needed him. There is no doubting his loyalty to the crown or to England.'

'He is a man who does not balk at torture, rape and murder.'

'Enough, John. Sit down.' The privy councillor's voice became quieter. 'Please, listen to me. These are desperate times. Spain will come with a yet more powerful fleet next spring or summer. And her agents continue to worm their way into the body of England – in secret ways which it is our task to stop. You are my longbow in this, John – but Topcliffe is the poison tip of my arrow.'

Cecil, small and precise and still, never lost his composure as he spoke. Their eyes met. At last Cecil smiled and reached out his hand in friendship. 'Come, John, we need each other. Let us speak of pleasanter things. Let us speak of a bright future for England. I need you – and I believe you need me.'

Acknowledgements

I AM INDEBTED TO many people, who have helped me in myriad ways. In particular, I would like to thank my agent Teresa Chris, and my editor Kate Parkin for their superb advice and unstinting support. I would also like to thank the toxicologist Professor Robert Forrest (any mistakes are mine, not his); Jean Bray, the archivist at Sudeley Castle; Cosy Bagot Jewitt at Blithfield Hall; and, as ever, my wife Naomi.

Books that have been especially helpful include: *Arbella Stuart* by P. M. Handover; *The Second Cecil* by P. M. Handover; *Robert, Earl of Essex* by Robert Lacey; *Arbella: England's Lost Queen* by Sarah Gristwood; *Palaces & Progresses of Elizabeth I* by Ian Dunlop; *Dr Simon Forman: A Most Notorious Physician* by Judith Cook; *Roanoke: The Abandoned Colony* by Karen Ordahl Kupperman; *Roanoke: Solving the Mystery of England's Lost Colony* by Lee Miller; *Poor Penelope* by Sylvia Freedman; *The Lady Penelope* by Sally Varlow; *St Thomas' Hospital* by E. M. McInnes; *Bess of Hardwick: First Lady of Chatsworth* by Mary S. Lovell; *Sir Walter Raleigh* by Raleigh Trevelyan; *Sir Walter Ralegh* by Robert Lacey.

Historical Note

QUEEN ELIZABETH IS a bit-part player in this novel, yet her relationship with 24-year-old Robert Devereux, Earl of Essex, stands at the heart of the story – and of the late Tudor age itself.

What did the 58-year-old sovereign want from this ambitious yet hopelessly inadequate young man? Yes, she loved his charm and good looks, but I believe she also enjoyed goading his beautiful mother Lettice, the cousin she despised for marrying her own great love, Leicester. It was as if she was saying 'You may have won Leicester, but I have your son.'

And what did Essex want from Elizabeth? He wanted money, because he was desperately short of the stuff, and he wanted power. Indeed, he wanted her job, as the world was to discover with his wretched coup attempt in 1601.

At his trial, Sir Robert Cecil accused him: 'You would depose the Queen. You would be King of England.' The Earl of Northumberland asserted that Essex 'wore the crown of England in his heart these many years'.

Essex's 'affair' with Elizabeth – and his deadly rivalry with both Cecil and Ralegh – dominated the Queen's declining years. The Earl had become her favourite courtier in 1587, yet the cracks were immediately apparent. In the summer of that year they had a furious and very public quarrel which set the scene for many rows to come.

That first fight was over the Queen's snub for his sister Dorothy when she was barred from the royal presence for a perceived misdemeanour. In a rage, Essex accused Elizabeth of listening to gossip from his rival Sir Walter Ralegh. The more he insulted Ralegh (who had nothing to do with the snub), the more the Queen threw back insults against Essex's mother, Lettice.

Essex stormed out in the middle of the night, taking Dorothy with him. The Queen sent a courtier after him to apologise and ask him back. And so the morbid, hot-and-cold affair of the ageing queen and the moody young swain began. He would walk out and sulk, she would beg him to come back.

Yet she never trusted him with the power he craved. He continually demanded promotion, but she invariably gave the best jobs to someone else and, in doing so, fed his paranoia.

He often defied her. During his 1591 military campaign in northern France, he knighted twenty-four officers against the express orders of the Queen. When she heard what he had done, she was livid. She would not normally knight half that number in a whole year, and he hadn't even won a battle, let alone a war.

The year of Essex's 'cheap knights' was the beginning of his drive for the top. By giving knighthoods – as he was entitled to do when leading an expeditionary force – he was buying loyalty. The following year Essex set about becoming a statesman. He took on the Bacon brothers, Francis and Anthony, and they advised him that intelligence gathering was the way to make a political impact.

His lust for power was stoked up by certain Machiavellian friends such as Gelli Meyrick and Henry Cuffe, but mainly by his ruthlessly ambitious sister, Penelope Rich. She pushed him to rebellion and was a prime cause of his downfall.

And then there was Arbella Stuart. It was easy to see how advantageous a match might be with the young girl, a serious claimant to the throne of England. Essex used his charm well. He supported her at court and flirted with her when others avoided her because of her haughtiness. There was court tittle-tattle about their closeness and he is also believed to have conducted a secret correspondence with the impressionable girl, though this does not survive.

Did he have plans to marry her? Surely he considered it. His marriage to Frances Walsingham was an inconvenient formality and easily disposed of if necessary. That was the way the Essex clan did things. His mother had married Leicester knowing that he was still married to Lady Douglass Sheffield. And many believed Leicester had murdered his first wife, Amy Robsart, to enable him to marry Elizabeth and share her throne.

And yes, Arbella did have a tutor called Morley who was sacked by Bess of Hardwick in 1592. Was he spying on Arbella? Historians have speculated that he was a Walsingham intelligencer (some have even suggested he might have been the playwright Christopher Marlowe, who had been a spy). After Walsingham's death, who controlled this Morley? By 1592, Essex House was quickly becoming one of the main centres of espionage.

In the end, Essex was a weak, contemptible character. He attempted a coup, but he accused others of provoking him to it, turning on Penelope with venom. He had nothing to gain for he was already under sentence of death, but he wrote a confession in which he laid the blame on her. 'I must accuse one who is most nearest to me, my sister, who did continually urge me on with telling how all my friends and followers thought me a coward, and that I had lost all my valour. She must be looked to, for she hath a proud spirit.'

It is easy to see parallels in the story of Macbeth – the proud but flawed soldier urged on to treachery by women. Shakespeare would have known the Essex tale at the time of writing his great tragedy. Penelope as Lady Macbeth? Or the three of them – Penelope, Dorothy and Lettice – as three witches stirring a cauldron of sedition?

In the event, Penelope (whose bedroom at Essex House was, indeed, draped all in black) was spared – probably because of her relationship with Charles Blount, Lord Mountjoy, who was winning victories in Ireland and was needed by Elizabeth.

Finally, Elizabeth allowed the axe to fall on the neck of the young man she had once loved, just as her father had severed the heads of two young wives he once loved. The brittle young moderniser Sir Robert Cecil had won the day, though he never won the love of his Queen, nor of the people.

Character Notes

As well as well-known historical figures, this book includes some lesser-known names worth discovering . . .

Charles Blount (1563–1606)
As a young courtier, he wounded the Earl of Essex in a duel over an insult – and won his respect. Later, he won the love of Essex's sister, the beautiful Lady Penelope Rich, even though she was married. They eventually wed in 1605 after she scandalised society by being divorced. Like all good romantic heroes, Blount was handsome, dark-haired, strong, silent and happiest on the battlefield. He became Lord Mountjoy on the death of his brother in 1594, and was acclaimed for his decisive victories in Ireland. King James I honoured him with the title Earl of Devonshire. His early death has been attributed to heavy smoking.

Christopher Blount (1555–1601)
A distant relative of Charles Blount (see above), Blount began and ended his life as a Catholic, though in his middle years he seemed to turn against Catholicism and may have worked for the spymaster Sir Francis Walsingham to bring about the execution of Mary Queen of Scots. He served the Earl of Leicester and, on the Earl's death, married his wealthy and beautiful widow Lettice Knollys, who was twelve years his senior. One

claim is that their affair began *before* Leicester's death – and that she poisoned her husband to leave her free to wed Blount. He became stepfather to the Earl of Essex, whom he vowed to serve 'until after I be dead'. In 1601, he played a crucial role in Essex's abortive coup and, like him, was beheaded.

Arthur Gorges (1550s–1625)

A close friend and cousin of Sir Walter Ralegh, he was a poet, courtier and sea captain. He was bereft when his beloved young wife Douglas Howard died, aged 18, in 1590. His grief inspired the 1591 elegy *Daphnaida* by Edmund Spenser. The following year, he visited his kinsman Ralegh in the Tower (he had been imprisoned for marrying Bess Throckmorton without the Queen's permission) and was injured in an altercation between Sir Walter and the gaoler, causing him to write that he wished both their heads had been broken. Ralegh, in his will, left him his 'best rapier and dagger'. Gorges was often short of money and probably died of the plague.

Robert Greene (1558–92)

Greene was a prolific playwright and writer of courtly romances, as famous in his day as William Shakespeare, whom he sneered at as an 'upstart' in his notorious tract *Greenes Groats-worth of Wit*. Born in Norwich, he went to Cambridge and prided himself on being one of the 'university wits', whereas Will Shakespeare did not attend university. Yet Greene was a mass of contradictions, for he was also deeply attracted to the seedy side of life: he left his wife at home in Norfolk and lived in London with the whore Em Ball, sister to the infamous master criminal Cutting Ball. He wrote entertaining pamphlets detailing the language and habits of London's underworld, and died in poverty, supposedly demanding more wine after eating a dodgy dish of pickled herrings.

Manteo and Wanchese (dates unknown)

Algonquian Indians brought to England – apparently voluntarily – by the initial Ralegh-sponsored foray into the New World, in 1584. They lived with Ralegh at Durham House and were presented to Elizabeth (swapping their loin-cloths for taffeta). Their extraordinary personalities and speedy learning of English helped persuade the Queen to back Ralegh's colonisation plans. They returned to America with the short-lived colony of 1585. Wanchese rejoined his tribe, but Manteo stayed with the settlers and went back to England with them the following year. He then returned to Roanoke with the 'lost colony' expedition of 1587. Manteo, from the friendly Croatoan tribe, was baptised a Christian, but Wanchese, from the more hostile Roanoke tribe, may have been in the raiding party that murdered the settler George Howe. The ultimate fate of both Indians is unknown.

Gelli Meyrick (1556–1601)

A bishop's son from Wales, his family was closely associated with the Essex clan (Meyrick's uncle Edmund was chaplain to both the Earl and his father). In 1579, Meyrick joined Essex, who was then a student, and looked after his horses. Soon his role had grown and he was organising his estates and finances. Meyrick became increasingly influential. He was unpopular with tenants in Wales for his tough dealings, but Essex always supported him. He, in turn, backed Essex to the hilt and died for it, being accused of treason for his part in the rebellion of 1601. He was hanged, drawn and quartered at Tyburn. There was said to be much rejoicing in the valleys of South Wales.

Sir John Perrot (1528–92)

A large, powerful man, he was generally held to be the illegitimate son of Henry VIII. Certainly, he was quick to anger like

Henry. A gifted linguist and a lifelong Protestant, he went to the royal court at eighteen, but soon became known as a brawler. There was no doubting his courage – he once saved King Henri II of France from a wild boar. His bad habits dogged him and he lost all his money through his passion for the tilt 'and other toys I am ashamed to tell'. He spent various terms in prison, fought battles at sea and served with the English army in Ireland, where he did well. But he made enemies and with the death of his main protector Walsingham, he was vulnerable. In 1592 he was brought to trial for treason, having called Elizabeth 'a base bastard pissing kitchen woman'. He did not deny saying the words and was condemned to death, but died in the Tower while awaiting execution.

William Segar (1564–1633)

A fine portrait painter, who took himself rather too seriously as an officer of the College of Arms. He was first employed as a scrivener by the courtier Sir Thomas Heneage, and soon became a herald. His expertise in the finer points of noble family trees did not, however, hamper his other career as a portraitist. He was patronised by the Earl of Essex and was also commissioned to do pictures of the Earl of Leicester and Queen Elizabeth. Under King James I, he was the victim of a heraldic hoax by a rival, who tricked him into awarding a coat of arms to the London hangman Gregory Brandon (who enjoyed the joke and ever after styled himself 'esquire'). King James was not amused – and briefly jailed both Segar and the hoaxer, saying he hoped to make Segar more wise and the trickster more honest.

John Watts (1550–1616)

A larger-than-life merchant and pirate who typified the go-getting adventurousness of the Elizabethan age. Arriving in London as a teenager, he married the daughter of a rich merchant and never looked back. He sent wave after wave of privateers to the Caribbean to prey on Spanish – and neutral – shipping, and became exceedingly wealthy. He took his own ships to fight the Armada and was involved in some of the fiercest exchanges around Calais. Later he became an alderman, a governor of the East India Company, Lord Mayor of London and was knighted by King James I. One Spanish envoy said he was 'the greatest pirate that has ever been in this kingdom'.

Roger Williams (1539–95)

One of the foremost military men of Elizabeth's reign, he first went to war aged seventeen and made his name in the Low Countries by fighting bravely in single combat against a Spanish champion. Neither man was hurt and they ended up having a drink together. Williams soon became the most trusted lieutenant of Sir John Norris, Elizabeth's top general, but later the two men became rivals. After fighting all over Europe and writing important military books (including *A Brief Discourse of War*), Williams was drawn to Essex and called him 'my great prince'. His main stumbling block to high office was that Elizabeth did not like him and once dismissed him from her presence, telling him 'begone, thy boots stink'. Williams died of a fever.

Lexicon

LANGUAGE IN THE sixteenth century was rich, poetic – and coarse. Here are a few of the many words I have gleaned over the years.

For a fuller lexicon visit www.roryclements.com

alderliefest: most dear
all amort: dejected, miserable
apple squire: pimp, a harlot's servant
argosy: a large merchant ship
arras: tapestry or hanging of rich fabric with woven figures and scenes
attaint: stain, disgrace, condemn; lose standing and property
arquebus, arquebusier, hagbut, hackbut: matchlock weapon, muzzle-loading. The trigger brings the end of a slow-burning match into contact with the gunpowder that discharges the ball
auto-da-fe: execution of sentence of the Spanish Inquisition, often including a parade and sometimes including burnings of heretics

backed: dead
ban-dog: ferocious dog kept tied-up
bark: a small ship with standard rigging and build

bastardly gullion: a bastard's bastard

baudekin: brocade of gold thread and silk (the richest cloth)

beast: Antichrist (Puritan view of the Pope and Roman Catholic priests)

bees, a head full of: full of crazy notions

bellman: watchman, town crier

belly-cheat: slang term for an apron

Bess o'Bedlam: madwoman

black book: prison register

blackjack: leather beer jug sealed with tar on outside

bluecoats: serving-men

bodies (a pair of): bodice

brabble: quarrel, wrangle, noisy altercation

broadcloth: fine, wide, black plaincloth (as a Puritan might wear)

breech-clout: cloth worn by American Indians about their waist

bridale: wedding feast

bruit: to spread by rumour

buckler: a small, round shield

buttery: larder, service room for ale and general food stores

caliver: light musket fired without a support

callet: whore or lewd woman

canary: light, sweet wine from the Canary Islands

careen: turn a ship on its side to scrape its hull of weed and barnacles, and caulk

carrack: large merchant ship which could be converted to be a warship. Three-master, square-rigged with high castles, fore and stern

catchpole: arresting officer, a sheriff's sergeant

churl: ill-bred, surly, base fellow; farm worker

coif: a lawn or silk cap

coining: forging money

coney, cony: a dupe

copesmate: comrade

coter: author, person responsible for a work

couch a hogshead: lie down to sleep

cozen, cozenage, cozener: to dupe or cheat, duplicity, one who cheats

cresset: iron basket (usually on top of a pole) in which pitch or oil is burned for light

crossbiter, crossbiting: swindler, swindling

culverin: long-range cannon with bore of about five inches, firing shot of 17–20 lbs

cunning man: a sort of local detective. Someone possessing keen intelligence or magical knowledge

daub: mud for building

dell: a young vagrant girl, a wench

doddypoll: fool

dogswain: sort of makeshift covers or bedding

doublet: a close-fitting jacket, with or without sleeves

doxy: loose woman, a vagrant's wench

drab: low, sluttish woman, a whore

drinkpenny: tip, gratuity

drolleries: comic entertainment of a fantastical kind

ducat: Spanish gold coin, eighth of an ounce. Silver ducat worth 5s 6d; gold ducat 7s

electuary: medicine, a medicinal conserve or paste mixed with honey or syrup

Essex's cheap knights: those he knighted after failed sorties such as that to the Azores in 1597

factor: collecting agent

fain: be inclined, compelled

fairy, faeric: spirit, often evil

fall in: copulate

figure caster: astrologer

flowers: menstruation, period

Flota: Spanish treasure fleet from New World

foreign officer: parish official charged with seeking out vagrants

foreparts: stomachers, ornamental clothing for women

frantic: insane

freebooter: plunderer

French-hood: fashionable hood for women

French marbles, pox, crown, welcome: venereal disease

frenzy: madness

gage of booze: quart of ale

gamekeeper: a keeper of whores

garnish: bribe, especially in prison

gentry cove: upper-class man

gentry mort: upper-class woman

gibbet: gallows, especially one where dead criminal was left to
rot

glaziers: eyes

gong: a privy or its contents

gong farmers, night-soil men: sewage collectors

gossip: friend, especially female, perhaps godparent

greased priest: Catholic priest (anointed with oil)

groat: coin worth fourpence

guarded: trimmed with lace or braid, as in 'guarded coat'

hair o' the same wolf: hair of the dog – a hangover cure

halberd, halberdier: long-staffed weapon with a point, axe on
one side and billhook on the other; man who carries one

halek: astrologer and physician Simon Forman's secret word
for copulation

hand-fasting: betrothal, solemnising of wedding vows

headborough: parish officer, petty constable

headsman: executioner (with axe)

hedge-priest: itinerant preacher

hewing and punching: slashing the neck followed by a stab in the belly

hogshead: large cask containing 52.5 gallons

hole: worst prison cell

hornbook: board with letters or prayers with thin, transparent horn covering

hospitaller: man in charge of admissions and discharges from hospital and seeing that funds and supplies were accounted for and that valuables brought in by patients were safeguarded

instrument: male member

intelligencer: spy

intrigant: one who intrigues

jakes, jaques, house of easement: privy, toilet

jerkin: close-fitting jacket, often leather

jet: strut about, swagger

jetty: protruding storey of house

ken: house, especially one where villains lodge or meet

kennel: surface street gutter

kern: Irish warrior, foot-soldier, one of the poorer class of the Irish

kersey: worsted cloth, coarse and narrow woven from long wool and usually ribbed

kine: cattle

king pest: the plague

kirtle: outer petticoat or skirt; the garment under the mantle

knell: bell-tolling to mark a death

languishing sickness: depression or any illness where energy is lost

lawn: a fine linen, resembling cambric

lewd: immoral and worthless

light-heeled: wanton, loose

link: torch made of tow and pitch (or wax and tallow) carried in the street at night

linsey-woolsey: thin flax-wool material, usually of inferior quality, or a dress made of the material

maling cords: ropes for tying packs on to horses

malkin: a kitchen slut or an effeminate man

manchet: high-quality wheaten bread flour or a small round loaf of the same

mark: monetary unit – two-thirds of a pound

maund: to beg

maunderer: professional beggar

meet: suitable, appropriate

mercer: dealer in textiles, especially expensive ones

miasma: foul vapours, unwholesome air carrying disease

mistress of the game: prostitute, brothel madam

mittimus: letter from a JP or other authorised official committing a person into custody (an arrest warrant)

mixen, midden: dunghill

mooncalf: born fool, simpleton

mortbell: funeral bell

motion-man: puppet-master

murrain: plague

murrey: dark, blood red

musket: long-barrelled weapon, fired using a stand and capable of penetrating armour. A heavier version of the arquebus, using same matchlock principle

Mussulman: Muslim

netherstocks: stockings, tights, hose

occupy: euphemism for copulate
ordinary: eating house, pub
ostler: person who attends horses at an inn

pack-saddle: saddle for carrying goods
palfrey: lady's horse
palliasse: straw mattress
pantoufles: slippers
petronell: a heavy pistol carried in the belt, used especially by
    cavalry
philtrous powder, philtre: a love potion or charm
pike, pikestaff, pikeman: long-handled weapon with a sharp
    point, man who carries one
pizzle: male member
platter: a flat dish of pewter or wood
poniard: a small, slim dagger
postern: a back door or gate, small private door – distinct from
    the main entrance
powder: gunpowder
powder corns: grains of gunpowder
prigger of prancers: horse thief
projector: agent provocateur
puckrel: witch's familiar spirit, imp
pursuivant: a state officer with power to enforce warrants
pynner: a coif with two long strips on either side for fastening
    (worn by women of quality)

quean: slut, whore
quent merchant: pimp

reiver: plunderer across the border. To reave – to rob (archaic Scots)

revenger: one who takes vengeance

rich-guarded: richly embroidered

roarer: one who swears a lot, a loudmouth, bully, roisterer

ruffler: sturdy beggar or rogue claiming to be ex-soldier

runagate: vagabond, fugitive, renegade

rutter: navigator's chart showing prominent coastal features; or a swindler

scarlet whore of Babylon: Roman Catholic Church (as seen by Protestants)

sconce: 1) small fortress 2) lantern or candlestick with screen to keep from wind 3) a bracket candlestick fixed to the wall

scryer: crystal-ball gazer, fortune teller

scutes: small fishing boats

searcher, searcher of the dead: a pathologist (person appointed to view dead bodies and to make report upon the cause of death)

seminary: Catholic priest from one of the European seminaries

smock: 1) shift or under-petticoat 2) wench, derogatory term for a woman

snaphaunce: an early flintlock weapon from Germany

snout-fair: handsome

solar: upper room with large window to get sunlight

sotweed: tobacco – worth its weight in silver, according to John Aubrey

souse: pickled pork, especially ears and trotters

sovereign: gold coin of varying values up to thirty shillings

stairs, water-stairs: landing stage on river

stayed him: stopped him in his tracks

stew: brothel

Stilliard, Steelyard: London premises of the Hanseatic merchants, from German *stalhof* (warehouse)

stomacher: ornamental covering for chest or abdomen, worn under the lattice of a bodice (also called foreparts)

stones: testicles

stow you: shut up

stranger: foreigner, immigrant

strumpet: loose woman

subtlety: an exquisite, sugary dish, often ornamental

sumpter: packhorse or mule, beast of burden

swain: a young man, a lover or suitor, particularly rustic

swive: copulate

tables: backgammon

tallow: cheap, smelly, smoky candlewax made of sheep fat

tilt-boat: large rowing boat, having an awning (tilt) – a river taxi

tipstaff: sheriff's officer, constable or bailiff

Tom o'Bedlam: madman or ex-inmate of Bedlam

tow: strands of flax, hemp or jute used in torches

toy: 1) trifle or small object 2) whim

trencher: large, flat plate of wood

trillibub: bag of guts, entrails

trug: slut, whore

trugging-house: brothel

turnkey: gaoler

unspotted lamb of the Lord: a Puritan

vaulting-house: brothel

verinshe: superior tobacco from Venezuela

viol: stringed instrument of 5 to 7 strings, played with a bow

wainscot: panelling

wanton: lascivious, immoral

wattle, wattlework: Twigs and poles for building; wickerwork. Used with daub

wheel-lock: matchless gun. A serrated steel wheel is spun against a plate – the resultant sparks ignite the gunpowder

wherry: light rowing boat used to ferry goods and people on rivers; a large river barge

whittawer: a glover, one who works with white leather

Winchester geese: prostitutes (Southwark, where many whores plied their trade, was largely owned by the Bishop of Winchester)

wink at: overlook an indiscretion

wit: cleverness

yard: male member

The third historical thriller featuring John Shakespeare,
available soon in hardback

Prince

RORY CLEMENTS

Spring, 1593. England is a powder keg of rumour and fear.
Elizabeth's Golden Age is truly tarnished.

Plague rages, famine is rife, courtiers scheme; Spain watches,
waits – and plots. Into this turmoil a small cart clatters
through the streets of London, carrying a deadly load. It is
the first in a wave of horrific bombing attacks on the Dutch
immigrant community that will change John Shakespeare's
life for ever.

His investigations take him from magnificent royal horse
races to the opulent chambers of Black Luce's brothel, from
the theatrical underworld of Marlowe and Kyd to the torture
cells of priest-hunter Richard Topcliffe, and from the elegant
offices of master tactician Robert Cecil to the splintering
timbers of an explosive encounter at sea.

Now read on . . .

www.roryclements.com

Chapter 1

FOUR MEN STARED down at the body of Christopher Marlowe. A last trickle of bright gore oozed from the deep wound over his right eye. His face and hair and upper torso were all thick with blood. One of the four men, Ingram Frizer, held the dripping dagger in his hand.

Frizer looked across at Robert Poley and grinned foolishly. 'He came at me.'

'Boar's balls, Mr Frizer, give me the dagger,' Poley said angrily.

Frizer held out the dagger. All the living eyes in the room followed the tentative movement of the blood-red blade. A sliver of brain hung like a grey-pink rat's tail from its tip. Poley took the weapon and wiped it on the dead poet's white hose. Suddenly, he struck out with the hilt and caught Frizer a hard blow on the side of his head. Frizer lurched backwards. Poley pushed him to the floor and jumped on him, knees on chest, hitting his head again, harder, pounding him until Nick Skeres tried to pull him away.

Poley stood back, shook off Skeres's hands and brushed down his doublet with sharp irritation. He was not a tall man, but he was strongly built and the veins in his muscled forearms and temples bulged out and pulsed. He kicked Frizer in the ribs. 'You were only supposed to gag him and apply the fingerscrew, you dung-witted dawcock. Not kill him.'

The afternoon sunlight of late May slanted in through the single, west-facing window. The presence of the men and the body made the room feel smaller than it really was. It was cleanly furnished; a well-turned settle made of fine-grained elm, a day bed where the body now lay, a table of polished walnut with benches either side and half-drunk jugs of ale atop it. The dusty floorboards were scuffed by the men's shoes; there was, too, a lot of blood and a few splashes of ale on the wood between the table and the day bed.

'And you . . .' Poley turned to Skeres. 'You were supposed to hold him. He was out of his mind with drink and you couldn't keep a grip.'

Ingram Frizer pulled himself painfully to his feet. He was doubled over, clutching his side where Poley's boot had connected.

Poley handed him the dagger. 'Here, take it. And listen well: it was *his* dagger – Marlowe's dagger. He came at you, pummelled your head with it. You fought back. In the struggle, the blade pierced his eye. You were defending yourself – it was an accident.'

Frizer took the dagger. He was slender with a lopsided face, the left eye half an inch higher than the right. The skin had been cut from the side of his head by Poley's beating. There was a livid gash, almost to the bone. His head and ribs throbbed, but he understood Poley's plan well enough. 'I liked this dagger,' he said, turning the weapon over in his hands and examining the ornate hilt and narrow, sharp-pointed blade. 'Cost me half a mark.' He tried to laugh.

'Well, it'll be Crown property now. Marlowe was always fighting. He was going to kill you. It's a simple story, remember it.' Poley turned to the third man, Skeres. 'And you, Mr Skeres.'

Skeres nodded. His bulbous face was sweating heavily. He mopped a kerchief across his brow. His gaze kept flicking towards the body, and then across to the fourth man, who stood close by the door. So far he had said nothing.

'No, let's change that,' Poley said, shaking his head slowly. 'Someone might recall that dagger. Say it was yours, Mr Frizer, but Marlowe snatched it off you, then you wrenched it away from him as he battered you. You struck backwards wildly, didn't know what you had done. Got that? And the knife didn't cost you half a mark, it cost you a shilling. The rest of the story holds.' Poley suddenly slammed his fist down on the table. 'Where's the screw?'

Ingram Frizer pointed to the floor beneath the window, to where a five-inch by four-inch vice of iron lay. It was designed to crush the fingers of a hand, slowly and painfully.

'Do I have to think for both of you? Pick it up!'

Frizer scurried across the room and brought the device back to Poley, who thrust it inside his doublet.

At last the fourth man spoke. He was heavy-set with a wispy beard. 'I'm going now. Wait two hours, drink some ale, then call the constable and the coroner. None of this comes back to me or my master. I was never here.'

'No,' Poley agreed. He understood well enough. There must only ever have been four men in this room, not five.

The man took one last look around the room and met the eyes of Poley, Skeres and Frizer. 'Not one word.' He lifted the latch and silently left the room.

The other three watched him go. A seagull landed on the sill of the open window, defecated, then flew off. 'There's a problem,' Skeres said, shaking the sweat out of his eyes.

'The only problem,' Poley said, 'is *you*. You're a flaccid prick of a man, Skeres.'

'We've got to say what they were fighting about, haven't we?'

'It was the bill, of course. The reckoning. Frizer said Marlowe had drunk more so should pay more. Mr Marlowe wanted to quarter the bill evenly.'

'The coroner will never believe it.'

Poley laughed. 'Pour the ale, Mr Skeres, then light me a pipe.

How has a concy like you ever lived this long? Hear that, Mr Frizer? Mr Skeres says the coroner will never believe it.' Poley laughed again, louder this time, and Frizer and Skeres laughed nervously with him.

Chapter 2

JOHN SHAKESPEARE SPOKE briefly to the constable standing guard, before entering the room. He was a tall man, about six foot, and had to stoop to get through the door. He glanced around, taking in the furnishings, the window, the body. It was a fair-kept room. He stepped closer to the bloody remains of Christopher Marlowe and stared intently into his eyes. One was open and opaque, the other a black-brown scab of dried gore and brain. He remembered those clever eyes as they had been in the old days when he had performed certain secret tasks for Mr Secretary Walsingham. Marlowe had been clever and dangerous. Well, he'd met someone more dangerous.

The other three men in the room stood quietly by the table. Shakespeare caught Poley's gaze. They knew each other well. There had been times when they worked together, back in the mid eighties. It had never been a comfortable experience for Shakespeare. Now he lifted his chin in acknowledgement, if not exactly in greeting.

'Who did this, Poley? Who killed him?'

'Mr Frizer here. Ingram Frizer. It was self-defence. You know what Kit Marlowe was like.'

Indeed he did. Marlowe had been a fighter, a drinker, a poet, a character in the drama of his own life. He was Tamburlaine, Dr Faustus and any other number of Bedlam loons and Shoreditch roarers, all rolled into one. He had been trouble;

uncontrollable. Yes, self-defence seemed likely enough, knowing what Marlowe was like, with or without strong ale in his belly. The nagging doubt was the presence of Rob Poley. Very little was accidental when he was in the vicinity. Shakespeare turned to the others. 'Which one of you is Frizer?'

Frizer took two steps forward. He held the cleaned dagger in front of him, laid across both palms. Shakespeare did not take it from him; instead he gestured with his head to the table. 'Put it down over there.'

From outside, the bellman called nine of the clock. The room was still light. 'When did this happen?' Shakespeare demanded.

'Six,' Poley said. 'He was cup-shotten from a surfeit of ale. Wouldn't pay his portion of the bill. Attacked Mr Frizer here – and Mr Frizer defended himself.'

Shakespeare nodded. It sounded reasonable enough. But he didn't believe a word of it. 'What were you doing here?' He addressed the question to Ingram Frizer.

'Playing at cards,' Poley said. 'Smoking sotweed and drinking good ale.' He nodded towards the now empty ale jugs. 'Eating, too. Ellie Bull roasts a fine head of young pig and most excellent sweetmeats.'

'Do you speak for all, Mr Poley? The question was for Mr Frizer.'

'We were all here – I was just answering your question.'

'Well, don't, unless a question is asked of you.' He turned once more to Frizer. 'So where, pray, are the playing cards?'

Frizer looked blankly at Shakespeare, then nervously towards Poley. 'I—they—'

'I have them here,' Poley said, fetching a pack from his doublet. 'If I am permitted to speak, that is.'

'Put them over there, by the dagger.'

Poley ambled over to the table and fanned the cards out with a final, crisp flick for the last one. He smiled at Shakespeare. 'Might I know your interest in this sorry affair, Mr Shakespeare?

It is naught but an everyday manslaughter and we were told to wait for coroner Danby. We have all stayed here in the proper way of things; none has attempted flight. What possible interest can this occurrence, tragical though it be, have for such an eminent servant of the Crown as Mr John Shakespeare, senior secretary to Sir Robert Cecil?'

Shakespeare ignored the question. He was here because this was most decidedly his business. He had been investigating Marlowe on the orders of Cecil and a special Privy Council commission of inquiry. Marlowe had been suspected of involvement in an unsavoury episode – a vicious written attack on the many foreigners now living in London. A placard posted outside the Dutch church in Broad Street insulted England's Protestant friends from the Low Countries and France who had sought refuge here. Marlowe's style seemed to be writ all over the poster: fifty-three lines of seditious doggerel – and not just insults and threats to slit the incomers' throats, but strong criticism of the Queen and her government for allowing them to come here.

And why, specifically, was Marlowe a suspect? Because the placard was signed Tamburlaine – the heathen warrior king of his most celebrated play.

Yes, thought Shakespeare, this death was most certainly of interest.

'You,' he said brusquely, turning to Skeres. 'Who else was here?'

Unlike Frizer, Skeres had enough presence of mind not to glance towards Poley for guidance. But he was sweating heavily, even though the warmth of the day was long since turned to evening chill. 'Us three and Marlowe. That's all.'

'What is your name?'

'Skeres. Nick Skeres.'

'Who is your master?'

'I am my own man. I have property. My family is in the cloth trade – drapers, tailors.'

Shakespeare had heard the name Skeres before. Like Poley, he had worked for Walsingham occasionally. His presence in this room stank of rancid fat.

'Sweat pours from you like a heavy rainfall, Mr Skeres. Are you afraid of something?'

'A man has died here. What Christian would not be shaken, sir?'

'Indeed.'

'Would you like me to tell you exactly what happened, Mr Shakespeare?' Poley asked, his face a guileless mask.

'Save it for the coroner, Mr Poley. I am sure you have it well rehearsed . . .'

The door creaked open. All eyes turned to see the slim figure of Joshua Peace entering the room. Shakespeare smiled in greeting and stepped forward to clasp his hand. 'Thank you for coming, Joshua. It is good to see you.'

'What's *he* doing here?' Poley burst out.

'Mr Peace? He is here to examine the body and the scene of the crime – if there was a crime, of course. We must not pre-judge these matters, Mr Poley.' Shakespeare studied Poley's face, but the man had recovered himself.

Peace strode towards the corpse, barely acknowledging the three witnesses. For a few moments he stood and stared at the dead face. 'Marlowe, eh? A fair playmaker in his day. Smells like a taproom in here.' Peace, the Searcher of the Dead, was a man in his mid to late thirties. His eyes shone with wit and humour, yet you would pass him in the street and not note him. He was almost bald save for a thin circle of brown hair that always reminded Shakespeare of a monk's tonsure.

The searcher rolled back his sleeve, then slid his right hand and forearm inside Marlowe's bloody doublet. He held it there against the dead man's still chest, the tips of his fingers in the armpit, for a full minute. At last he withdrew his hand. 'How long do you think he's been dead, John?'

'This crew of villains say he died at six – so that's three hours.'

Peace shook his head. 'No, five at least. Perhaps even six hours gone. He died between three and four of the clock.'

'Well, Mr Skeres, what do you say to that?'

'It's all lies—' Poley broke in.

Shakespeare thrust the palm of his hand into Poley's face, smacking his head against the wall to stop his mouth. 'Learn some manners, Mr Poley. Speak when you are spoken to.' He held Poley there, pinioned. 'Now, Mr Skeres, if you please.'

'Six of the clock. He died at six hours.'

Peace picked up the dagger and examined it. He held its tip to the wound over the eye, then slipped it slowly through the gore, four inches into the depths of Marlowe's head without resistance. 'Well, this is most certainly the weapon that inflicted the wound. A common enough assassin's strike, I would say.'

'It was an accident!' Poley shouted, wrenching his mouth from Shakespeare's grasp. 'It was a brabble. God's wounds, look at Mr Frizer's head. Look what Marlowe did to him first.'

Shakespeare pushed Poley's head back against the wall. 'Speak again unbidden and I will relieve you of your teeth, Mr Poley,' he said, then released his grip. Poley wiped his sleeve across his mouth.

For the next ten minutes the searcher examined the body in silence, looking for other wounds or evidence of poisoning. He opened Marlowe's mouth and peered inside, then spent some time over his right hand, which was clearly injured. After his examination of the corpse he turned his attention to the living men. He made Frizer stand still while he looked at the wounds on his head. He took notes on the spread of blood across the body of the corpse and the killer. He also examined the garments and heads of the other two men for signs of injury or blood drops. At last he stood back from his work and gazed at Shakespeare.

'Well, Joshua?'

'I have no doubt that the stab to the eye killed him, though from the stench of him you might surmise he had drowned in ale. The blade penetrated the brain and brought forth a great rush of blood. There is no evidence of any other lethal injury, nor poison. The blood on that man,' he nodded towards Frizer, 'makes it quite clear that he wielded the knife.'

'Could it have been self-defence?'

'Yes.'

'And could the injuries inflicted on the knifeman, Frizer, have been caused by an attack by Marlowe?'

'Again, yes. Or by anyone else who happened to be in the room. I would add, John, that Marlowe's finger is interesting. The middle one of the right hand has been injured in some way. The knuckle was torn at about the time of death.'

'From landing a punch, Joshua?'

Peace hesitated. 'Most likely, yes. Although—'

'Although what?'

'No, nothing. It's pointless to surmise.'

'But I would be glad if you would anyway.'

'Well, the injury is really quite severe. The bone is visible. One might think the knuckle and the forejoint of the finger had been scraped by a rough edge of iron. More than that I cannot say.'

Shakespeare stepped forward and examined Marlowe's fingers himself, then turned back. He held up the limp hand. 'Well, Mr Poley – how do you explain this injury?'

'Take a look at Mr Frizer's head. That's how Marlowe hurt himself.'

Shakespeare turned away and clapped Peace about the shoulder. 'I want you here at the inquest, Joshua.'

He shook his head. 'No. I'll write you a report. That'll be enough for Danby. It's straightforward.'

'Put in the time of death as you estimate it.'

'Oh yes, I'll do that. But Danby will pay it no heed.'

The witnesses did not leave the premises for a day and two nights. An obliging Mrs Bull, owner of the house, bustled about bringing them food and ale, and provided a bed for them in another room. Two of the men slept on the outer sides of the bed, heads against the wall, while the third, Skeres, slept in between them, his booted feet against their ears, his farting, snoring bulk hogging much of the mattress.

The body of Marlowe was as cold as earth by the time the sixteen-man jury of local Deptford yeomen was assembled in the room where he had died. The jurors stood along one wall, heads bowed and fearful, clutching their caps and looking anywhere but at the body. Then the coroner appeared, a dark and formal cape about his shoulders and a fur hat under his arm. He sat at the table and called the room to order for the Lord's Prayer. At the coroner's side, Richard Topcliffe, the Queen's servant, took a seat, his white hair and dread face caught in the morning light from the little window.

John Shakespeare stood close to the doorway. He glared at Topcliffe, who smirked back. What was Topcliffe doing here, close-coupled with the coroner? This inquest could be none of his concern.

The proceedings were as Shakespeare expected; there was no one to gainsay the testimony of Poley, Skeres and Frizer, who all knew their lines well. William Danby, coroner to the royal court, then attending on the Queen less than a mile away in Greenwich, listened impassively. His manner was grave. He read Joshua Peace's report, which had been placed on the table in front of him, then set it aside without commenting on it to the jury.

For a moment, Shakespeare considered interrupting the inquest to point out the discrepancy over the time of the killing. But it would have been a waste of breath. Danby would merely have instructed the jurors to discount the testimony of Mr Peace, as he himself had done, and might well have thrown Shakespeare out of the hearing. And anyway, the hour of death, in itself, proved nothing. It was the *manner* of the killing that counted for all in this room.

The verdict was a foregone conclusion: self-defence. The jurors – each of whom had been required to step forward in turn to view the body and the fatal wound at close quarters – had done the job required of them. Ingram Frizer was to be taken to the Marshalsea prison to see whether he should be charged or no. That was the prerogative of the Queen and her ministers.

It was not the verdict which caused Shakespeare most consternation, it was the presence of the man who had sat at the coroner's side: Richard Topcliffe – killer, torturer, rapist, blood-lusting dog with the ear of the Queen.

The loathing between Shakespeare and Topcliffe ran deep. Their paths had crossed too many times over the years. Shakespeare had married a Catholic and Topcliffe wanted his blood. He wanted the blood of every Catholic in England. And who was to stop him when he had Elizabeth's licence to act as priest hunter and persecutor? No man could oppose him, not even the Privy Council, because he was answerable only to her.

As the jury shuffled out, Shakespeare approached the table. Danby was collecting up his papers.

'You know, of course, Mr Danby, that they were all lying.'

The coroner looked up, eyes wide, as if he had not seen Shakespeare before. 'Mr Shakespeare?'

'Frizer, Poley, Skeres. They concocted that story. And the time of the killing. You had Mr Peace's note in front of you, yet you paid it no heed.'

Danby bridled, though his indignation would not have alarmed a mole. Indeed, he was much like a burrowing creature with his dark cape, nervous eyes and twitching whiskers. 'You presume much to speak to a royal officer so, Mr Shakespeare. In truth I would go further, sir; you presume a great deal to call in the Searcher of the Dead without my authority.'

'If I had waited on your pleasure, Mr Danby, it might have been too late. The body would have been as cold as winter. Mr Peace might not have been able to determine the time of death with such accuracy.'

'It is for me to say how accurate Mr Peace's conclusions are. And I say that he is a diabolical dabbler. He plays with dead bodies in a most unchristian way. I will have none of Mr Peace.' Danby swept past Shakespeare, then paused at the door. 'And mark me well: I will have words with my lord Burghley regarding your part in this.' With a final, puffed-up flourish, he departed.

Topcliffe bared his yellow teeth and chuckled. He prodded Shakespeare's chest with his silver-tipped blackthorn stick. 'That's told you, Shakespeare.'

Shakespeare brushed the stick aside with a sweep of his arm and glared into Topcliffe's gloating face. 'God blind you,' he said. 'You are a malign presence.' This whole business was putting Shakespeare in an ill-humour. He had not liked it from the start, when Cecil had ordered him to inquire into Marlowe's dealings. Anyone could have written those placards. And if it *had* been Marlowe, why would he have signed it *Tamburlaine*? Only a fool would draw attention to himself in such a way – and Marlowe, however hot-blooded and wild, had never been a fool.

'Now, now, Mr Shakespeare,' Topcliffe said, putting up his stick as if it were a rapier. 'Hear me out.'

'I want to hear nothing from you, Topcliffe. Have you not women or children to torment somewhere?'

'Wait, Shakespeare. I know we do not see eye to eye on much, but I have to tell you that I am with you on this. Marlowe was a dunghill of iniquity, but he had his fair parts. The verdict was wrong, I am certain. He was murdered.'

'Then why did you say nothing?'

'I had no evidence, Mr Shakespeare. Why did *you* say nothing?'

Shakespeare ignored the question. 'And what was Marlowe to you, anyway? Why are you here?'

Topcliffe took a smouldering pipe from the pocket of his fine doublet and thrust it in his mouth. He sucked hard and blew out two thin streams of smoke from his nostrils. 'Marlowe? I would happily have drawn out his entrails and hacked off his pizzle like a Papist girl-boy for his godless ways and playmaking. And yet—' Topcliffe's menacing growl almost softened for a moment. '—And yet I will admit, in other things his heart was right. His denunciation of the foreign incomers was something that should gladden all English hearts, for who can stomach these strangers overrunning our land, taking bread from stout English tables? Five years ago, Drake sank the strangers who tried to invade our shores. Now the Council welcomes so many ragtag beggars from France and the Low Countries that you scarce hear an English voice in London. Marlowe was right and I am with him. I would push every last one of them back into the narrow seas and cheer their drowning.'

The pall-bearers entered the room and lifted the body of Christopher Marlowe from the day bed to carry him away for burial.

Shakespeare turned away. Topcliffe understood nothing. This was not about Marlowe's views, this was about murder. The trouble was that in these days of famine and rising prices, when many men could not find a day's work, there were plenty who thought like Topcliffe, plenty who would do evil to the incomers and their wives and children, Catholic or Protestant. Their only crime? Not being English.